PENGUIN BOOKS

UK | USA | Canada | Ireland | Australia
India | New Zealand | South Africa

Penguin Books is part of the Penguin Random House group of companies
whose addresses can be found at global.penguinrandomhouse.com.

First published 2018
001

Copyright © Chris Mooney, 2018

The moral right of the author has been asserted

Set in 12.5/14.75 pt Garamond MT Std
Typeset by Jouve (UK), Milton Keynes
Printed and bound in Great Britain by Clays Ltd, Elcograf S.p.A.

A CIP catalogue record for this book is available from the British Library

ISBN: 978–1–405–93253–0

www.greenpenguin.co.uk

Penguin Random House is committed to a
sustainable future for our business, our readers
and our planet. This book is made from Forest
Stewardship Council® certified paper.

The Snow Girls

CHRIS MOONEY

PENGUIN BOOKS

For Ken and Becky Whitlow, and their amazing
daughters: Michelle, Taylor and Kali

Author Note

I want to tell you a quick but important story about the book you're holding in your hands. It will only take a moment, I promise.

Fifteen years ago, I wrote a book called *Remembering Sarah*. It was published in the US and several European countries, but never made it to the rest of the world. The book, my third, a story about a grieving father who refused to give up searching for his missing daughter, was nominated for an Edgar Award for best novel and, in the Netherlands, went on to become one of the top-selling books of the year. There was a lot I loved about *Remembering Sarah* . . . and a lot of things I wished I had done differently. A lot of things. I felt the book could have been so much better and wanted to revise it. That didn't come to fruition, for reasons I won't get into, so I moved on to my next project, a book called *The Missing*, which introduced Darby McCormick, a Boston-based forensic investigator with a traumatic past and a doctorate in deviant behaviour. I had always wanted to write a novel with a strong and resourceful independent woman as the lead character, and what I loved about Darby – what made her different, to me – was how she acted like *Dirty Harry* with a PhD in creeps. She was (and still is) smart, tough and oftentimes ruthless – I enjoyed my time with her.

It seemed others did too. *The Missing* became a global bestseller. Nine novels and millions of readers later, I've watched, with admiration and, more often than not, great trepidation, as Darby has gone head-to-head with the worst our world has to offer, some of whom are the people we encounter in our daily lives.

People always ask writers where we get our ideas. The honest to God truth is, we don't know. But a couple of years back, I was sitting at my desk, writing a difficult scene and finding myself stuck in the mud – a common occurrence. When this happens, I usually turn away from the computer and look around my office to give my mind a rest. I saw a copy of *Remembering Sarah* sitting on my bookshelf and that voice responsible for ideas spoke to me (completely normal, by the way, for us writers to hear voices). *If Darby handled the case of the missing girl,* this voice said, *things would have gone down very differently.* What really captured my attention, though, was the villain my imagination had in mind – a former priest who would be unlike anyone Darby had ever encountered. I listened to that voice for a few minutes, daydreaming, then went back to work.

My imagination, however, wouldn't let go of the idea – kept nagging at me, showing how the story could be bigger and more compelling than *Remembering Sarah*. You have to understand a writer is not in control of his or her imagination. It does what it wants. During my downtime and without my permission, the story kept taking shape, and I often found myself jotting down ideas for scenes, bits of dialogue, everything.

I'm not a fan of writers who take old stuff, recycle it, and pass it off as new. But the idea had taken root, and as

I mentioned earlier, there was so much about *Remembering Sarah* I had wanted to do differently. So I spoke with people, a lot of them fans who had read the book, told them the idea I had in mind, and expected them to say, 'Please don't do that.' Instead, they told me the exact opposite. I consulted my agent and editor and, much to my surprise, they also thought it was a great idea, so I went ahead and wrote *The Snow Girls*.

If there's one cardinal sin a writer can commit, it's cheating the reader. I would never want to do that to you, so just to be clear, if you've read *Remembering Sarah*, you may recognize some scenes in *The Snow Girls*, but I think you'll find this new story richer and more compelling, with a new villain who will change Darby's life. I hope you enjoy it.

I

Darby hadn't seen the inside of the Belham Police Station since her father was a beat cop. She had worked plenty of forensic cases in Belham, back when she was in the crime lab and then later, as a forensic investigator, but the last time she'd actually set foot inside? Had to be at least twenty years.

She parked her rental car in the lot shared by the station and the church. It was Friday, coming up on 7 a.m., the cloudless November sky already a bright, hard blue. Winter had come to New England this year, sending the temperature down to the low twenties and creating the kind of harsh, biting winds that made you question why anyone in their right minds insisted on living in such a climate. Thanksgiving was three weeks away, and the downtown area was already decorated with white Christmas lights strung around small bare trees planted on the sidewalks, the telephone poles holding green plastic wreaths and stringy, weather-beaten tinsel.

Some things from your childhood never changed. Belham Station was one of them. The outside still looked the same: an imposing brick building with tall windows that never seemed clean, no matter what time of season. It gave her the feeling she'd had as a kid, which was that this was the sort of place where you would never find comfort.

The security cameras, she noticed, were dented and

banged up from the weather and from having people throwing stones, Belham having the distinction of not only becoming Boston's most violent neighbourhood but also the leader in attacks against the police.

The station's interior, amazingly, hadn't changed – same concrete walls painted in light and dark blues; the same shitty black-and-grey-speckled linoleum floor and the same steam-heated air containing the same odd mixture of Lysol, body odour and . . . was that pork?

The desk sergeant sitting behind the dispatch-office window saw her sniffing at the air and said, 'No, you're not imagining it. It's pork. Sausage, as a matter of fact.'

Darby picked up the clipboard. 'Thought I might be having a stroke.'

'No, that's burnt toast, what people smell right before they have one. Look, I'll tell you the same thing I told the last one, which is "No comment".'

'Okay.' Darby signed her name and said, 'I'm here to see Detective Chris Kennedy. He's expecting me.'

'You're not a reporter from the *Belham Tab*?'

'Nope.'

'They send the real pretty ones down here to ask their questions – like *that's* gonna work. Your name?'

'Darby McCormick.'

His face changed, went from mildly pleasant to turn-around-and-get-the-hell-out. It didn't bother her as much any more. She had grown . . . not used to it but had simply accepted it. There was nothing she could do to change some people's minds.

'ID,' he said gruffly, not looking at her. She handed over her driver's licence, which was tucked in the same black leather wallet as her investigator's badge and conceal-and-carry permits. He handed it back to her, along with a visitor's pass, and then pointed to the bench near a couple of payphones. The bench had been painted, but it was the one where she'd sat as a kid, waiting for her father.

Darby sidled over to the bulletin board, the wall above it adorned with framed pictures of cops who had died in the line of duty. Her father, Thomas 'Big Red' McCormick, was in the top row, dressed in his uniform blues, the auburn-coloured hair she'd inherited from him hidden underneath his cap.

He looked down at her with a stern expression, as if to say, *What are you doing back here, with these people?*

Her gaze slid away, to the bulletin board full of papers advertising needle exchange and gun-buyback programmes, as well as a list of detox centres. Someone had tacked a torn piece of paper to the board, the handwriting neat and legible: *This is the place where hope goes to die.*

From somewhere inside the station – probably the holding pen, Darby guessed – she heard a long, drawn-out scream: the raw, painful kind she associated with someone experiencing either a psychotic break or suddenly realizing the soul-crushing horror of his or her fate.

There had been a time when hearing such a sound would have caused her heart to leap in her throat. The skin on her face would have tightened and flexed across the bone; she'd feel cold all over, and have trouble thinking and concentrating. Now? Now, the sound was as harmless as radio static, and she wondered when this shift had happened. Wondered if she had simply become used to it or maybe had just stopped caring.

'Should have been here an hour ago,' Chris Kennedy said to her. 'Woman came in here, a big ole smile on her face, carrying a pastry box. Guy manning the desk, Mr Personality back there, Charlie, he asked her how he can help her and she says, "I'm here to feed the pigs".'

Darby walked beside him as they navigated the halls, heading to his office.

'*Then*,' Kennedy said, his eyes bright and mischievous, 'she opens the box, takes out uncooked sausage and pork chops, starts smearing everything all over the window and counter.'

'Wow. Clever *and* original. What a combo.'

Her sarcasm made him smile. He was the only cop who looked at her in a friendly way. Almost everyone else either averted their eyes or deliberately glared at her.

Kennedy's face turned serious. 'Stuff like that's happening more and more these days in Bedlam.'

Back when Darby was growing up, people called the city 'The Ham'. The downtown area where she had spent most of her youth had been replaced by cheque-cashing stores and pawnshops, and the vacant buildings had been taken over by the rampant homeless population, which was made up primarily of heroin addicts that came from all walks of life. Now kids were snorting, smoking, ingesting and injecting heroin and bath salts. They had abundant access to handguns, shotguns, semi-automatic rifles and hollow-point ammo, and now almost every kid had 'active-shooter' drills at schools. The crime rate here had surged so much everyone referred to the city as 'Bedlam'.

'And you can forget eating anywhere in town if you're a cop,' Kennedy said. 'People spit in your food, rub it on their genitals, sometimes even stick shit in it. And by "shit" I mean actual shit. We're here to help them, keep everyone as safe as possible, and everywhere we go we're treated like the Gestapo. Not a good time to be in law enforcement. What's with the jacket?'

Darby wore a stylish black motorcycle jacket made of thick black leather. 'You don't think it makes me look like a badass?'

'You *are* a badass. I just thought women with fancy Harvard doctorates got dressed up all fancy – you know, shirts, skirts and heels.'

'You've got the wrong girl.'

'No, I've got the *right* one.' He smiled knowingly. 'This is me, right here.'

His office had the look and feel of an underground war bunker – no external windows, the small space feeling even more claustrophobic on account of the boxes stacked high against the walls, full of case files and forensic reports. Kennedy, she knew, had recently been placed in charge of Belham's cold-case squad.

He picked up a stack of files from one of the two chairs in the corner of the room. Darby looked out through the window, into the bullpen, where a handful of cops were openly staring at her in disgust and contempt.

Years ago, back when she was working an investigation for Boston's Criminal Investigative Unit, she had uncovered a decades-long string of police corruption that extended up to the commissioner and the FBI's Boston office. These same people who had sworn to protect and serve had also orchestrated the murder of her father, Big Red McCormick, who had discovered the seeds of a criminal enterprise operating within the Boston PD. He had been shot while on duty.

Her father was strong. He had lasted a month before her mother decided to take him off life support. Darby insisted on being at the hospital. She was thirteen.

The reason for the vitriol she was witnessing right now was a result of her committing the cardinal sin of law enforcement: going public with the truth instead of playing the role of the good soldier and keeping the matter confined within Boston PD, where the bureaucrats and spin doctors would work tirelessly to bury the matter. She was branded a rat, ostracized for not following their rules. Then she'd lost her job.

Kennedy saw where she was looking. 'Ignore them.'

Don't worry, I am. She said, 'You must've made a helluva lot of friends, asking me to come here.'

'You're the best at what you do. Granted, you have the subtlety and grace of a wrecking ball, but you *do* get results.' He chuckled. 'Have a seat.'

Kennedy was well into his early fifties but except for his hair, which had gone from black to a steel-grey, and maybe an extra ten or so pounds, he still looked like the same beat cop she remembered from her days in Boston – the tough and crafty baseball catcher who'd earned a free ride to Boston College. He would've gone pro if he hadn't suffered a devastating knee injury, one that tore both his ACL and MCL, during his junior year.

'Who'd you piss off?' Darby asked, looking around his office.

'That's a mighty long list. Could you be more specific?'

'You worked homicide; now you're stuck in Bedlam working cold cases.'

'I needed a change of pace.'

'What's the real reason?'

'Doctor's orders.'

'High blood pressure?' Every homicide detective she knew suffered from it. That or alcoholism. Depression. The list went on and on.

'That and the two heart attacks that followed,' Kennedy said.

'Why didn't you retire? You put your time in.'

'And do what? Take up golf? Besides, my wife would kill me, having me around all day. Can I get you coffee? Water?'

'I'm all set.' Darby took a seat.

'So,' he said, hiking up his trousers as he lowered himself into the chair. 'Claire Flynn.'

Two days ago, Darby had been in Long Island, New York, winding up her consulting gig on a possible serial killer who, over a three-year period, had dumped the bodies of six women, all prostitutes or runaways, in the dunes. Kennedy called her out of the blue, asked if she'd take a look at a case Darby had worked more than a decade ago, and one that still haunted her: Claire Flynn, a six-year-old Belham girl, who, on a snowy night eleven years ago, went up a hill with her slightly older friend and never came down. It had been Darby's first case. She'd flown in yesterday morning and spent the next twenty-four hours poring over the evidence, the police reports, everything.

'What's your verdict?' he asked.

'She's dead.'

2

The evening Claire Flynn vanished, Darby had been the first person from the crime lab to arrive at Roby Park, although no one ever called it that. Townies had called it 'The Hill', and, back when she was growing up, it had been nothing more than a long, wide stretch of grass, at the top of which was Dell's, the only place in town where two bucks bought you a large Coke and a burger served on a paper plate stacked high with fries or onion rings, your choice. Dell's was still there, along with D & L Liquors, but by then the Hill had fancy jungle gyms, a new baseball diamond with standsand, its real attraction, a floodlight set up high on a telephone pole that lit up every inch of the Hill, allowing everyone to go sledding any time they wanted.

Belham PD had responded quickly to the report of Claire's disappearance and pulled out all the stops – blocking off every road and searching every car; an Amber Alert over the radio and through emails and the department's social-media platforms. Darby had interviewed Claire's father, Mickey Flynn, inside D & L Liquors while the storm raged outside. She had assisted in the search that night, and again the next morning and in the days that followed, hoping to discover additional evidence beyond the finding of the girl's sled and Claire's broken glasses, which her father had noticed that night and pocketed.

There had been a single eyewitness to the abduction:

Daniel Halloran, a nine-year-old, also from Belham. His father was a patrolman. The next morning Peter Halloran had asked his son if he had seen a young girl in a pink snowsuit up on the Hill, and when Danny had said yes, his father took him down to the station, where the lead detective, Tom Atkinson, interviewed him at great length.

'Dead,' Kennedy said, folding his hands on his stomach. 'She has to be. It's been eleven years since she vanished.'

'To the *day*. Today's her anniversary.'

Darby caught something in his tone and said, 'You know something I don't? Something new?'

Kennedy shook his head. 'I've told you everything I know, which isn't much,' he said. 'And you know the case better than I do, since you worked it.'

'It was my first case.'

'And you arrived well before any of the other forensic people did.'

She nodded. 'I happened to be in Belham that night.'

'Right.' Kennedy nodded sombrely. 'Your mother.'

Darby had spent a lot of time in Belham the year Claire disappeared, because her mother had been diagnosed with melanoma – the invasive type. The tumour had been removed, as well as several infected lymph nodes, but the cancer had already spread into the body, placing Sheila McCormick in the worst possible category: Stage IV. Metastatic melanoma, one of the deadliest and most difficult cancers to treat, didn't offer much in the way of hope, although the surgeon had tried to reassure them both that there were some promising clinical trials, and he had several patients who had extended their lives with immunotherapy.

'What's your opinion on how the case was handled?' Kennedy asked.

'You mean initially?'

'Yeah, start there.'

'Belham PD had the whole park blocked off, as far as I could tell. It was half past seven when I arrived, already pitch black, and, again, it was snowing, so visibility was poor – why are you grinning?'

'You sound like you're on the witness stand, McCormick. Relax. You're not under cross-examination.'

'There wasn't an actual crime scene. Claire Flynn had been missing for a little over an hour by that point. Detective Atkinson was at the scene when I arrived, and he had called Boston PD, asked them to send forensics along, just in case.'

'Because you've got to pull out the stops when a six-year-old goes missing.'

Darby caught the subtext in his tone: you've got to put on the best show for the cameras. Seeing a forensic van and team members on camera played well on the news, especially in an age when everyone got their knowledge from watching reruns of *CSI* and *Law & Order*. Perception mattered just as much, if not more so, than reality.

'Atkinson was the lead detective,' Darby said. 'He had the father, Mickey Flynn, already sequestered inside the liquor store when I arrived. Mickey was pretty despondent.'

'And shitfaced, from what I was told. Could barely stand.'

Darby nodded. 'He'd let his daughter climb the Hill with his nine-year-old god-daughter, Ericka Kelly, so they could go sledding. Mickey and Ericka's father, Big Jim Kelly, were at the bottom. Ericka came down alone, told them about how she'd got into it with a bunch of kids at the top –'

'Thomas MacDonald and his crew.'

'MacDonald pushed Ericka down the Hill on her inflatable tube. She arrived alone. Mickey went up to get his daughter. He found her sled and the broken glasses, but he didn't find her.'

Kennedy studied her for a beat, his eyes searching hers – for what, exactly, Darby didn't know.

'I processed the glasses myself, at the lab,' Darby said. 'We recovered multiple partial fingerprints.'

'One of which belonged to the infamous Father Richard Byrne.'

Darby knew him – everyone in town did. He had been a priest at St Stephen's, where Claire Flynn went to school and to church.

Kennedy said, 'He had daily contact with her and every other single kid there. Several witnesses at the school said Claire's glasses were always falling off, especially when she was outside, playing. Kids and teachers would pick them up for her – Byrne included.'

'That's the same argument his defence attorney used.'

'The fingerprint evidence was never going to be enough to convict him. We all knew that. We didn't have a single witness who could put Byrne there that night.'

'Didn't have any witnesses who could validate his story about being at the rectory that night either,' Kennedy added.

'As for the one witness we did have, the Halloran kid, he was helping Claire look for her glasses when a man stepped up next to them. He didn't get a good look at the guy's face, and the guy never spoke to him.'

'It could've been Byrne.'

'*Could've* doesn't get you a conviction.'

'No shit.' Kennedy breathed deeply as he craned his head and looked up at the ceiling. His puffed his cheeks and blew out a long, frustrated sigh.

'Chris,' Darby said.

His eyes slid back to her.

'You've been on the job, what, four, five months?'

'About that,' he replied.

'You've got stacks of cold cases in here. Why Claire Flynn?'

'Because I don't like paedophiles,' he said. 'And I especially don't like how the Catholic Church, under the leadership of that arrogant prick, Cardinal Law, may he not rest in peace, knew full well that Byrne and those other priests were paedophiles. What did he do? He shuffled them around for something like fifteen years, put the reputation of the Church ahead of stopping child rape.'

Kennedy was right. Boston's Cardinal Bernard Law had, for nearly two decades, shuffled known paedophile priests to other parishes all over the Commonwealth of Massachusetts rather than reporting their crimes. It went on until 2002, when the *Boston Globe* broke the story, which went global. It seemed Law wasn't the only one who'd put the needs of the Church above the needs of humanity: hundreds of similar stories kept popping up not just in the US but also all over the world. The Catholic Archdiocese of Boston had sold many of its properties to help defray the staggering legal costs and the nearly $100 million settlement for the victims of sexual abuse.

'The state didn't have a mandatory reporting law,'

Darby said. 'Cardinal Law wasn't under any legal obligation to come forward with any sexual-abuse claims.'

'Doesn't make it right.'

'Didn't say it did.'

Kennedy waved his hands, as if surrendering. 'But we're not talking about that sick bastard Law. We're talking about our sick bastard. Byrne abducted two girls before Claire Flynn.'

'There's no evidence that supports he –'

'First church Byrne was sent to out of seminary was down in New Bedford,' Kennedy said. He was leaning forward in his seat now, elbows resting on his thighs, his eyes heated with anger, or frustration, or maybe a combination of the two. 'He was an English teacher at St Bartholomew, taught first and second grades. Was there for something like fifteen years.'

'Eighteen.'

'Right, eighteen. Sorry, senior moment. Now, we don't know too much about what happened back then. Totally different time period – nobody would believe a priest was capable of molesting kids and, because the victims were underage, their parents didn't want to go to the police, have it get around town. What we do know is that Byrne took a special interest in his female students, asked certain ones to stay after class, to come visit him alone in his office for talks that often involved their sitting on his lap. And now we know the Church, behind the scenes, came in and intimidated the hell out of the families, bought their silence. Cardinal Law didn't put a stop to it, even after Byrne's last year there, when Mary Hamilton vanished without a trace during a snowstorm.'

Darby had read the case file: how the Hamilton girl, who was roughly the same age as Claire Flynn, had been abducted while playing in a friend's backyard. The friend's mother, who had been out with the girl, supervising, had gone into the house to fetch her cigarettes. When she came out, Mary Hamilton was gone: her daughter told her that a man had come out of the bushes and grabbed Mary. She was never seen again.

The friend told the police that the man who had grabbed Mary Hamilton wore a priest's collar. She hadn't seen the abductor's face.

'A few months after that,' Kennedy said, 'the Catholic Church sends Byrne for a little R & R at that private spa resort they've got in upstate Connecticut for treating priests who like molesting kids. Our man spends not even a month there and the Church decides that's enough, he's rehabilitated, and Law sends him to another church – this one up north, in Nashua, New Hampshire. Year goes by, everything's hunky-dory, and what happens next? Ten-year-old Elizabeth Levenson disappears, again during a snowstorm. Mother called the school: Byrne had offered to give the Levenson girl a ride home, and did. He admitted to that.'

'The Nashua police found no evidence or eyewitnesses tying him to that crime – he wasn't even a suspect at the time. Same deal in New Bedford.'

'Then the Church ships him here and we know what happens next. This isn't a series of coincidences – it's a goddamn pattern.'

'Any particular reason you're so laser-locked on Byrne?'

'You don't think he's our guy?'

'I was wondering why you're so heated up about him all of a sudden.'

'It's got to be Byrne. Who else could it be? And please don't tell me Mickey Flynn's old man. I don't buy for one minute that Sean Flynn was behind his granddaughter's disappearance.'

'He made Mickey's mother vanish into thin air.'

'A theory that was never proven,' Kennedy said. 'I'm not saying it's a bad one. After all, what sort of mother would abandon her kid, leave him to be raised by an animal like Sean?'

'It happens more than you think. Anyway, we took a good, hard look at Sean. Guy was a contract killer for the Irish mob – and the only one that I know of who never got arrested. We couldn't find a motive, let alone evidence, that suggested he was behind Claire's disappearance. After that, we worked on the theory that Claire might've been snatched as retaliation or payback by one or more of his business associates, or, say, a family member of one of his long list of victims. Sean made a lot of enemies over the years.'

'But nothing ever came of it, right?'

Darby nodded. 'The Irish and Italian mobs were long gone by then, and what few guys were left were either in jail or wearing diapers and using walkers. Boston PD did a lot of the legwork on that. They had a hard-on for putting Sean behind bars. Probably still do.'

'You think Sean might have played a role in it?'

'How about you cut to the part where you tell me the real reason I'm here?'

'What are you talking about?'

'We could have discussed all of this over the phone. You wanted me to come here in person. Why?'

Kennedy sat back in his seat. As he crossed his legs, his eyes cut sideways to the glass partition. When they landed back on hers, something in his face had changed, but she couldn't tell exactly what it was.

'Byrne is back in Belham, living in his mother's house,' Kennedy said. 'He inherited it after she died – probably of shame and embarrassment.'

'I heard he was back.'

'From who?'

'The *Boston Globe Magazine* article published last week. I read it online yesterday. He's been back here for, what, almost two years now.'

'So you know Byrne is dying?'

Darby nodded. 'We talking months or weeks?'

'Days, from what I've been told. Since he moved back here, every morning without fail he attends the six o'clock mass at St Stephen's. He doesn't get together with any of the priests, and he doesn't have any visitors except for his hospice nurse, a woman named Grace Humphrey.'

'You have people on him?'

'Just concerned people in the community who like to report to us.' The way Kennedy said it suggested he had cops watching Byrne on an unofficial basis, so it wouldn't ever come back to bite him in the ass. 'Byrne stopped going to mass about two weeks ago. He's holed up in his house – final days, I'm guessing. Although I'm told he does occasionally still walk the trails behind his house.'

'Some of those trails lead to the Hill.'

'They most certainly do.'

'You try using cadaver dogs? I didn't see that mentioned anywhere in the file.'

'Tried the dogs once, but nothing ever came of it. Byrne used to be tight with this other priest from St Stephen's, Father Keith Cullen. He's going to give Byrne the sacrament of reconciliation.'

'Father Cullen told you this?'

'No. That would violate all sorts of, you know, clerical ethics. Byrne told me.'

Darby looked at him in disbelief. 'Byrne told you.'

Kennedy was nodding. 'He called me up out of the blue, said he wants to talk.'

'What did he say?'

'That's the thing,' Kennedy said. 'He doesn't want to talk to me. The only person he wants to talk to, it seems, is you.'

3

Darby wasn't often taken by surprise. She was now.

'*Me?*'

Kennedy nodded. 'You.'

'Why?'

'That,' Kennedy said, snapping his fingers and pointing at her, 'is the question.'

'I've never met the man.'

'Byrne told me he was close to your mother – very close, were his exact words.'

'Meaning what?'

'I don't know. That's why I'm asking. Did she ever talk about him?'

'No. Never.'

Kennedy's eyebrows jumped in surprise, his face practically screaming *bullshit*.

'My mother,' Darby said, 'was super Catholic. Church every Sunday, and she went twice during the week, when she was healthy. She also did charity work with St Stephen's for as far back as I can remember. But she never talked about that part of her life. She –'

'Surely your mother must have shared her feelings on Father Byrne, when the news broke.'

'You would think she would. But you've got to remember my mother was a product of a time when you never, under any circumstances, said anything bad about a priest or the Church. When the story hit about the Catholic Church shuffling around paedophile priests, it broke something in her. Did something to her faith. She didn't talk about it – at least with me – and when Byrne became the lead suspect, I asked her a ton of questions, wanting to know more about him. She didn't want to talk about it, called the whole thing sad.'

'Was he at her funeral?'

'No.'

'What about the wake? Maybe he swung by to –'

'By the time my mother died, everyone in the state knew who Byrne was,' Darby said. 'The guy was a pariah. If he came to the wake or the funeral, I would have remembered seeing him, believe me.'

'So you're saying he never swung by the house at any time.'

'This is starting to feel like an interrogation.'

'Darby, I'm just asking questions.'

'Questions you could have asked me over the phone. Instead, you hired me on the pretext of re-examining the Claire Flynn case –'

'Wrong.'

'Are we done?'

'Why? You've got someplace you need to be?'

'Yeah. It's called work.'

'That's why I hired you,' Kennedy said. 'To work.'

'You mean talk to Byrne.'

'And Mickey Flynn, while you're here.'

'Why? For what reason?'

'Mickey showed up at Byrne's house and almost killed him.'

'Again?'

'No, I'm referring to the incident early last year, shortly after Byrne moved back into his mommy's house. But now that Byrne's drawing his final breaths, I'm sure Mickey's hearing a clock ticking in his head and deciding to make a final run at him. I don't want him to do that, and have told him as much. But I think he might listen more to you.'

Memories came to her of summer days spent at a beach in New Hampshire, followed by wild nights of drinking and other . . . things. Darby shifted in her chair and felt her pulse race when she said, 'What makes you think he'll listen to me?'

'You two grew up together, went to the same high school. You understand these people – you're a part of that stubborn Irish Catholic clan that's still entrenched here.'

'You're Irish Catholic.'

'Ah, but I didn't grow up here, which, as you know, makes me a permanent outsider. And the fact that I grew up in one of the W-towns and went to Boston College – even some of the Belham cops treat me like I'm some privileged rich white asshole.'

'That's because you are a privileged rich white asshole.'

'Ah, I miss your sarcasm and ball-busting.'

'I was being serious.'

'I am too,' Kennedy said. 'I need you, Darby. I want to find out where Byrne buried Claire Flynn and the two other girls, so I can nail that prick to the wall. Will you help me do it?'

4

That same morning, just shy of 5 a.m., Mickey sat alone inside his truck, staring out at the Hill. He desperately wanted a cigarette but didn't want to ruin the smell of lilacs. They sat beside him on the passenger seat, wrapped in cellophane. He had them sent overnight, every year, on the eve of Claire's –

He sucked air sharply through his nose and held it as his vision blurred. He had never said the word, even in his private moments, and he refused to say it now.

The flowers' overpowering but pleasant scent filled the truck, taking him back to that one spring when Claire – she must have been all of three at the time – had asked if she could take some lilacs from the tree in the backyard and place them in her bedroom, Claire going on and on about how much she loved the way they smelled. He remembered propping her on his shoulders, and after they filled up one of her plastic beach pails, they headed upstairs and placed the flowers around her room.

No, Daddy put the flowers under *the pillows, not* on *the pillows*.

Her exact words but the voice was wrong. It was Claire's voice he heard, but it was stuck at three. He could recall how her voice sounded at three and the years before and after that, thanks to all the videos he'd taken of her, but he had no idea how her voice might sound now, fourteen years later, at seventeen. Yes, she would be seventeen by now. A young woman. She would have traded her glasses for contact lenses. The little-girl ponytail would be gone, and her ears would be pierced – just one on each ear, he hoped, simple and tasteful. She'd probably be wearing some jewellery, not much, and she would be interested in boys and choosing her clothes with great care, because, even when she was a little girl, she had strong opinions about what she wore. She would be a senior in high school, probably on the honour roll, because she was smart. She would be looking at colleges, a whole new life ahead of her.

If he saw her right now, would he recognize her? Would he be able to see some of the last, lingering traces of the little girl who thought tossing a Nerf football in the backyard was an awesome way to spend a weekend afternoon?

The National Center for Missing and Exploited Children had a computer program that could turn a photo of a kid into what he or she might look like at a certain age. Twice a year, NCMEC emailed him dozens of pictures of what Claire might look like now, at seventeen, and, as good as they were, all these dizzying combinations muddied his head. At night, he would lie in bed and try to settle on the one that spoke to him the most, but all he ever saw was the real Claire, the flesh-and-blood six-and-a-half year old he'd held in his hands and tucked into bed; the little girl with blonde hair and a gap-toothed smile who wore thick glasses and always smelled like a dog because she insisted on having Diesel, the big, burly bullmastiff puppy they'd adopted, sleep with her underneath her bed covers.

And now that version of Claire was fading too. The only time he could get a lock on her was when he drank, and he couldn't drink any more because of the court order. He couldn't do a lot of things now.

Mickey checked the digital clock on the console. He'd been sitting here for over half an hour. He needed to get going soon or he was going to be stuck in traffic and risk being late for his appointment in Boston. The court didn't tolerate lateness of any kind, for any reason. He left the engine running, grabbed the flowers and got out of the truck.

The winter sun was starting to rise behind the tall pines in the woods. As he walked, he thought about the other gaping wound in his life: his mother.

He had been eight the last time he'd seen her. They had been on their way home from the library, his mother picking up her weekly fix of paperback romances with titles like *The Taming of Chastity Wellington* and *Miss Sofia's Secret*, when the snow turned violent, the wind howling so hard Mickey wondered if the car would tip over. Traffic was backed up everywhere because of an accident, and they weren't the only ones inside St Stephen's Church waiting for things to calm down.

His mother had been a petite French woman who spoke perfect English, so small and light that Mickey would tightly clasp his hand around hers, afraid that if he didn't she might blow away. She flipped a page in one of her books, her face serious but relaxed, the way she looked when she prayed. The fingers of her other hand caressed a beautiful silk blue scarf. It was imprinted with ancient pillars, statues and angels, and looked completely out of place against her bulky winter jacket.

'*It's rude to stare, Mickey,*' she said in a soft voice. Even when she was mad, which was hardly ever, her voice stayed that way.

'*Where'd you get that scarf?*'

'*This thing? I've had it for a long time.*'

His mother's lies were as easy to spot as her bruises. She was careful never to wear it around Sean, his father. She put it on after she left the house; took it off and stuffed it in her jacket pocket before she got home. Mickey knew she hid it in a box marked 'Sewing' in the basement. Two Saturdays ago, after his father had left for work, Mickey had caught her in the basement, removing the scarf from the box – also the hiding spot for her photo albums.

His mother smiled at him – the smile that made men stop and take notice of her. That told him he was safe. It reassured him everything was going to be all right.

The next day she was gone. Her car, a Buick Century pockmarked with rust, was parked in the driveway when he came home from school. Mickey expected to see her in the kitchen, reading one of her paperback romances by the table near the window and smoking a cigarette, but the house was quiet – too quiet, he thought, and felt the hammers of his heart pound. He opened the basement door and descended the stairs, Mickey remembering how lately his mother had been spending a lot of time down there, lost in her photo albums. When he hit the bottom step, he saw the box marked 'Sewing' in the middle of the floor. He removed the top, saw that the photo albums and the blue silk scarf were gone, and right then he knew, with a mean certainty, that his mother had left without him.

Mickey widened his eyes and blinked the memory away.

The Hill's floodlight was always on and he could see the trails carved by sleds in the snow, and the places where people had gathered at the top. He walked to the monument that had been set up in memory of Claire and the two other missing girls, and placed the lilacs on the ground, next to its base. The fragrance of the flowers was strong even out here in the cold wind, and as he stared at the place where he'd found her sled: he imagined the powerful scent of these flowers riding through the air, blowing through other cities and states, blowing to wherever Claire was. Maybe she would smell the lilacs and it would trigger a memory of the room waiting for her at her home here in Belham, and maybe today she would pick up the phone and call.

Mickey knew the thought was ridiculous, but he didn't care. That was the thing about hope. It made you believe anything was possible. It made you believe in miracles.

Dr Donna Solares's Boston office had dark-grey walls that made Mickey think of storm clouds, and a beige couch and matching chair that were as rigid as her glass-top coffee table. With the exception of a pair of framed degrees, both from Harvard, the only other personal item was the oil painting hanging on the wall behind her desk, a wide canvas full of the kind of drips, squiggles and blobs found on a housepainter's drop cloth. The picture had a title: *Memory*.

She sat across from him, a copy of last Sunday's *Boston Globe Magazine* sitting on her lap. Mickey saw Post-it notes sticking out along the edges. He couldn't make out the handwriting.

'Why didn't you tell me about this?'

Mickey shrugged. 'Not much to tell.'

Her thin, pencilled eyebrows jumped in surprise.

'When Claire's anniversary date draws closer,' Mickey said, 'I call up some people and have them pull whatever strings they can, see if I can get Claire's name out there. It helps keep interest in her alive.'

Alive. Her eyes lit up at that word, Mickey knowing what she wanted to say: *You believe your daughter could still be alive.* These sessions had touched upon that, his inability, as she called it, to let go and grieve. He wasn't going to go down that road with her, so he said, 'It's been eleven years. The papers wanted to run an article, so –'

'I noticed your ex-wife didn't give an interview.'

Mickey said nothing.

'The reason I brought it up is so we can discuss the side story on your father.' She had a deep voice, husky, the kind he associated with a lifetime of cigarette smoke and hard liquor. Or maybe all the fat under her chins was strangling her vocal cords. Take away her designer suit and pearls, the expensive watch and makeup, and she'd look like any number of the obese soccer moms he'd seen splayed in chairs along the sidelines.

'I had no idea the reporters were going to talk with him, if that's what you're asking,' Mickey said. Which was one hundred per cent true. And he had to admit he was impressed by the reporters: they had not only managed to track down Sean in his hiding spot in Miami, but they had also somehow convinced him to talk.

'What was your reaction when you read the article?' she asked.

'I didn't have one.'

Dr Solares's gaze was fastened on him, watching, scanning him like an X-ray, probably searching for signs of what the court called his 'anger management issues'. The judge had sentenced him to a lengthy (and ridiculously expensive) anger-management course, followed by forty-eight mandatory sessions with this woman, to discover why he had attacked Richard Byrne, the man everyone knew was responsible for Claire's abduction.

Fortunately, this therapy bullshit ended today – as long as he kept his cool.

'This is the first time your father –'

'Sean,' Mickey corrected her. 'I've told you a hundred times, that man is not my father.'

'This is the first time he's spoken publicly about his granddaughter.'

'Claire's not his granddaughter.'

'I'm not following.'

'Sean never met her. Sean hasn't been a part of my life in a long, long time.'

'Since your mother left.'

'That, and the fact that the guy is a shitbag. It's good to keep your distance from a person like that.'

'The reporter asked your father if he'd talked to you since Claire's abduction.'

Mickey slowly drew the air through his nose. Sean Flynn had absolutely nothing to do with what had happened to Claire – and the woman knew that – but here she was, yet again, poking around the subject. She pinched one of the Post-it tabs between her sausage fingers and opened the magazine.

'Your father said, "Mickey and I haven't talked much since the day he got married. That's his choice. Some men need hate to get them through the day."' She looked up, waiting for a response.

Mickey didn't give her one.

'Any thoughts?' she asked.

'Not really.'

'I believe he gave this interview because he's trying to reach out to you.'

'To do what?'

'Make amends.'

Mickey couldn't help but smirk. 'Sean reaching out?' he said, leaning forward to pick up his Dunkin' Donuts coffee cup from her glass table. 'All due respect, I think you're the one who's reaching here.'

'The reason I'm pressing you on this is because I want to make sure you're looking at him the way he stands now and not through some leftover filter from childhood.'

'Filter from childhood,' Mickey said evenly.

'We tend to confound parents with their roles and not view them as people. I've noticed that you tend to view people in either/or categories – good or bad, smart or dumb. I can certainly appreciate your feelings regarding your father – and I'm certainly not trying to placate you by suggesting I have any idea what it was like growing up with a paternal figure who was unpredictably violent.'

'Don't forget murderer. Sean killed people for a living, remember?'

'For the Irish mafia, yes, you told me. Be that as it may, there's clearly another side to him – the one that raised you after your mother left, took you to sporting events

28

and the like. The side your mother initially fell in love with and, for many years, loved. If he was willing to share his feelings in print, maybe he would be willing to open up and share the truth about your mother.'

'You mean like how and when he killed her and where he buried her?'

Now it was her turn to be silent.

As she wrote something on her pad, Mickey thought about the pewter keychain in his front pocket: on the front of the circular disc was an etching of St Anthony holding the baby Jesus, on the back an image of a church in Paris, *Sacré-Cœur en Montmartre*. The keychain had been sent in an envelope to the home of his friend Jim Kelly a month after she left. Mickey still had the letter, had read it so many times he could recite the words: *The next time I write, I'll have an address where you can write to me. Soon you'll be here with me in Paris. Have faith, Mickey. Remember to have faith no matter how bad it gets. Remember how much I love you – and, most importantly, remember to keep this quiet. I don't have to remind you what your father would do to me if he found out where I was hiding.*

The second letter never came, but four months later, in July, Sean had come home from a three-day 'business trip', called Mickey out into the backyard and launched into a spiel about how his mother wasn't ever coming home. His old man had made the mistake of leaving his suitcase open, and when Mickey walked past Sean's bedroom and saw it, he did a little investigating and found an envelope holding a passport and plane tickets to Paris. Only the passport and the tickets were under the name 'Thom Peterson'.

'Your father is alive, Mickey,' she said. Then she paused, he guessed, for dramatic effect. 'It's my opinion that he will try to approach you in an attempt at reconciliation. How you choose to deal with this if it should happen is, of course, entirely up to you. My suggestion is to approach it with an open mind. Which brings us to Father Byrne.'

Mickey felt the heat climb into his neck.

'Father Byrne,' she began.

'He's not a priest any more. The Vatican finally stripped that from him. That was in the article right there on your lap.'

'Yes, I know. The article also said he's dying of pancreatic cancer.'

Dying. The word pressed against his chest like concrete blocks. It hurt to breathe.

'I'm worried his impending death might cause you to confront him again,' she said.

Mickey stared at the painting behind her desk and thought about how it didn't matter that Byrne owned a winter jacket that was an exact match to the one described by the witness, the boy on the Hill, Danny Halloran. It didn't matter that the next morning, Saturday, when the storm broke around nine, the bloodhounds had followed Claire's scent through the trails to the boyhood home of Richard Byrne, an old weather-beaten Victorian house where his mother still lived. It didn't matter that Byrne was a now-defrocked priest who had abducted three young girls, including Claire. What mattered was evidence.

Evidence, Mickey had learned, was the Holy Grail. No evidence, no case. The Belham detectives and Boston's top crime-scene investigators had gone in with all their collective forensic expertise and power. They examined every inch of Byrne's mother's house, the tool shed in the backyard and the battered Ford van he drove; yet they had failed to come away with the two most important elements: DNA and fibre evidence. That meant Richard Byrne could hold a press conference and play the victim, right down to asking the public to pray for the safe return of Claire Flynn. He could, if he wanted to, stand at the top of the Hill and watch little girls sledding. Byrne was a free man and free men could do anything they wanted.

Building a case takes time, Mr Flynn. You need to be patient, Mr Flynn. We're doing everything we can, Mr Flynn. Your daughter's case is our top priority.

The police were good men, he supposed, but they didn't understand what it was like, losing a child, even though a lot of them had kids of their own. Claire was *his* daughter, and to ask him to be patient while the mother-fucker who took his daughter went about his daily life . . . Mickey had reached his limit, couldn't stand the idea of dragging that knowledge with him to bed, waking up chained to it again the next morning. Something had to be done. Something *was* done.

'Mickey?' she asked. 'Did you hear what I said?'

'Yeah.' He swallowed, then cleared his throat. 'Yeah, I did.'

She studied him for a moment. Assessing. Prying.

'I'm sure the cops are talking to him,' he offered.

'As of today, you and I are officially finished with these sessions. You still, however, have another seven weeks left on your probation. If you make contact with him in any way, if you violate any of the other conditions of your probation, a judge will have no choice but to send you to jail. Are you still attending A A meetings?'

'When I can.'

'But not every day.'

'Hard to do when you own your own business and pay for things like therapy.'

'You need to work the programme as part of your recovery. That means attending –'

'I've been sober for almost two years,' Mickey said.

'And you need to stay that way well after your probation ends. You'll need a support system in place to help you deal with your alcoholism.'

Mickey felt the anger seeping past his face. He wasn't an alcoholic, hated it when she used that word – and she used it a *lot*. Got off on bringing it up every chance she had.

'You'll also need a structure in place for when Father Byrne – excuse me, when *Mr* Byrne dies.'

The anger had gone to work behind his eyes, pressing against the soft, vulnerable tissue like hot coils of wire – the signal that he was about to lose his shit. He gritted his teeth, telling himself to keep his mouth shut, stared at a spot on the carpet and started the visualization exercise he'd learned in his anger-management course. Instead of picturing an ocean or a woodsy New England postcard, or imagining himself placing his anger on a raft and watching it go down the river, or some other such bullshit, all he could picture was the $125 stuffed in his front pocket – the amount of her hourly fee. He had to pay for it out of pocket because his insurance didn't cover these visits, and, as he rubbed his face, the skin hot and damp, he imagined her lying against the floor and him sitting on top of her and stuffing crumpled $1 bills into her fat mouth one hundred and twenty-five times.

'Is there something you'd like to share?' she asked.

'Just practising one of those, you know, visualization exercises.'

She brightened. 'Does it work?'

'Yes,' Mickey replied. 'It works amazingly well.'

5

Mickey's probation officer suffered from a major case of little man's complex and approached his job with a strict, by-the-book mentality. Thief, arsonist, rapist, murderer, heroin addict, drug dealer or the father of a missing girl who had beaten the shit out of the man responsible for taking her and two other girls – in Frank Towne's world, you were all lumped together and afforded the same level of contempt.

Mickey had been on his way out of Boston, heading to a remodelling job he and his friend and business partner, Big Jim Kelly, had booked in Newton, one of the more upscale cities located west of Boston, when Towne called and told him to head over to the probation office in South Boston.

'I thought we were meeting tomorrow morning,' Mickey said.

'We are. This is one of your random drug tests. I need you to swing by, blow in the tube and piss in the cup.'

'I'm already out of the city.'

'So turn around.'

Mickey tried to bite his tongue, couldn't. 'Really? Today? Of all days?'

'What's wrong with today?'

You know today's the anniversary of my daughter's abduction, prick.

Mickey, though, kept his mouth shut. He was so close to putting this all behind him and didn't want to ruin it. And Towne, being the asshole he was, would have no problem telling the court that Mickey Flynn had refused to come to see his PO. So Mickey turned around and, for nearly two hours, fought the crushing gridlock traffic. By the time he got through his meeting with Towne and drove to Newton, the morning would be gone.

Towne, barely thirty and all of five-five and dressed in a suit his mother had probably picked out, dumped his well-worn leather briefcase on top of the counter in the bathroom down the hall from his office.

Towne handed him a plastic cup and said, 'Fill 'er up.'

The terms of Mickey's probation required him to take a piss test in front of his PO; it was the only way to make sure the urine sample was, in fact, his. Mickey unzipped his fly, and, once Towne saw that he was, in fact, taking a leak using his dick and not some elaborate tubing connected to a hidden bag holding someone else's piss, he checked out the condition of his gelled hair in the mirror.

Lying inside Towne's briefcase was a copy of today's *Globe*. The headline ELEVEN YEARS AND QUESTIONS STILL LINGER screamed at him from the front page. The reporters hadn't used the computer-enhanced pictures of what Claire would look like now.

Next to Claire's smiling face was a picture of Byrne dressed in a winter coat and using a cane. The photographer had captured Byrne's frailty, the deathly pallor of his skin.

Mickey, you are one lucky son of a bitch.

The voice belonged to his criminal lawyer, Alex Devine. Nearly a year ago, on a cold winter afternoon in early April,

Mickey had been gutting a kitchen in East Boston when his phone rang, Devine's secretary was on the other end of the line, telling him to drop whatever he was doing and get to the office ASAP. An hour later, Mickey was standing inside Devine's sixth-floor office, with its sweeping views of the Charles.

'I had a long conversation this morning with the DA,' Devine had said.

Mickey felt like his heart was going to explode inside his chest.

For the past three weeks, while Byrne lay in the hospital, recuperating from the attack that had left him with three broken ribs and a severe concussion, Mickey had tried to wrap his brain around the concept of possibly spending five to eight years of his life inside a prison cell. It seemed more like a foreign concept than an actual reality – like someone had asked him to pack for a one-way trip to the moon.

His only regret was that he'd go to jail not having found out what Byrne had done to Claire.

Devine was coming up on sixty, with white, wispy hair and skin that looked like sun-dried leather; he opened a folder on his desk with a wrinkled hand. Mickey's breath caught in his throat, a feeling of dread wrapping itself around his skin. Here it came, the verdict.

'Byrne wants to drop all charges,' Devine said. 'And he has stated he has no interest in filing a civil suit.'

Mickey exhaled.

'It's a smart play on Byrne's part,' Devine continued. 'Doing this shows the world he has compassion, that he's not a monster. You're one lucky son of a bitch, Mickey. You dodged a major bullet here – and, before you go thanking me, you'd better listen to the terms of the deal.'

His two years of probation included a mandatory five-week stay at an alcohol treatment programme. Alcoholics Anonymous meetings at least three days a week and a special breathalyser installed inside his truck that he had to blow into every time he got behind the wheel. If he had any booze in his system, the truck wouldn't start and the device would alert his probation officer. His probation officer could perform a breathalyser test at any time, and he had to submit to random drug testing – fail either and he'd be riding the bus to Walpole to serve a minimum of five years. Six hundred hours of community service at a place to be determined by the state. Mandatory anger-management classes and private therapy, everything paid out of Mickey's pocket.

Mickey capped the urine sample and placed it on the bathroom counter.

'Still on that job in Newton?' Towne asked.

'Still there.'

'How long?'

'End of the month.' Another part of his probation required showing proof of employment. That meant handing over cheque stubs, receipts – anything Towne wanted. Towne examined everything. Nothing was going to slide by him on his watch, no sir, no way. Frank Towne was going places, just you watch.

Towne held out the breathalyser. Mickey stared at it.

'There a problem?' Towne asked.

Mickey washed his hands. 'You guys made me install one of these things in my truck, remember? Costs me two

37

hundred a month, I have to blow into it every time I start my truck, and pull over when it asks me to blow into it again.'

'Your point?'

'If I'd been boozing, I wouldn't have been able to drive here, would I?'

'Are you refusing the breathalyser?'

Mickey took it and blew into the tube, inhaled and then blew into it again. The device beeped and spit out the reading on the display: o.o.

'Imagine that,' Mickey said. 'Clean and sober at eleven in the morning.'

'Joke about it all you want, but a lot of alkies booze it up in the morning, figuring I won't catch 'em.'

Mickey thought about correcting him, saying that even at his worst, he had never taken a drink in the morning, ever, or slipped behind the wheel after he'd had a few pops. In Towne's world, a drunk was a drunk and always would be a drunk, and Mickey wasn't about to justify himself to this punk midget suffering from a terminal case of asshole-itis.

'What time you kicking off work?' Towne asked.

'Around six or so.'

'And after that?'

'What do you mean?'

'What are your plans after work?'

'Home.'

'Make sure you stay nice and dry. Remember what happened the last time you got caught on the sauce?'

Strike two: Mickey had made the mistake of getting good and loaded last year on the eve of Claire's anniversary, doing it at home alone, when Towne decided to pay a surprise visit. Mickey flunked the terms of his probation – which he was sure delighted Towne no end – but the judge didn't send him to jail. Instead, the guy ordered another round of therapy sessions and another stay at an alcohol-treatment programme and more AA meetings. Mickey had had to start at zero again, work his way back up.

'You get caught drinking again,' Towne said, 'then it's strike three my friend, game over. You go to prison. Or you can behave yourself, do what you're told and get your life back. How you want to play this out is entirely up to you.'

Mickey opened the bathroom door, wondering what life Towne was referring to.

Mickey spent the early afternoon with Big Jim installing the windows for Margaret Van Buren's sprawling two-floor addition in Newton. At two thirty, they broke for lunch. The three young guys they had working for them were in their early twenties, single, and talked incessantly about the upcoming weekend: the bars they were going to hit, the different girls they were seeing and the ones they wanted to dump.

Jim picked up his lunch. 'I can't listen to this shit any more,' he whispered to Mickey. 'I'm locked in a house with four women who want to kill each other on a daily basis and these guys are having hot-tub parties with bikini models.'

If Death had a bodyguard, it would be Jim Kelly. He stood six-six and had shoulders as wide as a car fender and weighed three hundred pounds, most of it still solid muscle. He had a diamond stud in each ear and he wore a black-knit winter hat with a Harley Davidson logo pulled low over his wide forehead, and every time he ate, even back when they were kids, Big Jim shovelled food into his mouth with the quickness and ferocity of a starving man.

They sat inside Mickey's truck, eating the subs Jim had picked up downtown, Jim talking about last night's escapades with his twins, Grace and Emma, the ten-year-olds deciding 2 a.m. was a good time to get into a fight over a missing American Girl doll named Clara. Mickey tried to listen – tried to keep himself in the moment and out of his head. His head, he had learned, was a dangerous neighbourhood where he could get lost – and he was lost in it right now. As Jim talked about his crazy kids and his crazy family life, Mickey had the sensation that someone was sitting on his chest, then standing on it, then jumping, Mickey thinking all the while, *I'd chop off one or both of my legs right now, myself, if I could get just five minutes with my daughter. Just five minutes to tell her how much I love her.*

And then he thought of Byrne sitting inside his house, the seconds ticking by turning to minutes and hours – the monster was dying, and he was going to take the knowledge of what he'd done to Mickey's daughter to his grave. Mickey was gripped by crushing waves of loss and sadness and regret so powerful that he thought he was going to explode into tears.

Christ, I need a drink, Mickey thought.

And a voice answered: *Then go get one.*

'Something I need to tell you,' Jim said, his voice snapping Mickey back to the present. 'Got a call from Win this morning.'

Win, Mickey knew, was Stan Winston, a Belham plainclothes cop who was tight with Jim.

Jim took a bite of his Italian sub. 'Darby's back in town,' he said, chewing.

'Darby McCormick?'

'The one and only.' Jim turned his head to him and smiled, his eyes crinkling in humour. 'She had a private meeting with whatshisname there, the guy heading up the cold-case squad.'

'Kennedy.'

'Yeah. Him. Don't know what they talked about, but Win said Kennedy hired her to look into some shit.'

'Claire's case?'

'Dunno. Win wasn't privy, as they say, to the conversation. You know she's a doctor now? Not a doctor-doctor but a college doctor. Went to Harvard.'

'She was always smart.'

'Win said she's held up really well, still looks smokin'.' Big Jim chuckled.

'What?'

'I was just thinking of that time in our junior year, that party Todd Bouchard threw at his house when his parents went to Florida. Peter McGee went up and grabbed her ass and Darby – I mean she hauled off on him, broke his nose with one solid punch.' Big Jim grinned. 'That girl always knew how to fight.'

'That article in Sunday's *Globe* magazine,' Mickey said, changing the subject.

'What about it?'

'You read the interview with Sean?'

Big Jim nodded and took another bite of his sub, grinning as he chewed. 'Your old man missed his calling as a comic.'

'The ice queen thinks Sean's gonna reach out to me. You know, try to patch things up.'

'You serious?'

'She was,' Mickey said, and took another bite of his meatball sub.

'You should arrange a get-together. She spends a minute talking with him, I guarantee you she'll walk away feeling like she's got bite marks all over her skin.'

Or he'd just kill her, Mickey thought. *Bury her someplace where nobody will ever find her, like my mother. Like –*

No, he told himself. *Don't say it. If you don't say it, it can't be true.*

'Dotty Conasta called again,' Mickey said, wanting to stay out of his head. 'She has a couple of questions she wants answered before she signs. I'll swing by tonight, after we've finished up here.'

'Have you met her?'

'No. Why?'

'I was over there two nights ago, about to go over the plans for her addition, when she tells me to wait, wants her husband to join us.'

'So?'

'So her husband's in an urn.' Big Jim shoved the remains of his sub into his mouth and sighed. 'That job's got Excedrin written all over it.'

In his rearview mirror he saw a car pull in behind him – a white Honda Accord that looked like it had come straight from the car wash. The driver's side door opened to a flash of black leather and auburn hair, and when he turned around in his seat Mickey saw Darby McCormick striding up the driveway, heading right towards him.

6

The name Darby McCormick would forever remind him of lazy days spent on the beach, where the only cares you had were making sure your beer was cold and whether or not you liked the music pumping from the speakers. Mickey and Darby had gone to the same high school, but he hadn't really known her then, beyond bumping into her at some school thing or the occasional house party where they'd exchanged a few words, all surface stuff, nothing in the way of an actual meaningful conversation. It wasn't that he didn't like her – he did: Darby was seriously pretty and smart, not to mention confident and tough, man, she didn't take a lick of shit from anyone, what wasn't there to like? Thing was, she was a bit of a loner, and when he was around her she always seemed distant, sometimes cold, and she had this really intense 'Don't fuck with me' glare. A lot of guys – women too – thought she was stuck up, but they had it all wrong.

Darby was the type who preferred to keep her own counsel. She didn't suffer fools lightly, or gladly, or whatever the expression was, and she had erected a lot of walls to keep herself safe – and, really, who could blame her? First her cop father had been shot, and then she and her mother had been forced to make the God-awful decision to remove him from life support. Then, when she was fifteen, some crazy psycho had broken into her house and tried to kill her.

So of *course* Darby was aloof. Of *course* she had walls. How could that shit *not* affect you?

Mickey, though, admired her stubborn architecture. He had painstakingly built the same walls to protect himself, what with everyone in town knowing his old man was a contract killer for the Irish mob. Mickey could relate to the stares, people talking behind his back, all of it.

Mickey got to know her, really know her, by chance, the summer after high school graduation, when Heather's best friend Samantha and her parents moved to Newport, Rhode Island. Heather was going to spend the summer with them, working as a waitress at some fancy seafood restaurant, and the week before she left Heather told him she wanted to see other people, find out if what they had between them was real and meant to be and not the mutually shared neediness of two teenagers afraid of adjusting to life after high school.

In a weird way, Mickey had felt relieved. He had been with Heather all through their junior and senior years, and he and Big Jim had accepted a summer job up north, in Durham, New Hampshire, painting houses with a friend of theirs who had just finished his freshman year at UNH. Every Saturday morning, he, Big Jim and all the other painters who were sharing the house together on the college campus would drag their hangovers over to Hampton Beach and spend the day (and sometimes the night) partying with girls with teased hair and tats who wore lots of gold – chains, bracelets, anklets, rings, you name it – and liked to rock out to the king of the hair bands, Bon Jovi.

Except Darby, who also just happened to be working on the UNH campus that summer. Darby wore her auburn hair straight across the shoulders, like she did in high school, or tied back in a ponytail; and, unlike the other girls from Hampton Beach, she didn't feel the need to show off every inch of her skin. She read books by Hemingway and Faulkner and drank bourbon straight up while her friends read *Cosmo* and did body shots with drink names like Titty Twister and Screaming Orgasm.

On the last Saturday in July, a storm swept through and roughed up the waves. Mickey went bodysurfing, and an hour later stumbled back to his blanket and saw that everyone had gone off to play volleyball – except Darby. She sat in a beach chair, wearing shorts and a bikini top, and, as she drank a beer, alternating her attention between the sunset and the volleyball game, she seemed perfectly content.

Mickey plopped himself beside her, on the towels laid out over the sand, and saw Big Jim yank down his swimsuit and moon one of the girls. She screamed and ran away, giggling.

'You might want to tell him to use some Clearasil on his rear end,' Darby said, bringing the can to her lips. 'It'll clear those pimples right up.'

'I don't think he cares.'

'And that's what I love about him.'

'You got a thing for Big Jim Kelly?'

Darby laughed. It was one of those contagious laughs, and Mickey loved the way it rippled through him, made him feel lighter, almost hopeful of the world and his place in it.

'You know,' he said, 'me and you went to high school for four years, and this is the first time I've ever heard you laugh.'

'That's your fault, for not giving me the time of day.'

'*What?*'

'You heard me. Every time I tried to strike up a conversation, all you'd do was nod or grunt. This right here?' She pointed back and forth. 'This is the longest you've ever talked to me.'

Mickey didn't know what to say. When he looked back at her, she had turned her attention back to the sunset. Man, she looked good. No, she looked *great*.

A thought flooded his mind and turned his mouth dry, made his heart beat a little faster.

No way, a voice warned. *Not in a million years.*

But it was summer, he was having fun, and, hey, the mood felt right. Why not go for it?

'Sunset's better down by the shore,' he said. 'Want to go for a walk?'

'Sure.'

The one thing he knew about himself was that he wasn't good at pretending. When she asked him about community college – he was to attend Bunker Hill come September – he told her he was going to drop out and start a contracting business with Big Jim. Mickey liked working with his hands. It was a skill that had provided Big Jim's father, a guy with no college education, with a good house, his pick of trucks and enough money to cover his bar tabs. What was the point in taking out loans to attend classes that, when you got right down to it, added up to nothing more than a long, teasing and expensive hand job that left you feeling unsatisfied and ripped off?

'Congratulations,' she said.

'For what?'

'For knowing who you are and what you want and having the balls to go after it. Most people spend their whole lives checking off the boxes for the things they believe they're supposed to want instead of going after what they want. You should feel relieved.'

They slept together three weeks later. Years would pass, and Mickey would always be able to recall the vulnerable way Darby looked as she took off her clothes, the curtains swelling around her; the cool air filled with the smell of fried seafood wafting up from the restaurant below; the way his skin quivered when she first touched him; the way she stared into his eyes during that final, heart-twisting moment, Mickey knowing she was sharing something more precious and sacred than just her body.

It should never have ended but it did, during the last week of summer. Heather had come home from Newport in tears, telling him she had made a terrible mistake. She didn't want to see other people. She missed him and she loved him and she wanted to get back together. He said yes.

He waited until Darby went off to college before he told her it was over. He did it over the phone, and when she'd asked why, he said he was getting back together with Heather. Darby didn't buy it. When she kept pressing him, he started to dodge her phone calls because he could barely acknowledge the truth, let alone express it: his shared history with Heather was familiar and comfortable and as predictable as the tides.

Besides, how realistic was it to hope that someone like Darby would stick around for the long haul with a blue-collar guy without a college degree? He was going back to life in Belham, and Darby, well, she could go anywhere she wanted.

On an early Sunday morning, right before six, Mickey woke up to Darby banging on the front door of his house. He begged Sean not to open it.

'It's a big fucking deal when someone hands over a piece of their heart,' Darby said, loud enough to wake up the entire neighborhood. 'I know you're in there, Mickey. If you're going to shit all over me, then at least have the balls to look me in the eye and tell me why.'

Sean sat in a kitchen chair, smoking his cigarettes and grinning, delighted by the sound of Darby's fists pounding on the front door, her words. When she finally jumped back in her car and drove off, tyres peeling across the pavement and Mickey sitting on the foot of the stairs with his face buried in his hands and wondering if he'd made the biggest mistake of his life, Sean flicked his cigarette into the sink and said, 'She must've been one hell of a ride in the sack. The crazy ones usually are.'

The first thing Mickey noticed now was the confident way she carried herself. She had been confident back when he knew her, but this was something different – something that reminded him of a soldier who had endured a lot of battles and suffered many losses and used her experiences to make herself not only smarter but, perhaps, also purposeful and stronger. Seeing her, after all these years, he realized that was what had both attracted and frightened him the most: her unwavering sense of resolve and the force of her personality.

But her eyes told the real story. When she looked at you, the way she was looking at him right now, you saw someone who was not only devoted to helping you solve your problems but also someone who actually gave a shit about you, your pain. Someone who would go to hell and back to help you ease your suffering.

Darby offered her hand. 'Nice to see you, Mickey.'

'You too. What brings you back to town?'

'Consulting work.'

'As in my daughter's case,' Mickey saying it as a statement of fact, not as a question.

Darby smiled warily. Her face looked lean and chiselled, but not from stress. She had the healthy glow that reminded him of the younger generation who took an almost militant approach to their physical and mental wellbeing.

'You got a minute? If not, I can come back after you kick off work.'

'Now's fine,' Mickey said. 'How'd you know I was here?'

'I spoke to your PO.'

Of course, Mickey thought, feeling a spike of anger at how his constant whereabouts at every given moment of the day had to be accounted for, while Byrne could do whatever the fuck he wanted, whenever he wanted.

They stood near the back of his truck, the November sun warm on his face and clothes. Mickey slipped his hands into his jeans pockets, waited.

'It's about Byrne,' she said.

He felt his heart jump in his chest. His expression must have changed, because she said, 'I don't know anything new. That's not why I came here.'

'But you're working on my daughter's case.'

'I've been asked to look at it. Reason I wanted to see you is to get some . . . context, I guess.'

'Context,' Mickey said.

'How many times have you spoken to Byrne?'

'You mean one-on-one?'

'I mean any conversations you had with him – or tried to have with him outside of that one . . . incident.'

'It was just that one time.'

'Run me through it.'

Mickey stared off at the house and started with how he'd been drinking at home, alone. How he'd gone to Byrne's house late at night and banged on the door with his fist, the finger of his other hand pumping the doorbell button, until the front door swung open and there was Byrne, dressed in a wrinkled pair of khakis and a yellowed undershirt, his grey hair tousled from sleep and sticking up at odd angles as he blinked himself awake.

I didn't have anything to do with what happened to your daughter, Mr Flynn.

Where is she? Where did you bury her?

I didn't do anything. I'm innocent.

Innocent? Your name was on that list of priests who molested kids. You molested little girls. The only reason you're not in jail is because they were too terrified to testify against you. You're a piece of—

You're drunk, Mr Flynn. You need to go home.

Byrne went to shut the door. Mickey put out his hand and stopped it.

You're going to tell me what happened to Claire.

Only God knows what is true.

What? What did you say?

I can't give you what I don't have, sir. I can't give you back your daughter, and I can't take away the guilt you're still carrying for letting your little girl walk up the Hill all by herself.

It was true, what Byrne had said. He had let Claire walk

50

up that hill with Big Jim's daughter, Ericka, but the crushing guilt he felt had more to do with the fact that, earlier that afternoon, Heather had forbidden him to take Claire to the Hill. After Heather left, Mickey took Claire sledding.

But how had Byrne known that? That information wasn't in any of the papers, and Heather hadn't told him – hadn't told anyone, as far as Mickey knew.

Byrne straightened a bit, and Mickey was sure as shit the guy was suppressing a grin as he said, *Maybe if you had listened to your wife that night and put down the bottle, your daughter would still be alive.*

When Mickey snapped out of it, two uniform cops had him pinned to the foyer floor of Byrne's house. The former priest lay a few feet away, moaning. His body was deathly still, his face unrecognizable. As for how Byrne had got that way, Mickey was at a loss – still was. He had no idea what had happened, and he didn't find out until later that Byrne carried a panic button with him that could summon the police.

'You blacked out,' Darby said. 'From the booze.'

'And the anger. At least that was what I was told.'

'You've blacked out from anger before?'

'Once, I think. Maybe a couple of times,' he said. 'But I'd been drinking. Why'd they bring you into this?'

'I told you, to consult on –'

'But why now, eleven years later – *and* on the anniversary of my daughter's abduction?'

'They wanted me to take a look at the evidence, see if there's anything new.'

'And?'

'I can't find anything. But I'm going to talk to Byrne.'

'They've all tried talking to him, and he won't say shit. Why do they think you'll get something different out of him?'

'I've had a lot of experience dealing with his type over the years.'

'And what is he?'

'The clinical definition? My guess is he's a psychopath – a very clever one. Is there anything else that you can tell me about him?'

'He's dying.'

'Yeah,' Darby sighed. 'I know.'

'You think you can get him to talk?'

'I'm going to try, Mickey.'

'Better do it soon.'

She held his gaze for a moment.

'I'm sorry,' Darby said. 'For everything you've gone through – for everything you're still going through.'

He sensed she really meant it, that she wasn't paying him lip service like all the other cops. The anger and frustration he'd been carrying with him since his meeting with his PO – it didn't go away but it receded a bit.

'I heard about you and Heather,' Darby said.

'Happens a lot, I'm told. You know, couples who lose a kid. They often don't make it.'

'How long has it been?'

'That we've been divorced?' He shrugged. 'Three years or so.'

'I'm sorry.'

'Don't bother talking to her. She doesn't talk about it any more. To anyone. Not even me.' He saw the question in her face and said, 'Heather has decided to . . . She's let it go or made peace with it, I dunno.'

'The parents of the other two girls,' Darby said. 'Are you still in touch with them?'

'I've talked a lot with Judith – that's Elizabeth's mother – over the years. She's from New Hampshire. Nashua.'

'What about her husband?'

'Never met him. As for Mary Hamilton's parents – well, I should say parent. Nancy was a single mother, lives in New Bedford. At least I think she still does. Nancy was –'

'Sorry to interrupt, but what about the father? My case notes said he abandoned the family when Mary was two years old.'

'He did. He died, Christ, six, maybe eight years ago of a heroin overdose. I only met Nancy Hamilton once, at a press conference the police held shortly after they had focused on Byrne as the prime suspect. You know, one of those public pleas to see if anyone had any information about Byrne. Nothing came of it.'

'What was she like?'

'Nancy was . . . I don't want to say a cold fish. Maybe stand-offish. Like she really didn't want to be there. She didn't want to talk to me about anything. I got the feeling she was, you know, in a lot of pain. She developed an addiction to Xanax, I heard, had to go into treatment. What's with all the questions? Not that I mind, I'm just curious.'

'I was hoping you could do me a favour and get in touch with them, let them know I'll be calling.'

'Why? You think they won't speak to you?'

'I think they're wary of speaking to anyone who works as a consultant or a private investigator – and rightfully so.'

'Why's that?'

'Because some people will try to take advantage of

them, ask them for money to look into their case. Not all, but some. I don't want them to think I'm doing that here. And if you call them and let them know who I am, they'll be more willing to pick up when I call. Oh, and when you give them my name and phone number, tell them that I'm working with the Belham police.'

'Okay. Sure. I'll do that today. Anything else?'

'Not at the moment.' Darby reached into her back pocket, came up with a card and handed it to him. 'My cell is written on the back. If you remember anything else or if you just need to, you know, talk, don't hesitate to call me.'

'You staying in town?'

'Yeah. The Budget Lodge on Route 6.'

'Well if you've never had an STD before, you're sure to get one now.'

Darby laughed a little, and, just like that day on the beach when he'd first heard it, the sound lifted something in him, made him feel lighter.

Mickey was staring at the card, at the doctor title in front of her name, the Ph.D. at the end and the term FORENSIC CONSULTANT, when she reached out and hugged him – a real hug full of genuine emotion and warmth, not the awkward embrace he got from some women who acted like the abduction and murder of his daughter was an infection that could be spread through physical contact. She kissed his cheek, and, as she walked back to her car, he found himself thinking about his mother for some reason, Mickey wondering if she had come into his bedroom early on the day she'd decided to leave without him and maybe kissed him goodbye.

7

Darby had never been big on reminiscing. She didn't devote much time or energy to re-examining the past and constantly asking 'What if' questions. What was the point? The past – good, bad or indifferent – was still the past. The laws of nature and physics didn't allow you to time travel and perform a do-over.

Something happened in your life, you performed a forensic autopsy. You took a good, hard look at what happened, saw where you screwed up, what you could have done better, and hopefully learned some valuable lessons about yourself. Then you shut the door on it and moved on. Unless you were a victim of trauma, in which case confronting your past was key to recovery. Picking at the scabs of regret or indulging in make-believe, wishing and pining away for a different outcome, were not only completely and utterly useless but also the definition of insanity. A self-indulgent exercise that imprisoned you in a lifetime of pissing and moaning about life's random unfairness and cruelty rather than dealing with the reality. The world didn't care about you; it wasn't designed to care. Wishing for life to be fair and considerate, to show mercy and understanding, rather than stubborn, unwavering indifference, was the province of man, not nature. Wishing for the world to be different was about as productive as wishing that a leopard could change its spots.

But, as Darby drove away from the construction site, she found herself thinking about Mickey. More specifically, the summer she had fallen in love with him.

The power of first loves and the sway they hold over your life was a popular and endlessly mined theme that had made romance writers and Hollywood producers billions. Darby had known Mickey and his buddy Big Jim Kelly all through high school, had seen Mickey at various places all over town. While she considered him handsome and rugged, a hard-working farm boy who had traded his cowboy boots and Stetson for Timberlands and a Red Sox baseball cap, she had never entertained any romantic feelings about him until that summer in New Hampshire. There he had opened up about his life, his dreams and desires; shared the pain of having his mother pack up and leave without him; the awful truth of what it was like growing up with a man who was a full-time psychopath and contract killer; and the burden of knowing his father wasn't above killing his wife, whom he had used as a human punching bag, for abandoning them.

Mickey had shared all these things with her when he was sober too, which said a lot about him. It had been Darby's experience that most men did not share their fears, burdens or the secrets that ate at their souls like acid unless they were very drunk, and usually only after they had been endlessly prodded or nagged.

She was a virgin the first time they slept together. Mickey had been kind and patient, and had shown a level of respect and maturity that wasn't common in boys his age. He made her needs a priority, not his, and when it was over she had learned that two people could create their own private world where the problems and daily heartache of life couldn't penetrate. Mickey Flynn had renewed her faith that maybe heaven was, in fact, a real place, one that could be reached not by daily suffering and kneeling and praying in a church but by the rare and singular chemistry created between two people who had mutually discovered, together, the terrain of each other's souls.

Then Heather had wanted him back and Mickey had returned to her not so much out of love (although, at the time, Darby was sure he did still love Heather) but because the woman who would become his wife was a known quantity. Heather was safe and her ambitions were rooted in Belham and not in the world outside of it, and Mickey had gone back to her because, at the end of the day, his world was in Belham too. He had no desire to live, let alone explore, a life outside the city limits.

And now, after all these decades apart, she discovered that the scar left by the man she had first fallen in love with wasn't a scar at all but a wound that, while healed, was still as tender as it had been on the day she drove away from his house, hands gripping the steering wheel and streams of tears burning across her cheeks. That day she vowed never to let another man get so close. Then she had met Jackson Cooper, but by the time she was ready to reveal her true feelings to him she discovered that not only was he in love with another woman but also engaged. He lived in Virginia with his fiancée, and their once-close friendship had been reduced to the kind of short texts and emails shared periodically between colleagues and acquaintances.

That was all in the past, so why was she brooding over

Coop? Why was she feeling the way she did right now about Mickey, which was insane, given the circumstances in which she found herself? She was here to help solve the mystery about what had happened to his daughter. Was some part of her lizard brain searching for permanence? Did some part of her want to set down roots back in the city where she had grown up, a place that to her felt on most days like an open-air insane asylum?

Maybe she lacked perspective in her life. Or maybe it was because she didn't have a life. Take away her investigator's badge and gun, deny her access to a murder book or piles of evidence, and she would disappear, become . . . what?

She didn't know.

Her thoughts shifted to Byrne. She needed more information on the former priest, needed to get as many perspectives as possible before confronting him – even though another part of her wanted to go straight at him, discover the real reason why he'd asked to speak to her and only her.

She drove back to Bedlam.

A Boston 25 news van was parked on Byrne's street, the reporter standing in front of the former priest's house and doing a remote. Darby also spotted another reporter conferring with a cameraman and quickly drove down a side street, so she wouldn't be seen. She didn't want the media to know she was in town.

Darby didn't care for reporters. In her experience, they were more concerned about infotainment and becoming talking heads rather than doing actual journalism. She had learned the hard way that once the media discovered she was involved in a particular investigation, they would resurrect the same stories of how her father had really died, the number of psychopaths she had hunted down and killed, and how she had been almost killed by one when she was a teenager – a man the FBI called Traveller, who had gone on killing for decades until she confronted him again, this time inside an elaborate maze of horrors that had left him dead and her with a hatchet wound on the left side of her face. It had required extensive plastic surgery, including a brand-new cheekbone. The surgeons had told her she was lucky she hadn't lost her eye.

Since she was already in Belham, she decided to pay a visit to the man who probably knew Byrne the best: Father Keith Cullen. Cullen and Byrne had been at the seminary together, Kennedy had told her, and, from all accounts, the two had once been close friends. When Byrne became a suspect in Claire Flynn's disappearance, Cullen had stuck by him. Their friendship fractured when the news came out that Byrne was also possibly linked to the disappearance of several other girls, and when the Boston Archdiocese finally, under intense public pressure, released the list of paedophile priests, Cullen had severed all contact with Byrne.

St Stephen's still looked the same to her: a towering Gothic structure of brick and tall, stained-glass windows that seemed to want to devour souls rather than save them. This was where she had been baptized and received her first communion, and then, later, been confirmed. The burial services for her father and then her mother had been at this church. It didn't surprise her that she associated St Stephen's – all Catholic churches, really – with death and suffering instead of solace and hope.

Father Cullen, the prim, ancient secretary informed

her, was not at the office today and she refused to explain where he was. That changed when Darby took out her badge. It said 'Investigator', not 'Police Officer', but the woman didn't notice. All she saw was a badge and that was enough to alter her demeanour.

'I don't know the details,' the woman said defensively. 'I wasn't present when it happened.'

'Could you be more specific, please?'

'This morning's . . . incident with Heather Flynn and Father Byrne.' The woman looked puzzled. 'Isn't that why you're here?'

'What happened between Byrne and Mrs Flynn?'

'It's Miss now, and, as I said, I don't know the details.'

'Who does?'

'Father Cullen.'

'I'd like to speak to him, please.'

'He's not here. Would you like me to leave a message?'

'What I would like is for you to tell me where he is right now.'

The secretary glanced at the watch on her plump wrist. 'He's probably still at the track at Belham High School.' She smiled like a proud mother. 'Father Cullen is a competitive runner. He runs the Boston Marathon every year.'

'Yes, I know.' She knew Father Cullen from her school days at St Stephen's, had had him for several classes. He'd also taught cross-country.

She found him running by himself on the track, dressed in dark-grey sweats and a heavy, hooded navy-blue sweat-shirt. When he rounded the corner and saw Darby standing next to his gym bag, he slowed to a walk and pulled down his hood.

The man looked older and greyer but still had the lean frame she remembered from her childhood, the sad, almost rheumy eyes that seemed to be unable to bear the weight of what he heard in the confessional, what he saw in the world. Or maybe it was from drinking. Her father had once told her that Father Cullen worshipped at another altar – ones with polished mahogany bar tops and clientele who wore ties and could afford bar tabs for high-end whiskies and bourbons. Her father, who never held back his opinions on people, had also told her he found Cullen to be a smug and arrogant man who believed he was morally and intellectually superior to those he served in the parish, someone who relished talking down to his parishioners, putting them in their place. That had been her experience too.

'Dr McCormick,' he said, his voice sounding frail. Wispy.

'You remember me.'

'Of course. You've become something of a celebrity, if that's the right word, here in our hometown.'

Darby, catching the undercurrent of derision in his tone, grinned. 'I understand Heather Flynn had a run-in with Byrne this morning.'

He didn't seem surprised by her words, which made Darby believe the secretary had called and given him a heads-up.

'They're not married any more,' Cullen said. 'But, to answer your question, yes, Heather came by the rectory this morning to see me and bumped into Father Byrne.'

'He's not a priest any more.'

'Technically speaking, that's true. But a man of the cloth is always –'

'What happened?'

'You'd have to ask Heather. I wasn't present.'

'What was Byrne doing at St Stephen's?'

'He came to see me.' Cullen didn't volunteer any further information.

'About what?'

'Private matters.'

'Like asking you for last rites?'

He smiled knowingly. 'Being the good Catholic you are – or were, Doctor – you know I'm bound by the sacrament of confession, which means I can't, even in a court of law, reveal the contents of our conversation.'

Darby glanced out at the field. 'Richard Byrne is a paedophile.'

'If you say so.'

'You believe otherwise?'

'It's not a matter of belief, Doctor. Correct me if I'm wrong, but the crux of your profession relies on the burden of proof. Last I heard, no charges were ever brought against him.'

'Three girls disappeared in the parishes where Byrne was a priest – one of them right here,' Darby said. 'How do you explain that?'

'I can't. What I can say is that God has a plan for all of us. Even you, Doctor.'

'That's what I've always hated about being a Catholic,' Darby said. 'People like you are always quick to judge people like me when we do something wrong, but when we shine the light on your sins, well, that falls under the umbrella of God's great plan.'

Cullen glanced at his watch.

'A man – not God – a man named Bernard Law

knowingly and willingly, for decades, shuffled paedophiles all over the Northeast. Byrne was one of these men. Law moved Byrne – who was suspected of molesting several girls in New Bedford, and may have very well been the man responsible for the abduction of Mary Hamilton from her own backyard – up to New Hampshire. Then one day Elizabeth Levenson's mother calls and says she's got car problems, so Byrne gives the girl a ride home and Elizabeth disappears. Byrne says he's innocent, and the police believed him, because your boy Bernie kept all of Byrne's molestation stories to himself.'

Cullen drank from his water bottle.

'You ever think that maybe if Bernie had opened his mouth, then Claire Flynn – whom you baptized – might still be with us right now?'

Cullen swallowed and wiped his mouth with the back of his hand. 'I'm not sure what you're asking,' he said.

'Your opinion.'

'Am I ashamed at the way the Church handled all the sexual-abuse victims here in the state and, for that matter, all over the world? Of course I am. Did the Church ignore and betray the victims afterwards? Yes. It's abominable, quite frankly, and it makes me sick. Richard makes me sick. Is that the kind of honesty you came here seeking, Doctor?'

'It's a start. I'm told you and Byrne were very close back in the day.'

'*Were* being the operative word. Now, if you'll excuse me, I'm running a bit late for another appointment.'

'I'm not through with my questions.'

'Then I suggest calling my office and making an appointment.' He reached down and grabbed his bag.

'There's a man who's living in a daily hell, wondering what happened to his daughter.'

'And there's not a day that goes by when I don't think about how incredibly painful and difficult this is for Mickey and Heather and for Richard's other victims.'

'So you believe he's guilty.'

'I hope you make some inroads, Doctor. I'll pray for you.'

'All due respect, Father, prayers aren't what solves a case.'

'Then I'll wish you well.'

Darby turned and started walking across the stiff, cold grass, heading back to her rental car.

'Dr McCormick?'

Darby turned. Cullen was walking towards her, his gym bag gripped in a bony hand. 'I take it you're planning on talking with Richard,' he said.

'He asked specifically to speak with me.'

'About what?'

'He wouldn't say.'

Cullen turned his head to the side, his gaze darting back and forth across the tall pines, the sky. He looked as though he had aged a decade. Maybe it was the angle of the sun. He definitely looked troubled, though.

'There's this wonderful quote about the Devil that I believe is attributed to James Garfield, our twentieth president,' Cullen said. 'A brave man, he said, is one who looks the Devil in the face and tells him he's the Devil. It's a nice sentiment, very noble, and makes for a good story. But those stories don't talk about the consequences a brave man or woman suffers for doing such a thing.' Cullen turned back to her. 'I'd hate to see that happen to you.'

'I've dealt with his kind before.'

'And at significant physical and mental costs, from what I've read.'

'I appreciate your concern, Father –'

'But you're going to talk to him anyway.'

'The man is dying. If I can convince him –'

'Richard isn't going to give you what you want. He isn't going to tell you anything about those girls. That he asked to speak to you tells me he has something he can use to hurt you.'

'Such as?'

'I don't know. What I *do* know – what I can promise you – is that when you're done speaking with him, you won't be the same person. The man is evil, and that's a word I don't often use, Doctor.'

'But that didn't stop you from administering the last rites to him.'

'I denied him the sacrament,' Cullen said. 'I won't bore you with the specifics of canon law, but suffice to say that if someone refuses to show signs of repentance before death, the Church can refuse funeral rites, and a Catholic service. I denied Richard both. If he wasn't willing to confess his sins to me and ask God for forgiveness, what on earth makes you believe he'll confess anything to you?'

8

Heather Flynn had moved from Belham to Rowley, a town located thirty miles north of Boston and about as different from Belham as you could get: nicely kept suburban homes on ample-sized lots. She lived in a well-maintained white Cape with a two-car garage. Tiny white Christmas lights, the kind a lot of people now used all year round, had been artfully arranged on the branches of a bare tree in front of the house, the neighbourhood – the whole town, really – giving off the bucolic vibe she associated with rustic New England: farmhouses and fields, no Dunkin' Donuts and ATMs on every street corner, the streets quiet, pristine and undisturbed.

Darkness was creeping into the sky and a light snow had begun to fall when Darby pulled into the driveway. She had no idea if Heather was home, and she hadn't called ahead to see if the woman would be. After her conversations with Mickey and, earlier, Kennedy, who had told her that Heather practically all-out refused to talk to the police and reporters – anyone – about what had happened to Claire, Darby had the feeling she screened her phone calls, even more so today, the eleven-year anniversary of Claire's disappearance. Still, Darby needed to talk to her, had to try. It was always harder to say no to someone in person.

Darby rang the doorbell, and she felt slightly relieved

when she heard the sound of approaching footsteps. Now came the hard part.

For half a second, Darby didn't recognize the woman who had opened the door. Heather Flynn had blonde highlights now, her hair cut short and styled with a product that gave it a messy, just-got-out-of-bed look. And, while she had never been heavy, the woman had been carrying an extra twenty or so pounds when her daughter had disappeared. Now she, looked emaciated, her cheekbones more prominent.

The pleasant expression on the woman's face turned to surprise, then annoyance.

'My name is Darby McCormick. We met when –'

'I know who you are.' Her gaze flicked past Darby to the rental car parked in the driveway, then to the street.

'I came here alone,' Darby said. 'I was hoping I could speak with you.'

'I don't want to rehash what happened to my daughter – especially today. You *do* know what today is, I hope.'

'I do. And I didn't come here to speak about what happened to Claire.'

'Then why are you here?'

'May I come in?'

Heather Flynn weighed the question on her cold scales, tapping her thumb against her thigh. She wore stone-coloured khakis and a white shirt. Darby had the distinct feeling the woman had been expecting someone else.

'I don't have a lot of time, Miss McCormick, so you'll have to be quick.'

The warm foyer was eerily quiet. A rolling black suitcase sat next to the foot of the stairs.

'Going someplace hot, I hope,' Darby said.

'France.'

'Sounds nice.'

Heather shut the door and motioned to an archway that led into a small living room. Heather immediately took the chair, sitting ramrod straight as she crossed her legs and folded her hands across a knee, looking like a woman who had just been asked to give a deposition in a room full of hostile men.

Darby didn't take off her jacket. She unzipped it, though, and sat on the stiff couch. Everything in this room and the adjoining one looked stiff and unused, everything neat and clean, no dust. This house didn't look like anyone lived here on a daily basis. It didn't look or feel like a home either, no family pictures, nothing. It looked staged.

'Someone's coming by to pick me up and take me to the airport,' Heather said.

'Looks like I arrived just in time.'

'I'm not normally home when Claire's anniversary rolls around. I can't deal with all the well-wishers and friends dropping by, to see how I'm doing. The phone calls. Then there are the reporters and such who stop by un-announced wanting to ask their questions.' *People like you*, her eyes said.

'What about Mickey?' Darby asked. 'Are you two still in touch?'

'He usually calls every year, on the anniversary date. Although I haven't heard from him yet.'

'I saw him today – a couple of hours ago, as a matter of fact.'

'What do you want?'

'I understand you saw Father Byrne this morning at St Stephen's.'

She visibly stiffened.

'Did anything happen?'

'Yes,' Heather said coldly. 'The son of a bitch held the door open for me.'

'Is that all he did?'

Heather considered the question. 'He was standing there with this . . . this sick grin. He said, "You're looking well, Heather. Life in Rowley must really be agreeing with you." Then he held the door open for me.'

'And what did you do?'

'I told him that I hoped he was in a lot of pain and that he would rot in hell.'

'Did he say anything else?'

'I didn't stick around, for reasons I'm sure I don't have to explain.'

'Have you shared this with Mickey?'

Heather Flynn recoiled as if she'd been slapped. Her mouth hung open and her eyes were heated with insult. 'Why would you say such a thing to me? You think I want to torture him with what happened to me with Byrne *today*, on the anniversary of our daughter's abduction?'

'No, I don't think you want to torture him. I only asked because –'

'Mickey has a restraining order against him. If he gets anywhere within a hundred feet of that . . . thing, they'll arrest him. That's our great legal system at work.'

'I'm sorry, Heather.'

'I don't want your apologies or your prayers, even your

kindness or sympathy. What I want is for you to leave.'
Heather got to her feet.

Darby remained seated. 'They want me to speak with Byrne.'

'Why?'

'I've had experience with men like Byrne. Belham PD thinks I –'

'He won't tell you anything.'

'That's the same thing Father Cullen told me.'

'And he's right. It's rather arrogant, don't you think, that you believe you're going to be the one who's going to get him to crack?'

Darby didn't want to explain how Byrne had asked for her. Doing so might get the woman's hopes up that Byrne might possibly be looking to confess what he did to her daughter and the other girls before he died.

'What can you tell me about him?'

'He's a monster,' Heather said. 'Beyond that, I couldn't say.'

'But you had interactions with him in the past, at church and when your daughter was attending St Stephen's.'

Heather folded her arms and puffed up her chest – a subconscious, defensive gesture people often used when wanting to protect themselves, or to closely guard a secret. 'My interactions with him were limited. A quick hello, nothing more,' she said. 'Did Mickey tell you that son of a bitch used to call the house?'

'No.'

'This was early on, before he became a suspect. He'd call and talk to me, ask me how I was doing. And I'd cry on the phone, he'd listen and offer me all sorts of *wonderful* sympathy and support. He even came by the house a few times. He was –'

'Like he really cared,' Darby offered.

Heather took a deep breath, swallowed. Nodded.

'And after he became a suspect? Did he ever call you?'

'Several times,' Heather replied. 'I never talked to him, because I never picked up the phone. But he'd leave messages saying he didn't do it, to believe in God – all of that happy horseshit. The calls stopped when the news came out about him molesting girls. The police never told us about that; we had to learn about it from the papers and TV.' Heather said the last words with acid.

Darby had come here to listen and learn, not to engage in a debate about the harsh realities of police work. She said nothing.

Heather had turned her head to the window. She stared at something outside, her eyes filmed with thought.

'What?' Darby prompted.

'I was thinking about St Stephen's. The playground. Well, it's not a playground, just an area behind the school where the kids can run around. Byrne was always outside, watching the children with the other teachers during recess, and I always had this . . .' She shook her head, focused back on Darby. 'Forget it.'

'Please. Finish the thought.'

Heather sighed. 'Even before Claire vanished, when I saw him out there with the kids . . . he took an interest in the girls, and I always had this sense, this feeling, that he wasn't watching to make sure they were, you know, safe.'

'How was he watching them?'

'Like he was sizing them up, trying to find their weak

71

spots.' She rubbed her forehead. 'I'm probably not making much sense. In fact, I know I'm not.'

'You're doing fine. Why did you go to St Stephen's this morning?'

'To see Father Cullen.'

'To say goodbye,' Darby offered.

Heather eyed her coldly.

'When are you moving?' Darby asked.

'When I get back from my vacation with my . . . friend. Did Father Cullen tell you?'

'No.'

'Then how did you know?'

'It was just a guess. Your house has that showroom feel to it, everything perfectly staged. Does Mickey know? About your moving?'

'I don't see how that's any of your business.'

'It's not. It's absolutely none of my business,' Darby said. 'I only mention it because . . . Heather, you're the last link he has to your daughter. And, while you two may not see each other any more, there's still a part of him that's comforted by the fact that you're not that far away.'

'That's right, you're a shrink. I remember reading that somewhere. A *Globe* article, I think, from a couple of years back – the one that talked about how you were fired from the police department.'

'You should tell him, so he can prepare himself, is all I'm saying.'

'I'd like you to go.'

'The other two girls who disappeared,' Darby said, getting to her feet. 'What are their parents like?'

'Why are you asking me this?'

'I haven't spoken to them yet and was hoping you could give me your general impressions.'

'I've never met them.'

'But you've spoken to them.'

'No. *Never.*'

It was the emphasis Heather put on the word 'never' that took Darby by surprise, as though speaking to the families of Byrne's other two victims was completely and utterly ludicrous. It must have shown on her face, because Heather said, 'Did you expect us to, what, form some sort of support group?'

'Victims of a violent crime often –'

'My daughter is dead.' Heather's voice was flat, unemotional, but her eyes burned with the kind of pain and suffering Darby had seen far too often. 'Richard Byrne isn't going to tell you, God or anyone else what he did to Claire, or why, or where he buried her. She's never coming home. None of those girls are.'

9

Mickey's truck was parked on a side street, and he sat inside, smoking a cigarette and watching Byrne through the man's dining-room window.

The former priest sat at a table warped by water damage, sucking deeply from an oxygen mask. His skin appeared sunken, pulled tight against the bone, and his bulky black cardigan seemed to belong to a man twice his size. His hair, once grey, was now gone.

A thin, middle-aged woman, her hair in a braided ponytail, placed a glass of water with a straw in front of him. Byrne nodded his thanks as the spidery fingers of his free hand, the knuckles bent and twisted from arthritis, reached for the glass.

The woman had to be either a private nurse or a hospice worker, Mickey thought. She had that air about her, and he knew Byrne had no family. Heather's mother had battled lung cancer, and when it became crystal clear there was nothing more the doctors could do, she decided she wanted to die at home, in her bed. The hospice worker, an overweight, patient man with a warm smile who always smelled of a citrus-scented lotion, had been sent in to relieve her pain, make Heather's mother as comfortable as possible during her final hours.

Final. The word pressed against his chest, squeezing all the oxygen from his lungs and making him feel light-headed.

Byrne pulled his mouth away from the straw and started panting, as though the simple act of drinking had left him winded.

You need to turn around and leave.

Look at him. He could be dead tonight.

All he has to do is make one phone call and the police will haul your ass off to jail. You want that?

He can't see me.

Do you want to go to jail?

That afternoon, shortly after Darby left, Mickey had received word through Big Jim's cop buddy Win that Byrne had gone to St Stephen's to see his good buddy Father Keith Cullen. Win didn't know the exact reason why Byrne had gone there, but the word on the street was the ex-priest was looking to confess his sins to his old friend Father Keith. If that was true – if Father Keith had given him the sacrament of confession – no police officer, judge or jury could make Father Keith reveal the contents of whatever Byrne had said during confession.

He'd read Byrne was dying, but, seeing the man now, up close and in the flesh – the clock ticking inside Mickey's heart grew louder. Stronger.

The way Mickey figured it, if any bit of humanity was left inside of Byrne, if that side had been strong enough to seek out Father Cullen this morning and confess his sins, maybe that part of Byrne was still locked in there somewhere. Maybe that part of him was terrified of dying without having unburdened his soul. Father Cullen couldn't reveal the contents of the confession, but maybe he had mandated that in order to be *truly* forgiven in the eyes of God, Byrne had to confess what he knew and relieve the victims of their suffering. Maybe if he appealed to the man's human side, maybe Byrne would –

His cell rang. Mickey glanced at the console and saw Heather's name on the screen. He also saw the time: half past seven. She rarely called him this late – rarely called him at all. They hadn't spoken much after the divorce, and on the few occasions she'd called him it was usually about some financial matter involving a clerical error on their divorce paperwork – Mickey continually amazed by how many things had got screwed up, the number of incompetent people there were in the world who held jobs, and people who simply didn't give a shit.

He wasn't in the mood to talk about any of that now. He was about to let the call go straight to voicemail when he remembered he hadn't spoken to her today. He always called Heather on Claire's anniversary date. Mickey took the call.

'Hey,' he said. 'How's it going?'

'That's the question I was going to ask you. I didn't hear from you today.'

There was a lot of commotion in the background. Mickey placed his hand flat across the other ear and said, 'Yeah, about that. Sorry. I got tied up. Work-related stuff.'

'But you're okay.'

'I'm breathing. How about you? How are you, you know, managing?'

'I'm at the airport.'

'That explains all the noise I'm hearing.'

'I'm going on a trip for a few weeks.'

'Good. That's good.' He was looking at Byrne drinking through the straw again. 'Can I give you a call back? I need –'

'I'm moving,' Heather said. 'When I get back.'

Mickey felt a new and different fear brush against the walls of his heart. 'Where?'

'New York,' she said. 'A friend – well, a friend of a friend, actually, his business is moving to Japan. He owns this apartment on the Upper East Side and he's letting me sublet it for a few months. It's a beautiful place.'

He stubbed out his cigarette in the ashtray.

'Mickey? You still there?'

'Yeah,' he managed to say. The fear had found his vocal cords. He had to swallow several times before he could speak. 'Sounds expensive. New York.'

'It is. But I have the money my mother left me. The apartment's on the fifteenth floor. It has an amazing view of the city. It's just so beautiful.'

Mickey said nothing, his eyes on Byrne, watching him sucking greedily from the oxgen mask.

'I need to do this,' Heather said. 'I need to move on and –'

'Can you still see her?'

'I think about Claire all the time. I haven't forgotten her, Mickey, if that's what you're asking.'

He found himself getting angry and he wasn't sure why. It didn't have to do with her comments about Claire or selling the house; they had covered that ground before, numerous times. So why was he getting pissed off now?

It was New York. His only remaining connection to Claire was moving away. Leaving him.

'What I meant was, when you close your eyes, can you see her face?'

'Yeah. Of course I can. Why?'

'What about the way she looks now? You think she might look like those computer photos they gave us?'

'I remember her the way she was. I can't think about the way she'd look now because –'

'What?'

There was another long silence, Mickey about to fill it when she said, 'I say this because I care for you. You know I do. But you need to come to grips with –'

'I can't see her face any more. I can still hear her voice, the things Claire said, and I remember the things she did – what we all did together – but her face is always a blur, and I don't understand why. I didn't have this problem before.'

'When you were drinking.'

After Claire disappeared, he'd lie on her bed and close his eyes and see her as clear as day – when he'd been drinking. And the two of them would have the most amazing conversations until he passed out, Heather there in the morning shaking him awake, until she decided to leave him.

Mickey found it difficult to breathe. He slammed his eyes shut, fighting tears, as Heather said, 'This morning I was at a bookstore and this boy, he couldn't have been more than four, was in line with his mother holding a copy of *Make Way for Ducklings*. You remember the first time you read that book to her?'

Mickey swallowed. 'Claire was around three.' He took in a deep draught of air through his nose. 'You bought her the book for Christmas.'

'The first time you read it, Claire begged us to take her into Boston to see the ducks, remember?'

Mickey felt a smile reach his face. He remembered how disappointed Claire was to learn that the swan boats inside the Public Garden weren't actual swans. That disappointment nearly turned into tears when Claire saw the bronze statues of the mother duck and baby ducklings from the book. *Dees aren't the ducks from the story, Daddy, dees ducks aren't real!* During the ride home, though, Claire came up with an explanation: *Dose ducks are made of medal, Daddy, 'cause that way people can't hurt them. Dose kids sitting on the backs of the mother duck and baby ducks? If I had people sitting on my back all day my back would hurt real bad and dat's why they're made of metal so they won't get hurt. At night, when everyone's sleeping — dat's when they turn into real ducks and go swimming in the pond with the real swans!*

Claire had been sitting in her car seat in the back of his truck when she'd said those words. The windows were down, the wind whipping her blonde hair around her face; she'd been wearing a pink Red Sox hat and a pink sundress, both gifts from Heather's mother, and she had a chocolate ice-cream stain on the front of her dress. He remembered all those little details and more, and when he tried to see her face now it blurred again and started to fade. *No, baby, please don't leave me.*

Heather was saying something to him, asking him a question, maybe. He said, 'Sorry, I didn't get that.'

'I asked you if we can get together when I get back.'

'Yeah. Sure. Have fun on your trip.'

Mickey didn't give her a chance to say anything else. He hung up, dumped the phone on to the console and wiped at his face. His throat was bone-dry and his arms felt weak. He also felt light-headed and his chest felt tight, as though small rocks were blocking the arteries to his heart. But his thinking was crystal clear. He knew he couldn't allow Byrne to take his knowledge with him into the ground. He needed to find out what Byrne had done to her and where she was buried, even if that meant going to prison. If he didn't try, Mickey knew he would never be able to look at himself again. He got out of the truck.

10

The air was cold and raw, but there was no wind. Mickey shut the door softly and stuck to the shadows so Byrne couldn't see him from the dining-room window.

No one was outside. He was alone.

The house sat on the street corner. Mickey turned, stepping up on to the sidewalk, and looked at the front of the house. The same rotting waist-high redwood picket fence was here, although Byrne had nailed a pair of neon-yellow plastic signs made of reflective material to the front pickets: NO SOLICITING NO LOITERING NO TRES-PASSING <u>ALL</u> VIOLATORS WILL BE PROSECUTED.

Mickey flipped up the latch for the gate and was about to open it when he heard a voice behind him say, 'Stop.'

Mickey flinched, face flushed with guilt and anxiety at having been caught. He turned and saw Darby McCormick step out from the shadow of an oak tree on the sidewalk. She walked towards him, her hands stuffed in the pockets of her black leather jacket, puffs of steam blowing around her hard-set face.

'What are you doing here?' Darby asked. She sounded more concerned than angry, and he was sure he heard some sympathy in her tone.

He also felt a wave of relief. The business card she had given him earlier said she was a forensic consultant. She wasn't a cop any more. He was safe.

'You're violating the terms of your probation,' Darby said, keeping her voice low. 'If you don't turn around and leave –'

'What are *you* doing here?'

'You need to get out of here, Mickey, right now.'

'You're here to talk to him, aren't you?'

'Do you want to go to jail?'

'Answer my question.'

'You actually think he's going to talk to you?' Darby asked, Mickey noticing the way she glanced down the road, as if someone were hidden there in the dark, watching. 'That he's going to invite you in for a sit-down?'

'I could say the same thing to you.' He shifted his stance and leaned closer, holding her gaze when he said, 'You wouldn't have come here unless you'd found out something. Something you can use against him.'

'Mickey –'

'Tell me what it is.'

'I haven't found anything. I –'

'Then why are you here? And why are you following me?'

'I don't have time for this. Leave. I'll fill you in tomorrow, okay?'

'You're not a cop any more. You don't get to order me around.'

Darby took out her phone.

Mickey felt like she'd spat in his face. 'You're going to rat me out?'

'Mickey –'

'This is my daughter we're talking about. He hasn't got much time left – he may *die* tonight for all I know, and I have a right to know if –'

'You need to leave. Now. If you don't, I'll have someone come here and take you away.'

Anger exploded inside his head. His eyes burned and his limbs shook with rage. 'They were right about you, what they said. You *are* a rat.'

She flinched at the last word. Somewhere in the back of his mind he knew he had crossed a line – knew too that what he'd just said wasn't entirely true. She had exposed crooked cops and crooked politicians, one of them the Boston Police Commissioner, the first woman who'd ever held the job, for getting in bed with a well-known Irish gangster Sean had worked for once upon a time. She had stood up and done the right thing, and she'd lost her job because of it.

Her voice was calm when she spoke. 'You're a good man, Mickey. I've always respected you, and I can't even begin to explain how truly sorry I am for your situation. And you probably won't believe me when I say this, but I'm on your side, and I'm trying to protect you. Which is why I'm going to ask you one last time to leave. I won't ask you again.'

Mickey looked away from her, at the dimly lit windows of the house, and felt as though every inch of his skin were wrapped in barbed wire.

Get arrested and risk going to jail, or trust her to do whatever job she's come here to do?

Darby's gaze dropped to her phone. She began to dial. Mickey turned around, his heart tearing in half, and when he took that first step, heading back to his truck, he was so light-headed he thought he might pass out.

11

Darby unlatched the front gate, Mickey's parting comment about her being a rat still ringing in her ears. It was one of the things she detested about Belham, the whole 'code of silence' bullshit she'd grown up with, the lifers carrying it around like a badge of pride – and Mickey was a lifer, the guy never having travelled anywhere beyond New England. It was one of the main reasons why their relationship had been doomed from the start: Mickey was the type of guy who wanted to live within borders; Darby the type who, for as long as she could remember, needed to bust through them.

As she marched across the walkway and up the front steps to the roofed porch, Darby again wondered what Byrne's true agenda was.

Time to find out. She rang the doorbell, stepped back and slid her hands into her jacket pockets. Her ears were numb from the cold and the rest of her felt numb too, and that didn't have anything to do with the temperature.

Darby heard a deadbolt slide free. The door cracked open and she saw a pair of old-fashioned security chains no one used any more because they were useless.

The small, thin woman who answered the door had the type of round, pleasant face Darby associated with people who had grown up in the Midwest – kind, friendly, decent. She wore drab khaki slacks with a dull grey sweater and white nursing clogs. The hospice worker, Grace Humphrey.

'I'm here to see Mr Byrne,' Darby said.

The woman straightened a bit, glancing past Darby to the street, expecting to see a cameraman, perhaps.

'I'm not a reporter,' Darby said. 'He's expecting me.'

She frowned. 'He didn't tell me he was having any visitors this evening. Your name?'

'Darby McCormick.'

'Let me check.'

The woman didn't invite her in; she shut the door. Darby heard the deadbolt slide home.

Why? Did the woman think she was going to, what, kick down the door? Or had the nurse simply done it out of habit?

While Darby waited, she took a good look at the house, with its peeling grey paint and the porch's weathered floorboards, the newspapers and soup cans packed in the recycling bins, the heavy dark curtains drawn over the front windows – the perfect home, she thought, for a dying monster. There was no solid evidence to suggest he was, in fact, a monster. No evidence had been uncovered (and, she secretly believed, never would) to connect the former priest to any of the abductions, but there was a solid pattern of behaviour, as Kennedy had said earlier this morning.

She also believed Byrne had no intention of confessing what he'd done to those girls or where he had buried them. The true agenda of a psychopath was always the same: manipulation.

And pain. Lots of pain.

The deadbolt slid back again, and the door cracked open. Both security chains were still in place.

'Father Byrne isn't feeling well,' the woman said from

behind the chains. Her voice was tight, and she had the frantic, fearful look of someone who had seen or overheard something she wished she could erase. 'He told me to tell you to come back tomorrow afternoon.'

Darby sensed the woman had more to say. She moved closer to the door. A wave of heat brushed against her face – it felt like Florida in there – and she could smell the unmistakable odours of stale cigarette smoke and cooked food.

'What's your name?' Darby asked.

'Grace. Grace Humphrey.'

'You're Byrne's hospice worker.'

'I'm also a nurse.'

'You seem uncomfortable.'

The woman didn't reply. She swallowed, her throat working.

'Do you need help?' Darby asked. 'I'm working with –'

'I know who you are. Father Byrne told me.'

'He did?'

The woman nodded. 'He said you're an investigator of some sort.'

'That's right.'

Darby waited for the woman to elaborate. She didn't.

'Did he say anything else?' Darby asked.

Grace Humphrey's face twisted in discomfort. 'He asked that . . . He wanted me to tell you to –' She cut herself off and her eyes slammed shut as she drew in a sharp breath. When she opened her eyes again, she studied the ratty-brown carpet beneath her clogs. 'He wants to see you tomorrow, at one. He said you should wear something pretty. Sexy.'

The next morning, a few minutes shy of seven, Darby headed to Coolidge Corner, the birthplace of former president John F. Kennedy, to speak to Danny Halloran. Kennedy had given her Halloran's address and phone number.

It was Saturday, and traffic heading into the city was light. She didn't call ahead, not wanting to give Halloran a chance to hang up on her and then head out somewhere, avoid his apartment. It was early enough; she was hoping to catch him at home, asleep.

Halloran had been nine and was the last person to have seen Claire Flynn before she vanished. He was also the only one who had seen her at the top of the Hill. Darby had read through his interviews when Kennedy first asked her to review the Flynn case, and she had read them again last night. She wasn't holding out any hope of discovering anything new from him.

So why was she going to speak to him? Police reports were dry and factual, devoid of feeling. Talking to him in person, hearing him retell his story, would give the event life, and maybe, by talking with him, she could place herself on the Hill that night, see what happened through his eyes. Maybe she might notice something he hadn't.

Halloran lived in a corner apartment building across the train tracks used by the Green Line. No one answered his door, and he didn't pick up his phone when she called. She didn't leave a message.

Darby stood out in the cold. She was determined not to leave Boston empty-handed.

The great thing about working freelance was that she didn't have to deal with the kind of red-tape bullshit created by overworked city and state lawyers, and by bureaucratic jerkoffs who woke up every morning with a flowchart depicting whose ass they had to kiss and for how long. She could, when needed, skirt around a lot of legal issues and save valuable time and energy. It came in the form of technology, and most of it was readily available on smartphones.

Darby stayed away from the computer stuff. It changed so fast she could hardly keep up, found herself not wanting to keep up. She knew people who did this stuff for a living, and the person who came to mind was her friend Sue Michaud, who worked as a private investigator for Shapiro & Hager, one of Boston's largest and most prestigious law firms. Darby called her cell.

'You do realize most people sleep well past eight on a Saturday morning,' Sue said when she answered.

'You've always told me you're up every day no later than six, including weekends.'

'What if I had a date last night? What if you woke me up while I was sleeping in some hot guy's bed? Would you feel bad about it?'

'If any of what you just said was true, you wouldn't have picked up the phone.'

'Always the detective.' Darby could hear the smile in her friend's husky voice. Sue was direct, no-nonsense, which was why Darby liked her, and she had a deep, infectious laugh that terrified men.

'I heard you were back in town,' Sue said.

'Good news travels fast.'

'You should see these guys when they talk about you. The look on their faces, it's like someone's holding a flame right under their nut sack.'

'I need a software recommendation.'

'To do what?'

'I want to track someone's phone, see where they are – like those find-a-friend apps.'

'With those apps, the person has to give you permission, through the software, for you to track their phone. Is this person a friend?'

'Not yet,' Darby replied. 'But I hope to make him become one with my winning personality.'

'Let's make this easy. Give me the number and I'll trace the signal for you.'

'How long will it take?'

'Not long. I'm already in front of my computer. What's the number?'

Darby gave it to her as she headed back to her car, the wind strong against her back. She ducked into an alley between two buildings and the wind stopped blowing and she could hear Sue typing on the other end of the line.

'This is interesting,' Sue said.

'What is?'

'The number you gave me, it says here it belongs to Daniel Halloran. You're working on the Flynn case, aren't you?'

Darby emerged on to the street, the morning sun bright

and hard, and fished her keys out of her jacket pocket. 'I'm consulting for Chris Kennedy from Belham.'

Sue sighed. 'Those poor girls.' A beat of silence followed. 'You think what's-his-face, the priest, is going to unload the goods before he kicks the bucket?'

'Halloran – or I should say, Halloran's phone – is in Boston. At the moment, it's transmitting from 1595 Washington Street.'

'Are you going to be in the office for a while?'

'Sadly, yes. Like you, work is my life.'

'Would you mind keeping an eye on the signal, let me know if it moves?'

'I live to serve. Anything else, my queen?'

'Not at the moment. But I'm sure I'll think of something else.'

'Oh, yes,' Sue said. 'Of that I have no doubt.'

The address Sue had given Darby was that of a bakery in Boston's South End. Back when she was growing up, during the 1980s, the neighbourhood of tree-lined streets of old Victorian homes, brownstones and red-brick bowfront townhouses could be summed up in four words: stay the fuck out. Crime and poverty were rampant, the streets dangerous, even during the daylight. The upside? Rent was dirt cheap. Waves of artists and young gay men and women flocked to the neighbourhood and renovated the homes, parks, gardens and buildings, turning the South End into trendy fashion and culinary hotspots. The gentrified area was the city's most culturally diverse – and one of its most expensive real-estate markets.

Flour sat on the corner of Washington and Rutland,

across from a pair of community gardens that, during the spring and summer months, gave the area of brick-faced buildings and sidewalks a hint of suburbia. Darby bypassed the long line, entered the bakery and scanned the faces of those seated inside the tiny collection of tables that could be moved apart or pushed together. It wasn't difficult to find Halloran. He was the only one with red hair.

Halloran sat in the far corner, his attention locked on the man seated across from him – a twentysomething who wore a stylish knitted beanie and a down Patagonia jacket. Halloran was completely engrossed in whatever his companion was saying. When Halloran saw Darby, his eyes widened in fear, and he removed his hand from his friend's, gripped the edge of the table and stood, getting ready to run.

13

Halloran decided against leaving. Maybe he didn't want to make a scene, pushing his way through the crowd, or maybe his decision had to do with his friend, who had reached out and tried to take Danny's hand. Danny wouldn't let him.

The point was now moot. Darby blocked his path.

'Hello, Danny. I'm sorry to interrupt, but I need a moment of your time. My name is Darby McCormick.' She showed him her badge, but he didn't look at it. His friend did. His face tightened, the olive skin flexing across the bone. He sat up straight in his chair, looking to Danny for an explanation.

Danny slid back into his seat and leaned forward across the table, his voice low as he tried to calm his friend. 'It's okay, Vic. It's not about –'

'You promised,' Vic said, then lowered his voice. 'You promised me you were clean.'

'I *am*. It's not about that.'

'No,' Darby added. 'It's not.'

'So why did you want to run?' Vic asked.

Danny rubbed his mouth with the back of his wrist. 'I'll explain everything later, I promise. I'll meet you back at your place. This won't take long.'

Vic didn't look happy about it. He looked downright hurt as he waited for a hug goodbye. Danny's face flushed, and he offered up a pained smile, his gaze dropping to his lap, not wanting to show any sign of affection, she guessed, because he wasn't officially out of the closet yet, or maybe he just didn't want her to know.

Darby took Vic's seat. It was warm, and his cologne lingered in the air.

'Have we met before?' she asked.

Halloran shook his head. He seemed so delicate, like he was about to crack. Or maybe she thought that because of his porcelain features.

'My father told me you might be looking for me,' he said.

Halloran's father, Kennedy had told her, was a Belham cop. 'And he gave you, what, a physical description?'

'I didn't know who you were, so I looked you up online.' He kept twisting his hands on his lap. He had the kind of long eyelashes women envied, a narrow jaw and full lips that were chapped from the cold. 'I saw your pictures and that story about the guy who kidnapped people and hunted them down in that dungeon or whatever it was. Who told you I was here?'

'What does it matter?' Darby smiled. 'I'm here, and I want to talk to you about that night on the Hill.'

He rolled his eyes. Then he glanced to his right, where two men were sharing a sticky bun, engaged in a conversation about yet another nor'easter that was expected to hit the city sometime later next week.

Danny turned back to her and leaned his chest against the edge of the table, his hands still on his lap. 'Look,' he said, keeping his voice low, 'all due respect, this is harassment. I've talked to I don't know how many cops over the years, FBI agents – I even spoke to those guys they have from that group that specializes in crimes against kids.'

'Investigative Support Unit.'

'Right. I even did hypnosis back when I was a kid, to see if I remembered anything from that night – and I didn't. Everything I knew, I told.' He didn't hide his frustration, and she saw a barely concealed anger burning in his blue eyes – a rare colour for a redhead. 'I've told all of you the truth from day one.'

'No one's accusing you otherwise.'

'So why do you people keep acting like I'm keeping secrets from you? Why do you keep coming around bothering me?'

'You're the only one who saw him.'

'I *didn't* see him. How many times do I have to say it? The guy who stepped up next to me – he could have been the Cookie Monster for all I knew. I didn't *see* his face. I didn't see *a* face.'

'Danny,' she said. 'Byrne is dying.'

That took a bite out of him. 'Yeah,' he said, bowing his head. 'Yeah, I know,' he sighed.

'I'm just asking you to walk me through it.'

He stared down at the table, as though the answers he needed were buried somewhere on the scarred wood surface. He bounced a leg up and down, and he gave off the kind of manic energy that made her wonder if he were about to push the table aside and bolt for the door.

'You mind telling me why you're so nervous?' she asked.

He looked up at her and studied her face, testing the seriousness of her question.

'Everyone is expecting me to pull a rabbit out of my ass, come up with some last-minute . . . miracle that'll show that Byrne is, you know, *the* guy. What you people forget is that I was nine. I was there that night to try out my new snowboard.' He closed his eyes for a moment and shook his head. 'I should never have helped her.'

'Helped her?'

'Claire Flynn. I didn't know who she was that night; I found that out later. She was . . . Okay.' He sighed again, resigned to the fact that he had to share his experience again. 'Okay,' he said again, and folded his hands on the table. He leaned forward, so they could talk privately, and kept his voice low. 'I read you're from Belham.'

'Born and raised.'

'So you know the Hill.'

Darby nodded. 'Spent plenty of time there as a kid.'

'So that night, it's, like, five or so, and it's already pitch black. The snow had picked up and at the top there's . . . not a line but it's really crowded. I was on the farther side of the Hill, the place near the entrance for the parking lot, because that's where the older kids went sledding, you know, to keep away from the little kids, so we wouldn't run into 'em. That's when I see Ericka Kelly. I knew her from school. Everyone knows her because everyone in town knows her father.'

'Big Jim Kelly.'

'You know him?'

'I went to school with him.'

'Okay, so you know how *massive* the guy is. Six-foot-six, three bills, has a diamond stud in each ear and a sleeve of tats on each arm. One look at the guy and you can feel your nuts shrink. My point is everyone in town knows who Big Jim Kelly is, and this meltdown from school, this kid Tommy MacDonald – he's on the welfare-project crew, getting into it with Big Jim's daughter 'cause she's holding everyone up to help this little girl in a pink snowsuit get on her sled – the girl we all find out later is Claire Flynn.' He snorted. 'You know he's dead, right? Tommy Mac?'

Darby nodded. It was in the report: Tommy MacDonald, driving drunk when he was seventeen, had crashed into a telephone pole in Belham and killed himself and the two friends he had with him in the stolen car.

'Tommy Mac looks like he's going to clock her,' Danny said. 'Instead, he forces her on to her inner tube, one of those inflatable jobs that fly across the snow, and pushes her down the Hill. After that bit of fun, I notice the little girl in the pink snowsuit is walking away – only she's moving towards the part of the Hill where you can't sled because of all the rocks and trees and shit. There's, like, a ledge there, and I'm thinking, "Shit, what if she trips and falls." That's when I go to help her.'

So far everything he'd shared jibed with what she'd read in the reports. He'd told this story so many times, to so many detectives, that it sounded as though he had memorized it by rote.

'When I reach her,' he said, 'she's balling like someone chopped her arms off. I can't get her to calm down, and she's going on and on about her glasses, how she can't see without them, she can't find her glasses. I couldn't just, you know, leave her there, so I get down on my hands and knees, searching through the snow while she's bawling, and that's when a guy I *assumed* was her father steps up next to her. Not me – *her*.'

'Why did you think the man was her father?'

'You're not listening. I just *assumed* he was. I wasn't, you know, paying attention. It's not like he was carrying rope or some shit or wearing a sign that said "Warning: child abductor". I was nine. What was I supposed to think?'

'Danny, I'm not blaming you. It's just a question.'

He rubbed his forehead. Then he folded his hands on the table and looked out of the window, at the people waiting in line, and sucked in air sharply through his nose. His nostrils flared, and, when he looked back at her, she saw traces of the nine-year-old who had grown into a confused young man, unable to understand why this event had been visited upon his life, which had been changed in ways he could never have expected.

'Where I was, there wasn't a lot of light,' he said. 'Some of the cars in the parking lot had their lights on, because the snow had turned bad and the wind had picked up, so some people were leaving. He's standing sort of sideways, with his back to me. Her back is to me too.'

'How far away were you?'

'Four, maybe six feet. I'm down on my knees when he stepped up next to her. I looked up and saw a guy of what I thought was average height.'

'But you said you couldn't see his face.'

'That's right, I couldn't. I *assumed* it was a guy because he's wearing the kind of coat a guy would wear. It was navy-blue or black – definitely dark – and it came down a little past the waist. You know, a big, bulky thing. The coat had a hood and he had it tied down at the neck so it wouldn't blow off. The hood was lined with fur that made me think of a raccoon. I remember thinking his jacket looked like the one Han Solo wore at the beginning of *Empire*, you know, that scene on Hoth, in all the snow?'

'In the report, I read something about a scarf.'

'I *think* it was a scarf. I caught a really brief glimpse of something wrapped around his mouth and nose – you know, the way people do when it's really cold out – and it was getting colder out, I remember that. But I couldn't tell you if he was white, black, whatever.'

'And then you spoke to him.'

'Correct. I says, "She lost her glasses, I'm trying to help her find them." I said that 'cause she's still crying, and I'm thinking he's going to blame me for hurting her or something. He says *nothing*. I couldn't tell you if he moved his lips because, like I said, I can't see his face. I can't tell you if he heard me or if he ignored me. Then he reaches down and grabs the girl's hand. *She* yanks it back.'

'Did she say anything?'

'If she did, I didn't hear it. What people forget is that there was a lot of noise up there – you know, people talking and shouting and laughing. Then you had the wind and the cars in the lot – the engines are running, tyres crunching across the snow. That stuff. That was another reason why I went over there to help her. I didn't want her to get hit by a car.'

'What ran through your mind when she yanked her hand away?'

'I thought she was being just a typical kid. When they get upset, you can't reason with them, do anything to calm them down. You just gotta let 'em ride it out.'

'What happened next?'

'He got down on one knee and got real close to her. That's when I noticed the blanket. He had it tucked under his arm. It looked heavy, like wool, maybe, and it was a solid colour – a dark blue, maybe black. Again, I couldn't see his face, and it wasn't like I was looking at him. I was looking to get out of there.'

'Why?'

'Because I didn't want to get in trouble,' he said. 'I just assumed this guy was thinking that I'd done something to his kid, when I hadn't. I'd just been trying to help her.'

'And Claire, what did she do when he wrapped the blanket around her?'

'Nothing. Not a thing. That was the last thing I saw. I decided to pick up my snowboard and leave.' He was studying her face again. 'I'm sorry, okay?'

'For what?'

'For not being able to give you or any of the others what you want. Every time I do this, you all get the look you have right now. Disappointment.'

'You didn't do anything wrong.'

'And yet you all make me feel as though I did, which is why I keep apologizing, again and again and again.'

And Darby saw how it still ate at him: the guilt for not remembering tiny details that even an adult would have been unable to recall; for not paying more attention; for not knowing something was wrong and for not doing something about it, even though he realized, deep down, there was nothing he could have done.

'You did nothing wrong,' Darby said, hoping he heard the genuine empathy in her voice.

'That's what everyone keeps telling me.'

'I'm not bullshitting you. Hey, look at me. I was fifteen when someone broke into my house and tried to kill me. I had barricaded myself in my parents' bedroom, and downstairs this guy was holding a knife to my friend, using her to try to lure me out.'

'What did you do?'

'I ran for help.' She could see he didn't believe her. 'Go online and you'll find the story.'

Darby took out her card. 'I know the names of a couple of great therapists who specialize in survivor's guilt. You want their names – anything – you call me.'

She slid her card across the table. When he reached out for it, she saw the track scars in the webbing between his fingers.

He saw her looking and said, 'I'm clean.'

'Good. That stuff will kill you.'

'You ever done it?'

Darby shook her head.

'So you don't know what it's like,' he said. 'How it just . . . rights everything wrong inside you. It's like this glue that mends all your broken pieces, puts you back together the way God made you when you were born.'

'You didn't do anything wrong that night,' she said again.

'You going to tell my father?'

'About what? Our conversation?'

'I meant my . . . sexual preference.'

So that's why he was so nervous, Darby thought. 'Don't be ashamed of who you are.'

Her words didn't reassure him. He looked scared.

'It's none of his business,' Darby said. 'It's not anyone's business but yours.'

'So you won't say anything.'

'Of course not.'

'Good,' he said, glancing at his needle scars. 'I've already disappointed him enough.'

Driving back to Belham, Darby kept replaying that moment up on the Hill when the man wrapped the blanket around Claire Flynn and spoke softly into her ear, no doubt reassuring the six-year-old over and over again there was no reason to cry. *I'm not going to hurt you*, Darby imagined her would-be killer saying. *Just come with me and we'll call your mommy and daddy. Everything's going to be fine, you'll see.*

14

Mickey woke up that morning thinking about confession.

Not with a priest. He'd done that bullshit way back when, during his childhood, when going to mass weekly and on important Catholic holidays was a mandatory part of the school curriculum, as was weekly confession. He got the whole point about squaring yourself with God, showing that you were truly sorry, but as an adult he figured that God, if He cared, could look into his heart or soul, or even his head, any time He wanted to. If He did, He'd know Mickey Flynn was a good, decent person who loved his wife and his daughter, and was always trying to do the right thing – not perfectly, and a lot of times falling short, but trying.

The main reason, though, had to do with priests – not the ones at St Stephen's but all priests. They were men, and, like all human beings, priests had their own set of character defects. He'd known priests who drank too much and passed out drunk; priests who loved to gossip; and priests who looked down on others from their high horse of moral and spiritual authority. Why would anyone in their right mind want to share their deepest, darkest and most embarrassing secrets and monumental fuckups with a guy who might get shitfaced and decide to entertain everyone with stories of his clientele?

No, there was no need for a middleman. If you screwed

up and hurt someone, the best, most practical thing you could do was to go to that person and confess.

The refrigerator was bare, and he didn't have any coffee left. He could go out and grab something to eat, or he could bite the bullet and go do the one chore he loathed: grocery shopping. He decided to get it over with, grabbed his keys and headed downtown, thinking about Heather.

He had been straight up with her about what had gone down the night Claire was abducted. What he wanted to confess to her was something intimate, something he had shared with no one, not even Big Jim. He'd held on to it for eleven years, and when it crept up on him, and it often did, he wanted to reach for the bottle to drown the guilt – and often did. At least until that God-given right had been stolen from him by the court, which cared more about the rights of a paedophile priest than those of his victims.

As he pushed his trolley down the aisles, his mind shifted to an incident that had occurred at the Hill the month before Byrne snatched Claire – and that's exactly what it was, an incident, and a very minor one at that. Heather, though, kept referring to what had happened as an accident, and calling it that had made the event a much bigger deal than it actually was.

And it really *wasn't* a big deal – a little scary, okay, but it didn't warrant a trip to the ER. Mickey had been navigating the toboggan, Claire seated in front of him, when a sled piloted by a drunk teenager crashed into them and sent Claire tumbling across the snow, where she whacked her forehead on a patch of ice. Heather, queen of the helicopter parents, came running, and, while Claire had cried a bit, there was no blood or even a cut, just a slight bump, the skin a slight red from the impact. Heather, though, had acted as if Claire had been thrown from a speeding car and insisted on taking her to the ER, where a young doctor informed them it was just a bump, not a concussion. Heather wasn't buying the guy's expert medical opinion and went to work on badgering him, trying to get him to agree to X-ray Claire's skull. The doctor patiently explained that X-rays couldn't detect skull fractures – you needed an MRI for that – so she tried to wear him down into signing off for an MRI, the doctor finding all sorts of polite ways to say no until he grew tired of it, telling Heather she was more than welcome to get a second opinion, which, Heather said, she would.

On the way home Heather informed him – them – that sledding at the Hill was over. Claire was in tears, begging her mother to reconsider. Heather, Mickey knew, wouldn't back down. Once she said something, in her mind it became law. *You're too small*, she'd told their sobbing daughter. *I've told your father that place is too rough and too dangerous for someone your size – and I was right. I should never have agreed to it.*

The statement didn't come as much of a surprise, Mickey having grown numb, by that point, to Heather's extreme reactions when it came to their daughter. Every time Claire's glasses fell off – Claire screaming for help finding them because her eyesight was so bad – or every time Claire took a tumble or bumped her head, Heather would swoop in and take her daughter into her arms, telling her that she was fine: *You're safe, baby, everything's fine.* Heather always acted as if she'd rescued Claire from a burning building. But all these little meaningless rescues added up over time and slowly turned Claire into a frightened little girl. If Mickey didn't put a stop to it soon, Claire would grow up into a terrified young woman.

Which was why he decided to take Claire sledding that night – after Heather left. She was in charge of St Stephen's annual spring fair to help raise money for the church's after-school childcare programme, and had a meeting at the school at four. The moment her car pulled away, he helped himself to the bottle of Knob Creek bourbon he'd stashed in the back corner of one of the high kitchen-cabinet shelves. Heather had been up his ass about his drinking, saying he was hitting the bottle too hard, how the hard stuff wasn't good for his health, even though he was perfectly fine, healthy as a horse. He admitted to drinking more these days, Mickey explaining to her how it was the way he dealt with stress after a long day, how the booze unwound him and helped him to sleep. What he didn't tell her was how bourbon was also the glue holding their frail marriage together, how he would have packed up and left by now if it weren't for their daughter.

Mickey thought he was in the clear, but then Heather had forgotten something at the house, and when she returned Claire told her where Dad was taking her that night, and Mickey could hear their shouting all the way upstairs, over the spray of water in the shower. Heather marched upstairs and confronted him. Words were exchanged – heated ones; hurtful, mean ones, Heather calling him a sneak and a liar, just like his old man. Then Heather left for her meeting – and what did he do? He

105

committed one of the cardinal sins of parenting: he sided with the child. He filled up his flask and took Claire sledding.

Was he wrong for going behind Heather's back? No question. Still, he knew he was right. Real life, with its constant ass kicking and sucker punches and bone-weary bullshit, was waiting for her. You only got to be a kid once. His job – his *duty* – was to show Claire how strong she could be. Yes, life kicked you in the ass and scarred you and robbed you of the things you loved the most – like your mother, when your old man had killed her. Life didn't offer you an apology or a helping hand. Sometimes it kicked you again, harder and meaner, and your job was to pick yourself up. You couldn't let fear rule you.

Standing in the falling snow at the bottom of the Hill, which was crowded with other adults, Mickey half listening to Big Jim and covertly taking belts from his flask as he tried to keep an eye on Claire through the curtains of falling snow, he couldn't get his mind off Heather. She still looked like the young woman he'd fallen in love with back in high school. She still wore her dirty-blonde hair long and she still looked great in a pair of jeans. She still could, with a simple touch or a slight tilt of her head, make him feel as though he were the most important man in her world. But, as for whatever private battle was raging behind her eyes, he was completely lost.

And maybe it wouldn't have pissed him off so much if she'd always been that way. There had been a time not that long ago when she'd actually enjoyed having fun – like their first Christmas party at the house. Sixty-plus people crowding the basement and Billy Joel pumping from the stereo speakers – the old Billy and not the pussy-whipped Billy, the mad genius who sang songs like 'Scenes from an Italian Restaurant' and made you feel as if he'd stolen those lyrics right from your own heart – and here was Heather singing along to Billy's 'Only the Good Die Young' and hanging tough until the last person left. Heather still looking for fun an hour later, at two in the morning, when she sat on the edge of the pool table, not drunk but definitely close to it as she sang 'She's Got a Way' and unbuttoned her jeans with a wicked smile on her face. That night she had kissed him like he had something she needed in order to keep breathing. Back then when they made love, they walked away bruised and exhausted, the sex filling them both up, making them – or at least him, anyway – feel like they could conquer the world.

The first miscarriage came a few months after the Christmas party, followed by one in the spring. The year after that, she lost three pregnancies and the doctors couldn't explain why. Claire was born – early, a preemie – and that was when Heather changed. It turned her into a hyper-aware, vigilant and anxious parent, and the woman he'd fallen in love with wasn't so much gone as had been put to rest. Every time he hugged her Mickey felt like he was holding on to something hollow and incredibly frail.

The snow had picked up, but he could still see Claire. She came down the Hill in her plastic red sled, Ericka right behind her, on an inflatable inner tube. Claire looked around, saw him, waved and smiled.

He heard Heather's voice in his head: *What if she falls and gets hurt real bad this time? What if she breaks a leg or cracks her head open – Jesus Christ, Mickey, look how small she is. If she –*

What if she has fun, Heather? You ever stop to think about that?
You're putting her life at risk. You're —
I'm done, Heather. With you. With us. I can't take living with
someone who is constantly terrified of life, who refuses to allow me a
say in anything I want as a father or husband. I'm sick and tired of
it, Heather, and I'm sick and tired of you. I don't want you any
more, and I don't want this life. I want fucking out.

It seemed God had been listening that night. Heard his prayers and took away his life by taking away his daughter. God, being the all-loving and all-forgiving guy He was, ignored his pleas for Claire's safe return. But what had Mickey expected? If God had abandoned His own son at his most desperate hour, why would He agree to return his daughter unharmed?

That night, Mickey had taken Claire sledding because he wanted her to have fun. But, as he got some distance on what had happened that night, he wondered whether his real motivation was to get back at Heather. If he hadn't been so pissed at her (and a little drunk — okay, fine, he'd admit to that), he wouldn't have let Claire go up the Hill with Ericka, because his daughter *was* small. At six, Claire was the smallest kid in her class, and he constantly worried about when her growth spurt would kick in, help her to catch up with the rest of the first graders. A part of him knew he should have kept a closer eye on her, but he had been too pissed at Heather; he had reached his limit, and prayed for a way out. And God gave him one.

Mickey wanted to tell Heather and he didn't want to tell her. He wanted to unburden himself and ask for her forgiveness, even though, deep down, he knew she probably wouldn't give it to him. But he still needed to get this off his chest. He'd been carrying it for too long. What was it they said in those AA meetings about being as sick as your secrets? How could you ever truly be free of the past unless you made amends?

Mickey was thinking about how he would broach the topic with Heather when he turned the corner for the dairy aisle and saw Father Cullen, dressed in jeans and a sweatshirt, examining a container of yoghurt through his bifocals.

The priest saw him. Put the container back as though he'd been caught reading a porn mag.

'Mickey,' he said, and forced a smile.

Why does he look nervous – and why is he looking over my shoulder?

Mickey turned, looked and saw Richard Byrne standing twenty or so feet away.

15

Mickey had seen what the final stages of cancer looked like up close, when Heather's mother had been dying. In the last month of her life, she'd lost almost sixty pounds: chemo and radiation had taken away all of her hair and her strength to fight, had turned a vibrant, active woman who loved gardening, golf and running into a zombie – no light in her eyes, just a frail sack of skin and bones.

Seeing the man out in the open was very different from watching him sitting at a dining table, struggling to breathe. Byrne, using a cane, shuffled instead of walked, and he was clearly in pain. Suddenly Mickey realized just how close to death Byrne actually was. Not days now but hours.

Byrne had two men with him. They wore overcoats over their rumpled suits, and they were both thick and wide and dressed in clothes straight from the Bada Bing! fashion line. One guy, with a shaved head, picked up a carton of orange juice and placed it in his trolley. The other one was a few inches taller and had curly hair and was walking swiftly towards Mickey.

Mickey, however, couldn't keep his eyes off Byrne. The oxygen mask Mickey had seen him wearing the other night had been swapped for a nasal cannula. It was connected to a portable oxygen concentrator hidden inside a black bag that he wore slung across his shoulder, like a woman's handbag.

'Hey, Mickey,' the man with the curly hair said. 'How you doing?'

'I know you?' Mickey's eyes were on Byrne, who was gimping towards him.

'I know your old man.' Curly snorted and scratched the area under his nose with his thumbnail, his eyes downcast when he said, 'Look, I take no pleasure in doing this, but I've gotta ask you to, you know, leave.'

Mickey turned to him. 'Who the fuck're you?'

Byrne answered the question. 'He's with me,' he wheezed, the veins popping out on his neck. 'He's here to protect me. From *you*.'

Curly swallowed, his face and tone full of empathy when he said, 'Come on, Mickey, you know the drill.'

Mickey didn't move, his mind filling with images of Claire standing on top of the Hill, frightened, her vision terribly blurred without her glasses; Claire crying out for help and swatting away the strange hands so eager to touch her.

'You're in violation of your probation,' Byrne wheezed. 'I have my cell phone – and witnesses. Right, Father Cullen? Go ahead, Paul, make the call. Mr Flynn is refusing to –' He cut himself off when Mickey lunged.

Curly and his partner were quick and strong, and they stopped Mickey. Father Cullen too: the priest sank his fingers into the meat of Mickey's bicep, Cullen's back towards Byrne and his breath hot against Mickey's ear as he hissed, 'Leave him to God.'

Mickey could only see Byrne. 'YOU'RE GOING TO PAY FOR WHAT YOU DID TO MY DAUGHTER!' Spit flew from his lips and the words scraped his throat raw. They were trying to drag him away. Mickey fought them but his eyes never left Byrne's. 'I DON'T CARE WHAT IT TAKES OR WHAT IT COSTS, I'M GONNA MAKE SURE YOU FUCKIN' BURN!'

Byrne licked his lips, his eyes gleaming.

16

Winter, Coop liked to say, was one fickle bitch. Darby couldn't speak for winter in the rest of the country, but, here in New England, winters had turned into a roll of the dice when it came to temperature. Yesterday the high was in the low forties, accompanied by the kind of sharp and biting wind that had enough power to remove a layer of skin. Today the wind was gone, the temperature in the mid sixties – not exactly swimsuit weather but warm enough to melt the snow on the roofs and roads, make you open up your windows and get some fresh air.

But the nice weather couldn't warm the chill at the centre of her core or change what she felt every time she had to speak to a paedophile or child killer – the feeling that, if left up to her, she would have them all euthanized, preferably by a bullet.

In the unforgiving bright afternoon sunshine, Byrne's dark-grey Victorian home, with its weathered roof and heavy curtains covering all the windows, looked less like a haunted house and more like a canker in the neighbourhood of small but well-maintained homes full of young families, the driveways full of minivans and SUVs, those stick-figure stickers, representing a family and all its members, affixed to their back windows.

A kid, maybe a group of them, had egged Byrne's house. She saw dozens of frozen yolks splattered across the front door and windows, broken brown shells littering the porch floor and the front steps.

Darby didn't have to ring the doorbell; the hospice nurse Grace swung the door open as Darby marched up the steps. The grave-faced woman wore the same clothes as she had the previous day – stone-coloured khakis and a white shirt, Darby figuring that the woman bought them in bulk, wore them as a uniform. As she stepped inside the dim hallway where the sunshine never reached, she wondered what sorts of conversations, if any, the woman had with Byrne, the mental compartmentalization process Grace Humphrey must have gone through in order to care for the town pariah.

The foyer had a lime-green-and-brown linoleum floor that was probably popular in the fifties and fleur-de-lis-patterned wallpaper she'd seen in older funeral homes. The wallpaper was curling along the edges, the wall decorated with framed pictures of a woman taken at various stages of her life. The woman in the pictures glared at the camera in what looked like anger and suspicion, as if the lens were somehow going to capture the real person living behind her horse-like features.

'His mother,' Grace said tonelessly as she shut the door, sealing Darby inside the house. It was packed with a dry and suffocating heat, the air smelling of soup and the furtive odour of menthol. 'He's waiting for you in the kitchen.'

Darby followed, taking in the house. A humidifier hissed in a small living room – what her mother would have called a parlour – and before she passed through the archway into the kitchen she glanced into another small room, this one with an old cathode-ray TV. A TV tray holding crumbs and half-filled glasses of water and either ice-tea or booze sat next to a well-worn recliner made of brown fabric the colour of mud. The shades were drawn to keep out curious eyes, and she saw cheap silk flower arrangements collecting dust, and hardcover books the size of medical texts scattered haphazardly over the floor and couch.

Richard Byrne sat at a small circular table by a pair of windows overlooking the side street. Here the shades had been pulled back; dust motes swam in the strong sunlight. Like the rest of the house, the kitchen belonged in another century; but the faux brick floor and the yellow linoleum counters looked relatively new. On one worktop pill bottles stood in two rows, a Post-it note with instructions written in a feminine hand placed in front of each one.

Grace went over to the stove and stirred a pot of what looked like tomato soup. She had also made four grilled-cheese sandwiches and placed them on a white plate, which she picked up and brought to the table. Darby stood in the centre of the room, taking in the kitchen, her gaze roving over each object, committing it to memory.

'There's no reason to be shy, Dr McCormick,' Byrne said, the words drowning in phlegm. He was slumped in his chair, wheezing, his shoulder resting against the window, his rheumy eyes looking her up and down. 'Please, sit. I promise I won't bite.'

His greasy smile revealed his tiny yellow-and-grey-coloured teeth. 'Grace was kind enough to fix us lunch,' he said. 'Nothing fancy, I'm afraid. I'm on a limited budget these days.'

'Thank you, but I'll pass.'

'Goodie. More for me.' His eyes remained locked on Darby as Grace brought over a bowl of tomato soup and a stained napkin. 'I hope you won't mind if I eat. Dying, you will one day discover, is a strenuous business. You've got to keep your strength up. Grace, before you go, be a dear and bring me a bottle of Irish whiskey.'

Grace opened the kitchen cabinet above the pill bottles: the shelves stocked with booze. She was reaching for a bottle when he said, 'No, not the cheap stuff. The bottle of Midleton's. It's on the top shelf. We have a doctor joining us today – a Harvard PhD! What is it in again?'

'Abnormal psychology,' Darby said.

'Sounds fascinating.'

'Not really. Creeps, losers and moral cowards aren't all that interesting.'

Byrne let loose a wet laugh that broke into a coughing fit. He leaned forward, his face turning the colour of a plum as he coughed, and Grace ran over, fitted the cannula over his nose and turned on his oxygen tank. She looked like she wanted to grab her handbag and keys and rush out of the house, praying she wouldn't have to return.

Byrne wiped the spittle from his mouth and chin using the back of his hand. 'You must be very careful with Dr McCormick.' He spoke to Grace, but his attention was locked on Darby. 'This one here doesn't mince her words. Her mother, Sheila, was the same way.'

Grace looked as if she had swallowed a razor. 'Do you need anything while I'm out, Richard?'

'No, dear, I'm fine. Take your time. Treat yourself to a

lovely afternoon. If I need anything, I'll call.' His hand, pale and wrinkled and covered in liver spots, patted an old flip-phone cell.

Darby unzipped her jacket. She didn't want to take it off, but it was stifling in the kitchen, and she wanted to give the appearance of casualness, as if coming here to speak to him was something she had wanted, not him.

Grace collected her things. As she left, Darby hung her jacket on the back of a chair. Then she opened the window next to it, pulled out the chair and sat at an angle, so she could cross her legs and look out at the kitchen as they talked. She wanted to appear relaxed and aloof – wanted Byrne to work hard to engage her attention.

'You didn't wear anything pretty,' Byrne lamented.

'Not true. I wore my best clothes just for you.'

'A white shirt and jeans?' He chuckled. 'I highly doubt men get hard looking at you in *that*.'

Darby smiled. 'What's the point, Mr Byrne? I'm not –'

'It's *Father* Byrne.'

'I'm not your type.'

'Oh? And what, exactly, is my type?'

'Little girls who are light years away from puberty.'

Byrne smiled. 'Let's set up a few rules before we start the dance.' He uncorked the whiskey and poured it into two glasses – although it was more splashing than pouring, the way his arm shook. 'First, you *will* call me Father Byrne. No matter what you or that liberal dipshit currently heading up the Vatican says, I'm still a priest.'

He pushed a glass towards Darby. 'Second rule. I did not molest a single girl, not in my entire life. I would never engage in such a cruel and disgusting act.'

117

'But you would admit to taking an avid interest in your female students and parishioners.'

'Only some.'

'Why?'

'I wanted to help liberate them.'

'From what?'

Byrne picked up his whiskey. He held it with two hands, and, as he slurped from the glass, an image filled her mind – Byrne brushing away a lock of a young girl's hair, maybe even tears, as he reassured her everything was going to be okay, that the pain, humiliation and fear he was about to inflict on her was not only normal but fully sanctioned under the eyes of God.

The thought of his doing such a thing was, naturally, repulsive and sickening, and made her want to pick up the bottle and smash it across his face. But you could never let on that you felt that way. You couldn't allow your feelings to reach your face or change your body language in any way. You had to appear relaxed and interested, as though you understood their insanity, make them feel as though the way their brains were wired was, in fact, completely normal.

'What did you talk to them about?' Darby asked.

'Their favourite subject: their awful, toxic parents. Christ, what monsters they were. You may find this interesting, being a tortured Irish Catholic yourself, but in all my years of serving the Lord I've discovered that the ones who are truly sorry for their sins generally don't seek out confession. They tend to share their sins and secrets with their spouses, friends, sometimes even their children. But the ones who are actually seeking forgiveness?

They treat the confessional like the town dump. They come in, throw out their shit, and then come back the following week and throw out some more of the same shit because they truly believe God's love and forgiveness is bottomless, when, of course, people like you and me know it's not.'

'I don't know anything about that.'

'Of course you do. I know you're a believer – no, there's no reason to refute it, I can see it in your eyes. The Good Lord above has given us all a role to play. But, back to my point: how many fools have you caught in your line of work who professed to be sorry, how, should they be given just one more chance, they'd go back into the world and actually live like a human being? And you know they're lying. They're going to go right back out and kill again, molest, whatever, because that's their nature. They can't help it. It's the job of people like ourselves, Doctor, to make things right. Because that is *our* God-given nature.'

Darby said nothing.

'God,' Byrne said, 'makes no mistakes. That is why He put us on this earth – to do what he created us to do. Do you see?'

'I do.'

'No, you don't.' He sighed, his lungs crackling. 'We were discussing confession. Have you by any chance spoken to Judith Levenson?'

'Elizabeth's mother?'

'Yes. Her. She still lives in Nashua, New Hampshire, waiting for her little Lizzy to come home.'

'I haven't spoken with her yet.'

'Well, you're in for quite a treat. Judith is, to use the

parlance of your profession, a complete and utter whack job. The woman should be committed or, preferably, euthanized. But I digress. Judith was a nymphomaniac. She went to bars and picked up men – the more dangerous, the better – and took them to seedy motel rooms where she performed various sexual acts that ended with her being spit on or choked. It was the only way she could achieve orgasm.'

'She told you this?'

'Several times, under the confidential seal of confession. I cast no judgement or aspersions on her sexual proclivities, or on the fact that she'd had an abortion, which, as you know, is a big no-no in the Church. What I took exception to was Judith's weak moral fibre, how she'd imprinted her sick psychosis on her daughter. Poor little Elizabeth didn't know what to do. It was eating her alive, the way her mother physically and psychologically abused her. I took it upon myself to inform Elizabeth about her mother's – and father's – true natures. I helped to alleviate her suffering.'

How wonderfully kind of you, Darby thought. 'And Elizabeth? What happened to her?'

'Who's to say? I can assure you she's in a much better place, wherever she is.' Byrne smiled again. 'Judith was very quick with the belt and the wire coat hanger – she was New Hampshire's version of Joan Crawford – and now the poor woman doesn't have anyone to abuse any more.' Byrne hung his head in mock sadness.

Byrne's deflection didn't come as a surprise. Killers who enjoyed talking about themselves would often bring you close to the edge of discovery about their crimes and what they'd done to their victims, only to back away suddenly, trying to throw your attention on to some other gruesome or sensational topic.

'I can see you're doubtful,' Byrne said. 'Maybe you should hear Judith in her own words.'

He leaned over the side of his chair facing the wall, reached down and came up with an old tape recorder, a once-popular model she remembered vividly from her childhood – a vintage Magnavox the size of a thick hardcover book.

'You recorded her confession?' Darby asked.

'*Confessions.*' Byrne smiled brightly. 'For educational purposes, you understand. Did I neglect to tell you I have a degree in psychology? Granted, it's not as *illustrious* as one from Harvard, but, still, we *do* fish in the same stream, don't we?'

Darby felt a sense of violation she couldn't put into words. While she was no longer a practising Catholic, she had grown up as one, attending Catholic school and church until her high school years. Byrne had abused the single most important sacrament provided by the Catholic Church, one that granted privacy so absolute that a priest could not divulge its contents, even if the confessor admitted to murder. A priest who did such a thing was automatically excommunicated.

He rested his index finger on the 'Play' button and she saw a predatory light come into his eyes. It was the same one she had seen up close and in person in several highly intelligent psychopaths; it was the look they got when they believed they had their victims trapped and at their mercy, their human mask dissolving and making way for the creature that lived beneath the skin.

'I don't want to hear it,' Darby said.

'I admire your ethics. Truly, I do.'

He pressed 'Play'. The plastic key clicked as it locked into place. The cassette tape turned and a woman's voice spoke over the small speaker: 'I don't know what to do, Father. I don't know what to do.'

It wasn't the voice of Elizabeth's mother, Judith Levenson.

The voice belonged to Darby's mother.

17

Darby felt the skin of her face stretch tightly across the bone.

A man's tender, sympathetic voice filled the sunny kitchen: 'You're human, Sheila. Everyone makes mistakes. God knows this.'

It wasn't Byrne. The voice belonged to Father Keith Cullen.

'I can't forgive myself,' Sheila said. Darby could tell her mother had been crying. 'I don't see how God can forgive me.'

'Have you told Red about the affair?'

'No,' Sheila replied, choking on the word. 'If I do, he'll – I don't think he'll stick around this time. In fact, I know he won't.'

This time, Darby thought, and her heart dropped. Was her mother saying she'd had a previous affair?

From across the table, Byrne watched her like a lion that had sighted prey. Darby could feel his eyes on her. She kept her attention locked on the recorder, a storm of anger and embarrassment and vulnerability roiling inside her. She wanted to shut it off and another part of her wanted to keep listening to her mother showing an extremely private and wounded side to her personality.

'Sheila,' Cullen said, 'I can't advise you about what to do on a personal level. If you decide to tell Red, I can recommend an excellent marriage counsellor.' His voice was surprisingly empathetic. 'The important thing, what I want you to understand and believe, is that God can see what lives in our hearts. He forgives those who can truly forgive themselves first.'

Sheila broke down in tears. She drew in a sharp breath, and was about to speak when Darby calmly reached across the table and hit the 'Stop' button.

Then the only sounds she heard were the slight hiss of oxygen from Byrne's tubing and the click of a grandfather clock coming from one of the adjoining rooms. She felt sick all over and her hands were shaking. She folded them on her lap, underneath the table, and stared at a space above his shoulder as fragments of her conversation with Father Cullen ran through her mind: *Richard isn't going to give you what you want . . . That he asked to speak to you tells me he has something he can use to hurt you . . . When you're done speaking with him, you won't be the same person. The man is evil . . .*

'Your mother,' Byrne said, 'goes on to say she's frightened about what will happen if she tells your father – frightened that you'll ending up hating her if she and your father get divorced.' Darby heard the smile in his voice. 'Did she ever tell you about the affairs?'

Affairs. Darby slid her gaze to his, her stomach filling with acid as she fought to keep the pain from reaching her face.

It didn't work.

Byrne nodded in mock sympathy. 'I see,' he wheezed. 'I'm so sorry. I thought you knew. I should then also assume your mother didn't tell you she was with one of her lovers the night your father was murdered.'

Blood pounded in her ears and through her limbs, and she stared at the curtains of loose flesh hanging from his chin, at his fragile neck.

Don't engage him, she thought. *That's what he wants.*

Byrne finished his whiskey and poured himself another. 'Are you sure you wouldn't like that drink?'

'I'm fine.' Her voice sounded far away, unrecognizable to her own ears.

'You certainly don't sound it – or look it. If you don't mind my saying so.'

'We're here to talk about you.'

'Your father developed quite a drinking problem, according to your mother. I think she might have told him about her infidelities.'

Darby wasn't going to talk about it – and not because it wasn't out of the realm of possibility that Byrne might be recording this conversation. She wouldn't speak to him about her mother or father or anything personal because he wanted to see more of her pain and she had already given him enough – too much.

'Your mother – I don't know if it's on this tape or another one – she carried a lot of guilt about the boy she and your father gave up for adoption, back when they were high-school sweethearts.' His features suddenly relaxed, his eyes widening slightly, his mouth forming an *o*. 'Oh my,' he wheezed. 'I guess this is the first you're hearing of this. I'm so sorry.'

He's playing you, she thought. *Don't let him play you.*

Darby slowly got to her feet.

'Would you like to know his name?' Byrne asked.

She picked up her jacket.

'You haven't asked me about little Claire Flynn yet.'

Darby slid into her jacket, her face hot, as though she were standing in front of a fire.

'I know where Claire is buried,' Byrne said.

She zipped up her jacket.

'If you leave,' Byrne said, 'I'll never tell you.'

Darby slid her hands into her pockets, balled them into fists.

Waited.

'First, a small favour,' he said. 'I want to see you.'

'You're seeing me right now.'

'Yes. And you look lovely. What I'd like to see is the way God made you.'

It took her a moment to find her voice. 'You're asking me to take off my clothes.'

'And stand before me, right in this good, strong, winter light, in all your beautiful glory. I want to see every inch of you.'

Darby said nothing.

Byrne's eyes danced with a merry light. 'I'm offering you a chance to solve the case,' he said. 'To bring those poor little girls home.'

Darby said nothing.

'If Mickey Flynn were here,' he said, 'what would he ask you to do?'

'That's all you want. To see me naked.'

'You won't have to touch me, if that's what you're worried about.'

'What a relief.'

'But I *will* touch you. That condition is non-negotiable.'

Darby turned her head and looked out of the window, at the snow banks crusted with ice and dirt.

'So how about it?' Byrne asked. 'Would you like to bring little Claire home and end the mystery?'

'Is she nearby?'

'Oh my, yes. I like having all my girls nearby so I can visit them.'

My girls. The words made her flesh crawl. 'What about Elizabeth and Mary?'

'Don't get greedy.'

Darby took in a deep breath and held it.

'Little Claire is waiting,' Byrne said.

She came around the table and stood in front of Byrne. His eyes took on a dreamy, lascivious quality. He held his glass with two hands and took a sip of his drink. Some of it dribbled down his chin.

'Strip down to your bra and panties, if you please.'

Darby looked out of the window again.

'Don't worry about being interrupted,' Byrne said. 'I gave Grace the afternoon off. We have all the time in the world, which means you can undress slowly. You can start by getting rid of that awful leather jacket. It's doing you no favours. Makes you look like a dyke, quite frankly.'

'Mind if I have that drink?'

'As much as your heart desires.'

She leaned forward for the glass and grabbed the air tube instead and yanked it from his nose.

Either Byrne lacked the strength to fight, or the inclination. Or maybe he was too stunned by what she had done. He knew he was in trouble, and he turned to the table and reached for the inhaler. Darby scooped it up with her free hand and then she pulled the tubing from the tank and leaned the small of her back against the edge of the kitchen counter. She folded her arms across her chest, the tubing dangling from one hand as she sighed.

'I feel so much better now,' she said, smiling. 'Don't you?'

The way his mouth opened and closed reminded her of a fish marooned on land.

'You,' he wheezed, his face mottled with both rage and fear. 'You just made a grave –'

'Let's start with something easy, like the tapes. Where are they?'

Byrne didn't answer. Darby watched his growing panic at having been deprived of his oxygen. She could hear the raspy wheeze grow louder with each breath, as though his lungs were being squeezed.

'I gave you a gift,' Byrne said, looking genuinely hurt. 'I offered you a wonderful gift, and all you had to do was –'

'Tell me where the tapes are, and you get to breathe for a bit. Then I'll go find them, come back, and you'll get to breathe some more. That's a fair trade, don't you think?'

'Possession of these tapes is not a crime. A judge will never sign off on a search warrant.' Byrne smiled in sour triumph.

'We're in court right now,' Darby said. 'Right now, I'm your personal judge and jury, Richie. Now, would you like to keep breathing?'

Byrne didn't answer. He gulped at the air, wheezing.

'Go ahead, think about it,' Darby said. 'You gave Grace the afternoon off, remember? So take your time. Well, don't take *too* much. It sounds like your lungs are filled with quicksand.'

'I don't have to put up with this.' Shakily, he tried to get to his feet.

Darby came off the table and used the sole of her boot to push him back down in the chair. He stared at her defiantly, the way a child would. He clutched at his neck, as though an invisible hand were strangling him.

'I . . . can't breathe.'

'Neither can your victims,' Darby said. 'Now you have something in common with them. How does it feel, Richie?'

'You'll . . . you'll never . . . know . . . what happened.' His lungs made a sick, whistling sound. He looked like he was going to cry. 'Our Father, who art . . . in heaven . . .'

As she watched his mouth working, trying to draw in air between the words of the Lord's Prayer, it occurred to her how all her efforts at trying to do the right thing – her whole eye-for-an-eye philosophy and the feeling not necessarily of comfort but of completion after dealing with men like Richard Byrne – it was all for nothing. The dead would still be the dead. The victims would suffer, dragging their guilt and hopelessness and their piercing sense of loss that never fully healed through the rest of their days, the only cure their faith that whatever world lay beyond this one would grant them a sense of serenity and peace.

The cycle would never stop. She wasn't a cure. If anything, she was a Band-Aid, a temporary fix.

'. . . thy kingdom come . . .'

Byrne slumped forward and fell out of his chair.

Darby hooked the tube back up to the oxygen tank and turned the valve. A hissing sound filled the kitchen.

'Answer my question and I'll hand this to you right now.'

'Give us this day . . .'

He's going to die, an inner voice said.

So let him die.

If he dies —

He's not going to tell me or anyone else what he did to Claire Flynn and the others.

This isn't about the Flynn girl or any of the others. This is about his taking advantage of you, and your wanting him to suffer. If you let him die, you won't have another chance with him.

Darby didn't move.

Don't let him take away what little humanity you have left. Don't become like him. Don't —

Darby stepped forward and pressed the heel of her boot on Byrne's shoulder, rolling him on to his back. She dropped the air tube on his chest.

Byrne wouldn't take it. He stared up at her, glassy-eyed, his lips moving silently. She got down on one knee and placed the tubing around his nose. Then she retrieved the inhaler from her pocket and stuck it in his mouth and pressed down on the aerosol container. Medicine hissed out of the tube but his eyes didn't focus on anything. She pressed down on the container again, then a third time, and then she saw his wormy lips wrap around the plastic nozzle and suckle it like a hungry newborn as his hand, ravaged by arthritis, wrapped around hers. It felt like sandpaper against her skin.

His eyes refocused, locked on hers, and she could smell the sour odour rising from his clothes, his breath foetid, like the rotting remains of food left at the bottom of a dumpster in summer, and he grabbed the back of her head with a furious strength, pulled her towards him and kissed her. He shoved his tongue into her mouth and she felt it mash against her teeth, and before she could react he let go of her head and slumped back to the floor.

Darby drained the glass of whiskey, but she didn't swallow it. She swished it around her mouth, gargled and spat it on him. She eyed the tape recorder, thinking about the tape in there, and made a gut decision to leave it behind. When she reached the archway separating the kitchen and the hall, she felt compelled to look back at him, and did.

He was still lying on his back against the floor, his eyes now closed, and he was smiling, blissfully lost inside his version of heaven, finally alone with the cherubs who delivered a harvest of nightmarish thoughts, images and memories that calmed his frantic, dying heart.

18

Darby had promised Kennedy she would call him the moment she got back to her car. She didn't want to call him. She wanted to go to her hotel and take a long shower, and to follow it up by using an entire tube of toothpaste to scrub her mouth, and then gargle with bleach instead of mouthwash.

As she drove away, she kept looking in her rearview as if expecting to see Byrne there, following her.

She gripped the steering wheel to keep her hands steady. All she could think about was the tape.

From all outward appearances, her parents had had a solid marriage. They loved each other and laughed a lot and they didn't snipe at each other or trade passive-aggressive comments at the dinner table like most married couples from that time. They weren't perfect – what couple was? – but, from everything Darby had seen, her parents were good, decent people, kind and loving and considerate, and always standing up to do the right thing. And now Byrne had shared a small snippet from a tape that had poisoned not just the memories of her parents but also how she viewed them as people, which was worse.

Had Byrne been telling her the entire truth, though? That was the question.

The answer, she suspected, was yes. Byrne had in his possession the sort of secrets he knew could flay her soul, and the evidence was sitting in a cassette recorder back at his house. She wondered if she had made the right decision, leaving it behind.

Being a good cop required that you know a good deal about the law. Massachusetts Statute Chapter 272, Section 99 – otherwise known as the 'Wiretap Law' – dealt with the interception of oral and written communications. Created in 1968, the law came into being in order to give law enforcement the investigative power, under strict judicial supervision, to combat the growing threat of organized crime. It also detailed what citizens can and cannot do with a tape recorder.

Massachusetts was one of a handful of states that required 'all-party' consent. Recording audio of someone, or a whole bunch of people, without their explicit consent was a felony with a maximum five-year sentence.

Possession of such a tape, however, was not a crime. There was no solid evidence that Byrne, in fact, had made the recording. Add that to the fact that Father Keith Cullen's voice, not his, was on the recording. For all she knew, Father Cullen had been the one who had recorded the confession. If that was true, how had Byrne got his hands on it?

Her phone rang. It was Kennedy.

She decided to take the call.

'*Well?*' he asked, drawing out the word, his voice spiked with hope.

Darby wondered how he knew she had left the house; then she remembered he had people watching it. *Someone must have called him.*

'How did it go?' he asked.

Where to start?

Never make it personal. That was the first rule of the job. Darby quickly collected her thoughts.

'He asked if I wanted to know where Claire Flynn was buried.'

'Hold up,' Kennedy said. 'He *confessed* to burying the Flynn girl?'

'No. He asked if I wanted to know and I said yes.' Then, in a cold, clinical manner, she told him about Byrne's proposition, leaving out the part about what she'd done to him inside the kitchen.

A long silence followed after she finished.

'I know you're going to think I'm an asshole for asking this,' Kennedy began.

'I didn't wipe the floor with him, if that's what you're wondering.'

'Then what, may I ask, *did* you do to him?'

'I left him.'

'In one piece?'

'You think I beat the shit out of him?'

'Did you?'

'I'm gonna pretend you didn't ask me that.'

'Were his bodyguards there?'

'His bodyguards?'

'He hired two guys to watch him.'

That made her straighten a bit. 'Are you serious?'

'Dead serious,' Kennedy said. 'I take it they weren't there.'

'No. Who are they?'

'Nick Rossi and Paul Ward. They work for a place in Boston that specializes in security and investigations, do a lot of work for Byrne's lawyer. This morning they took Byrne out grocery shopping and guess who they ran into?'

'Mickey was there?'

'You got it. Mickey went after him. Or, I should say, he tried to go after him. Byrne's hired muscle dragged him out of the door, Mickey screaming his head off about how he's going to go after him. This is according to multiple witnesses – including Father Cullen.'

'Did something happen? Did Byrne provoke him?'

'Byrne wanted him to leave the store – which, legally, Mickey was required to do.'

'The restraining order,' Darby said.

'Right. It must've set him off. Byrne, being the kind, wonderful soul he is, didn't file any charges. Let's go back to you: specifically, why Byrne wanted to talk to you.'

Darby's thoughts turned back to the tape. Once she told him, there was no turning back.

Did she trust him?

'I need to tell you something in confidence,' she said.

'Okay.'

Darby took in a deep breath and held it for a moment.

'Byrne had a tape. An audio cassette,' she said. 'My mother was on it. She was in the confessional.'

'With Byrne?'

'Cullen. She confessed to having an affair. That's why he wanted to see me, Chris. He wanted to play the tape for me, see my reaction and put it into his spank-bank for when he jerked off later.'

'Ladies – especially ones with degrees from Harvard – should not use terms like "spank-bank" and "jerk off". That's very crude.'

135

'Duly noted.'

'What else was on the tape?'

'I didn't listen to the rest of it. He alluded to having audio cassettes of confessions from other parishioners – namely, Elizabeth Levenson's mother, Judith.'

'Did he play them for you?' Kennedy asked, his tone urgent now.

'No. And I didn't see any other tapes lying around.'

'It's not going to be enough to get a search warrant. The problem we have is that the person on the tape – your mother – is dead, and there's no way to prove she didn't give consent.'

'When you go to confession, the right to privacy is implied.'

'Correct, but there's no way to know for sure that recording was made inside a confessional, is there? For all we know, Cullen had that conversation with your mother inside his office, where a lawyer could argue consent.'

Kennedy, unfortunately, was right.

'And there's the issue of possession,' Kennedy said.

'Possession is not a crime, yeah, I know.'

'Where's the tape now?'

'I left it back at the house. I thought – my gut reaction was that it was a set-up. Legally, if I took the tape, he could charge me with theft.'

'And you could have charged him with blackmail.'

'He knew I wouldn't do that.'

'Why not?'

'I think he's made a very careful study of me,' Darby said. 'He knows I don't give interviews, and he's smart enough to know I wouldn't want to expose myself in that way. But I didn't take the tape mainly because that's what he wanted me to do. He wanted me to take it and then he'd imagine me listening to my mother confessing all these secrets about her, my father, God only knows what, and getting his rocks off. I also think . . . never mind.'

'No, tell me.'

'When he started playing the tape, I got this feeling that some part of him was trying to goad me into killing him.'

'In other words, a normal day for you.'

Darby didn't reply. She was thinking back to Byrne's proposition, the lust he was barely able to keep out of his eyes and voice.

'Really?' Kennedy said. 'Not even a chuckle?'

'I was just thinking about Byrne's request.'

'Why? You thinking about going back there and giving him a lap dance?'

'Would you stop me if I said yes?'

'Darby, to solve this thing, I'd consider throwing my mother down a flight of stairs. Actually, I've been meaning to do that anyway. Bad example.'

'He's not going to tell me, you or anyone else where he buried those girls.'

'Something else is eating at you. I can hear it in your voice.'

'He wanted to see me naked,' Darby said. 'Paedophiles aren't interested in adult women.'

'True. But he's an old guy now, he's dying, the world knows he's a paedophile. He doesn't have access to kids any more, so he uses the only weapon he has left.'

'Humiliation.'

'You got it. But what do I know? I'm having a problem

following this guy's thought patterns. Why do I get the feeling he has some sort of endgame in place?'

'He knows he's dying, and he wants to go out creating as much damage as possible. He said Judith Levenson had peculiar sexual appetites.'

'Like what?'

'It doesn't matter,' Darby said. 'But if it's true and her tapes made their way into the public domain, imagine the shame and embarrassment she'd go through. That's what he's after, what this is all about. He wants all the attention turned on him when he decides to release those tapes.'

'And there's no way I can get my hands on them legally.'

'I doubt they're even inside the house. My guess is he has them stored somewhere.'

'Guy doesn't drive, though. The only one who visits him is the hospice lady. And now the two bodyguards.'

'So maybe she's brought stuff to him from a safety-deposit box or maybe something from his lawyer's office. Or Byrne's hired muscle could also act as delivery boys.'

'I'll look into it.' Kennedy blew out a long stream of air. 'Cagey prick, ain't he?'

'Slick.'

'How's your head?'

'Still attached to my shoulders.'

Kennedy chuckled a bit at that. 'I don't know what to say other than thank you. That and I'm sorry for putting you through this.'

'Do me a favour.'

'Name it.'

'If we end up finding those tapes, I know you'll have to log them into evidence. Just promise me you'll limit who has access to the ones involving my mother. Byrne isn't the only psychopath who gets off on people's pain and misery. Some of them work in your office.'

'Don't worry about them, McCormick. I've got your back.'

Kennedy hung up. Darby dialled Father Cullen's cell number: a recorded greeting on the other end of the line told her that the number was no longer in service.

She drove to the rectory.

The office was warm and fragrant with coffee, and she found the secretary on the phone, jotting down the details for a funeral. The woman ignored her, and after she hung up she busied herself with paperwork.

'I need to speak to Father Cullen,' Darby said.

'He's unavailable.'

'When *will* he be available?'

'He's on vacation.'

'Where?'

'I don't know, and I didn't ask because it's none of my business.' The woman's gaze flicked to Darby. 'Or yours.'

'Why did he change his number?'

'I'm under no obligation to give it to you.'

Darby knew she wasn't going to get anywhere with this woman. 'You know what? You're right. The next time you speak to Father Cullen, tell him I found his tapes.'

'His tapes?'

'Yeah, the recordings he made of his parishioners in the confessional.'

The woman blanched.

19

Mickey bolted awake, his heart twisting from a dream in which he had been trapped inside a house with a never-ending maze of rooms, Claire crying out for him: *Daddy! Daddy, I need you!*

After he caught his breath, he laid his head back against the damp pillow. He shut his eyes and thought about how Claire would crawl into bed with him and Heather when she'd had a bad nightmare – and she had them a lot when she was three and four. Claire somehow had convinced herself that there were monsters under her bed and the only way to get rid of them was to turn on a flashlight and leave it under the bed all night. When she realized the monsters had moved into her closet, she kept a light on in there too.

He could remember other events as well – like the time she had sneaked out of bed sometime during the night and gone downstairs to the kitchen, where she'd grabbed a handful of Sharpie markers. The next morning, he'd found her standing on her bed, smiling proudly as she pointed to the squiggles and stick-figures she'd drawn on the wall. Even now, all these years later, he could recall the drawing – a brown-and-purple house and a green sun and yellow grass. He could recall the drawing and other little details and yet he still couldn't see her face and it terrified him.

'I haven't forgotten about you, sweets,' he whispered in the dark. 'Daddy's just having trouble remembering.'

Daddy.

Were you still a father if your only kid was missing? Dead? What if he never –

His phone rang, the sound shockingly loud in the quiet room. He reached for it on the nightstand. The caller ID said UNKNOWN.

'Hello.'

Wheezing on the other end of the line.

'Hello?' Mickey said again.

'I know you were outside my house tonight,' Byrne replied. He sounded like someone had crushed his windpipe. 'I have you on camera.'

Mickey scrambled to think of something to say when Byrne said, 'You stay away from me or so help me God I'll call the police and send you off to prison. I'm going to die in peace, Mr Flynn. You're not going to take that away from me. Not you, not the police, not the press.'

Byrne hung up.

Mickey was about to redial the number, then stopped. The conditions of the restraining order clearly dictated that he couldn't call Byrne. If he called Byrne back, Byrne would call the police, and they would have a record of the call. Not to mention that, if Byrne were telling the truth, he already possessed evidence of a clear violation of Mickey's restraining order.

But why had Byrne called? He had never done that before.

The phone rang again.

The caller was Detective Chris Kennedy, from Belham PD.

'I'm sorry to bother you at such a late hour,' Kennedy said, 'but I need you to come down to Roby Park.'

Mickey's heart was beating in his throat. 'What's going on?'

Kennedy hesitated, and Mickey was about to speak again when the man said, 'It's best if I explain everything when you get here.'

20

It was half past four on Sunday morning, and the sky was dark. A single cruiser, its light turned off, blocked the entrance to the Hill. Darby pulled alongside it as she rolled down her window, and when the cop rolled down his she gave him her name. He nodded and waved for her to continue on ahead, where a crowd of cops was gathered around the Snow Girls memorial.

Darby had never seen the sculpture up close and in person, but she had seen pictures of it online. It had been commissioned by Belham as a way of honouring Claire Flynn – to show the public that the town hadn't forgotten her. The city set up a committee, and for several months it went over submissions from Massachusetts-based artists. The winning bid went to a Boston-based artist who had, according to a member of the committee, submitted a design for a sculpture that 'reflected the city and its core values of community'.

The artist, however, decided to ditch her original design. She would later tell reporters that she'd needed to follow her creative muse and create a sculpture that reflected the hard truth about the Catholic Church, especially here in Boston. The city discovered the woman's new design the day the sculpture was unveiled to the public.

The bronze sculpture affixed to a marble base showed a depiction of Jesus hanging on the cross. A priest stood behind him, covering Jesus's eyes with a blindfold, while Claire Flynn, Elizabeth Levenson and Mary Hamilton knelt in the snow, bundled in jackets and scarfs, their gloved hands clasped together in prayer, their faces twisted in pain and fear.

The sculpture and the artist who created it made national headlines for weeks.

Diehard Catholics who never questioned the teachings of the Church or its moral failures, as well as leaders from the Church and the Boston Archdiocese, thought the sculpture was in poor taste. The Archdiocese and its well-stocked stable of lawyers and PR people mounted a crusade to get the sculpture removed. The public, however, thought the sculpture was an accurate portrayal of the Catholic Church and fought back, and when polls showed that negative perceptions of the Church were reaching epidemic levels, the Vatican stepped in and, not wanting to add any more oxygen to an out-of-control fire, pulled the plug on the fight.

Darby reached the top. The floodlight affixed to the telephone pole was on. To the far right of it was the memorial. It was hidden underneath a white crime-scene tent.

Darby parked in front of Dell's. The store lights were on and through the windows she saw the owner Debbie Dallal, restocking shelves. Kennedy sat in a booth, his attention locked on the screen of a MacBook.

Debbie looked up from her work when Darby entered.

'I've put on a fresh pot of coffee,' she told Darby. 'Go on behind the counter and help yourself. Doughnuts there too.'

Darby thanked her and walked over to Kennedy. In the

harsh fluorescent light he looked like he had aged a good ten years since yesterday morning. He had thrown on jeans and a Red Sox baseball hat, and wore his badge on a lanyard over a grey Harvard sweatshirt, the cuffs worn thin.

'Where'd you get the tent?' she asked.

'Trunk of my car. Always carried one during my homicide days, never took it out. Crime lab are on their way.'

'Did you –'

'No. Didn't touch a single thing. Everything is safe and secured, I promise. Take a seat. You need to see this.'

Darby sat across from him. Kennedy turned his laptop around so she could see the screen.

In the picture, Richard Byrne, bundled up in a heavy winter coat and wearing boots that came up to his knees, stood by the monument. Given the light in the sky, it was early morning – just as dawn was breaking, or during twilight, she wasn't sure which. One gloved hand gripped his cane while the other held a bouquet of cellophane-wrapped flowers. He held the flowers against his face, as though inhaling their scent.

Jesus, Darby thought. 'Where'd you get this?'

'On Insta-crap, or whatever it's called.'

'Instagram.'

'All this social media stuff is, frankly, beyond me. Guy at the station is the one who brought this picture to my attention. I'm only on Facebook, and I joined to shut up my wife. Did you know only old people like you and me use Facebook?'

'I've heard that.' Darby stayed off all social media. She had no use for it, didn't want to invite any more attention to her private life, which, thanks to the Internet, wasn't so private. 'Who posted this?'

'Kid named Neal Sonnenberg,' Kennedy replied. 'He's sixteen, a born-and-bred Belham boy. He and a few of his buddies apparently like to follow Byrne around town, take pictures of him with their phones. They call him the Belham Boogeyman. That has a nice ring to it, don't you think?'

'As a matter of fact, it does.'

'Sonnenberg and his buddies make a game out of it.'

'A game?'

'Yeah. Who can get the most pictures of Byrne, that sort of shit. There're about two dozen or so pictures posted on this private account they've set up, which only they can access. They've got pictures of Byrne out walking and more than a handful of ones taken through windows. Don't ask me why they're doing it, 'cause I don't know – at least not yet. I'll be talking to them later on this morning, see if they've glimpsed anything interesting, something that maybe they didn't want to post.'

'How long have they been doing this?'

'Couple of months, from what I'm told,' Kennedy said. 'Neal took that picture this morning. There's a place across the street where the bus picks him up for school.' Kennedy removed his cap and ran a hand vigorously over his scalp and yawned. 'Why the fuck has Byrne come back here – especially now, after that article that came out? Why isn't he hiding away in that haunted-looking house of his?'

Darby shrugged, her attention locked on the picture. 'Who left the flowers? Mickey?'

'Yeah. Leaves them every year on the anniversary date.

146

And what's with the shrugging? You're the one with a diploma in dipshits. You know how these guys think. Is it more than just wanting to relive the event in their minds?'

'They have active fantasy lives. But, generally speaking, they typically engage in reliving the event at the place where they tortured and killed their victims. You tell Mickey about these pictures?'

Kennedy shook his head. 'Don't plan on telling him either. Mickey sees that one of Byrne smelling the flowers he left for his daughter, it'll push him over the edge. He'll go charging into that house.'

'I agree.'

Kennedy turned his head to the right and glanced over his shoulder, at the cops gathered around the monument. Darby looked too. Thinking about what was in there made her stomach clench, feel like it was packed in ice.

When Kennedy turned back to her, she saw his face had changed. She knew he was thinking about what was in there too.

'You ever encounter something like this?' he asked.

'No.' She inhaled sharply. 'Never.'

'You speak with the other two mothers yet?'

Darby shook her head. "Neither Nancy Hamilton nor Judith Levenson has returned my calls.'

'Can't say I'm surprised. I had to chase them down too.'

'I drove up to Nashua, hoping I could catch Hamilton. She wasn't home, so I checked in with Nashua PD and went over the case, checked back at the house. Nothing. A neighbour thinks she and her husband are out of town.'

'Picked a good time to get away. When the news about the jacket gets out, it's going to be a media shitshow.'

'I'm going to try Levenson today, head down to New Bedford.'

'I told you, Levenson is a waste of time. She wouldn't talk to me about her daughter. She's not going to talk to you.'

'I've got to try.'

'The woman told me that she knew her daughter was dead, that she had grieved and moved on with her life.'

'She said those exact words?'

'More or less.'

A pair of headlights washed through the parking lot. 'This must be Mickey,' Kennedy said.

Darby saw Mickey's truck come barging up the Hill. She closed the laptop.

Kennedy swallowed and his breath caught in his throat. He fitted the baseball cap back over his head so the visor hid his eyes, and, as he got to his feet, Darby saw an expression on his face that matched exactly how she was feeling – how Kennedy wanted to press a button and transport himself out of this room, this town and this state – this world – and go someplace where he'd never be tasked with having to deliver yet another piece of awful news to an already grieving victim in another ring of hell.

21

The last time Mickey had set foot inside Dell's was the morning after Claire was snatched from the top of the Hill. A storm broke for a couple of hours later that morning, and the lead detective, a guy named Atkinson, and his people had used Dell's as a makeshift base of operations to help organize the volunteers who searched the wood and then later Belham, Boston, Logan Airport and airports in Rhode Island. They were armed with colour printouts of Claire's face, alongside her age, height and weight – her six years of life compressed into a single sheet of 8 × 10 paper, the word MISSING written in bold red letters at the top, right above Claire's smiling face. Atkinson had also brought in a Belham cop whose sole job was to get Claire's picture out on to the Internet and to the FBI and other agencies who specialized in child abductions.

Mickey saw Darby first. He tried to read her face but she didn't give him anything.

Kennedy put out his hand. 'Thanks for coming.'

'What is it? What's going on?'

'If you'll follow me, I'll –'

'Answer my question.'

He expected Kennedy to turn guarded, maybe even defensive, the way all cops did. His face, though, had softened. 'There's something I need to show you,' he said softly. 'This way.'

Kennedy brushed past him and went outside. Mickey followed him, his legs feeling hollow and his brain scrambling, trying to figure out what was going on, what was so goddamn urgent, when he saw a white tent covering Claire's memorial.

'What's a tent doing there?' Mickey asked.

Kennedy, walking several feet ahead of him, didn't answer. Mickey turned to Darby.

'He wants you to take a look at something,' she said.

'What?'

She didn't answer. They were standing outside the tent now. Kennedy pulled back a flap held in place by Velcro with one hand, his other holding a flashlight. 'Don't touch anything, okay?' he said.

Mickey ducked inside and saw a flash of pink and his breath died somewhere in his throat.

'I need to know if this is your daughter's jacket,' Kennedy said, handing the flashlight to Darby.

Claire's pink snow jacket was fitted over the cross, the hood draped across the top.

His daughter's winter jacket was here.

On a *cross*.

His first, immediate thought: *This has to be a prank*.

Early on, during those first couple of weeks when the police had been investigating Byrne – no, fuck that, well after Byrne became the prime suspect – Mickey's physical mailboxes and email box were flooded with anonymous letters from people professing to know what had happened to his daughter. Some were from prisoners doing serious time, murderers looking to trade what turned out to be made-up stories about who had taken and killed Claire in exchange for a reduction in their sentence. Nearly one hundred per cent of every email and piece of mail he'd received was completely bogus, and he had been the victim of a select few who got off on mailing pieces of a pink snow jacket to him, usually with a printed letter that went into great, gruesome detail of the things done to his daughter before she was killed.

The letters were bullshit. Heather usually bought Claire's clothes in pairs, Claire being the type of kid who really did a number on them, going through them quickly. The replacement snowsuit Heather had purchased was sent to the FBI lab and the report came back with specifics: it was manufactured by a North Carolina company called Bizzmarket, the pink model being one of the company's most popular: it was sold all over the Northeast exclusively at Target.

And now some sick fuck, some bored asshole who hated his life, had decided to come out here during the night and place a look-alike jacket on top of the memorial's cross.

Kennedy's hands were covered in blue latex gloves. He gently removed the hood and Darby pointed the beam of her flashlight at the jacket's tag.

'Whenever you're ready,' Kennedy said gently.

Mickey leaned in, slow and uncertain, as if the jacket might suddenly reach out and grab him.

CLAIRE FLYNN was written in black lettering across the jacket's white tag.

Mickey didn't recognize the sound of his own voice in his ears when he said, 'That's Heather's handwriting.'

'You sure?' Kennedy asked, his tone still gentle. Sympathetic.

Mickey nodded, remembering the day at the kitchen table when Heather had written Claire's name on the fabric tag with a black Sharpie marker. Claire's name on the inside tag was a detail that hadn't been made public. *I can remember Heather writing Claire's name on the tag and the type of marker she used, but I can't remember my daughter's face. I can't remember it unless I look at a picture of her. What's wrong with me?*

Kennedy said something to him. Mickey couldn't recall it.

'What did you say?'

'I asked if you'd take a look at the pocket,' Kennedy said.

Mickey had to move around the memorial to see it.

The edge of the left pocket had a small tear in the stitching – another detail that hadn't been made public. Claire's puppy, Diesel, had done that. Now Diesel was dead and Claire was –

Mickey's eyes snapped shut. When he opened them, Claire's jacket was still there.

And it was Claire's jacket. There was no question in his mind. It was Claire's jacket and here it was, eleven years later. Claire's jacket.

Mickey didn't know his heart could beat this fast.

Darby brought Mickey a cup of coffee. Mickey wrapped his hands around the mug, grateful for the warmth.

This isn't happening. Your missing daughter's winter jacket doesn't suddenly show up eleven years later in the middle of the night.

Darby pulled up a chair. Kennedy sat across from him. The fluorescent lights above them hummed.

It occurred to him they were waiting for him to speak, so he did.

152

'The jacket. Who found it?'

Kennedy answered the question. 'Deb did. She came in around four, like she usually does, to get everything ready for when she opens up at seven. She pulled in and saw the jacket.'

Mickey caught something in the man's voice – a sense of hesitation – and when he looked up he saw Darby exchange a look with Kennedy.

'What?'

Kennedy shifted slightly in his seat. 'Someone had collapsed in the parking lot,' he said. 'She thought the person was hurt, so she took out her phone and called 911.'

'Who was it?'

Kennedy's expression changed, his eyes flicking to Darby.

Darby said, 'It was Byrne.'

A white noise filled Mickey's head.

'It seems Byrne walks around a lot at night and during the early morning, when it's dark,' Kennedy said. 'During the day, he's pretty much a shut-in. People who recognize him – some have thrown rocks, whatever. Others have pushed him. A couple of months back, he claimed someone tried to run him off the road. So he only goes out when it's dark, and he usually disguises himself.'

'And visits the place where he abducted my daughter,' Mickey said, the words strangling his throat.

Kennedy looked to Darby. She said, 'The problem is Deb didn't see Byrne plant the jacket on the memorial. If she had –'

'Where is he?' Mickey squeezed the mug. 'And the answer better be jail.'

Darby leaned against the table. 'Listen to me, Mickey.'

'Don't say it.'

'Listen to me. Byrne called 911 roughly five minutes before Deb did. The police were already on their way.'

'So he fell down and called for help. So fucking what?'

Darby was shaking her head. 'He called about the jacket.'

Mickey slowly ran his hands through his hair, squeezing his skull.

Kennedy said, 'I understand you're upset. Trust me, I get it. What you need –'

Mickey slammed a fist down on the table. '*You've had eleven years!*' His voice boomed through the store and blood exploded against his ears and he shoved a finger in Kennedy's face and screamed, 'Eleven *fucking* years to build a case against him, and now you've got an eyewitness who can place him right fucking next to my daughter's jacket – that's *her* jacket out there. The fuck you waiting for? For Byrne to ring your doorbell and say, "Hi, I did it"?'

Kennedy said nothing. He didn't look away – didn't look ashamed or embarrassed, his face getting that blank, impassive expression all cops got when they shut down. Talk, scream, yell – share any intimate detail about yourself or break down and cry, all they did was give you this blank look of nothingness, like he was discussing the weather or how to make a ham sandwich, whatever, instead of a missing kid – *his* missing kid, *his* missing daughter.

Darby, though, didn't have that look. She looked genuinely sad and frustrated in equal measures, and for some reason it made him want to lurch across the table at Kennedy, grab the guy by the back of the head and smash that stone-cold look of his against the table until it shattered. Instead, he grabbed the edge of his seat and squeezed so hard his arms shook.

Kennedy said, 'You're aware that Byrne's dying.'

'Well, there's a fucking news bulletin. Thanks for sharing that.'

Darby said, 'What Chris means is, where do you think Byrne's most likely to talk to us? In a jail cell or sitting in his favourite chair in his house where he's comfortable?'

'*Comfortable?* Are you –'

'The jacket,' Kennedy said, 'will be at the lab first thing this morning. It's our top priority. Darby will be there with me, we'll make sure the lab does every single test it can. She's the best in her field, which is why I brought her into this. When we find anything out – *anything* – I give you my word I'll call and tell you. Why don't you head on home, get some sleep?'

Mickey stared down at the table. 'How long?'

'How long what?'

'For the jacket,' Mickey said, his voice raw.

'It's our top priority, like I said.'

'And Byrne's caretaker, nurse, whatever she is – you talk with her?'

'We will.'

Again that tone in Kennedy's voice, like he was holding back something. Mickey looked up, knew what the man was going to say before he said it. 'I need you to stay away from her.'

'I'm pretty sure she isn't part of my restraining order.'

'Mr Flynn –' Kennedy began.

'Oh, it's Mr Flynn now.'

Kennedy folded his hands on the table. 'I got a report that a truck was parked on a side street near Byrne's house. Unfortunately, the person who called it in didn't get a good look at the driver's face, the truck's licence plate, or its make and model.'

Mickey's gaze cut sideways to Darby before he could stop himself.

'It wasn't Dr McCormick,' Kennedy said, 'if that's what you're wondering.'

'Then who was it?'

'Doesn't matter. What *does* is your restraining order. You go near him – if you so much as say hello – all he has to do is pick up the phone and call us and you'll be doing five to eight. And there's nothing I'd be able to do for you. The judge won't cut you any slack.'

'Man with the best lawyer wins, right?'

'The thing about cell phones?' Kennedy said. 'They're constantly sending out signals to towers, tracking your location minute to minute. If your PO, a judge, whoever – if someone decided to pull your records, they would get a detailed history of your movements throughout each day. And if the records showed that you were parked near Byrne's house . . .'

Mickey rubbed his forehead, trying to wrap his mind around everything. Christ how he needed a drink.

'What I'm trying to tell you,' Kennedy said, 'is that you need to let us do our jobs.'

'You're saying this is all my fault.'

'I'm saying we're running on borrowed time here. I think I've got a way to get what I need from Byrne, but for it to be done right you've got to stay away from him, the nurse, all of it. Darby and I will worry about Byrne. Just go back to your normal life.'

'I don't have much of a life any more,' Mickey said, glaring at him. 'And I can guarantee you what's left of it is anything but normal.'

22

O'Neil's Pub was on the edge of town, near Chelsea. Any time Mickey set foot inside the bar, it reminded him of a black-and-white drawing of purgatory he'd seen in a catechism book as a kid – souls denied entrance to heaven lying in hospital beds, their faces twisted in pain. They seemed no different from the people who came here, a collection of the world's lost and angry and rejected, people who cashed their Social Security, disability and welfare cheques and spent their days holed up in a box with dim lighting and dark corners, wondering why God had singled them out, turned their lives to shit.

The bartender was somewhere in his early twenties and wore a black T-shirt, both arms so heavily inked with tattoos that they looked like they had been dipped in paint.

'Shot of Jack with a draught on the side,' Mickey said.

'What kind of draught? I've got –'

'Surprise me.'

One drink. That's all he was going to have, just one. Normal people came home from work every day after busting their hump and unwound with a drink or two, their reward for putting up with the daily grind and all the bullshit that came with it. He had earned this drink – fucking *deserved* it after the day he'd had. The booze would singe his nerve endings and drown out the voices in his head, and then he could go back home and sleep. No way his PO was going to call or stop by for a random breath-alyser at this hour.

And if he did? Fuck him. Fuck everyone.

The bartender came back and placed the shot and the draught in front of him. Mickey ran his tongue over his front teeth, the voice of his inner addict whispering in the back of his mind, encouraging him to pick up the shot and knock it back, promising him that this would feel better than the world's greatest fuck.

There was another voice speaking to him. This one was calm and spoke with a quiet authority – the voice, he supposed, of what AA called his 'higher power' or higher self. *You're feeling sorry for yourself*, this voice said. *Accept it and own it.*

So what if he was indulging in a little self-pity? And why was he bound to a set of rules that dictated his every waking moment, while that piece of shit got to go wher-ever he wanted, whenever he wanted? Where was the justice in that?

Mickey picked up the shot glass and brought it to his lips, the smell of booze filling his nostrils as that calm inner voice said, *One drink is going to turn into two and then three and then four and five, because you're an alcoholic – you* know *you're an alcoholic. You know you're incapable of having just one drink. You know you're going to get good and fucked up, and then you're going to drive back to Byrne's and find a way to get your hands on him, do whatever you need to do to rip the truth from him. You want to knock back that shot, fine, go ahead. But realize you're pissing everything away. You go to prison, you'll have no one to advo-cate for your daughter.* No one. *If you don't have a problem, then go ahead and get good and shitfaced.*

His hand trembled as he put the shot glass back on the bar. He dug out his phone from his pocket and dialled the number he knew by heart.

'You ever wonder what the difference is between purgatory and real life?'

'Father Cullen? That you?' Big Jim asked, his voice thick and groggy with sleep. 'I swear, Father, I haven't been touching myself in my no-no place.'

'They found Claire's jacket on top of the Hill an hour ago.'

'Where are you?'

'Staring down a shot of Jack Daniel's at O'Neil's.'

'*That* dump? Jesus, Mickey, if you're going to fall off the wagon, at least do it in style. Did you know they had to close that place down for a day about a month ago, because of head lice? Just hang tight, okay? I'm on my way.'

'I saw him at the grocery store.'

'Byrne?'

'Yeah.'

'What happened?'

'I went after him.' On the other end of the line, he heard Jim open and close the door to his truck. 'Didn't get to him. His bodyguards pounced on me, dragged me outta there.'

Jim's sigh exploded across the receiver. Mickey heard the diesel engine turn over as he walked Jim through what had happened. He told Jim about how, on the day of Claire's anniversary, he had gone to Byrne's house, only to get intercepted by Darby.

'Sounds to me like Darby did you a solid,' Big Jim said. 'If you'd gone ahead with it, you'd be calling me from jail.'

'She wouldn't tell me what she was doing there.'

'Maybe she can't, you know, legally or some shit.'

'Claire's *my* daughter. I'm her *father*, and they won't tell me anything?'

'You think maybe they're afraid you're gonna go all Clint Eastwood on him again?'

'Someone needs to. They found Claire's jacket.'

'*What?* Where?'

'On the monument at the Hill,' Mickey said. 'Byrne found it.'

Big Jim was silent. Mickey rubbed at his face, trying to ignore the tinkling sounds of the glass bottles that were making his mouth water. 'I'm not gonna say I understand what you're going through right now, 'cause I don't,' Big Jim said. 'No one does, except for the parents of Byrne's other victims.'

'Mary and Elizabeth.' Saying their names opened up a cavern inside Mickey's chest, the girls, like his daughter, having become footnotes. A lot of people, too many, forgot the names of Byrne's victims, but they always knew Byrne's name. Always.

'It's been an hour, and I still want to kill him.'

'Here's a funny story,' Big Jim said. 'Me and the wife went out to dinner tonight to that new steak joint on Route 6. I ran into our boy Joey Boots and his new gal-pal, Brittney. You met her yet?'

Mickey watched beads of moisture rolling down the beer glass. 'Nope.'

'Well, you're in for a real treat. This broad's dumber than a Kardashian.'

'Impossible.'

161

'Oh, yeah? Brittney thought pork came from a mushroom. And that reminds me: we're not going to Boots's house next Sunday to watch the Pats game. Seems he's taking an unexpected trip to Arizona. Now ask me why.'

'I take it it's not to go see the Grand Canyon.'

'Try day spa,' Big Jim said. 'Brittney wants Boots to drop some serious pounds. He's going to be eating wheat-germ pancakes for breakfast, doing yoga and taking mud baths, getting coffee enemas.'

'People do funny things when they're in love.'

'That fat bastard even got his teeth bleached. I says to him, "Boots, why didn't you just buy a bottle of Wite-Out and paint your Chiclets just like you did before our senior prom?"'

'You're breaking up.'

'I'm hitting that dead patch on Carter Road. Hang tight, I'll call you right back.'

Mickey tossed the phone on to the bar and stared at the shot glass.

One shot. That's all he was asking for, just one shot to settle his nerves and keep the nightmare of what he'd just seen at bay for just a little bit, so he could think, figure out how he was going get himself alone with Byrne and –

Someone reached for his shot glass. Mickey looked sideways and saw Darby standing next to him.

23

Darby grabbed his shot. She knocked the shot back, winced.

'Jesus,' she said. 'How can you drink this shit?'

'You following me?'

'Damn right I am. Got to keep an eye on you, make sure you don't do anything stupid.' She grabbed his beer glass and pushed it to the side.

'They ask you to babysit too?'

'No,' Darby said. 'I came here on my own.'

She leaned sideways against the bar. Her eyes were intense, but he was sure he saw some compassion in them, too. Or maybe it was pity.

'You don't deserve any of this,' she said.

You're goddamn right I don't. Mickey kept quiet.

'And I get why you're pissed off and frustrated. I truly do.'

'Really?' he asked, trying to sound casual and knowing he was failing. 'You've got a kid I don't know about who got snatched?'

'You have any idea how many cases like this I've worked over the years? You think this shit doesn't affect me? That I don't care?'

'Didn't say that. But you get to go home, put that shit on a shelf and forget about it for a few hours. I go home and see an empty bed, so, all due respect, don't try to tell me you know what I'm going through, because you don't.'

Darby held up a hand and dropped her head a bit, conceding his point. She looked at the mirror behind the bar, her eyes travelling across the galaxy of black spots covering the glass.

'You want another one?' Mickey asked, pointing to the empty shot glass.

When she looked back at him, her expression had changed. It reminded him of the way she had looked at him that first night they slept together in New Hampshire, the walls coming down to reveal that private part of herself she carefully hid from the rest of the world.

She leaned in closer, Mickey smelling the whiskey on her breath when she said, 'A monster broke into my house when I was fifteen. I managed to escape to the bedroom, thought I was safe when the doorbell rang. Melanie Cruz and Stacey Stephens had come over.'

'I know.'

'What you don't know is that after this psycho slashed Stacey's throat, he used Melanie to lure me out of the bedroom. Said if I came downstairs to talk, he wouldn't hurt us. I didn't believe him, but I didn't want him to hurt Melanie either. So I unlocked the door and headed downstairs.'

Mickey turned slightly in his seat, gave her his full attention.

'I'm heading downstairs,' Darby said, 'and that's when I saw the blood. Right then I knew there was no way he was going to let us live. So I ran back upstairs to the bedroom, locked the door and jumped through the window. You know what happened next.'

He did. Stacey Stephens was found dead in Darby's house, and Melanie Cruz had vanished.

164

'There's nothing I could've done to have changed the outcome,' Darby said. 'I know that intellectually. I know there's nothing I could have done to save her, but that doesn't mean I don't carry that shit with me. I still ask myself what would have happened if I had just *tried* to talk to him. Maybe it would've, I don't know, bought Melanie some time to get away from him and escape. What if I had said this or done that, would Melanie still be alive? Maybe if I'd done something different, Melanie's mother wouldn't have died without knowing what had happened to her daughter.'

Mickey wasn't sure why she was sharing this with him. But he was glad she was. It had calmed something in him, and he was no longer thinking about having that drink.

'I'm not certain of many things in life, Mickey, but I'm certain of this: creatures like Byrne are a special breed, what we call a highly organized psychopath. What gets them off, what feeds them, is watching people suffer. They never deviate from that script.'

His eyes narrowed in thought. 'Why are you telling me this?'

'If Byrne placed your daughter's jacket on the monument —'

'*If?*' Mickey said, loud enough to draw the attention of the nearby customers. He leaned closer to her and, while he lowered his voice, there was still plenty of anger in it. 'Who else could have done that?'

'Police Work 101 is assume nothing and keep an open mind, even if it seems obvious. You don't do that, you're almost certain to miss something crucial. Now I've got to talk to you about the jacket. First thing Monday morning, I'm taking it to the lab –'

'You and Kennedy said you were going to take the jacket to the lab today.'

'I know, that's why I'm bringing it up. I had a talk with Kennedy right after you left, convinced him to wait until first thing Monday morning.'

'What, the lab isn't open on Sundays?'

Her eyes clouded. 'Let's just say it will be to your benefit to do it,' she said.

'How about speaking English?'

'Trust me on this one, okay? Can you do that for me?'

'That's why you followed me, isn't it? To give me this little talk to make sure I play nice, don't screw up your plans.'

'I followed you because I wanted to make sure you were okay, to make sure you didn't do anything stupid, like drink a shot and a beer.'

'By Monday he could be dead.'

'You can't beat the truth out of him, Mickey. He's not going to give you what you want. He'd rather die than do that.'

We'll see, Mickey thought.

'You do realize you're doing exactly what he wants,' Darby said.

'What're you talking about?'

'*If* he put that jacket on the monument, he did it to activate you, to put you into motion. Don't you get it, Mickey? He *wants* you to go to him. He *wants* you to beg and cry, and then, after you lose your shit and go after him again, he'll play the victim. He'll hold press conferences from his hospital room, probably with his lawyer by his side, tell everyone how he understands your pain and frustration and how we should all pray for you. He'll maintain his innocence, while inside he's getting off on the whole theatre he's created around him. But what's really going to give him a major hard-on is knowing you're suffering, alone inside a holding cell, waiting to be shipped off to court, where a judge will have no choice but to send you off to prison. Is that what you want? To be the guy's bitch?'

Mickey stared down at the bar, his nostrils flaring, his bottom lip pinched between his teeth.

'Just hang tight, okay? . . . Mickey, did you hear what I said? Look at me.'

He got to his feet, trembling, the rage and sorrow moving beneath his skin like razors. He grabbed the beer, and the moment the cold liquid slid past his lips, that internal pilot light, quiet for so long, came roaring back to life. When the cold beer hit his stomach, his mind turned as calm and still as the surface of a lake, and the fist squeezing his heart let go of its grip; and none of it had anything to do with the beer and everything to do with what he had to do next.

24

Bright and early Monday morning, Darby followed Kennedy through the revolving doors and into the main lobby of the Belham PD headquarters, a startling large space of imported brown-and-black marble. She had been only a couple of months into her job as a crime-scene technician when she first worked on Claire Flynn's abduction, and now here she was, over a decade later, holding an evidence bag containing the young girl's winter coat and heading back to the lab. Returning to a bureaucrat pit run by men who cared more about how their spreadsheets balanced and how to spin a story to their advantage than doing the next right thing for the victim of a violent crime.

She signed in and was given a guest ID, then she followed Kennedy to the elevators and rode one to the top floor. Kennedy had called ahead to let the lab know he was coming with the jacket. He hadn't mentioned she was accompanying him.

Her lower back was stiff from a weekend spent sitting in her car. Yesterday, she had travelled to New Bedford to speak to Judith Levenson about her daughter, Elizabeth. Levenson wasn't home and none of the neighbours knew where she was. Darby had called the woman as well as Nancy Hamilton repeatedly over the weekend, hoping they would, at the very least, return her calls. They didn't.

When the elevator stopped and its doors slid open, she wasn't surprised to find the director of the crime lab, Leland Pratt, waiting for them in the reception area.

Leland, closing in on sixty, had the personality and charm of a used Band-Aid. He also, she was sure, had the qualities of a closet sadist. For as long as she had known him, he got off on saying no to his people and, Darby sensed, he secretly enjoyed watching their frustration and anger at the obstacles he put in place.

'Good morning,' Leland said. He looked only at Kennedy.

Leland's hands were tucked in his trouser pockets. He wore an expensive suit and the kind of garish accoutrements – a gold tie clip and cufflinks and a big Rolex watch – that gave him the swarthy air of a Lamborghini salesman from Long Island.

'Lab all ready?' Kennedy asked.

'It is.'

'Great. Thanks for accommodating us at such short notice.'

Leland's smile was tight. 'There's one small matter we need to discuss,' he said, and slid his eyes to Darby.

Darby showed no reaction, which, she was sure, disappointed him greatly. The man loved a good argument.

Kennedy said, 'She's consulting with us on the case.'

'Yes. I've heard. Be that as it may, the lab is for qualified personnel only.'

'She's not qualified?' Kennedy chuckled, but it carried a warning: he was ready to climb into the ring and go head to head.

'Of course not,' Leland scoffed. 'Dr McCormick is well

known in her field. But she does have a prior relationship with the family of the victim.'

'You mean Mickey Flynn,' Kennedy said.

Leland nodded. 'I consulted with the district attorney about it this morning. Given the highly volatile nature of this case, he explicitly stated that under no circumstances is Dr McCormick to be allowed inside the lab while the jacket is being processed for evidence. All it will take is for Mr Byrne's lawyer to point out during the trial –'

'There isn't going to *be* a trial. The man's dying, in case you haven't heard.'

Leland shrugged. 'We have our orders.'

Kennedy, Darby knew, wasn't about to go up against DA Tommy McMannus. His hands were tied. But he didn't back down. 'Get Tommy on the phone,' Kennedy said.

'He's in federal court. He'll be tied up a good part of the day.'

Of course he is, Darby thought, taking out her phone to check her messages.

Leland said, 'What would you like to do, Detective Kennedy? It's your call.'

Kennedy began to twist in the wind. Darby said, 'It's fine, Chris.' Then, to Leland: 'Who's going to work on the jacket?'

'No one you know,' Leland said pleasantly. 'Everyone you know has moved on, I'm afraid.'

'How much time have they racked up working major cases?'

Leland bristled a little at that. 'I can assure you, they're highly qualified.'

'But not experts.'

Leland's eyes were working, trying to figure out where she was leading him, what she had planned. They widened in surprise and, Darby supposed, shock when she gave him the names of two pioneering forensic scientists – an older man and woman who had both gained celebrity status by working on and solving some of the world's most difficult criminal cases. They had appeared on so many true-crime shows and documentaries over the years they were practically household names.

'I don't see what relevance those two people have to the matter at hand,' Leland said.

'I spoke to them both at length over the weekend,' Darby said. 'They've agreed to volunteer their time and help the team working on the jacket.'

'As much as I'd like to have them here at my lab, the reality is the jacket is ready to be examined now. I've rescheduled cases and resources in order to accommodate –'

'They're on their way from the airport. I just got a text.' Darby showed Leland the phone and took great pleasure in watching him squirm, Leland shuffling as though he had a hot coal pinched between his cheeks. 'Of course, this is *your* lab, as you kindly reminded us, so you can say no. Granted, I'm not as versatile in the art of kissing ass as you are, but what do you think the DA is going to say if you refuse to allow the top two forensic specialists in the world to examine the jacket?'

Leland straightened, his throat working.

'And if your mind just ran to your spreadsheet, thinking about operating costs, you don't have to worry about Boston picking up the tab,' Darby said. 'The bill has been paid in full.'

'By you?'

Kennedy answered the question. 'By my department.'

Leland turned his attention – and anger – to Kennedy. 'I don't appreciate being manipulated.'

Darby said, 'I'm sure Mickey Flynn will be very grateful that two experts agreed to take time out of their demanding schedules to work on his daughter's case. I know how much you'd hate to disappoint a grieving father – not because you have a heart but because of the bad PR it'll generate if you act like a supremo asshole here.'

Leland's throat had reddened but his face was the colour of bone. 'Anything else?'

'Besides upgrading your mouthwash? No,' Darby said. 'Now run along and call the DA. We'll wait here.'

Leland was working double-overtime to keep the defeat from reaching his face. He calmly walked away to make the call, and, when he shut the door to his office, Kennedy leaned into her and whispered, 'I am so in love with you right now.'

25

When you use the media, they end up using you. The mother of one of Byrne's victims, Judith Levenson, had drilled those words into Mickey's head early on, during the first few months after Claire's abduction. *Always remember they're after your tears. That's all they care about. They want you to cry, scream, swear – they want you to have a breakdown on camera, and the only way they can try to make that happen is by provoking you with the sort of questions that will make you want to beat the living daylights out of them. When they ask these questions – and they will, over and over again – always remember to focus on your daughter. Always remember that alongside every stupid question are cameras and tape recorders that are going to take whatever you say and do and run it on TV and online, along with your daughter's story and picture. The longer you keep Claire out there, the more likely it is that someone will come forward with useful information. You stand there and be as nice as pie to them because there will come a day when you'll need them.*

For the next five days, no matter where Mickey went, when a journalist cornered him, he would, in a strained but pleasant tone, answer the same mind-numbing questions over and over again, answer them as though hearing them for the first time. Yes, I'm sure it was my daughter's jacket on the monument. No, I can't explain why Byrne called 911 and reported finding the jacket. No, I don't know the status of the jacket, what the police found – all I know is that they're working hard on it. No, I don't know why the police haven't arrested Byrne yet. I don't know much of anything at the moment. You have to talk to the police. Go to the police. Speak to the police.

The day after Byrne called the police about finding the jacket on the memorial, police searched Byrne's house. If they found anything, they weren't saying. Chris Kennedy held two press conferences – smoke-and-mirror shows of 'We're working on several leads at the moment', followed by the ever popular 'No comment'. Kennedy was holding his cards close to his chest; he wasn't going to give away any information.

Darby hadn't conducted any interviews and, as far as he could tell, her name hadn't appeared in any news stories. Mickey had reached out to her a few times, hoping to get the inside line, but she never answered her phone, and she hadn't returned his phone calls. She had, however, sent him a text promising to get in touch with him soon.

By the end of the work-week and with nothing fresh to feast on, the media went into a temporary state of hibernation. Reporters, cameramen and news vans were still lingering around Belham, and mostly around Byrne's house, hoping to capture fresh footage of the dying recluse.

Mickey's PO, Frank Towne, decided to pop Mickey's job site for an unannounced breathalyser and piss test. Mickey had passed the breathalyser but had forgotten to lock the urine sample, and it had spilled inside Towne's briefcase. The man left in a huff, and it brought Mickey the first genuine smile since . . . well, he couldn't remember.

Every morning, from five to six, even in the dead of winter, Father Keith Cullen ran the track at Belham High

School. Mickey knew this because back in high school he used to run the track in the early morning to keep in shape for football. Oftentimes they ran together and talked about any number of subjects, the priest not at all shy about voicing his opinions on Sean Flynn.

On a drizzling Friday morning, Mickey headed out to the high school. Father Keith wasn't there, so Mickey called the man's cell. Back when they were married, he and Heather had synched their phones using the same computer and shared the same list of contacts.

Father Cullen's number was no longer in service. Mickey drove to the rectory, only to be told the priest was unavailable. The secretary promised to give Father Cullen the message. The priest never called back.

That night, Mickey went home, to sleep in his own bed. Since the story of the jacket broke, he'd been sleeping on Jim's couch to stay away from the media, which had, for the past week, been pretty much parked out in front of his house. Thank God they were gone.

The next morning, he awoke to someone ringing his doorbell. He glanced at the clock on the nightstand. 5.12 a.m.

The doorbell rang again. Again.

Has to be a goddamn reporter, Mickey thought, sliding out of bed. They had no shame, ringing the doorbell and knocking at all hours; cameraman coming up to the windows, hoping to catch some footage. He was willing to bet they didn't pull this shit at Byrne's house.

He went to the bedroom window and looked out at the driveway and street. He didn't see a news van or any vehicle to indicate the presence of a reporter or TV cameraman, and from this angle he couldn't see who was standing at the front door. Whoever was there was now knocking on the front door in addition to ringing the doorbell.

Mickey padded barefoot downstairs, dressed in a pair of boxers and an old and nearly threadbare Budweiser T-shirt. He punched in the code for the alarm and then undid the locks and cracked opened the door to Sean Flynn.

'The fuck you doing here?'

'Good morning to you too,' Sean replied.

'What do you want?'

'I've got some important news that pertains to you and what happened to my granddaughter.'

Mickey bristled at him using the word 'granddaughter', but he let it slide, more interested in trying to read his old man. He didn't have that particular talent when it came to Sean – no one did. Anyone who had tried to figure out what was going on in Sean's head at any given time, what made him tick, usually walked away sweaty and pale, shaken.

'You gonna invite me in?' Sean asked. 'It's colder than the hinges of hell out here.'

Mickey reluctantly stepped aside. Sean came in, dressed in jeans, gloves and a brand-new goose-down North Face jacket. He took off his Scally cap as Mickey shut the door.

'You're looking good,' Sean said. 'Lean and mean, as always.'

The same could be said of him. Sean was lean, always had been, the meanness and hair-trigger rage somehow preserving him. His hair was greyer, his tanned face a bit more weathered from decades spent baking in the sun, but his old man, even at seventy-whatever-the-fuck-he-was, unquestionably still possessed the confident, youthful

176

swagger that had made him a successful street brawler and killer.

'Police know you're in town?' Mickey asked. They were standing in the kitchen.

'No, and I'd appreciate it if you kept that quiet.' Sean started to unzip his jacket.

'Keep it on,' Mickey said. 'You won't be staying that long.'

If the words affected Sean in any way, he didn't show it. He turned his attention to the kitchen table, which was stacked with mail, a lot of it letters from crazies claiming to know what Byrne had done to Claire. There were a lot of prayer cards, too, from people he'd never met, and a lot of letters from so-called psychics. Sean picked up a piece of pink stationary, the words MADAME CLARA, WORLD RENOWNED INTERNATIONAL PSYCHIC printed at the top, along with her picture.

'Christ,' Sean said. 'This broad hit every branch of the ugly tree.' He tossed the paper back to the table, shaking his head. 'I hope you're not entertaining any ideas about those people. They're evil.'

'You said you had something important to tell me.'

'All this time, your circumstances, I thought it would've made you a bit more forgiving.'

Mickey thought of Dr Solares's comments about Sean reaching out, looking for forgiveness, and said, 'You want forgiveness, St Stephen's is in the other direction.'

'You know Byrne's dying,' Sean said. 'I mean he's going to buy the farm any day now.'

'That's your newsflash?'

'His nightstand and kitchen table are full of all kinds of

meds – morphine, Demerol, Prozac, you name it. It's amazing the son of a bitch can walk, he's so doped up.'

Mickey started to speak, then stopped.

Sean had been inside Byrne's house.

'You mind if I take off my jacket and sit and talk?' Sean asked. 'Or would you still like for me to go?'

'What were you doing inside Byrne's house?'

'Put on some coffee.'

Mickey did, Sean lighting a cigarette with a gold lighter embossed with the Marine emblem, the lighter a fixture from Mickey's childhood for as long as he could remember. He had finished nearly half his cigarette when Mickey returned to the table with an ashtray and sat.

Sean smoked, eyeing him up and down, as if trying to come to a conclusion.

'Lot of weird shit going down in that house,' Sean said after a moment. 'Guy's got Christmas lights and decorations hung around his bedroom and living room. He's got toys all over the place too, these –'

'Toys?'

'What I said. Paul told me –'

'Paul who?'

'You gonna let me talk, or are you gonna cross-examine me?'

Mickey leaned back in his chair, arms crossed over his chest.

Sean took a long drag from his cigarette. 'Paul is Paul Ward, one of Byrne's bodyguards. I hear you met him the other day at the grocery store.' Sean smiled.

Mickey said nothing.

'Paul did some babysitting for Byrne for a bit way back

when, after that number you did on Byrne. The priest was afraid you'd go after him again. Now, with my granddaughter's jacket being found, Byrne gave Paul a call again. Paul and this other guy are with him around the clock.'

Sean stubbed out his cigarette. 'This shit with Christmas decorations and toys, it's called regression. Byrne's hospice nurse said that can happen when a patient is dying. He goes back to happier times in his life, know what I mean?'

'She told you this?'

'Of course not. I had a – a whatchamacallit –' He snapped his fingers impatiently. 'Had an intermediary get the info 'cause she's under strict orders from your friends on the force not to say so much as hello to you.' Sean lit another cigarette, peered at Mickey through the smoke. 'When Byrne's lucid, which isn't much of the time, he talks a lot to his lawyer. He's terrified of dying in jail, our hometown priest. Lawyer keeps telling him not to worry.'

Jesus. He's bugged the place.

'I think it's time Byrne talks,' Sean said, Mickey hearing that effortless, magnetic confidence in the old man's voice and remembering how his mother had responded to it time and time again, believing he'd keep his anger in check the next time, promise not to drive his point home with his fists.

'I'm not asking you to get involved,' Sean said.

'What are you asking?'

'When I'm done with him, if the police come around and start asking questions, I may need an alibi.'

Not once had Mickey crossed the line into his old man's other life. Growing up, when any of Sean's low-life friends had stopped by to play cards or talk business, Mickey would leave the house. He didn't want to know Sean's business, terrified he'd accidentally overhear something that would slowly devour his soul.

'So,' Sean said. 'Can I count on you?'

'Let the police handle this.'

Sean took a long drag from his cigarette, eyed him through the smoke.

'That what you really want?'

Mickey nodded.

'You think the cops are doing such a great job, why'd you drop by Byrne's house last week?'

'You do anything to screw this up, you get involved in any way, I swear to Christ, Sean, I'll tell the police about this conversation.'

Sean's eyes took on a disturbing vacant quality. 'The night you went after Byrne? You were at McCarthy's, downing that cheap-ass whiskey that tastes like paint thinner.'

Mickey had no memory of seeing him that night.

'You and I had ourselves a real heart-to-heart,' Sean said.

Mickey wanted to call bullshit. Even at his worst, he wouldn't share anything with Sean. Then again, he didn't remember much from that night. It was amazing, really, in the state he was in that he had not only arrived at Byrne's but had also got there in one piece.

'What you did to that piece of shit?' Sean said. 'I was real proud of you.'

'It was an accident.'

'That the crap you sell yourself when you're shaving in the mirror?' Sean chuckled. 'There's nothing wrong with taking pleasure in your work. If it were me, though, I would've –'

'Stay away from this.'

Mickey's phone rang. It was sitting on the kitchen table, right next to his wallet and keys. DARBY MCCORMICK appeared on the screen.

Mickey didn't pick up the phone.

'Go ahead and answer,' Sean said, smiling. 'I'll get us some coffee.'

Mickey took the call, his eyes tracking Sean.

'Hey.'

'Hope I didn't wake you up. You told me you're an early riser, like me.'

'No, I'm up.' Mickey watched his old man rooting around the cabinets, searching for the mugs, and felt a sense of violation he couldn't quite put into words.

'I wanted to see if we could talk,' Darby said. 'I'm about five minutes away from your house. I can –'

'Let me take you to breakfast.' Mickey did not want Darby to meet Sean – didn't want her to know that Sean was back in town. The police had a major hard-on for Sean, wanting to put him away. Mickey didn't want his life complicated any further by cops coming around, asking questions about his old man.

'You don't have to take me to breakfast,' Darby said.

'I want to. To apologize for being, you know –'

'A complete and utter asshole?' Darby offered.

'Yeah. That.' Mickey chuckled. He couldn't remember the last time he'd felt a sliver of relief, tasted a bit of humour. 'I'll meet you at J & M in ten.'

'It's still around?'

'One of the few things left from when we were growing up. See you in a few.'

Mickey hung up and got to his feet.

Sean said, 'You're putting all your chips on Big Red's daughter?'

'They brought her in to –'

'Consult,' Sean finished for him. 'Yeah, I know all about it.'

Of course you do, Mickey thought.

'McCormick talked to the priest,' Sean said. 'Had themselves a little sit down.'

Mickey nodded. He had got word from Jim's cop buddy Win that Darby had spoken with Byrne, but he didn't know the contents of their conversation – and he desperately wanted to know, it was eating at him, not knowing what Byrne had said (or hadn't said), if the lab had found anything on his daughter's jacket – he had a laundry list of questions to ask her.

'She tell you what they discussed?' Sean asked, saying it in a way that suggested he had a transcript of the conversation.

And maybe he did. Sean had bugged the house. Had he recorded the conversation?

The thought of it loosened the tightness Mickey had been carrying in his chest since discovering his daughter's jacket. He straightened a bit, Sean catching something in his expression or body language or both because Sean had that grin on his face, the one that announced he held something valuable to you – only he wasn't going to give it to you right away. First, he was going to dangle it in front of your face. Taunt you with it, make you beg.

'She didn't tell you, did she?' Sean said.

'She gave me the broad strokes,' Mickey lied. 'Did you record the conversation?'

'No.'

'But you heard it. What did Byrne say?'

'Why you asking? You said she already told you.' Sean took a sip of his coffee. 'I hope you're thinking with the head on top of your shoulders and not the one dangling between your legs.'

'Thanks for stopping by, Sean. Always a pleasure.'

'Hey, I'm just looking out for you. But, since she's back in town, you should tear yourself off a piece, get your pipes cleaned. It'll help you think straight.'

Sean put down his mug and then crossed his arms over his chest, his eyes turning thoughtful. Serious.

'Byrne talks a lot in his sleep. I haven't been able to make out much, but when he goes to bed, he plays these . . . these recordings, I guess you could call 'em.'

'Recordings? Of what?'

'Hard to say. He keeps the volume down low, so I can't make out what's being said. But I hear crying. Sounds like little girls crying to me.'

Mickey felt his muscles seize up. His stomach dropped and kept dropping, the edges of his vision turning black.

'You get sick of being jerked around and want to get to the truth – when you really want to find out what he did to your daughter – my granddaughter,' Sean said, 'call McCarthy's and leave a message with the owner there, George. He knows how to get in touch with me.'

26

The J & M Diner was in downtown Belham, about three streets over from the police station. Darby opened the front door, a bell tied with ribbon clanging above her head, and she felt as though she had stepped through a portal and back into her youth. She saw the same scuffed and chipped ivory Formica tables and stiff red plastic chairs; the same dull grey, L-shaped counter and stools made of red imitation leather. She didn't see any cops – at least any cops she recognized. She didn't recognize anyone in here. The faces she saw looked tired and haggard and weary, and the people stared into space as if lost.

She grabbed a seat by the window, her mind returning to the countless times she had sat here with her father. This was one of his favourite haunts, and what she always remembered, what she loved the most about him, was that no matter how old she was, he would ask her questions and then genuinely listen, give her his full attention, invested in hearing her thoughts and opinions.

It was then she realized why she didn't like coming back to Belham – not because it had changed (and, arguably, for the worst) but because the city had become one big cemetery to her, places like J & M acting as headstones, reminders of a life that had been torn from her by violence and lies and greed and people whose moral compasses were constantly pointing at whoever could line their pockets and perform the kind of quiet, back-door favours that often left their victims searching for peace and comfort and understanding at the bottom of a high-ball glass or the sting of a needle.

And now here came Mickey Flynn, the man who had taken her virginity, the first man she had ever loved; a man she still liked and respected. And now she was going to blow up his world again. Darby wondered how many blows the human heart could take before it decided to quit.

She was going to shake his hand when he reached out and hugged her, the way close friends did. He squeezed her a little harder, as though he wanted to take something from her and absorb it, and then he kissed her cheek, broke away and sat down across from her. His face was guarded. Wary.

'Rough morning?' Darby asked.

'Hard time sleeping. What's up?'

Darby didn't have a chance to answer. The waitress, a girl no older than twenty by the looks of her, came to their table, set down two thick white mugs and started to pour coffee, asking them if they were ready to order. Mickey knew what he wanted. Darby hadn't had a chance to read the menu and wasn't particularly hungry but knew she needed to eat and, in the interest of saving time, ordered the same thing Mickey had.

When the girl left, Darby picked up the blue folder she'd placed on her seat and put it on the table. She made sure no one was standing nearby and then opened the folder and showed him an 8 × 10 colour photo of his daughter's jacket. A ruler had been placed next to it for measurement purposes. The hood wasn't folded back, the way it had been when it was found on the memorial.

It was open, and she watched Mickey lean forward and look at the three quarter-sized red-brown smudges on the left side of the hood.

Mickey swallowed several times. 'Those marks, are they –'

'Yes.'

'Claire's?'

Darby felt her muscles tighten, as if expecting a blow. She nodded.

Mickey looked like he'd been dunked in ice water.

'The lab ran the DNA and a hair analysis,' Darby began.

'Hair? They found Claire's hair in the hood?' He didn't look up from the picture. His face was pale, almost bloodless, and his voice had changed, as if someone else were speaking.

'They found three blonde hairs stuck in the jacket,' Darby said, hating that she had to be the one to tell him this. But it was the right thing to do. After all the shit he'd been through, he deserved to know. 'One of them had a root bulb, which means they could extract DNA from it. That's where they lucked out, because they couldn't get DNA from the blood. That's because –'

'I thought you could get DNA from blood.'

'You can. The problem is, the blood on the hood is what we call a degraded sample. It means they couldn't extract DNA from it. But the root bulb they found on one of the hairs did contain DNA, and they matched it against the DNA sample you gave Belham PD.'

'Her toothbrush,' Mickey said tonelessly. 'I gave them her toothbrush and her hairbrush and her pillowcase.

And fingerprints. Heather had her printed when she was four or so, at the police station – one of those child prevention things you do because if you do it you tell yourself bad things won't happen to your kid.'

He rubbed a hand vigorously over his mouth, thinking.

'What?' Darby prompted.

'That night you guys showed me her jacket. Kennedy folded back the hood so I wouldn't see the blood.'

'Anything about the jacket jump out at you?'

Mickey shook his head.

'The white fur lining the outer rim of the hood,' Darby said. 'It looks relatively clean.'

'You saying, what, he stored it?'

'When the crime lab went through his house a couple of days ago, they walked away empty-handed, which is why Belham can't build a case against Byrne. The thinking now is he might have hidden stuff at an offsite location, a storage facility, maybe even a safety-deposit box.'

'Atkinson, the detective in charge of her case, said he checked into all that.'

'He did check into it.' Darby had read the notes in the case file. 'Kennedy did too. But they checked records using Byrne's name. If he used an alias, forged the paperwork . . .' Darby shrugged. 'Kennedy is digging into that area.'

'I don't understand why he'd keep the jacket. That's evidence.'

'Serial offenders often keep souvenirs of their crimes so they can . . . you know . . .'

'No,' Mickey said. 'I don't know.'

Darby took a moment to organize her thoughts.

'No,' Mickey said. 'Don't do that.'

'Do what?'

'Give me the sanitized version. Don't hold back because you're afraid I'm gonna – just talk to me like a real person, okay? I need to hear it straight or I'll . . . you need to be direct with me, okay? No bullshit. It'll help me . . . you know, close the door.'

Darby sensed he was both repulsed and comforted by saying those last five words. She gave it to him straight.

'Owning a piece of the victim's clothing, a piece of jewellery – I know of a particular killer who collected women's driver's licences – we call them trophies. Serial killers and serial paedophiles often keep things belonging to their victims because it's a way for them to relive their crimes. It's also another way of maintaining control over their victims.'

'You make it all sound so . . . rational. Predictable.'

'Creatures like Byrne – ones who are highly intelligent and very organized – almost every one of them follows the same predictable patterns of behaviour to the letter. When Claire's anniversary day rolled around each year, Atkinson put people on Byrne, to see where he went, what he did. Atkinson even went so far as to collect Byrne's garbage and sift through it.'

'That legal?'

'Once it's placed on the street, it becomes city property,' Darby said. 'Men like Byrne, they're often very methodical and very patient. In other words, they know how to cover their tracks.'

'So why would he put Claire's jacket on the memorial?'

'Perfectly rational question,' Darby said. 'Unfortunately, I don't have a perfectly rational answer to give you.'

'So you don't know why.'

'What I do know – what you need to understand – is that these types of offenders don't think the way you and I do. When they commit certain acts, it doesn't make any rational sense to us. Many of these offenders have a desire to get caught. The desire can be subconscious. Some get caught because they get sick and tired of playing the game and secretly wish for the police or the FBI to come in and catch them. Some make a game out of taunting the police, wanting to show how smart they are. Some, when they get caught, start to brag about their crimes.'

'And where does Byrne fall?'

'All I have is speculation.'

'So speculate.'

'Putting the jacket on the cross and risking a return to living under the microscope – especially when he's dying and, from all accounts, wants to die in peace – it defies logic. If I had to guess – and that's all it is at this point, a guess – I'd say Byrne is terrified of being forgotten. Finding the jacket and finding him close to it puts him back into the spotlight.'

'And back under the microscope.'

'Like I said, it's not rational. They don't think like us.'

Mickey slurped his coffee. His hands were not steady.

'I do have some potentially good news,' Darby said. 'The lab also recovered two synthetic fibres from the jacket. One of them matches the fibres on Byrne's winter coat. The other is a grey hair. It didn't contain a root bulb, so the lab can't do DNA, but the hair is a strong match for Byrne's.'

Mickey stared at her for a long moment.

'Kennedy is getting his ducks in a row,' Darby said. 'He's

consulting with the DA as we speak, but the goal is to arrest Byrne. His lawyer will request a bail hearing, but, given the way judges are inclined towards paedophiles these days – even one who is dying – there's a strong chance a judge will deny bail or, if he or she grants it, set an amount so high Byrne won't be able to make bond. Either way, he'll go to jail.'

'And die there.'

'That's where we might have some leverage,' Darby said. 'Kennedy will agree to let Byrne die at home in exchange for certain pieces of information – namely what happened to your daughter and the other two girls, where he . . . buried them.'

'You said a few minutes ago that you think he won't share that information.'

'I don't,' Darby said. 'But if we threatened him with dying alone in prison . . .'

Mickey stared down at the picture of the jacket. Darby closed the folder when she saw their waitress heading their way, carrying plates of food.

'I don't know how to feel,' Mickey said after the woman left. 'I should feel . . . I dunno, vindicated somehow. Relieved. I should feel something. But what I'm feeling right now is . . . hollow.'

'That's shock.' She reached out across the table, put her hand on top of his. 'I'll be with you through every step.'

'Where'd you get this stuff?'

'You see the news – the two forensic investigators who were all over the TV because they came into town to work on the evidence?'

Mickey nodded.

'They're colleagues of mine,' Darby said.

'That's why you wanted me to wait until Monday, wasn't it? So they could do this.'

Darby nodded. 'This report hasn't been released to Kennedy yet. It's got to stay between you and me.'

'Thank you,' Mickey said. 'And thanks for this stuff. And for being –' His throat seized. He swallowed and tried to clear it and speak but he couldn't form the words. His eyes grew wet and he looked away, embarrassed.

Darby squeezed his hand tighter, feeling surprised and a bit relieved when he squeezed back. Then he gently withdrew his hand and propped his elbows on the table and rubbed his eyes.

'I keep having these dreams,' he said. 'Claire sleeping in her room and she's crying.' He opened his eyes and Darby saw the fatigue there and a jittery look that reminded her of a downed power line, its torn edge sparking. 'She won't stop crying.'

She sensed he had more to say and waited.

Mickey took in a deep breath and continued. 'In the dream, every time, I grab a pillow and hold it over her face. The other night I had another dream where we're in a car and Claire is crying and I kick her out. Me. Her father. Why would I be having dreams like that?'

'Maybe she wants you to let go.'

Mickey crossed his arms over his chest and looked out the window again, the early morning sunlight bathing his face, Darby watching him and seeing the same look she'd seen hundreds of times in the families of victims of violent crime, that hell wasn't an imaginary world from the Bible but a real place that, for those unfortunate few, took up residence in your soul.

27

The gig couldn't have been simpler: babysitting a Q-tip days, maybe even hours, away from becoming worm food. Nick Rossi had practically grown up in the business, starting off doing security for his old man's bar in Southie before moving off to work some of the major clubs, where broads practically dressed in tissue paper, wore dental-floss undies, and got high and horny on Molly. Breaking up fights between drunks didn't bother him. Usually just seeing his size and his shaved head, the tattoos running up and down his arms, the ones along his hands and his neck, and the yahoo would downshift his attitude, put it in neutral. All it took was a fuck-with-me-at-your-own-risk glance and a firm hand and a little bit of muscle and you were good to go.

Usually.

Posers were the problem. Fortunately, they were as easy to spot as a turd in a punchbowl – legit and wannabe gang bangers and juice-heads with lots of tats and wearing muscle shirts and cock-walking around the bar or club, acting like they owned the place and itching for trouble. Nick had never had a gun pulled on him – thank God for metal detectors and a liberal pat-down policy – but one time this group of Mattapan punks decided to get into it at a club, and by the time he'd broken up the fight, all three douchebags where collapsed on the floor, collecting their broken teeth. He also had a switchblade stuck in his lower back.

An ER surgeon had had to cut him open to repair the punctured kidney – and thank the sweet Lord Jesus and his family for the wonderful gift of opiates. While Nick lay in the hospital, doped up on Oxy, this humongous black dude dressed in some seriously expensive threads popped into his room and said how impressed he was by how Nick had handled himself that night at the club. Dude's name was Booker and he owned a private security company in downtown Boston and wanted to know if Nick had any interest in a full-time gig with a nice salary and health benefits and paid sick time, holidays and three weeks' vacation. Nick said yes.

That was almost five years ago, and, during that time, Nick, now coming up on forty-three, had carved out a nice life for himself, the only steady woman in his life a sweet white pit bull he'd named Snowball. His job took him all over the world, so he got to travel for free, but his favourite gigs were doing crowd control on movies filming in Boston, providing security for actors and actresses, consulting on the local scenery, whatever was needed. He also did a lot of 'protection-service details' for a big-time Boston lawyer named Mark Nelson, providing his clients with what amounted to full-time babysitting – like this Richard Byrne dude.

Since 6 p.m., Byrne had been sitting in a rocking chair, an Afghan blanket draped over his lap, staring out of the window overlooking his backyard. It was now one in the morning and the ex-priest was still up, still rocking and still staring out of the window. What was the point of sleeping when you knew you were dying, right? One look and you could tell the guy was on his way out: air tubes in his nostrils, portable oxygen tank on the floor, thin blue and purple veins bulging from beneath his egg-white skin, a vacancy sign already hanging in his eyes. Nick had seen that look so many times throughout his life that he instantly recognized it.

The weird thing? Actually, there were several weird things, but the one Nick was thinking about now was how a guy clearly so close to death would get a second wind or whatever, decide it was a good time to go out for a walk. Nick hoped the guy wasn't planning on doing one of his witching hour strolls tonight: the air was so cold outside it could shrink your balls to the size of raisins.

Nick heard a toilet flush from down the hall and a moment later Paul Ward came into the living room, today's *Herald* tucked underneath his arm. Paul was Nick's partner. With these gigs, you always worked in pairs.

'Get you something to eat or drink, Mr Byrne?' Paul asked.

Byrne, his gaze pinned on the window, mumbled something under his breath.

'Sorry, what's that?' Paul asked.

The ex-priest didn't answer, which didn't surprise Nick. Byrne liked to speak silently to himself, not hearing you or ignoring you, Nick wasn't sure which. The guy was probably praying. He did that a lot. Nick was never able to make out what the guy was saying but he figured the man was asking for forgiveness, if such a thing was possible, for molesting those girls and making a handful of them disappear into the ether, never to be seen or heard from again.

Did Byrne really believe that the Big Man in the Sky was actually going to forgive him for the pain and horror he'd inflicted? Nick wasn't big on religion, but he had learned a lot about God from TV and movies, and he couldn't reconcile the idea of some powerful but benevolent being actually rubber-stamping Byrne's sins. More likely God was turning to His son, Jesus, with a big grin and saying, *This guy Byrne actually thinks I'm going to take him in just because he was a priest. Can you believe this shit?*

Byrne could pray 24/7 and Nick was sure it wasn't going to make a lick of difference. After what he'd done to those girls, the guy was destined for hotter climates.

Paul turned to Nick and said, 'I'm gonna make myself a sandwich. You want anything?'

Nick shook his head. Paul walked away and disappeared into the kitchen, and Nick turned his attention back to playing *Candy Crush* on his phone.

'Sister,' Byrne croaked in a wet voice.

Nick looked up. 'What's that, Mr Byrne?'

'Your sister.' Byrne had stopped rocking. His eyes were locked on Nick's, the guy suddenly looking wide-awake and alert. Lucid. 'Your sister's name is Michele.'

'Excuse me?'

'That article in the *Globe* about the opioid epidemic,' Byrne wheezed. 'It talked about a woman named Michele Rossi from Southie. She died of an overdose. Heroin. She was your sister.'

Byrne wasn't asking him a question but rather talking like he already knew the answer – and he was right: Nick had had a sister named Michele who had died from a bad batch of heroin. The guy who had written the story was a buddy from the neighbourhood – a guy who'd had his own problems with H – and he wanted to talk about the heroin epidemic in Boston. Nick's mother had jumped on it, wanting the world to know that her youngest daughter was more than a junkie who'd died in a motel room so disgusting bed bugs refused to live there.

That article had been run in the papers two, maybe three months ago.

'I understand,' Byrne wheezed. 'The hurt can sometimes be too much for us to bear. The Lord understands that, Nicholas. He doesn't condemn – He embraces. Don't hold on to the hurt. If you let it go, the Lord will free you – He will heal you. Do you understand?'

Nick got to his feet, his knees cracking.

'I can help heal you. Take the pain and guilt away,' Byrne said. 'Would you like me to hear your confession?'

'I'm all set, padre, thanks.' Nick walked out of the living room and into the kitchen.

Paul saw the look on his face and put down his sandwich.

'What's up?'

'Nothing,' Nick said. 'Just stepping outside for a smoke. You mind?'

'Smoke the whole pack if you want. Guy's not going anywhere.'

Nick grabbed his black Navy pea coat from the rack and shoved his arm into the sleeve, finding it suddenly too small.

Not his coat; it was Byrne's. The guy owned a similar one.

'This guy ever sleep at night?' Nick asked.

'Not the times I've been here.' Paul shoved a handful of Doritos into his mouth. 'I think he's got that narco thing.'

'Narcolepsy.'

'Yeah, that. Jesus, man, you look wiped. After you finish your smoke, grab some shuteye.'

'What about you?'

'I just downed two Red Bulls.'

'Okay. Thanks.'

Nick put on his coat and stepped outside, on to the back porch.

Morphine-induced psychosis. That was the term Byrne's lady nurse used to describe the guy's inability to remember simple things – like where he'd put his reading glasses or keys – yet easily cough up memories from his childhood and months-old newspaper articles. Nick had seen it happen before, to his aunt Trudy. When the breast cancer had finally taken hold of her vital organs, she'd sometimes have trouble remembering who he was, and then, outta nowhere, she'd start listing the ingredients for some recipe her great-grandmother had written on a card that was stored in a box somewhere in the kitchen. Morphine could make you spit up these random bits of memory, just as Byrne had done with the newspaper article.

The air felt so good, so cold and sweet and clean. Spend an hour in that guy's house, the windows sealed shut and the baseboard heating percolating all of Byrne's sneezes and hacking coughs and his halitosis breath, and it made you begin to appreciate the small things in life.

The neighbourhood was so nice and quiet too, no

more reporters. They had pretty much petered off. Last night, Byrne had decided to go out for one of his midnight strolls with his cane. His walker sat in the corner. He refused to use it, even in the house.

Nick leaned forward, grabbed the walker's handles and used it to stretch out his back. First time his sister had tried to kick her habit, going cold turkey, she was so dope sick she'd had to use a walker to shuffle back and forth from the bed to the bathroom. Michele had suffered through every kind of detox and gone to every kind of meeting, and had prayed and used her support network. She had tried every gimmick under the sun and yet none of it could stop her deep and endless love for the needle.

Maybe if he hadn't been thinking about his dearly departed sister, may she rest in peace, he would have heard the dry flick of a lighter or seen the jumping flame. But his ears were working just fine, and, when he heard the crunch of footsteps running across hard, compacted snow, he looked up and saw a tall flame spinning through the darkness, then a glass bottle shattering against the railing, splashing gasoline on his clothes and face, engulfing him in flames.

28

'Homemade Molotov cocktail,' Kennedy was saying. 'A glass bottle hit the porch, turned the poor bastard into a human candle. Guy hurled himself off the back porch and started rolling around, what little good it did him.'

Mickey lifted his tool-box into the back of his truck.

They were standing in Margaret Van Buren's driveway in Newton. It was Wednesday, a few minutes past one, Mickey wrapping up half a day of work.

'Bodyguard wasn't the target, though,' he said, watching Mickey from behind a pair of tough-guy Oakley sunglasses. 'Coat Nick Rossi had on? It was similar to Byrne's, and the perpetrator couldn't get a good look at who was standing on the back porch 'cause there weren't any lights.'

Mickey dumped a box of tile samples on to the front seat.

'So it's dark out there, Rossi's standing next to the walker – I mean, it could have been Byrne, *should* have been Byrne,' Kennedy said. 'If someone hadn't unscrewed the bulbs from the pair of sensor lights out back, maybe Rossi wouldn't be clinging to life inside a burns unit at Mass General.'

Mickey slammed the door shut. 'Anything else?'

Kennedy sighed, his hands deep in his coat pockets. 'You know what I've got to ask. Where were you last night?'

Mickey fished his keys out of his pocket. 'What's the deal with my daughter's jacket?'

'Still waiting for the lab results,' Kennedy replied.

Mickey brushed past Kennedy and opened the door to his truck. He closed it as he climbed behind the wheel. He had started the truck when Kennedy appeared by the window, rapping a knuckle on the glass.

Mickey rolled down his window. 'Problem?'

'You didn't answer my question.'

'I've decided to take a page from Byrne's rulebook. Talk to my lawyer.'

'Mickey, all I need –'

'Talk to my lawyer,' Mickey said as he rolled up the window, wondering if Kennedy was going to bust out the cuffs and arrest him, drag him down to the station. The guy looked pissed enough to do it.

'I'll have a search warrant by the time you get home,' Kennedy said.

'There's a key under the mat on the back porch. Knock yourself out, chief.'

WBZ news radio had the story in heavy rotation.

'In what police are calling a deadly case of mistaken identity, Nicholas Rossi, one of two men hired to protect defrocked priest Richard Byrne, is listed in critical condition after suffering third-degree burns and inhalation injuries resulting from a fire-bombing attack during the early-morning hours. Richard Byrne, an alleged –'

Mickey shut off the radio, a barely suppressed scream rising in his throat. He gripped the steering wheel so hard his knuckles formed white half-moons.

Ever since he found out about what had happened to the bodyguard, Mickey's thoughts had turned to one person: Sean. His old man was capable of doing such a thing, no question in his mind. But Sean's specialty was making people disappear. Setting a guy on fire didn't seem like his style; then again, when it came to his old man, what did Mickey actually know? Back in the day, Sean had shot people dead while they were sitting in their cars or standing next to a payphone or coming out of a store. He had kidnapped people and taken them to a beach in Southie and to parking lots and shot them in the head and left their bodies there. Maybe Sean had thrown that Molotov.

So why did it sit so wrong with him? Was it because it felt sloppy? Sean would have made sure it was Byrne standing on the back porch before he lit the match. And Sean, Mickey was pretty sure, would have broken into the house so he could have some special one-on-one time with Byrne, get him to talk about Claire.

His phone rang. He picked up his cell, saw that Darby was calling and put the phone back down. He'd been hoping it was Heather.

He had left her a message and sent a couple of texts, telling her about the discovery of Claire's jacket, but Heather hadn't texted or called back. He knew she was still in France and it was possible she hadn't put an overseas calling option on her phone. But the news about Claire's jacket being found – and Byrne being found lying twenty feet away from it – had made CNN, and *USA Today* had run the story on the bottom half of their front page.

The phone rang again. Darby. He ignored it, thinking of how hotels, at least in his experience, gave their guests complimentary copies of newspapers like *USA Today*. They had TVs and access to American cable channels like CNN and Fox.

Darby tried calling again.

And even if Heather wasn't reading a paper or watching the news – things you didn't necessarily do when you were travelling – she was still in touch with plenty of friends back home, and at least one of them had to have found out about the jacket and reached out to her. Everyone he knew checked their email at least once a day, and he was sure she had Facebook and Twitter. There was no way Heather could *not* know about Claire's jacket, so why hadn't she called and asked what was going on, looking for an update?

Mickey came to a stop at the light. Sweat had gathered beneath his clothes; a dry pasty coating lined his mouth. He was in downtown Newton, it was a bright and beautiful winter day, and everywhere he looked he saw families out and about doing errands or maybe grabbing a late breakfast or an early lunch, and for a reason he couldn't explain he wanted to jump out of his truck and scream. He felt like he was coming apart at the seams and he didn't know why and he wondered if he was having some sort of breakdown.

Then his gaze landed on a neon sign hanging above a pair of big, dark windows facing the street. The sign was for a beer garden and he found himself looking for a place to park when his phone rang – Darby again – and he took the call not because he wanted to talk to her but because he didn't want to spend any time in his head thinking about hitting a bar and getting loaded.

Darby, being the blunt and brutal instrument she was, didn't mince her words: 'Have you lost your goddamn mind?'

'You actually think I did *that*?'

'Then what's the shit about you getting lawyered up? Kennedy just told me he's getting a search warrant.'

'That asshole just came by my job site asking me where I was last night.'

'Yeah. It's called a *police investigation*. Given your past history with him, you're what we call a *prime suspect*. You went after him once and nearly killed him, and you went after him the other day in the grocery store where, according to *multiple* witnesses, you threatened to burn him alive. You really need me to explain this shit to you?'

Mickey stepped on the gas, and when he drove by the bar he felt a sense of loss that shamed him. 'I love how you people always expect me to drop whatever the fuck I'm doing and answer your questions, but when I've got one, you all turn blind, deaf and dumb.'

A long, frustrated sigh exploded on the other end of the line. 'We've been over this,' Darby said.

'I asked Kennedy about the lab results on the jacket.'

Silence on the other end of the line.

'I didn't tell him about anything you told me,' Mickey said. 'I just wanted to see if he was going to come clean and –'

'I can't believe I'm hearing this.'

'Tell me the truth. As usual, he denied –'

'You've got a serious hearing problem, Mickey, you know that?'

'I've got rights here. You people keep forgetting that this is *my* daughter we're talking about.'

'You're right, Mickey. We're all a bunch of heartless pricks. That's why Atkinson, before he died, kept you in the loop on everything. And how'd you repay him? By turning around and beating the living shit out of the main suspect because you felt the police weren't doing their job.'

'If you guys had done your job he'd be behind bars! At least I'd have that satisfaction! At least –'

'Byrne didn't hire bodyguards and install panic buttons all over his house because he's scared of the police,' Darby said, her voice exploding across the line. 'You want to throw blame around, fine. Be my guest. But don't play the perennial victim card with me. You're the one who got drunk and went full Rambo on the guy. Not us; *you*. It's time you start owning your shit.'

Blood slammed against his eardrums, Mickey feeling it pounding across his forehead and behind his eyes.

'And Kennedy,' Darby said, 'being the heartless prick he is, went out to *your* job site so *you* wouldn't have to make the trip down to the station and deal with the media shit storm. Guy's trying to do you a favour, and, in typical Mickey Flynn fashion, you turn around and kick a two-by-four up his ass. You –'

'I'd love to see what you'd do if the one person you loved more than anything was –' His throat seized. He tried to clear it and felt his love for his daughter burning deep inside his chest, felt his hope rising and falling, rising and falling. He thought about her jacket on the cross and then he thought about how, if given the opportunity, he'd gladly cut off his arms, his limbs, anything, if that meant discovering what had happened to Claire. Because knowing whatever nightmare she had endured, alone, without him – knowing it, no matter how painful it would be, had to be better than this hell in which he found himself exiled right now.

He took a deep breath and tried to put his feelings into words.

'Finding Claire's jacket . . . it's supposed to mean something. And I . . . I can't walk around any more with this . . . this *mountain* on my chest. I can't do it any more, okay?'

Mickey pulled the phone away and wiped at his eyes with the back of his hand, Claire still there in his chest, telling him no, he had to keep fighting.

'Mickey?' Darby said, her voice a bit softer but still clearly pissed. 'Mickey, you there?'

'Yeah.'

'Just tell me where you were last night – and don't bullshit me.'

And then, for a reason he couldn't explain, he felt that need to fight for his daughter dry up.

'Mickey?'

'I swung by Big Jim's house to drop off some stuff – some contracts.'

'What time?'

'Around seven,' Mickey said. 'I ended up staying the night.'

'Why?'

'Because I –'

'You what? And don't lie to me, Mickey. If you lie to me, I swear I'll –'

'I didn't want to be alone,' he said. 'I was scared to be alone, okay?'

'You have any idea who may have done this?'

I sure as hell do, Mickey thought. 'Byrne has a list a mile long of people who want to see him burn alive,' he said, hoping – *praying* – nothing in his tone gave him away. Heather had always told him he wasn't a good liar, which explained why he never lasted long in poker. 'I'm sure Kennedy has a list. Why are people constantly sticking it up *my* ass? Why don't you –'

'Where are you right now?'

'On my way home.'

'You know where Highland Auto Body is?'

'Yeah. Why?'

'Meet me there. I'll take you in and you can give your statement.'

'I just told you where I was last night. Why do I have to go to the station?'

'Kennedy just sent me a text,' Darby said. 'The bodyguard, Rossi, just died. We're dealing with a homicide, and right now you're the lead suspect.'

29

Darby hung up on Mickey and slid her phone back into her jacket pocket as she turned around and faced Byrne's house.

The side street where she now stood was the same one Mickey had furtively travelled when he had decided to approach the former priest. Both ends of the street were blocked off by patrol cars, and behind her was a long row of trees, most of them towering pines and oaks, with trails leading into the Belham woods. Trails that could be taken all the way back to the Hill where the kids went sledding.

There were more vehicles parked on Byrne's street and more cops working crowd control, trying to keep the media at bay. She could hear their voices mingling in the air, the occasional shouts and threats, the crackling bursts of police radios. Kennedy wasn't here – wasn't coming back any time soon. He was on his way to the station to wait for Mickey. She was waiting for the detective in charge of the crime scene, a man named Jerry O'Toole, to come out of the house.

The early-morning fire had caused damage to the porch but not enough to require Byrne to vacate the premises. Darby stood on the other side of the five-foot fence, her gaze roving over the black scorch marks. They fanned across the porch floor and snaked up the pillars, the air filled with odour of charred wood. She followed the blackened footsteps down the porch steps and into the yard, her attention resting on the spot of melted snow and blackened, burnt grass where Nicholas Rossi had rolled around, trying to suffocate the flames. Byrne's other bodyguard, Kennedy had told her this morning, had remembered spotting a fire extinguisher underneath the sink, grabbed it and sprayed Rossi down first before turning back to the porch.

Mickey couldn't have done this. Lurking in the shadows and throwing a Molotov was cowardly, and, besides, Mickey needed information from Byrne, and that meant getting close and up front with the ex-priest, not lobbing a Molotov. Kennedy had agreed with her, but he still had to clear Mickey as a suspect.

'But I do have a guess who might have done something like this,' Kennedy had told her as their conversation this morning drew to a close. 'Guess who's back in town?'

'Sean Flynn.'

'The one and only. We're looking for him right now.'

Sean had killed plenty of people in his day, but he had been . . . clean. Precise and orderly, the way a professional killer was. This seemed too messy for Sean. If Sean had decided to go after Byrne, he would have tortured the former priest for information on where, exactly, the man had buried his granddaughter.

But she was thinking of the old Sean Flynn. The Sean Flynn of today was in his early seventies. Maybe he wasn't as sharp and careful as he once was. Maybe he didn't give a shit.

Or maybe someone else was behind this. Byrne had a long list of people who wanted him to suffer.

A pair of crime-scene techs from the Boston lab moved through the backyard, which was a pretty good size for a house in Belham. Most had postage-stamp-sized lawns, but Byrne's backyard could fit a shed, a rickety, tilting thing that looked like an old animal about to gasp its last breath before keeling over. She got the attention of one of the techs, a young guy by the looks of him. He wore a ski cap and latex gloves and sunglasses.

The guy came over to her because she was in 'the safe zone', the area designated for cops and other personnel. She didn't have a badge – and she hoped the guy wouldn't ask to see one.

'I'm working with Detective Kennedy,' she told him.

'I know who you are. The forensic consultant.' He said the words without a trace of antagonism, and Darby was relieved when he offered his hand. 'Nice to meet you. Barry Stein.'

'What have you found so far?'

'Cigarette butts and a lighter over there behind the shed.'

'Footwear impressions?'

'One looks like it has some tread marks that could be helpful in identifying a brand of boot, sneaker, whatever. We're –'

A whistle tore through the air. Darby turned to her right and saw a tall man with his fingers in his mouth. He whistled again then shouted, 'Barry. Back to work.'

The tech seemed puzzled. He shrugged and walked away.

The man who whistled was a detective. He wore a beaten leather jacket the colour of rust and the badge hanging from the lanyard rested on top of a substantial beer gut. The hostility was evident in his face and in the way he lumbered over to her.

Be polite. She forced a smile and, putting out her hand, said, 'My name –'

'I know who you are, and I've got to ask you to leave.'

'Detective Kennedy –'

'Kennedy transferred the crime scene over to me, which means I'm in charge and calling the shots. So, again, I'm asking you –'

'I'm not *at* the crime scene. I'm outside of it.'

'Yeah, and distracting my people. You want a forensics rundown, get it from Kennedy.'

Darby studied his lumpy face through the green tint of her sunglasses. 'Are you trying to be an asshole, or are you always an asshole?'

He grinned. 'Just with rats.'

'Might want to be careful with your word choices,' she said.

His grin broke into a smile. 'You want to take a swing at me, put on a show for the cameras, be my guest. Either way you cut it, you're leaving. You can do it on your own or in cuffs. What's your preference, cupcake?'

Darby glanced at the window and saw Byrne sitting on the other side of it, at his small table. Their eyes locked and he smiled at her and then blew her a kiss.

30

As much as people believed that she enjoyed being combative, the truth was otherwise. Dealing with bullshit and bureaucratic agendas and stupid people and the garden-variety assholes everyone encountered in their daily life often left her feeling addled, drained to the bone. Instead of seeking refuge inside a bottle, the way most cops did, Darby turned to the one place she had discovered that recalibrated her thinking.

CrossFit called it a 'box', which was their name for a gym. An online search revealed Belham had one. It was located downtown, the inside pretty much like all the ones she had visited, a garage-like space big enough to accommodate an adult version of a jungle gym. It had pull-up bars of various heights and ropes for climbing and gymnast rings hanging from the high warehouse ceiling. The floors were padded, and the weights were made entirely of rubber or coated in it. The box was warm and smelled of sweat and determination and chalk, and the clanging sound the weight bars made as they were dropped to the floor relaxed her in the same, soothing way as if she had been listening to the ocean.

For the next hour, she threw herself into a gruelling workout that left her collapsed on the floor, her lungs on fire and soaked head to toe with sweat. Her body was pleasantly exhausted, which was great, and her mind now felt wiped clean but also invigorated, which was even better. She showered, dressed, and then drove back to Belham, to St Stephen's, where Cullen's secretary told her that the priest was still unavailable.

When she returned to her hotel, Darby headed into the sad-looking lounge draped with thick velvet curtains and a glowing, neon-blue mirror to show people how cool and hip the place was. It had a solid lunch menu and a pretty decent selection of bourbons. She ordered a double Bulleit neat and an Angus burger stacked with all the fixings, opened a tab and took her glass over to a booth in the far corner of the room, wondering why Kennedy hadn't called her. She took out her phone and found out why: she had muted her phone at Byrne's house, wanting to focus on the crime scene. She found the constant buzzing and pinging sounds of her phone distracting.

Kennedy hadn't called her, but someone else had. A green text box message held a local phone number she didn't recognize. It also told her the caller had left a voicemail. She listened to it now.

A wet, crackling sound filled the phone speaker before the voice spoke.

'I was hoping to catch you before you left,' Byrne said. He struggled to breathe, his throat and lungs drowning in phlegm. 'I remembered a detail about your brother I thought you might find helpful, in case you decide to look for him. Oh, and one other thing. Your father engaged in an extramarital affair of his own shortly after your mother's peccadillo. She lives in Belham. The woman, not your mother, obviously, as Sheila has long since passed. Please don't hesitate to call if I can be of any help. May God bless you and keep you safe, Darby.'

The message ended.

She had to give him credit. He really knew how to set the hooks.

But her words were facile, and she knew it. His words had bypassed the logical and intellectual centres of her brain – gave them the finger and headed straight down to their intended target: her heart. She felt them twisting inside there, her heart trying to pump them away and failing because Byrne had, in his possession, incredibly private information regarding her mother, her father, her family. He knew intimate details of their lives, things she didn't know about and would never know about. Byrne would never pass the information on to her, and she knew he would never give her the tapes either, because he wanted to torture her with them. He wanted to use them to break her down until she begged. Pleaded. Cajoled.

That was never going to happen.

As for the tapes themselves, she suspected Byrne had either destroyed them or put them someplace where they would never be found after he died. Having the truth come out about her parents' private lives wasn't nearly as fun or as satisfying as watching her twist on the hook, knowing it was eating her alive. He would take his knowledge with him into the ground, and thinking about that made her want to drive to his house and beat it out of him – the same tactic Mickey Flynn had already tried.

Besides, if she went after Byrne in his current physical state, he would die – which, she firmly believed, was what Byrne desired. Going out on a violent note was a far more interesting and far more powerful end to his story than withering away inside his house.

Darby also had another thought – one that had been quietly nagging at her for the past couple of days. Byrne playing the tape of her mother's confession, telling her about her parents' infidelities and the story of how they had given a child – a boy – up for adoption – and now, leaving a cryptic message to torture her mind further – yes, all of it had thrown her, and yes, she was, in all likelihood, still in a state of shock, her brain trying to process everything, come to terms with it. And maybe that was the point. If she were consumed by her own personal turmoil, it would divert her time, energy and attention away from Byrne. Sure, he got off on seeing how it had hurt her, but what if he had a secondary agenda – namely, throwing her off the scent, trying to keep her mind occupied on herself instead of discovering something she could use against him?

But that was the one thing she hadn't found. The guy was a walking cypher. She had been relentlessly working the phones, trying to dig up information on Byrne, talking to anyone she could to learn more about the man. The Boston Catholic Archdiocese refused to speak to her about Byrne in any way, shape or form – or the Belham police, for that matter. After Kennedy had tried – again – and hit a wall – again – Darby had enlisted Sue Michaud to help, hoping Sue could work some back channels, dig something up. Sue, though, hadn't got anything beyond dry biographical information. Nobody knew Byrne – and, if they did, they weren't talking about him.

Father Cullen was the only one who really knew him, and the man was MIA. She had left several messages with his insufferable secretary, and he hadn't called. And then there was the matter of the mothers of Byrne's other two victims, Nancy Hamilton and Judith Levenson. They still hadn't returned her calls.

Mickey had described Nancy Hamilton as 'stand-offish'. Darby thought she might have better luck focusing her efforts on Judith Levenson, who was probably the better choice, anyway, since Byrne had discussed her and her daughter that day in his kitchen. Darby took out her phone and called, unsurprised when the woman's voice-mail picked up. Darby checked her frustration and left another message.

Her food came. Her burger, fries and salad, even the bourbon – it was all as tasteless as Pablum.

Her phone rang when she was paying the bill. It was Sue Michaud.

'I have a present for you,' Sue said.

'Great. I could use some good news. What is it?'

'Father Keith Cullen got himself a new cell phone.'

'And you have his new number.'

'I do. I also know, thanks to GPS tracking, where he is at this very moment. Now, before I tell you, I need your assurances that you will not hurt him or do anything that will get you into trouble and, by proxy, me, since this gift I'm about to give you is technically illegal.'

'I'll be on my best behaviour. You have my word.'

'All right, then. I've been tracking Cullen's cell signal, and, according to what I'm seeing here on my screen, he just walked into 29 Huntington Avenue in Boston. Address belongs to a restaurant called Camilla Rose. Hey, speaking of Cullen, I did some digging, because I was curious about him.'

'You find anything good?'

'Unfortunately, no. Everything points to his being a boring, ordinary priest. Then again, on paper, I could say the same thing about good ole Father Byrne, and we know that's not true. You think there's something there with Cullen?'

'Hard to say.' Darby hadn't told Sue about the recorded confession Byrne had played for her.

'Well, if there's anything I can do on my end to help, don't hesitate to ask.'

Darby felt the words on her tongue, surprised herself when she said them out loud. 'Actually, there's one thing you can help me with – not about the Flynn case but about something else. Something ... personal. About my parents.'

Sue waited. Darby closed her eyes and took in a deep breath, wondering if she wanted to set this ball in motion.

'I was told they had a kid – a boy,' Darby said. 'This is before I came along, so he'd be older. I was told they gave him up for adoption when they were in high school.'

'Who told you this?'

'I'd rather not say right now.'

'Is this source credible?'

'To some degree.'

'Well, if you can get me your parents' social-security numbers, that would be a huge help. That opens a lot of doors. Until then, give me their full names, and as many details as you can.'

Darby rubbed her forehead. 'Okay.'

'This thing with your parents, how long have you known?'

'A few days.'

'I asked because, well, I'm sure I don't have to explain this to you, but, in situations like this, I find that people don't really think through the long-term implications of what they truly want. People want to know details but not *all* the details. You can't cherry-pick.'

'I understand.'

'Take some more time and think this over. Thing like this, when you reach the end of the road, it's not going to end the way you wanted it to. You're not going to be in some Disney movie where you get to the end and everyone is happy and singing songs together, while unicorns shit rainbows. But you know this better than anyone, am I right? . . . Darby, you there? Hello?'

31

Darby had been to Camilla Rose once, a few years back. Coop had taken her there for her birthday. Actually, he'd *insisted* on it, wouldn't take no for an answer. Despite being a jeans-and-T-shirt guy, Coop harboured a secret love for haute cuisine and fancied himself as something of a foodie; and, although he would never admit to it, she suspected he liked getting dressed up. Darby, a lover of diners and burger joints and dive bars, never understood the point of dropping wads of cash on big fancy white plates that contained hardly any food, and dressed up only for weddings and funerals, and then only because it was mandatory.

Still, she agreed to go because she saw how it excited him, and because she relished any time she could spend alone with him.

Thinking about him now – how they hadn't spoken in over a year, how they had drifted apart once she found out that he was engaged to be married – formed a knot in her heart. She had never put much stock in marriage until she'd met him. She'd never bought into the whole soulmate notion either, until she'd met him. Jackson Cooper had changed her, and now he was lost to her, in love with another woman, and even after all this time it still *hurt*. Darby walked into the restaurant, a knot twisting in her heart.

When she stopped near the entrance to the dining room, with its high ceiling and artful lighting and expensive décor, she wasn't surprised that she recognized many of the faces seated at the white linen tables – the current Massachusetts senator dining with a former mayor who had tried to run for president; the owner of the New England Patriots; a popular radio personality; and two former players for the Red Sox. Camilla Rose, one of Boston's oldest and most expensive restaurants, was also one of the city's de facto hot spots for power brokers.

The maître d', an older gentleman himself, and wearing a three-piece suit, sidled up next to her. He glanced at her jeans and black leather jacket and said, 'May I help you?'

Darby kept scanning the room. 'Just looking for a friend. Don't worry, I'm not staying for dinner.'

'Be that as it may, our guests are required to wear –'

'I'm here on police business,' Darby said, and turned to him. 'That a problem?'

He stiffened, swallowed. 'No, it's not a problem.'

Darby smiled. 'Didn't think so.'

'But I would ask that you show some discretion. Our patrons –'

'Ah, there he is. This will only take a moment. Thanks for your concern, Jeeves. Have a wonderful evening.'

Darby moved through the dining room, heading to the far right-hand corner where Father Cullen sat at a table with three other men. She recognized the fat one holding court: Stewart Worthington, one of the city's most prominent trial lawyers. She had met him several times over the years, in court and at various social functions. Worthington fancied himself as Boston's version of Brad Pitt, only he was Jabba the Hutt with a bad Boston accent and big, capped teeth as white as a toilet bowl.

Worthington was an odd dining partner for a priest, Darby thought. Or maybe not. Worthington, she remembered, had gained a lot of press and notoriety when he agreed to lend his services and those of his legal firm to the Boston Catholic Archdiocese during the sexual-abuse scandal.

Worthington saw her approaching and smiled expansively, flashing his enormous choppers. Father Cullen saw her too – was staring right at her with the flat, expressionless gaze she had seen time and time again in prisoners, recidivists and criminals-in-training – an empty look that said you weren't worth their time or attention.

'Well, look who it is, Boston's celebrity sleuth,' Worthington said, his eyes bright with alcohol. His voice was loud too, which told her he'd already pounded back a few. The table was packed with crystal highball and wine glasses and plates holding fancy, artfully arranged appetizers. 'Long time, no see. How's it hanging, Doc? What brings you by?'

Her eyes never left Cullen. 'I'd like a word with Father Cullen.'

'Pull up a chair and join us,' Worthington said.

'Another time, Stewie.'

'Why do you always have to call me that?' To the table: 'Doctor D here loves breaking my balls, it's a thing with her.' Then, back to Darby: 'Come on, sit down, take a load off. We're all friends here.'

'I'd like to speak with Father Cullen privately.'

Cullen didn't move, but Worthington reached to his

side and clamped his meaty hand on the priest's forearm, to prevent him from getting up. 'Any questions you want to ask Father Keith, you can ask in front of me.'

'Why? Are you representing him?'

'I am.'

'Oh? Since when?'

'Since now. You've got that crazy look in your eyes, the one that says you're about to go postal.'

'I wasn't aware of Father Cullen having been accused of a crime.'

'He hasn't.'

'So why would he need legal representation?'

'He doesn't. I'm being proactive here, making sure my friend's reputation doesn't get dragged through the mud.' Worthington smiled, his eyes crinkling with amusement.

Darby kept her attention on Cullen. 'I've left you several messages. Care to explain why you're avoiding me?'

Worthington said, 'The better question is, how'd *you* know he was here?'

'I've got friends everywhere, Stewie.'

'Friends are important. They keep us in check, prevent us from saying or doing stupid things. And I'm being a friend to you when I say you're overstepping your bounds. You're not a cop any more, which means you're no longer allowed certain privileges – like stalking and harassing people.'

Darby dug her tongue into her back molar. 'Is that what you told him, Father Cullen? That I've been stalking you?'

The priest didn't answer. Worthington said, 'So, Doc, before this escalates, maybe you should do the right thing and leave nice and quietly.'

Darby felt someone sidle up beside her. She turned,

saw the maître d'. He'd brought two men along with him, middle-aged guys with faces that had been knocked out too many times in the boxing ring.

Almost everyone in the restaurant had turned to stare. The waiters watched. Cullen sipped his scotch. Worthington drummed his fingers against the table, waiting to see what she was going to do.

Darby sighed. She turned around, took a step forward and then stopped and addressed the diners.

'Ladies and gentlemen, I'm sorry for the disruption. I just stopped by here to ask Father Keith Cullen, from St Stephen's parish in Belham, why he recorded confessions with his parishioners and shared them with Richard Byrne, a defrocked priest who molested and murdered three girls – the Snow Girls. I'm sure you've been reading all about them lately.'

Darby turned back to the table. Father Cullen stared down at the table, slack-jawed, his face as white as the dinner plates.

'Enjoy your evening,' Darby said.

Worthington shook his head, grinning. 'You never disappoint, McCormick.'

Darby had almost reached Belham and was still on the phone with Kennedy, running down what had happened at the restaurant, when she got an incoming call. She glanced at her screen.

The caller was Danny Halloran. Had he remembered something else about the night Claire disappeared?

'I've got to take this,' she told Kennedy.

'Keep me in the loop.'

Darby hung up. 'Hey, Danny.'

'You said I could call you if I needed something.' Danny's words were slurred and dulled either by booze or drugs, or a combination of both. It sounded like he was barely conscious.

'What's going on?'

'Vic said I should call you. Said I had to call you.'

'Vic?'

'Victor. The guy I was with that morning at Flour.'

'Right.'

'I'm with him right now, at his place.'

'What's going on?' she asked again.

He didn't answer.

'Danny?'

'I need to . . .' He took a sharp intake of air. Swallowed audibly. 'I haven't been entirely . . . truthful with you about what happened that night on the Hill. And some of the stuff that happened after. With Father Byrne.'

'What happened with Father Byrne?'

'Vic says I need to come clean. He says it'll be the only way I'll *get* clean, get off this shit.'

'He's right. Tell me what's —'

'I can't live like this any more. I've got to put everything out on the table. *Everything.* You know, make amends, but I don't know where to start.'

'Start with me. Let me help you.'

'Can I trust you?'

'Yes. Absolutely. Start at the beginning, okay? Start with that night on the Hill.'

'I don't want to do this over the phone. That's the cowardly way out. Vic says I've got to do this face to face.'

'Okay. Where do you want to meet?'

'Can you come to Vic's place? I'm not in any condition to drive, as you can probably tell already.'

'Give me the address.'

He did, and told her she could park at the back of the building, in Space Number 6. Victor had his own parking spot – a rarity in Boston.

'How far away are you?' he asked.

'Probably an hour. Let's stay on the phone and –'

'No. No, in person. And alone. Just you, me and Vic, okay? No other cops, or I'm not going to talk.'

'Okay, Danny. Just relax, I'm on my way.'

'No cops,' he said again. 'I got your word on that?'

'You have my word. We'll take this one step at a time.'

'I might need, like, a lawyer.'

'Let's talk first. Remember, one step at a time.'

No matter what time of day, Boston traffic was always a nightmare. The maze of narrow streets was crowded with too many pedestrians. There were too many lights and too many cars and always too many roadworks. By the time she reached the South End and had parked behind Victor's brownstone, in Rutland Square, almost two hours had passed.

Victor, Danny had told her, lived in the first-floor unit. Darby was walking through the lot, heading for the alley between the two buildings, when her phone rang again. The caller ID said UNKNOWN. She took it, turning her back to the wind so she could hear.

'McCormick.'

'I had *nothing* to do with those tapes,' Cullen said, trembling with rage. 'I didn't even know they existed until a few days ago.'

She ducked into the alley. The wind stopped howling and she could see her breath steaming in the air in front of her. 'How many does Byrne have?'

'I will not let you or anyone else ruin my legacy because of that . . . that *abomination*. Watch where you step, Doctor, or we will *destroy* you.'

Cullen hung up. She stared at the phone for a moment, wondering what her next play should be and then shut down her thinking. She would deal with him later. First, Danny. Darby slid her phone back into her pocket, heard movement behind her. She turned and caught a glimpse of a man wearing a black ski mask, a black down jacket and dark jeans. He swung from his hip with the speed, agility and skill of a trained boxer, throwing his weight into the punch.

32

The solar plexus is a complex network of nerves. When the blow hit her in the stomach, her breathing stopped. The area around her lower ribs cramped and she couldn't draw a breath and she doubled over, knowing she shouldn't, knowing she couldn't let him get behind her. But her muscles had contracted and she staggered forward and fell sideways against the back of a sectional couch someone had discarded next to a Dumpster. She still couldn't draw a breath and her lungs were screaming for air and her brain was screaming for her to fight because he was already behind her. She managed to get her hands on the couch and he managed to slip something around her neck.

It was a rope.

Now he had her pinned against the couch and she couldn't fight him because she still couldn't draw a breath. Her jacket was still zipped up to the neck and she couldn't reach her handgun, and he was squeezing the rope and her mind was feeding her important but ultimately useless facts she'd learned from strangulation cases – how it took anywhere from seven to fourteen seconds for the victim to lose consciousness; how death would occur in a minute or less, depending on the amount of pressure applied. He was applying a lot of pressure, squeezing with all of his strength, trying to garrotte her, and she could hear him panting.

Her right hand had already found the leather strap near

her belt buckle. Her eyes were wide and hot and wet, the edges of her vision already beginning to fade as she pulled the strap and felt the snap-button pop off. She threaded her index and middle fingers through the buckle and pulled, freeing her concealed knife from its hidden leather sheath. She had a solid grip, and so she swung the knife around and felt the six-inch blade sink deep into the meat of his right leg, along the side.

The man howled. He lost some of his strength and a bit of his grip but he didn't let go of the rope. He did when she twisted the knife and yanked upward, the sharp blade slicing through muscle and sinew, stopping when it hit the curved, flat bone underneath the kneecap.

He roared and pushed himself off her, Darby collapsing to the cold, hard ground and grasping at the rope still around her neck, the nerves in her solar plexus still misfiring, still refusing to let her breathe. He hobbled away down the alley, one hand gripping the wound in his knee. She got the rope off her neck, and, as she managed to get to her feet, she saw him duck out of the alley, on to the main street, and knew there was no way to catch him.

This wasn't a random attack either. Who knew she was coming? Danny Halloran knew. Darby stumbled her way through the alley, gasping for air, her face raw from the cold. She turned the corner and held on to the railing for balance, as she moved her way up the concrete steps of Victor's brownstone. Standing underneath the building's outdoor light, she found a bronze-plated call box to the left of an entry door painted a bright red. She pressed the button.

Danny didn't answer.

The call box had buzzers for six units. She pressed all of them. When the door buzzed a moment later, she entered a warm foyer with a winding staircase made of mahogany, the steps and the foyer covered in a carpet such a dark red it almost looked black.

Victor's place was on the first floor. She staggered her way to the white door, her breathing growing a bit steadier with each step. She turned the doorknob, surprised to find it unlocked.

The condo had tall white walls and blond-oak hardwood floors. The place looked expertly decorated too, Darby half wondering, as she removed her sidearm, what Victor did for a living to be able to afford such a place.

She called out Danny's name, heard the rasp in her voice, and tried again.

No answer. The home felt deathly quiet.

She cleared the first level, staggered her way up to the second. The bedroom across from the top of the stairs had chocolate-coloured walls and teak furniture. Danny Halloran and the man named Victor, dressed in jeans and T-shirts and sockless, lay unconscious on top of a white ruched duvet cover. Danny had used a belt as a ligature around his bicep in order to find a good vein, and he'd left his 'kit' – a zippered, black leather pouch holding a hypodermic needle, cotton balls, a lighter and a spoon used to melt heroin – beside him on the bed.

Darby checked Danny for a pulse. She couldn't find one. She pulled him off the bed and on to the floor, where she began to perform CPR, knowing it was hopeless and hoping it wasn't.

33

Darby didn't know the Boston detective who caught the case. If he recognized her name, he didn't show it. And if he knew who Danny Halloran was, he didn't show that either.

The detective's name was John Bace. His hair had gone prematurely white and he spoke in such a quiet, gentle voice she had to lean in close to hear him, Darby figuring the guy did this both to calm the victim down and to build intimacy. He had kind, soulful eyes, and, as they stood near the base of the stairs, Darby ran him through exactly what had happened when she entered the apartment.

She did not tell him about the reason why Danny had called her, the part about his wanting to speak to her about Richard Byrne. She knew Kennedy wouldn't want Boston PD interfering in his investigation, people playing politics trampling all over it.

Kennedy was on his way into the city. He had been her second call, after she'd got off with the 911 dispatcher.

Bace's eyes kept flicking to the rope burns along her neck.

'It's fine,' she rasped. 'Minor trauma.'

Her words took him by surprise.

'I've been through worse,' she said, trying to make light of it. She didn't want him or anyone else to treat her as a victim. She refused to take on that role, ever. 'The rope he used is on the counter over there. I placed it on a clean plastic garbage bag – I found a roll of them under the sink. I used another one for the buckle knife.'

'Buckle knife?'

'It's a hidden knife, slides right here into your belt.' She showed him.

'Who did you say you were again?'

The front door opened. The patrolwoman manning it motioned to Bace. He stepped outside and came back in a few minutes later with Kennedy, his cheeks ruddy from the cold. Bace didn't seem to mind having another detective there.

Bace and Kennedy moved up the steps to the second level. Darby followed.

'Christ,' Kennedy muttered under his breath, when he entered the bedroom. Darby remained in the doorway.

When the EMTs arrived, they had tried injecting Danny with naloxone, to counter the opioid overdose. It had failed to revive him because he was already dead. They were both as lifeless as a pair of dolls.

Bace said, 'You didn't tell me how you got access to the condo.'

'Someone let me in through the main door. After that, I checked the door for the condo, found it unlocked and went inside.'

'You said your attacker was wearing a mask.'

'Black ski mask.'

'How was he dressed?'

'Didn't really pay attention. It was dark out, and I was too busy trying to, you know, breathe.'

'I ask because we've got a guy here who's attacking gay

men and women at night in the South End. Beats them up, sometimes robs them.'

'Beats them up with what?'

'Pipes, mostly. I know he likes to kick a lot.'

'He try strangling anyone with a rope?'

Bace shrugged. 'Maybe.'

'Well, it sounds like you're on top of it.'

Kennedy shot her a look.

'The guy fled to the main street,' Darby said to Bace. 'I'm sure there are cameras out there.'

'We'll look into it.'

'What's the deal with Victor? Who is he?'

Bace flipped a page in his notebook. 'Full name is Victor Flores. He's thirty-three, works at Mass General in the ER. Trauma surgeon.'

'Any history of drug use?'

'Can't say. Although it's been my experience that doctors who are heroin addicts generally go the pill route. They usually have more access to opioids. You said Daniel Halloran called and asked you to come by.'

Darby nodded. 'He wanted to talk to me.'

'About what?'

'I don't know.'

'How did he sound?'

'Like he was on drugs.'

'This opiate epidemic . . .' Bace sighed and shook his head. 'I've got to ask you to go to the station, give a statement about what happened to you and about what happened in here, everything you did. Standard procedure.'

Kennedy said, 'I'll take her.'

He didn't speak until they were alone in the car.

'So,' he said, starting the engine. 'What do you really think?'

'That guy was waiting for me in the alley. He knew I was coming.'

'And you think he, what, used Halloran to lure you there?'

'Halloran calling me up, asking me to come and talk to him, to share something about the case – I knew it was too good to be true.' Darby sighed, shook her head. 'I should have been paying better attention. All the signs were there.'

'What signs?'

'Danny wanting to know how long it would take me to get into town, how he kept stressing about having me coming alone, no other cops. How he insisted on talking in person and not on the phone. He specifically told me to park in Vic's spot. It was a set-up.'

'So this guy uses Halloran to lure you there and, after he calls you and hangs up, this guy makes them shoot heroin, has them OD?'

She heard the scepticism in his voice. 'Would you shoot heroin if you had a gun to your head?' It sounded thin, but still it was possible. 'That guy Victor? I bet you he has no history of drug abuse. He was there the morning I met Halloran, thought I was there to bust Danny on a drugs charge and got real upset at him. Danny swore he was clean.'

'Was he?'

'He was when I spoke to him. The other thing is . . . that morning at the bakery, the moment Halloran saw me, he practically jumped to his feet. He was going to run, Chris, I'm telling you. And the entire time I spoke with him he kept fidgeting, acting real nervous. At first I thought it was because I'd caught him in what he perceived to be an *in flagrante delicto* situation – holding hands with his boyfriend or whoever he was to him. He was afraid I was going to out him to his father – said he had disappointed him enough. He still works for Belham, right, the father?'

Kennedy nodded.

'You tell him I was going to speak to his kid?' Darby asked.

'No. Why?'

'Halloran said his father had called and told him I might be coming by to visit him.'

'A lot of people saw you at the station that morning. Word got around.'

'Halloran also said he recognized me from some online pictures. What if he was lying? What if someone was threatening him?'

'All great questions – and ones we'll ask when we find the guy who attacked you.' Kennedy was staring at her neck.

'I'm fine,' she said.

'Plus side to almost getting strangled to death is that you've got one of those smoky, sexy lounge-type voices.'

'There's that.'

'Seriously, are you okay?'

'The guy really knew how to throw a punch.'

'Let's take a ride to the hospital, have that –'

'I wasn't attacked by some guy who's trolling for gay men and women,' Darby said. 'When you strangle someone, it's up close and personal. That happens, generally, in a sexual type of situation or when you know the vic, want to make a statement.'

'Did he say anything to you?'

'I don't think so. But there was a lot of rage there. It was definitely personal. Look, having this guy use Halloran to make that phone call and lure me there – I get it, it sounds weak. But I don't think we should discount it. It's too neat, how it all ended up, don't you think?'

Kennedy blew out a long breath. 'I don't like it. Not one damn bit.'

'I also have one more piece of interesting news.' She told him about Cullen's phone call. 'I think we should take a serious look at him.'

'You think a priest ordered a hit on you? What is this, a Dan Brown novel?'

'What if this is something that's bigger than just Byrne? What if Cullen is involved?'

'Well, *you* can't do anything with Cullen, not after that stunt you pulled at the restaurant,' he said. 'I got a call on my way down here. Cullen's going to file a restraining order against you, says you're harassing him.'

'That's bullshit.'

'Still, I've got to be careful here. You violate the restraining order, there's nothing I can do to protect you. And let us not underestimate the mighty power of the Catholic Church.' He smiled but there was no humour in it. He sighed as he looked out through the windshield, his gaze sweeping across the streets. 'And now your attacker's somewhere out there in the wind.'

'But hobbling,' Darby said. 'I did some serious damage to his knee.'

'With that hidden James Bond knife-trick shit.'

'Guy's in a lot of pain.'

234

'And pissed off, I imagine. At you.'

'That's the good news.'

'Oh? And why's that?'

'Because he's going to come after me,' Darby said. 'At some point he's going to want to finish what he started.'

34

Mickey had heard through Big Jim's contact inside Belham PD that Byrne's other bodyguard had quit. After what had happened to Nick Rossi that night in his backyard, Byrne couldn't get anyone else to watch over him. Bryne was back to living alone, his only regular visitor his caretaker, Grace Humphrey, who visited him during the day. She never stayed over at night, he'd been told.

It was half past two in the morning and the roads were deserted, the world dead asleep. Mickey had been expecting to find a patrol car parked somewhere nearby, keeping an eye on the house. He didn't see one, which didn't come as much of a surprise. The backyard crime scene had been processed, he'd been told, so there wasn't the need for Belham PD to protect it, and Byrne hadn't asked for police protection. Byrne said he didn't see the point, telling the detective that he believed he had only days to live anyway.

Mickey parked his truck directly in front of Byrne's house, knowing he was being recorded by one of the man's surveillance cameras and not caring.

A downstairs light was on; he could see its glow from behind the front curtains.

Byrne was awake.

Mickey got out of the truck and stared at the house, thinking about Claire, how he could finally see her face clearly again. He saw her in his mind's eye as she stood on the edge of Salmon Brook Pond, her pink winter jacket zippered to the top but her hood down, her face as clear and bright as day. Her mouth was open, and the tip of her tongue was out, rubbing against her bottom lip.

'Look, Daddy, look!' Claire wasn't skating so much as shuffling her way across the ice, her arms flung out at her sides, like wings.

He skated up next to her. It was a perfect winter day: sky a hard blue, air cold but lacking that angry bite that drove you indoors. The kidney-shaped pond was packed with kids and parents. Here, out in the sunlight, every feature on her face seemed magnified: her evident joy and the dimpled cheeks on her pale face; the blueness of her eyes.

'Daddy, we have to do the twirly-bird jump.'

'You know I can't do that, sweets.'

Claire came to a stop. She looked up at him and pushed her glasses back up her nose. 'But that's how they judge us,' she said.

He frowned, trying to decipher her thoughts.

'On TV, remember? The man and woman skated around and they got numbers.'

'Oh, you mean the figure skaters.'

Claire nodded so vigorously her glasses almost slipped off her face. 'The man picks up the girl and holds her up in the air and the judges give out numbers.'

'That I can do. You ready?'

'Ready,' she said, and offered her hand, Mickey gripping it, its smallness reminding him of the early hair-trigger days she'd spent in Mass General's NICU, the hospital's unit for preemies, all three pounds and two ounces of her hooked up to wires, her vitals being constantly displayed on monitors. She was fighting to breathe on her own because her lungs were underdeveloped and she had contracted

237

and, thank God, successfully fought off an infection that had almost killed her.

'Daddy!'

'Yeah, sweets?'

'The judges are waiting for you to pick me up and hold me out front.'

He did as instructed, scooping her up and holding her in front of him, his arms locked — an easy thing to do, since she weighed only forty pounds, Claire so tiny for her age.

Claire spread apart her arms and legs, forming an x.

'Starfish!' *she called out.*

'Well done!'

'Now you do one.'

Mickey lifted up his daughter and placed her on his shoulder. He wrapped one arm around her shins and, hugging her close to his chest, held his other arm out in front of him in a straight line.

'How's that?' *he asked.*

'Call out what you're doing, Daddy!'

'Arrow!'

Claire bowed her head, holding her glasses against her face, and frowned at him.

'The judges won't like that name.'

'What should we call it, then?'

She straightened, thought it over for a moment.

'Fighting fish!'

Mickey walked up the front steps, his footfalls announcing him, echoing in the night. He wasn't afraid or angry or anything, just calm. Claire was with him.

An inner voice suggested he check to see if the door was open. He did. It was locked.

The doorbell, then. He was about to ring it when he

thought he heard someone crying. It was low, the kind of trick his mind often played on him, especially in the beginning, after she was gone, Mickey coming out of a room or walking into the house and willing to swear on a stack of Bibles that he had heard his daughter. Then he remembered she wasn't there, her voice echoing in his heart.

Mickey heard it again, the low cry. It sounded like it was coming from above him or maybe behind him, he wasn't sure. He walked off the front porch and stopped, straining to listen . . .

There, he heard it again, very low – and it was coming from *above* him. He looked up at Byrne's house, at the windows. The one on the right was dimly lit, the curtains drawn.

But the window was cracked open. He'd seen the curtains stir in the wind and the crying had turned into wailing. An awful, terrifying thought came to him: was someone inside the house with him? A woman or, God forbid, a child?

A little girl?

Don't be ridiculous. There's no way –

'Daddy, where are you?'

Mickey recoiled as if the air itself had shocked him.

It's the dream, he told himself. His heart was pumping so fast, so erratically, he thought he was going to pass out. *The dream's still floating around in your head and your imagination is making you hear –*

'DADDY!'

Claire's voice. It was his daughter's voice and she was calling for him from inside the monster's house.

Mickey bolted up the porch steps.

Kicked the front door.

It wouldn't budge. He kicked it again, near the strike plate, throwing all of his weight into it, and it wouldn't give an inch – it was too thick. He bolted back to his truck to grab a crowbar from the tool-box and, when he saw the hammer, he took it and ran back to the house. He used it to smash the front window. Glass shattered, the sound. filling the night, and a warm gust of air came from inside, smelling of spoiled food and death, and he heard his daughter scream: '*I want my daddy. I want my mommy.*'

Mickey used the hammer to knock away the remaining shards of glass so he wouldn't get cut. He threw the hammer inside, saw it bounce on a throw rug and went in headfirst. He rolled across the floor and grabbed the hammer; then he stumbled to his feet. He found himself standing in front of a fake Christmas tree, complete with ornaments and the kind of lights he remembered from his childhood: thick bulbs in different colours, some blinking. He stumbled away from it, searching for Claire's voice, searching for the stairs.

Down the hall he went, and then up a set of steps with a dirty lime-green runner. More Christmas lights – tiny white ones – were wrapped around the railing and bannisters, illuminating the stairs like a runway at night. Mickey, taking them two at a time, nearly tripped when he reached the top.

'*Daddy,*' Claire wailed, her voice much louder now. '*Daddy, where are you?*'

The light was dimmer here, but he could see the watermarked wallpaper and the threadbare runner in the hall.

But even in his panic and fear he knew Claire's voice was wrong. It was her voice, no question, but it was her *old* voice – her six-and-a-half-year-old voice. Claire would be seventeen now. Her voice wouldn't have that high-pitched, reedy quality to it. It would be deeper, maybe.

'Claire,' he yelled. 'Tell me the name of your dog.'

No answer. Mickey moved across the rug, to the closed bedroom door. A sliver of light burned along the bottom, where the door met the carpet.

'Tell me your favourite colour, Claire.'

No answer from Claire and no sound of movement either, just the noise of his heart banging in his chest, blood pounding in his ears. And then he remembered what Sean had told him about Byrne going to sleep each night listening to a tape of little girls crying.

He lunged for the door, got his hand on the handle and rushed inside.

He found himself in a bedroom, and he assumed it was one that belonged to a child, because what he saw immediately were toys – seemingly hundreds of them, and all from another time: legions of old army figures, and lunchboxes hinged with rust, and metal spaceships and rockets, and other stuff crowding the bureau tops and shelves. The overhead light was on, and he saw old cowboy posters on the aquamarine-coloured walls. He saw an unmade bed with a bright yellow quilt; white sheets looking grey and dingy from multiple washings. He saw prescription bottles scattered on the nightstands, along with books and more toys – and on the other side of the bed he saw Byrne, kneeling in the corner. Byrne wasn't wearing trousers, just a black shirt with his priest's collar, and his head hung forward, suspended. A leather strap was tied around his neck: it was connected to a rope that was tied to an exposed ceiling beam. Byrne's bloated face was the colour of an eggplant, his bulging eyes were lifeless, the size of meatballs, wide open and staring down at the photographs of three young girls, smiling, happy, alive.

35

Richard Byrne was buried a week later, on a Friday morning.

His last will and testament called for a private service – absolutely no outsiders. It also requested that Father Keith Cullen handle all the arrangements. Cullen, Mickey discovered, was also the executor of Byrne's estate.

For his time and efforts, and possibly for his early years of friendship with Byrne, Cullen was given a tidy sum of money – $25,000, according to the will – along with ownership of Byrne's home. $20,000 was given to Grace Humphrey, Byrne's hospice nurse, 'for her wonderful care, love and attention'.

Mickey had found these details online. Someone had leaked a copy of Byrne's will to the *Boston Herald*. Other media outlets found out and ran with the story.

What made all this even more interesting was that the week before he died, Byrne had called his lawyer and asked for two more people to be put into his will: Dr Darby McCormick, for her 'kindness, patience, understanding and friendship over the years', and Detective Sergeant Benjamin Kennedy of the Belham Police Force, for 'protecting the values of the Catholic Church, and steadfastly believing in my innocence'. Each was given the sum of $10,000.

'Byrne wants to control the narrative even after death,'

Darby explained to Mickey again, as they sat in her rental car, watching the funeral from afar. It was the same thing she had told him days ago, when the news broke. 'He added my name and Kennedy's name to his will at the last minute so we'd be thrown into the spotlight and taken off the case because of possible ethical conflicts. He wants to take everyone he can down with him. And no matter how much Chris Kennedy and I explain ourselves, Byrne's stink of suspicion will follow us everywhere.'

The media showed up in droves at St Stephen's Church. While Father Cullen, who had come back from his vacation to handle the service, had barred reporters and cameras from attending the church service, he couldn't prevent people from setting up shop on public property. Cameramen lined the main street, along with onlookers and groups of protesters, with Belham PD performing crowd control. Mickey had heard through the grapevine that a lot of cops had refused to work the detail. He'd also heard that Father Keith had paid a visit to the station before the funeral and made a personal appeal to the officers, many of whom were Catholic, urging them to leave judgement in God's hands and to do their job. Many Belham PD officers still said no to the lucrative overtime. Boston PD had stepped in.

The cameramen jumped to attention when the front doors to the church opened and the pallbearers, four young men on loan from McGill-Flattery Funeral Home, stepped out with the casket. Flashbulbs popped and cameras clicked with the rapidity of machine-gun fire. The police detail had to clear a path for the hearse.

Mickey watched all this from the passenger's seat. They

were parked across the street, away from the mob. Even though the day was overcast, he wore sunglasses.

'The cemetery's going to be just as bad,' Darby said. 'Probably even worse.'

Mickey didn't respond, just sat there, staring at a small group of protesters huddled together on the kerb. It was hard not to stare at them. For starters, they all wore white winter coats and white hats, this mix of men, women and children. They didn't talk to each other or to anyone else, just held protest signs high over the heads of the crowd, the words printed in large block letters against bold rainbow colours: SODOMITES BURN IN HELL and GOD HATES YOUR PRIESTS and AMERICA IS DOOMED. Mickey spotted one that read ABORTION = HELL!!!

'Did you hear what I said?' Darby asked.

Mickey nodded, eyeing a small girl of around seven or eight holding a sign that read DIE FAGS & JEWS. 'Who are those people? The ones dressed all in white?'

'Members of a fringe hate group from Kansas called Soldiers of Truth and Light.'

'What are they doing all the way up here?'

'They tour the country protesting at funerals of priests and soldiers. Abortion clinics. They protest everything – homosexuals, the Jews, the Catholic Church, school shootings.' She must have seen the question in his eyes, because she said, 'They believe God sends these shooters to the schools to execute His judgement.'

Mickey glanced at his watch. 'We should get going to the cemetery.'

Darby took in a deep breath.

'I have to go there,' he said.

'But you still haven't explained why.'

'I just need to.'

'Mickey, cops can keep the press out of the cemetery, but we can't keep them from holding their cameras up over the cemetery walls. They've already set up shop on Evergreen. They're standing on the roofs of their vans to get a better view of the graveside. You go in there and they see you, your face will be playing all over the news.'

'If you don't want to take me there, I can have someone else take me.'

Darby sighed again. She put the car into gear.

Downtown traffic was light. They pulled on to Parker Avenue and drove up a steep hill, and when they passed Evergreen – a long street of tract housing for the terminally homeless and addicts wanting to kick booze and drugs to start a new life – Mickey saw a lot of people gathered on the streets and on their front steps and porches, their hands trembling as they lit cigarettes and drank coffee and watched reporters get their hair and makeup touched up. News vans were parked up on the sidewalks; satellite feeds extended into a sky threatening to burst with rain and possibly snow.

Darby wasn't the only one who had wanted to know why Mickey insisted on going to the cemetery today. It was difficult to put into words, this . . . compulsion to be at the grave when Byrne was buried. He figured it might have something to do with the dreams he'd had following Byrne's death, ones in which the ex-priest had been laid on an autopsy table, his last words visible in a pool of blood inside his mouth, floating like scrambled letters in a bowl of alphabet soup. All he had to do was to pick out the letters, sort them out, and he'd have the answer – to what, Mickey didn't know. But the coroner or whatever he was called started to sew Byrne's mouth shut and Mickey was outside the room, pounding on an unbreakable window, screaming for just a few minutes alone with Byrne. There was still time, he screamed. There was still time.

His cell phone vibrated in his jacket pocket. He took it out and glanced at the screen: NO CALLER ID. *Another reporter*, he thought, and let the call go to voicemail. The bastards wouldn't stop calling.

Darby hooked a left on to Hancock. Two cruisers were parked near the entrance to the cemetery. She rolled down a window and waved to the patrolman, who turned around and opened the gate. Mickey knew Darby had made these arrangements in advance with Kennedy.

They drove into the cemetery. When Darby pulled over to the side, Mickey saw, up on the Hill and in clear view, the rectangle of dirt where Byrne was about to be buried and felt a bullet of fear tear through him.

Darby put the car into park. 'How much have you had to drink this morning?' she asked gently.

Only two, he thought. Which was somewhat true. He'd only had two glasses of bourbon – two big glasses, to remove the bite from his hangover.

'I'm fine,' he said.

She took in a deep breath, about to launch into a lecture, he was sure, when he cut her off. 'What business is it of yours?' The words sounded lifeless in his ears; he didn't have the energy to argue. 'He's dead, remember? The order of protection no longer applies.'

Mickey opened the door.

Darby gripped his arm. 'I'm sorry, but I've got to say this again. Kennedy is doing this for you as a favour. His ass is on the line, so don't do anything stupid.'

'You worried you won't get your ten K?'

The skin of her face stretched tight across the bone, but she said nothing.

Mickey got out of the car and his phone rang again. NO CALLER ID. By the end of today, his voicemail would be full.

He walked alone up a slope of damp grass, heading towards what looked like a utility shed. To its right was a small patch of trees that hadn't been cleared.

He had no intention of creating a scene this morning. What was the point? Byrne was dead: the priest had decided to create his own exit, suffocating himself while he jerked off in the corner of his bedroom.

Mickey saw the contraption that would lower Byrne into his final resting place and took a couple of belts from his flask. Thank God bourbon was back in his life. It was keeping his mind glued together.

The hearse and limousine pulled on to Evergreen. A half-dozen or so blue uniforms assigned to traffic duty went to work to clear the area to let the vehicles through. A few minutes later, the hearse and limo had parked near the gravesite.

The young pallbearers got out and carried Byrne's coffin up the slope, Father Cullen sombrely trailing behind them, the man looking like a lumberjack dressed in his priestly robes.

The pallbearers placed Byrne's coffin on the thick black belts of the lowering device and then stepped back, bowing their heads and folding their hands behind their backs. Mickey wiped the sleeve of his sweatshirt across his damp forehead.

Father Cullen opened his Bible. 'Let us pray.'

'Mickey.'

Wide awake with that middle of the night terror that tells him something is wrong with the baby. Heather is coming up on Week 22 of her pregnancy, her swollen belly holding the girl they're going to name Claire, and now something's wrong – something's clearly wrong.

His keys and wallet are on the nightstand, so he doesn't have to hunt for them in the middle of the night. He grabs them as he sits up in bed.

'No, Mickey, it's okay. Give me your hand.'

He does, and she places it on her belly.

Kicking. The baby was kicking.

'Can you feel it?'

He did. Claire is kicking up a storm. Mickey smiles and Heather lies back down, and, as he begins to relax, easing himself on to his side, he keeps his hand on her belly, feeling the life forming beneath her skin. Just give me this, God. Just give me this and it will be enough, I swear. I swear to you, God, I'll never ask you for another thing.

A rumble of gears tore Mickey from the memory. He watched the coffin as it was lowered into the ground. He thought of his dreams – Byrne on the morgue table, those letters floating inside his bloody mouth – and felt so light-headed he thought he might pass out.

Only God knows what is true.

The coffin was in the ground now, hidden from view, waiting to be buried.

'Amen,' Father Cullen said, and closed his Bible.

It was over.

Mickey dug his fingers into the bark of the tree. It kept him from screaming.

His phone vibrated – not a call but a text. He welcomed the distraction.

The text was from Jim: 'Heather called me. She's been trying to call u & says u won't pick up & wants u to call her.' He gave Mickey a long list of numbers, which confused him. Then he figured it out: it was an international number. Heather was still running around Europe or wherever.

He didn't have to call her. She was calling him again.

'Mickey?' It *was* Heather, her panicked voice having an odd echo to it.

'I can barely hear you.'

'I'm calling you from France.' Her words came out in such a hurry that she sounded winded, as though she had just completed a long, gruelling run. 'I just found out. I've been staying out on a farm. There's no TV, and they don't have the Internet – it doesn't matter. I just booked a red-eye. I'll be home tomorrow. Are you okay? Where are you?'

Mickey's attention ran up the hill of dead grass, stopped at Byrne's headstone.

'Mickey? Can you hear me?'

'I'm at Byrne's grave.'

A long silence followed.

'Why would you do that to yourself?' Heather asked.

The need to scream was building inside his chest. He needed to reel it in, needed to look away from the headstone and grave and couldn't.

'You've got to stop doing this to yourself,' Heather

said, her sympathy feeling like spit on his face. 'How many times have I told you – I don't blame you for what happened.'

I'm done, Heather. With you. With us. I can't take living with someone who is constantly terrified of life, who refuses to allow me a say in anything I want as a father or husband. I'm sick and tired of it, Heather, and I'm sick and tired of you. I don't want you any more, and I don't want this life. I want fucking out.

'It's my fault,' he said. 'I took her there that night.'

'Remember that time at the grocery store? Claire was with me and I turned my head for a second and she was gone. They started to tear the place up and five minutes later I found her outside talking to a woman. Claire thought it was the mother of a friend and she had followed her out and –'

'You don't understand.'

'What don't I understand?'

That night on the Hill I let Claire walk up the Hill by herself because I was pissed at you. That night I prayed for a way out and God gave me one.

'Please,' Heather said. She sounded on the verge of tears. 'Please let me in. I want to help you.'

Mickey wanted to say the words. He needed to say them. He opened his mouth to speak and a moan escaped his lips. The guilt, the anger, the love he still carried for his daughter and the life they had once shared – everything he had carried for the past eleven years and everything he wanted to say was lost, drowning in his sobs.

36

While Mickey spoke with the priest, Darby watched the exchange from her car. The stay-away distance in her restraining order was 300 feet.

Mickey didn't want to talk about his conversation with Father Cullen. He didn't want to talk about anything. Darby sensed he seemed ashamed and embarrassed at having broken down at the cemetery. He had put on his sunglasses to hide his swollen eyes, and during the drive he turned his head away from her and stared out of the window.

She was taking him to Melrose, a city north of Boston. Mickey was staying at a friend's condo, so he didn't have to deal with the media. News vehicles had been parked day and night on Mickey's street since the news of Byrne's suicide broke.

Mickey cleared his throat. 'The autopsy,' he croaked.

Darby waited.

'You told me you were planning on, you know, being there for it.'

'Couldn't make it happen,' she said.

Mickey turned to her. 'Why not?'

'I'm not an officer of the law and, as such, not allowed to attend an autopsy,' Darby said. Which was technically true and, for the purposes of this conversation, the simplest answer. She didn't tell Mickey that an exception could have been made, given her forensic background and the fact that she had attended many autopsies in Boston over the course of her career. The reason she'd been denied access had to do with petty politics. Not only was Belham PD unhappy that Mickey had broken into Byrne's house and found the former priest's body, they were also downright hostile to her because, after Mickey had telephoned her, she had decided to enter the house and take a look at the crime scene instead of calling Chris Kennedy and remaining outside the house. She'd had no legal authority to enter and secure the scene herself.

'The police were inside Byrne's house for two days,' Mickey said. 'At least that's what the news is saying.'

'That's what Kennedy told me.'

'I heard they found more tapes,' Mickey said.

'Who told you that? Your source in the department?'

'Is it true?'

'Yeah,' she sighed.

'Two, right? Two more tapes?'

His source, whoever he was, seemed to have an inside line on the case.

'What's on them?' he asked.

'I haven't listened to them,' Darby replied. Which was true.

'But you know what's on them.'

She did. Kennedy had told her, but she didn't want to get into specifics with Mickey – at least not today, not in his present mental condition. She believed he would torture himself with the information. 'Let's talk about this another time, okay? Right now, I think –'

'No, we're gonna talk about it now.' Mickey swung his

head back to her. 'I have a right to know – and I want to know. I deserve to know.'

'Your source didn't tell you?'

'I didn't ask. I wanted to ask you in case I had questions, and because you're the only person I trust. So tell me. Please.'

Darby shifted uncomfortably in her seat. 'The two tapes are recordings, I'm told, of the girls . . . crying.'

'For their parents.'

And other things, Darby thought, Kennedy telling her how there were parts where the girls could be heard screaming – whether in pain, or fear, or a combination of both, wasn't clear. Kennedy had told her Claire Flynn had screamed for 'it' to stop – but there was no way of knowing what that was. She had begged to go home to her parents.

She didn't tell this to Mickey, nor did she explain how some serial killers used such things to relive their crimes, to satisfy their dark, and often sexual, urges. And Mickey, fortunately, didn't want to pursue the subject. He leaned forward and, with his elbows propped on his knees, rubbed his eyes and the sides of his head with such force it was as if he wanted to crush his skull.

'The photographs I saw on the floor,' he said. 'Did they find any others?'

'No, just what was on the floor.'

Mickey turned to the window, no doubt thinking of the pictures he'd seen of his daughter. There had been twenty-six in all, each one a 5 × 7 or 4 × 6 of Claire Flynn and the other two Snow Girls, Mary Hamilton and Elizabeth Levenson. The photographs, taken from what she assumed was a long-range lens, showed the girls in public places where someone with a camera wouldn't stand out – parks, playgrounds, fairs, swimming pools and community centres. A good number of photographs showed the girls in bathing suits or summer clothing. All the girls were smiling. Happy.

'I want those pictures of Claire,' Mickey said. 'I know that sounds odd, maybe even sick, given the fact that Byrne took them and touched them with his bare hands and did only God knows what else with them. But seeing those pictures of Claire, it's like . . . it's like Byrne stole something from me. I want them back.'

'I understand.' Darby didn't know what else to say.

'When will they give them back to me?' Mickey asked.

'Hard to say. They're part of the investigation.'

'What investigation? Byrne is dead. My daughter is dead.'

Darby wanted to say that until her remains were found – if they were ever found – the photos would most likely stay in the case file.

Mickey, though, didn't press the matter. He had lapsed into silence.

It was impossible to tell how Mickey was handling everything. He had seen Byrne – had seen the pictures of his daughter and heard his daughter's scared and wailing voice playing on the recorder. Given what he'd seen, she didn't begrudge him seeking relief inside the bottle.

Only he wasn't going to find any relief there. When the booze wore off and the hangover sank its razor-sharp teeth into the meat of his brain, the images he'd seen, his feelings – all of it would eat at him with the power and fury of a starving lion dropped into a petting zoo. That was the nature of the alcoholic mind.

'Kennedy,' Mickey snorted. 'He actually thought I'd done that to Byrne – you know, strung him up and all that.'

'He had to question you about it, Mickey.'

'It's bullshit.'

'I hear you. But you were the one who found him – and you broke into his house. Because of that, Kennedy had –'

'Why'd he have his trousers off? Byrne?'

'It's not important.'

He spun round to her. 'Don't be like the rest of them. Don't be . . . you were always straight with me. Always, even when I was a complete and utter asshole who flushed away the best thing I ever had in my life.'

'Why did you?' Darby asked, wanting to change the subject.

'If he wanted to commit suicide, why'd he put his trousers down?'

'I don't think he wanted to commit suicide.'

'Meaning, what? It was an accident or something?'

'An accident, I think.'

'But why was he, you know, doing what he was doing in the first place?'

She didn't want to get into this level of detail with him, not in his current condition, alone and grieving. But she'd rather he heard the truth from her.

Darby spoke by rote, in dry clinical terms. 'He died of auto-erotic asphyxiation. It's a sexual act generally performed by men who fall into the category of hardcore masochists. They believe that depriving themselves of oxygen during climax heightens an orgasm.'

'I know what it is. I mean, I've heard about it, you know, on the news.'

'When practitioners engage in this activity by themselves, the risk of instantaneous death is extremely high. The ligature puts pressure on the vagus nerve, which sends a message to the heart to shut down, resulting in sudden cardiac arrest.'

Mickey had turned away from the window. He leaned forward, his elbows on his knees. 'Jesus Christ,' he whispered to himself, about to bury his face in his hands when he suddenly straightened and looked out of the front window. 'Where the hell does Kennedy get off thinking I would break into the guy's house and stage something like that?' There was no anger or heat fuelling his slurred words, just a cold and weary acceptance. 'If I wanted to kill him, I would have done it with my bare hands.'

Darby could feel Mickey circling around what he wanted to talk about, but she wasn't sure he could – or maybe should – do so. Seeing the suspect responsible for the disappearance of his daughter and two other young girls dead from auto-erotic asphyxia, pictures of Claire and the others strewn about the floor – Mickey's psychological trauma might still be too severe.

He exhaled loudly, the sweet odour of bourbon filling the car. 'I wish I had done it.'

'He wouldn't have told you.'

'I should have confronted him that night. If I had, he might've –'

'Mickey, I want you to listen to me very carefully . . . Are you listening to me?'

'Yeah.'

'Trust me when I tell you there is nothing, absolutely *nothing*, you or anyone else on the planet could have done to get him to talk. Believe me, I tried.'

'So why did Kennedy go after me like that? Byrne killed himself – accidentally or otherwise. You were there.'

'When you have a suicide by hanging, you have to pay close attention.'

'To what?' He sounded like he was nodding off.

'We don't need to talk about this now,' Darby said. 'Go ahead and sleep this off. I know where we're going. I'll wake you up when we get there.'

He sat up abruptly. 'I'm awake. I want to talk about it now. Don't shut me out.'

Darby sighed. 'Sometimes a crime scene is staged to make it look like a suicide by hanging when it is, in fact, a homicide. With a homicide involving strangulation, you find defensive wounds on the victim's hands.'

''Cause they're fighting the person off.'

'Right. The medical examiner or pathologist will also find two sets of ligature marks. A person strangles the victim in one place, then moves him or her to another location and stages a hanging. Byrne had only one set of ligature marks, and they matched the rope. He also had what's called petechial haemorrhaging – the burst blood vessels you find in the white lining of your eyes. It's a distinctive sign that someone died from asphyxiation.'

'You said Byrne had only one set of ligature marks.'

'He did.'

'But you just said you weren't at the autopsy.'

'I wasn't. I spoke to the forensic pathologist who performed it.'

'Why? Because you think something was odd or whatever?'

'I just wanted to follow up on it. Habit of mine when a case is closed.'

Mickey turned to her. 'It's not closed,' he said. 'My daughter's body is still out there somewhere.'

Darby wasn't about to debate with him. 'Bad choice of words on my part. I'm sorry.'

Mickey said nothing. He went back to looking out of the side window, his forehead pressed against the glass.

'He talked about her in his sleep,' he said.

'Who talked about who in their sleep?'

'Byrne did. About Claire.'

'How do you know this?'

'It's not fair,' he said, more to himself than to her. 'He took my daughter and he took pictures of her, he recorded her crying and screaming, and he gets a funeral and a headstone, and what does my daughter get? Dumped someplace where I can't even go —' His throat seized up. He cleared it several times, and from the corner of her eye she could see fresh tears rolling down his hollowed cheeks.

No matter how many times she had to console a victim, it never got easier. As a victim herself, she understood his pain and anger and rage, and the only way she could try to bridge it, the only way she could try to convey to him that she fully understood the haunted landscape he found himself in, was to reach across the console and grab his hand and hold it to let him know he wasn't travelling alone.

37

After she dropped Mickey off in Melrose, Darby drove back to the Belham, thinking about Richard Byrne. More specifically, she was thinking about the offer the ex-priest had made to her that day in the kitchen – stripping down to her birthday suit in exchange for the location of Claire Flynn's body.

Most paedophiles had zero interest in seeing a grown woman naked – or, for that matter, how a woman dressed. Not all, but most. Kennedy believed Byrne's requests were an attempt to manipulate and humiliate her. He wasn't wrong – manipulation and humiliation were the two main governing traits of a psychopath – but if Kennedy had been with her that day in the kitchen, he would have seen the lust in Byrne's eyes. The man had made no effort to hide it. The monster formerly known as Father Richard Byrne was sexually aroused at seeing a grown woman's flesh – the desire of a heterosexual male, not a paedophile.

And – *and* – Byrne hadn't come up with that idea off the top of his head. To get to that goal – and that was his ultimate goal, seeing her naked body – he had spent a considerable amount of time ruminating on the best way to coerce her into cooperating. The point? The desire had been there – had always been there, and it bothered her. It didn't fit.

The only person who knew Byrne was Father Cullen, and now Cullen had lawyered up and put out a restraining order on her. Why? What was he so afraid of her finding out?

Grace Humphrey had spent time with Byrne – had seen Byrne at his weakest. Had he tried to manipulate and humiliate her? *Or maybe my encounter with him was an isolated incident – an act, as Kennedy suggested, designed to humiliate her in particular?*

Grace Humphrey's neighbourhood was a big step up from the area around the cemetery: duplexes separated by long, thin driveways; small, nice front lawns sectioned off by chain-link fences. Here there was no stink of desperation or decay. The houses had fresh coats of paint, manicured shrubs and fresh flowers.

Number 53 was a triple-decker with a front porch and steps and floorboards painted gunmetal-grey. Darby parked on the street, got out and jogged up the flagstone walkway and up the steps to the door on the left. She rang the buzzer, relieved to hear the sound of footsteps. A bolt snapped and the front door opened with a soft *swoosh*.

Grace Humphrey's smile was genuine but a little hesitant.

'Dr McCormick.'

'I'm sorry for dropping by unannounced, but I was in the neighbourhood and was wondering if you had a few minutes to talk.'

'Of course,' Grace said. 'Please, come in.'

Three steps and Darby was standing inside a large, rectangular room of hardwood flooring and bright yellow walls. Sunlight flooded the warm room, pouring in from windows that overlooked a backyard where a group of four or five toddlers took turns kicking a soccer ball.

The woman looked haggard. She wore jeans and a black cardigan, a plain gold chain and gold crucifix worn proudly around her neck. It was the only jewellery she wore. No earrings or rings – no makeup either.

'How are you holding up?' Darby asked.

'My phones won't stop ringing. Reporters keep calling with questions, wanting to know about him. I had to unplug my landline and shut my cell phone off. I feel like a prisoner in my own home. You?'

'They're calling me too.'

'Would you care for something to drink? I don't have any coffee, but I do have tea and Pepsi.'

'I'm all set, thank you.'

Grace sat down on one end of a chocolate-brown couch. It was the only place to sit. Darby took a seat on the other end. She unzipped her jacket but left it on, along with the scarf. It hid the rope burns on her neck.

'You have more questions about Richard,' Grace said.

'More?'

Grace looked puzzled. 'Detectives came by earlier in the week.'

'Detective Kennedy?' He hadn't told Darby about any visit.

'No,' Grace said. 'A detective named Blake – Roger, I think – and another man whose name I've forgotten.'

Darby kept her face neutral, wondering if Kennedy had been given the boot. She felt sure he had. 'What questions did they ask?'

'They wanted to know how Richard was acting the day he died, if he'd said anything.'

'Had he?'

'He was in a lot of pain, which made me believe he was getting to a point where he'd have to go into a hospital or hospice. He made it clear to me, right from the beginning, that when the time came, he was going to die at home.'

'Did they tell you how he died?'

Grace nodded. 'He hanged himself. In his bedroom.'

Given the woman's expression, her tone, it was clear she hadn't been told the grisly details surrounding Byrne's death. *Good*, Darby thought. Sometimes cops accidentally shared key details of a case with witnesses. So far, the press hadn't got wind of what Byrne had been doing when he died. If word got out, the media would come running back to Belham.

'I offered to stay with him but he wouldn't hear of it,' Grace said. 'I respected his wishes, and, as I was gathering up my things to leave, he made a point of thanking me for everything I had done for him. Told me he appreciated my kindness and loyalty. He'd never said those words to me before, so I knew he was saying goodbye, in his own way. But I had no idea he was going to take his own life.'

Which was another thing nagging at her – how Byrne had died. Darby was sure that it wasn't his intention to go the way he did, the evidence spread out across the floor. Byrne, she was sure, wouldn't want to be remembered that way – would want to die a mystery. Unsolved cases lingered in the public consciousness, sometimes for decades. Some serial offenders achieved, at least in their own, twisted thinking, a sort of immortality, someone who would never be forgotten.

'It surprised me, quite frankly,' Grace said. 'The man was a priest. He knows suicide is a sin.'

Darby nodded absently. Then she rubbed her forehead, thinking about how best to broach the sexual questions she wanted to ask.

When it came to discussing sexual acts – especially those of a deviant nature – most people got uncomfortable, even embarrassed. Some shut down, while others would try to change the topic, and, when that failed, more often than not they would deliberately not share key information or details in order to kill the conversation. Darby sensed it would be better to ease into the topic with Grace instead of adopting her usual approach, which was to be blunt and direct. She didn't want the woman to shut down.

'I'm trying to learn more about Richard Byrne. To learn more about the man and not what I've read and heard from others.'

Grace nodded, attentive.

'You spent a good amount of time with him,' Darby said. 'You may have seen things other people wouldn't know about.'

'Have you spoken to Father Cullen? They were friends for a long time.'

'*Were* being the operative word.'

'Still, they were close for a number of years. And they reconciled.'

'Reconciled?'

'That was what Richard told me. He was insistent that Father Cullen should be the one to handle his affairs. Father Cullen finally relented and came by a couple of times.'

'When?'

'The day you visited,' Grace said. 'When I returned, Father Cullen was here. They were going over Richard's final arrangements. Richard wanted Father Cullen to perform the service.'

'And the other time?'

'The day Richard died. That morning, when I arrived, Father Cullen was here, to deliver last rites. He —'

'Sorry for interrupting,' Darby said, 'but how do you know Father Cullen was here to deliver the sacrament?'

'That's what Father Cullen told me.'

Which was the complete opposite of what Cullen had told Darby, the day she had spoken to him out on the track. Cullen said he had denied Byrne the sacrament and a Catholic service because Richard wasn't willing to confess his sins and ask God for forgiveness. It made sense. Cullen had given Byrne a Catholic funeral, so it stood to reason he had also given the former priest the sacrament.

Why the change of heart? Darby could come up with only one answer: the tapes. Cullen knew about the tapes. Had Byrne blackmailed him? The tapes in exchange for a proper Catholic send-off?

'Richard told me the same thing,' Grace said. 'He said Father Cullen had given him last rites. No, wait.' Her face clouded for a moment. 'Richard didn't use those words. He said Father Cullen gave him something called an "apostolic pardon". I'd never heard of that, which isn't surprising, since I'm a Christian but not a Catholic.'

'I've never heard of it either.'

'I looked it up. In the Catholic Church, an apostolic pardon brings total forgiveness before death. Remember from the Bible, when Jesus promised the Good Thief on Good Friday he would join Our Lord and Saviour in paradise? An apostolic pardon works that way – sort of a "Get-out-of-jail-free" card, like in the *Monopoly* game, only you get to enter heaven.'

Grace stiffened, making no effort to hide her distaste. Darby said, 'And you don't agree.'

'I know you're Catholic, so I don't want to –'

'How do you know I'm Catholic?'

'I just assumed. Everyone from Belham is. It has a very high Catholic population.'

'I *was* a Catholic.'

'I see,' Grace said. 'May I ask why you're no longer one?'

'I have a major problem with how the Catholic Church conducted itself over the last decade, with how it treated the victims of paedophile priests.' *And their view on certain social issues*, Darby added privately.

'If I'm being honest, I too share your viewpoint about the Catholic Church. Father Cullen granting Richard an apostolic pardon, last rites – call it whatever you like – but a man like Richard is *not* going to heaven. Not after what he did.'

Grace looked embarrassed by her little diatribe. She grinned shyly and brushed the thighs of her jeans. 'But you didn't come here to talk about the evils of the Catholic Church. We were talking about Richard. I don't know if Detective Kennedy shared this with you, but Richard and I became quite close. We never spoke about his . . . crimes, but, well, about other things. I know that sounds odd, even monstrous to some degree, but when people are in a terminal situation, it's not all that unusual for them to open up, even to strangers. Richard didn't have any friends, unless you want to count his lawyer, but that's not really a friend, is it? I think he considered me a friend. Maybe that's why he gave me the money. I'm not keeping it, by the way.'

'There's nothing wrong with –'

'I can't. Not in good conscience. Are you keeping yours? No, wait, don't answer that. It's none of my business.'

'I'm not. I'm going to give it to a charity.'

'As am I. I was thinking about donating it to that organization that helps missing children, N-C-something.'

'NCMEC,' Darby said. 'The National Center for Missing and Exploited Children.'

'That's it. I'm told they do good work.'

'They do. Did Richard tell you why he asked me to visit him?'

Grace shook her head.

'Why do you think he wanted me to come by?' Darby asked.

Grace shifted in her seat. 'I thought maybe he had reached the point where he was ready to . . . unburden himself. Confess what he'd done to those poor girls. Which, obviously, he didn't.'

'I want to share with you what happened,' Darby said, and gave the woman a dry, by-the-numbers account of Byrne's proposition. She left out the salacious details and the part about Byrne having recorded confessions, as those aspects of the case needed to be kept private. It wasn't pertinent to her goal, anyway, which was to create a bond with Grace Humphrey by sharing the embarrassing details of her sexual encounter.

When Darby finished, Grace folded her hands on her lap and gazed out of the window, reflecting on some internal thought. The colour had drained from the woman's face. She looked like someone who had swallowed something sharp.

'Did he ever proposition you?' Darby asked gently. 'Act inappropriate in any way?'

'No,' Grace replied, her throat working. 'Never.'

'If he had, would you tell me?'

Grace whipped her head back to her.

'I need to know if he did,' Darby said. 'I wouldn't ask if it wasn't important.'

'He never did anything remotely like that.' Grace paused, searching Darby's eyes. 'I'm telling you the truth.'

'I believe you,' Darby said. She did.

'If something like that had happened, I would have left. I wouldn't have put up with that. No one should. He was nothing but professional with me. And kind. He was always asking me questions about my family, my childhood.'

That made sense. Darby was all too familiar with how psychopaths and sociopaths manufactured kindness, charm and charisma in the early stages of relationships with other people, in order to gather intelligence and find ways of exploiting their weaknesses.

'Did you ever see any pornographic materials lying around the house?' Darby asked. 'Not child pornography but heterosexual pornography. Magazines, maybe films.'

The woman's back straightened a bit, Grace clearly put off by the question. 'I didn't go snooping around his home.'

Darby held up her hands. 'I wasn't in any way suggesting you did. I was just wondering if you came across anything like that by accident.'

'No. Whatever Richard did to . . . whatever . . . urges he had, he kept them well hidden from me. Not once did I ever –' She cut herself off, her attention turning inward.

'What?' Darby prompted.

'He . . . Well, he watched the news a lot. The TV was on constantly – especially after he'd found that girl's jacket. He watched the news religiously then.'

That wasn't a surprise, as most high-functioning psychopaths were narcissists. Byrne would not only watch the news to feed his ego but also to try to stay one step ahead of the police.

'He gave me a key to the house, and I'd let myself in,' Grace said. 'Sometimes he didn't know I had arrived. His hearing wasn't that good, and the pain medication he took made him less aware of his surroundings. Sometimes, when I went into the room to bring him a meal or water or just to check in on him, he didn't even know I was there.'

Grace didn't know what to do with her hands. Finally she sat on them and stared down at the floor. 'The morning after the jacket was found, I went into the house and found him in the living room, on his recliner, covered by a blanket. The news was on, talking about the discovery of Claire Flynn's jacket, which led to a discussion about what had happened to her and the two other girls. Their pictures were on the screen, and Richard, he . . .' Grace swallowed.

Darby's phone vibrated twice. Someone had sent a text. Grace heard it too, and looked visibly relieved when she said, 'Go ahead and take that.'

'It can wait. Please, continue.'

Grace's gaze moved around the room, looking anywhere but at Darby.

'Richard's mother had these photo albums of when he was a child,' Grace said. 'There were photographs of his mother in there too, back when she was young. Those were the only pictures in there – either of him, or of his mother, or of the two of them, no one else. He showed the photos to me often, and would share childhood stories. You could see the love in his eyes, hear it in his voice. That morning, when I went into the living room, he was looking at the girls on the TV the same way, with that same love.'

The window next to them was open a crack, and the sound of the kids playing outside, giggling, filled the room. Grace watched the children for a moment, kept her attention on them when she spoke.

'I also saw this . . . calmness come over him,' Grace said. 'The way he shut his eyes and sighed and swallowed – it reminded me of my father.'

'Your father?'

Grace nodded. 'I got home early from school one day and found my father alone in the kitchen, pouring himself a glass of whiskey. He'd been sober for ten years, I think, by that point. He didn't know I had come home – didn't know I was watching him. He thought he was alone. He took a sip of whiskey and when he swallowed, he closed his eyes and everything inside him relaxed. It was like he had been finally reconnected with his one, true love. That was the way Richard had looked at those girls.'

Darby's phone vibrated again as Grace said, 'That was

the only time I saw something that made me truly believe he killed those girls. That he was guilty.'

'And yet you stuck around.'

Grace turned to her, anger flaring in her eyes.

'I'm not judging you,' Darby said.

'I thought about leaving. The night when you came by and he told me to tell you to, you know –'

'Wear something sexy.'

Grace's face coloured a bit – not in a prissy way but in indignation, Darby thought.

'I'm sorry about that,' Grace said.

'No reason to be. You were just delivering the message.'

'The side of Richard everyone else saw, it wasn't on display when I was with him. Which isn't that much of a surprise, really, since he relied on me. It was in his best interests to be nice to me. Kind. I was the only person he had in his life who was helping him. So, in a way, yes, I guess he *did* manipulate me.'

'So why did you stay?'

'I'm a Christian,' Grace said. 'And, while I wanted to judge him – and I did, in fact, judge him – my pastor told me that such judgement was to be left in the hands of God. So that's what I did. I left judgement to God and I did my job. I never saw the demon, monster, whatever you want to call the thing living beneath his skin. I just saw the man.'

'Did you ever try to broach the subject with him?'

'No. Never.'

'Did he ever make any overtures?'

The woman seemed confused by the question. Darby rephrased it. 'Did he ever appear as though he wanted to talk to you about his crimes? Sometimes people like Byrne want to confess – especially towards the end.'

Grace shook her head. 'He never spoke about it – at least not to me. Maybe to Father Cullen, but not to me.' She sighed, her expression turning reflective. Sad. 'Maybe I should have tried harder to get him to talk. But he was deteriorating rapidly. During the day, all he wanted to do was to sit in his rocking chair and go through his photo album and play with his toys. He kept a box of old toys from his childhood. A lot of them do that when the end is approaching – revert back to their childhood. They'll want to look at old pictures, hold toys and objects from their past, listen to their favourite music and rewatch their favourite TV shows and movies. It's a comfort mechanism. He asked me to get down a couple of boxes of Christmas lights from the attic. He wanted me to help him string lights around the living room and stairs. That made him happy. He would sit in his chair and stare at the lights. Just sit there and be quiet with his thoughts. The lights calmed him, I think. That, and the medication. He cried a lot.'

'About what?'

Grace shrugged. 'He would never tell me,' she said. 'He was such a lonely, lonely man, and I got the sense that the loneliness hurt him deeply.' She shook her head, looking visibly sad.

Darby's phone vibrated again. Another text. 'You liked him,' she said, sliding her hand into her jacket pocket.

'When people reveal themselves to you, when you see them in pain and know they're dying, terrified . . . it's hard not to feel something for them. When I was training, they taught me not how to block it out but how to manage it.'

Darby looked at her phone, found two messages from Chris Kennedy. The first said, 'Call ASAP.' The second message, which came seven minutes later, said, 'ASAP means drop what you're doing and CALL NOW. Better yet, just come to the station.'

'I appreciate your time, Miss Humphrey. Thank you.' Darby reached into her pocket and came back with a business card. She handed it to her and said, 'If there's anything else you remember – anything that you think might be helpful – please give me a call.'

'I will.'

'If I have any additional questions, may I call you?'

'Yes. Of course. I'll write down my numbers.'

'No need. Detective Kennedy gave them to me.'

Grace Humphrey remained seated. Darby sensed the woman had more to say, waited.

'Are you by any chance going to see Mr Flynn? I ask because I wanted to send him a sympathy card, but I didn't feel it was appropriate,' Grace said. 'If you see him, could you please tell him that I'm keeping him and his daughter in my prayers?'

38

If he was going to go through with it, he knew he had to do it in the daylight.

The day after the funeral, Mickey drove slowly down his street, red-eyed and sweating and a little drunk. It was a little after 11 a.m. and the street was mercifully quiet, not a single reporter or cameraman to be seen. With Byrne dead and buried, the media had mercifully moved on to some fresh new horror.

Bouquets of cellophane-wrapped flowers, cards, extinguished candles and blown-up pictures of his daughter packed his front steps and most of the walkway. He parked in the garage, where his truck would be out of view. He didn't want anyone to know he was home.

The inside was cool, the air stale. He had turned down the heat and drawn the shades and curtains before leaving for the condo in Melrose a few days ago. In the gloom he could see the dirty dishes and empty coffee mugs scattered along the kitchen counters. He was about to check on his mail when he remembered he'd put a hold on it the day he'd left. He would have liked to put a hold on it permanently. The idea of having to go through mountains of awkwardly written condolence cards, notes and letters made him want to scream. These people, he knew, had the best of intentions, but how could you write to someone and say, Gee, I'm real sorry that the sick son of a bitch who abducted and murdered your baby girl accidentally offed himself and didn't tell anyone where he buried her body? *Hallmark really needs to step up, come up with a section of sympathy and anniversary cards for the parents of dead kids*, he thought, tossing his keys on to the counter.

His house felt as cold and silent and welcoming as a crypt. He took his phone out of his pocket and turned it off. He didn't want any interruptions. He dropped the phone on the counter and went into the basement to gather what he needed.

Upstairs in Claire's room, he pulled back the black-out curtains. The room filled with strong sunlight. Her smell, that essence of her that had been trapped on her pillows, sheets and clothes, was long gone, faded away by time. Everything else remained the same: the drawing table by the window; the autographed picture of Tom Brady given to her by Big Jim; the stack of Barbie toys in the corner – Barbie's dream house, car and private jet. Barbie even had her own private McDonald's right next to her mansion.

Four framed photos hung over Claire's white four-poster bed: a picture of Claire taken in the delivery room; one of Heather holding Claire for the first time; Mickey holding her for the first time; and one of Claire sleeping in her bassinet. The pictures had been her idea, Claire amazed and fascinated that she had once been that small. Mickey had shown her the first time he had held her, a picture taken inside the NICU, where Claire, all three pounds and six ounces of her hooked up to all sorts of wire and tubes, fitted neatly in the cradle of his hand.

So small, he thought. She had been so, so small as a

premature baby. She had been one of the lucky ones: she had survived and thrived.

On the last morning that he would see her alive, he had walked into this very room and kissed her on the head, the same ritual he performed every morning before he left for work. He did it because he loved her, but there was another reason: he was terrified something would happen to her. Every morning when he went in to kiss her good-bye, he said a prayer, asking God to keep her safe. If Mickey did it enough, he believed God would spare him the heartache and terror of having the person he loved the most taken from him.

And yet God looked down on him and said, Sorry, I'm taking your daughter too. Nothing personal, Mick. But don't worry, it's all part of my divine plan. I'll fill you in on it someday.

Were Claire and his mother looking down on him right now? He pictured them together in heaven, forever and ever, amen. He had to believe in heaven. He had to believe that there was something more to life – to his life. The pain and suffering, it all had to amount to something.

Before Mickey had become a parent, Big Jim and other guys had told him how his life was going to change – not just his ordinary, day-to-day life, but his inner life. They told him how your kids filled you up with equal amounts of love and fear. That sometimes you'd look at your kid and your heart would expand until you thought it was going to burst. You didn't know that kind of love until you had a kid, until you changed their diapers, held them when they cried and teethed or got fussy, when they pissed and shat at all hours of the day and night, or when you lay next to them when they were sick, scared, angry or sad. Until they looked into your eyes that first time – really looked into them – and smiled, you couldn't comprehend how rare that kind of love was, or how it would change everything about you.

But Mickey had already experienced that kind of love, that kind of fear. His mother had packed up and left without him. And then, while she was getting herself set up, making plans to come back and get him, his old man had found out where she was hiding and flown halfway around the world to kill her. Okay, that hadn't been proven in a court of law, but it didn't mean it wasn't true. Big Jim and the other guys, they had no idea what it was like to go through life with a black hole in the centre of your chest.

Make that two black holes. One for his mother, one for his baby girl.

That morning he had looked at Claire sleeping and he knew this was enough. If this was the only thing life gave him, he would die happy. Fulfilled. And he had meant it.

But that life was gone. He couldn't have it back.

She'd been born premature and survived against the odds and grown into this wonderfully, beautifully stubborn little girl who –

You've got to let her go, Heather had told him. *You've got to move on.*

Move on to what?

You'll figure it out.

I don't want to figure it out. I want my daughter back.

That life is gone.

My life is gone.

Not true. If you miss your daughter and mother so much, you can join them.

He thought about the 9-millimetre he had stored in the gun safe underneath his bed.

Mickey shook the idea away and then rubbed at his face with the back of his hand, his thoughts turning to the brand-new bottle of Maker's Mark – the high-end stuff, Maker's 46 – sitting inside his truck. He wanted a drink or two, but knew that if he left the room he wouldn't go through with what he had to do.

He started with the Barbie dolls. One by one he picked them up, everything covered in dust. He hadn't kept up with the cleaning, not as he had in those first few years, when he would come in here pretty much every weekend to clean, Mickey wanting everything to look spotless for the moment when he received the news that Claire had been found. Then he had cleaned the room to try to stay close to her; and, during these last few years, to try to keep his memories of her from fading.

The toys, the clothes and the furniture – those things he would donate to charity. The pictures hanging on the wall would stay here until he was ready to deal with them. The items that held stories and special memories – like the yellow-and-blue teddy bear with the words YOU'RE SPECIAL printed on its belly – he had purchased it at the hospital gift shop the day Claire was born and had left it on her incubator and, later, her crib – these he would box up and bury in the attic, next to his mother's things.

Mickey took a long, hot shower in Claire's bathroom. He wrapped the towel around his waist and padded barefoot to his own bathroom, where he shaved and vigorously brushed and gargled with Listerine until his mouth burned and his eyes watered.

Downstairs, he opened the fridge, took out a bottle of water and drank it down. He had to stay hydrated.

And he had to eat. He realized he hadn't eaten anything since last night. He wasn't hungry but he knew he had to eat, because only a fool drank on an empty stomach.

His food options were limited. The milk had turned sour and the deli meat smelled funky. He found some Saltines in the cabinet, and, while his stomach welcomed them, it wanted something more substantial, which meant either going out to get food or ordering for delivery. Delivery it was. He turned on his phone, and, as he dialled the number for the sub shop down the street, he heard the steady chime of missed texts and calls coming across the phone's screen, a steady and annoying *ping-ping-ping*.

After he called in his order, he scrolled through his messages and calls, found several from Big Jim and Heather, both of whom were checking in to see how he was doing. Darby had also sent him a couple of texts asking if he was okay, if there was anything she could do.

Seeing Darby's texts made him smile a bit. Beneath that hard, no-bullshit exterior, there was a side to her that only a few people, he knew, got to see – the part of her that would have your back, no matter what. It was one of the many reasons why he'd fallen for her all those years ago.

His phone rang. The Belham Police Station was calling. He answered it, thinking it was Kennedy.

It wasn't.

'So you're going to let me rot,' Sean said.

'What?'

'You heard me.' Sean sounded out of breath, his voice pinched tight, like a man who had narrowly escaped from drowning. 'Knowing you, you probably jumped for joy when you heard the news.'

'I don't know what you're –'

'The hell you don't. It's all over the news.'

Mickey hadn't seen today's paper. He hadn't listened to the news in the car or been on the Internet. His gaze travelled to the kitchen table, where his laptop was, and he moved to it.

'I don't give a rat's ass what they say,' Sean said. 'I didn't do it.'

The laptop was already on; the screen came to life when he opened it. He used the touch pad, clicked on the browser, and, after it loaded, he hit the 'Home' button, which took him to the homepage for the *Boston Globe*.

'You hear what I said, Mickey? *I didn't do it.*'

Right there on the front page was a colour picture of Sean in handcuffs, two Boston cops standing on either side of him. The headline above the picture read: ALLEGED HIT MAN FOR IRISH MOB ARRESTED FOR MURDER OF DEFROCKED PRIEST'S BODYGUARD.

'I'm not using some goddamn public defender,' Sean said. 'Give me the name of the guy you used. He got you a good deal.'

Mickey was speed-reading the article, words and phrases jumping off the screen: solid evidence linking Sean to the murder of Byrne's bodyguard, Nicholas Rossi, who had died from complications he suffered after being burned;

Sean's 'alleged' connection to various Mafia figures over the years and his 'alleged' involvement in the murders of nearly two dozen people.

'*Are you listening?*' Sean hissed. 'I only got five minutes.'

'What do you want?'

'*Call* him.'

'Call who?'

'Your lawyer!'

'He died. Use yours. Guys like you have 'em on a retainer, I'm sure.'

'My guy is staring at a wall and drooling inside a nursing home. You need to get me a criminal lawyer – a good one. The best.'

Sean was having a hard time keeping his fear at bay – was sounding like he was coming apart at the seams. Which surprised Mickey. His old man was a pro at keeping his feelings hidden – especially fear, because showing fear to anyone was showing weakness.

Then he remembered Sean's terror of tight, confined spaces. Sean never came out and admitted this, of course. It occurred to Mickey as sort of an epiphany one rainy Sunday afternoon during high school, when he was watching *The Deer Hunter* on cable. Those scenes in which De Niro and Walken were stuffed inside bamboo cages, prisoners of war – that had once been Sean. Sean had been a prisoner of war, and then Mickey finally understood Sean's almost pathological insistence on taking the stairs or an escalator instead of an elevator; why Sean refused to fly when he could take a train or drive – but only in a large car, like a Cadillac. No small cars for him. ('There's no goddamn escape room in those rice burners. You get into an accident, you're dead.')

'So you'll take care of this, right?' Sean asked. 'The lawyer?'

Mickey was thinking about the attic. His mother's items – the few he had managed to save – were stored inside a shoebox. A month or so after his mother left for Paris, Sean had collected all of her clothes, the pictures – just about every personal item she had left behind – and burned them in an aluminum trashcan in the backyard.

'Mickey?'

Mickey didn't answer, grinning at the thought of his old man stuck in a small space, terrified.

'You rotten prick,' Sean said and hung up.

39

Darby thought Kennedy was texting to tell her that he had been officially removed from the Byrne case. It wasn't a matter of if but when. The man suspected of the kidnapping and murder of three girls had left a tidy sum of money in his will to the detective investigating him, so the police had no choice but to suspend Kennedy and open up their own investigation, to see if Kennedy had done anything unethical or, worse, illegal.

So she wasn't surprised when, after she got Kennedy on the phone, he told her he had been suspended, with pay, until Internal Affairs completed their review. Kennedy was no longer involved in the Byrne case – or in any of the other cases that had been on his plate. He also had more news to share: her services were no longer needed.

'Figured as much,' Darby said, driving away from Grace Humphrey's home.

Kennedy sighed. 'I get that I have to be sidelined until IA clears me. What I really resent, what is pissing me off, is how the media is spinning the story, making it seem like I might've given the son of a bitch a free ride because he was a priest and I'm still a practising Catholic. I want to hold a press conference, tell my side – tell them the goddamn *truth* – but the dopes in charge here put the kibosh on that, and my lawyer said it was a stupid idea.'

'He's right, unfortunately. Once you open your mouth, you'll only be adding fuel to the fire.'

'And by not opening my mouth, I look guilty. My picture's everywhere. People are shooting me looks that say they wouldn't stop to piss on me if I were on fire.'

'I'd stop,' Darby said. 'To piss on you.'

'Ah, you're sweet. How are you holding up?'

'I'm ignoring it. You should too. Who'd they put on the Byrne case? Is it this Blake guy?'

'Who told you?'

'Grace Humphrey. I stopped by her place yesterday, after the funeral. She mentioned that a detective named Blake came by and questioned her.'

'Yeah, the brass put him in charge of wrapping things up – and it's done, Darby. The Claire Flynn case is, for all intents and purposes, closed.'

Unless something new comes along, Darby thought. 'Blake any good?'

'Roger Blake is the Kanye West of homicide detectives – arrogant and too fucking stupid to know he's too fucking stupid. Which automatically makes him prime management material. But I'll let you form your own judgements when you speak to him. He wants you to come to the station, pronto.'

'For what?'

'To explain why Sean Flynn insists on speaking to you and only you.'

Darby straightened in her seat.

'What is it with you and the people who live here?' Kennedy asked. 'First Byrne, now Sean Flynn. What are you, the Asshole Whisperer?'

'I'm missing something here. What's going on with Sean Flynn?'

'You taking a day off from the news?'

'I was at the gym. What's going on?'

Kennedy gave her the rundown of Sean Flynn's arrest. Darby didn't have a chance to ask any follow-up questions; Kennedy had to take an incoming call. Before he hung up, she told him she was on her way to the station. Kennedy was there, at his office, tying up some loose ends before he went out on paid leave.

Twenty minutes later, she was sitting in Kennedy's office, speed-reading through the forensic report on the Molotov that had ended up killing Byrne's bodyguard. The evidence stacked against Sean Flynn was rock solid, but she was having a hard time buying into it. Sean wouldn't be so careless. If he went after Byrne, he would get up close and personal.

And then there was the man who had tried to kill her. He was still out in the wind.

Kennedy came in holding two paper cups of coffee. He handed her one, took the seat beside her.

'So,' he said. 'Sean.'

'Like I told you when I got here, I have no idea why he asked for me.'

'So let's go and find out.'

'I thought Blake is in charge of this.'

'He is.'

'Then why aren't I talking to him? Where is he?'

'He called and told me he's tied up in Boston. There are a lot of people who want to put Sean Flynn away – he's consulting with them, see what other charges, if any, can be brought up against him.'

'The forensic stuff in here is pretty solid,' Darby said, tapping the file on her lap.

'Feel free to share that with old man Flynn while you're in there: impress upon him the gravity of his situation, get him to cooperate with us.'

Darby chuckled. 'Sure. After that, I'll pull a rabbit out of my ass.'

'Just do it, will you? Who knows, maybe you'll make friends along the way.'

'Because if I don't, Blake will, what, try to get my investigator's licence pulled? Go to the state with some bullshit ethics violation regarding the Byrne payout?'

Kennedy gave her a sardonic smile. 'Nothing gets past you, does it?'

'What's his beef?'

'Let's just say he's not a fan of people who are —'

'Whistle-blowers?'

'I was going to say people who take a stand. People who are courageous and do the right thing. That's a foreign concept to him. You're dealing with a guy who not only thrives in a bureaucracy but also knows how to deal with it. Guy's barely thirty and he already knows how to kiss ass up, down and sideways.'

'How long has he been working homicide?'

An amused light worked its way through Kennedy's eyes. 'A little over a year.'

'And they put him in charge of the Flynn case,' Darby said flatly.

'So what does that tell you?'

'They're grooming him for bigger and better things.'

'Exactly. Brass wants a guy like that in a leadership

286

position – he does what he's told and looks good and does well on camera. They handed Flynn to him on a silver platter. Blake puts him away – and he will, I have no doubt in my mind that's going to happen – it'll be a major coup for him and the department.'

'And if I stand in his way, he and, I'm sure, his superiors, will work tirelessly behind the scenes to do everything in their power to crucify me, to the point where I'll never be able to so much as investigate a parking ticket.'

'It's like you're psychic.'

Darby's head throbbed. She had no use for petty politics, or for the people who played them. She said, 'Sean isn't going to confess to anything. He's too smart for that – and he's too smart to leave evidence behind. I'm not buying him for this.'

'Not our problem,' Kennedy said, rising from his seat. 'Come on, let's get this over and done.'

'Who's Sean's lawyer? I'm sure he has one.'

'No idea.'

'I have one condition.'

'Of course you do.' He sagged back into his chair.

'I want to take a look inside Byrne's house,' Darby said.

'You've already been inside his house, remember? Mickey called you that night instead of calling 911, and you went straight inside instead of calling 911 right away.' Kennedy shot her a look to make sure she knew he was in a lot of shit for that.

Darby said nothing.

'Forensics ripped the place apart,' he said. 'The only stuff they found is the stuff you saw – the photographs of the girls and those two audio tapes.'

'He must have had other tapes – I'm talking about the ones of those recorded confessions.'

'They're not in the house.'

'As far as you know.'

'Like I said, forensics ripped his house apart. Those tapes aren't there. I'm guessing he destroyed them.'

'Or gave them to someone,' Darby said. 'Humphrey told me Father Cullen visited Byrne the day I saw him – and on the morning he died.'

'That's not a crime. And, as previously discussed, possession of those tapes is not a crime, so don't go asking me to look at Cullen, because that's not going to happen.'

'The guy lawyered up.'

'Darby, there's nothing we can do with him, so –'

'The day I met Cullen at the track, he told me he'd refused Byrne last rites. He told me Byrne was evil. Then he visits Byrne not once but twice and then ends up giving Byrne a Catholic service. Humphrey told me Cullen gave Byrne an apostolic pardon. It's an "All sins forgiven, go straight to heaven" trump card. What's that say to you?'

'I don't know,' Kennedy said, making zero effort to hide the weariness in his voice. Right then, Darby knew he had already mentally checked out of the investigation – maybe even the police department, his thoughts now focused on his wounded ego, how he was going to fill his days during his forced suspension. She had been there. She didn't blame him. And he had the added burden of having suffered two heart attacks.

'You have a copy of Byrne's autopsy report?' Darby asked.

Kennedy shook his head. 'Glassman hasn't forwarded a copy yet. I've got a call into him.'

'Why? You don't think it's a suicide?'

'Byrne coming up with some elaborate plan to get me to strip down for him – no, don't say it was strictly about humiliation. There's more to it than that. You weren't there. You didn't see the lust in his eyes. A paedophile doesn't look at a woman like that.'

'I hear you,' Kennedy said. 'Still, you're assuming it was lust. For all you know that lust you were seeing had to do with the impending excitement of humiliating you.'

'He's done this thing to other women.'

'You got any names?'

'Not yet, but I'm sure I'll find them.'

'Darby,' he began.

'The whole crime scene looked staged to me. You saw the pictures on the bedroom floor – they were neat and clean. If Byrne had stored them in that floorboard underneath his bed, they would show some wear, right?'

'Possibly.'

'The pictures weren't sexual, Chris. Doesn't that bother you? Speaking of which, did you find any child-related pornography in his house?'

Kennedy didn't answer, but she saw that her point had struck home.

'We both know a suicide can be staged,' Darby said. 'Granted, it's tough to do, but not impossible. I've worked cases where I've seen it done.'

'I'll pass this along to Blake.'

'He's not going to do anything with it.'

'You're right. And neither are we. We're off this.'

'I was attacked on my way to Danny Halloran's place. Don't you think that's an odd coincidence?'

'I do. But it doesn't –'

'What's the latest from Boston on that?'

'No suspects.'

'Look, I get where you're coming from, I truly do. You're pissed at the media for turning you into a human piñata, and you've got your health to think about. All I'm asking is for you to get me into the house, so I can take a closer look at the crime scene. If I find something, I'll tell Blake. If nothing comes of it, what's the harm?'

'Blake isn't going to let you go in there all by yourself.'

'So tell him he can come.'

'And if he disagrees?'

'You want me to play nice, go in there and talk to Sean, I want –'

'You don't go in there and do your part, Blake – hell, probably everyone at Boston PD – will take turns jamming it up your ass. You really want to take that risk, have them pull your licence?'

'I want to see the house. Today.'

'Okay.'

'I want to hear it from Blake.'

'I'll make it happen. I give you my word.' Kennedy glanced at his watch and said, 'We've got to get this done before they take Sean to the courthouse. Come on, let's go.'

Darby got up and followed him out of the office and through the halls.

Kennedy stopped in front of the door leading to the holding pen. 'You've got twenty minutes,' he said. 'After that we're going to transfer him over to court. Remind him there's no way in hell he's going to make bail.'

Her phone rang. Mickey. She took the call, motioned for Kennedy to wait.

'Did you hear about my old man?' Mickey asked.

'I did. In fact, I'm on my way to see him right now.'

'Why?'

'It appears he asked to speak to me.'

'About what?'

'I was about to ask you the same question.'

'I have no idea. But I spoke to him about an hour ago. He wants me to hook him up with a lawyer.'

'Did you?'

'No,' Mickey said. 'That's why I'm calling you. I have an idea for something, and I need your help.'

40

Darby found Sean Flynn in the last cell. He sat hunched forward on the bottom bunk, his hands wrapped around a paper coffee cup. Despite the coolness in the room, dark rings of sweat were visible on the armpits of his blue collared shirt. His face was damp and he looked pale, like he was suffering from the flu or a stomach bug.

Mickey had told her Sean was claustrophobic. What she was seeing here, though, pointed to something more serious – something along the lines, possibly, of a post-traumatic-stress reaction to being caged inside a confined space. She knew about Sean's time spent as a prisoner of war.

For a brief moment she wondered if Sean Flynn might have been the man who attacked her. A quick glance at his right leg dispelled that theory. His leg was fine, no injuries.

She stood in front of the bars, the air packed closely with day-old sweat and urine and Sean's smoke-filled clothes. He hadn't touched his food – it sat on a cardboard tray on the floor – and he didn't look up at her.

'I liked your old man. Solid, no bullshit,' Sean said, his voice pinched tight. His fingers were stained yellow from nicotine, and what was left of his black hair had been trimmed close to the scalp. Sweat ran down his face. 'I'm sorry how he went out.'

'Why did you want to speak to me, Mr Flynn?'

'Pull up a chair.'

'I'd rather stand.'

Sean swallowed several times, Darby noticing how he stared hard at the floor, keeping his eyes there instead of on the bars.

'I grew up with this guy named Andy Ferreira. He and I enlisted at the same time. We were in Vietnam together. This one time, it was at night, we stepped into a village that was supposed to have been levelled. Andy happened to be looking the wrong way when a gook with a flamethrower turned him into a walking barbecue. A man screams a certain way when he's burned alive. A sound like that never leaves you.'

'And what sound does someone make right before you blow their brains out?'

'I'm not going to jail for someone else's mess.'

'The beer bottle used for the Molotov?' Darby said. 'Forensics pulled your fingerprints from some of the glass shards.'

The news didn't faze him – not even a ripple.

'The police also found cigarette butts in Byrne's backyard, behind the shed,' Darby said. 'They're the same brand you smoke. They're processing them for DNA as we speak. If that comes through, it's another nail in your coffin.'

Sean said nothing.

'And then there's Byrne's neighbour, the kid who's in an army training programme,' Darby said. 'As luck would have it, he was playing around with his night-vision goggles. Police gave him a six-pack to look at – you know, a group of six pictures. Guess who was identified as the man he saw unscrewing the light bulbs on Byrne's back porch?'

'They find any fingerprints on the light bulbs?'

They had, but none of them belonged to Sean.

When she didn't answer, Sean said, 'What I thought.'

'The gold lighter they found in the snow? Your prints were on that too. Are you starting to see the full picture here?'

'Last time I had that lighter was at McCarthy's. That's a bar over in East Boston. Someone stole it out of my jacket. Go ahead and call George McCarthy, he'll tell you.'

'Someone's trying to frame you?'

'You're goddamn right.'

'Why?'

'I don't know. But I intend to find out the minute I get out of here. Which brings me to why I asked to speak to you. I need –'

'I understand Boston PD caught up with you just as you were getting ready to blow town.'

'I was heading back to Florida. I've got a place there.'

'I think you're going to have a tough time selling that story.'

'You were in my spot, who would you call for legal advice?'

'Why is it you wanted to see me, Mr Flynn?'

'I need a lawyer. A good one. I figure you'd know several.'

'Why me, though?'

''Cause I know you're tight with my kid, trying to help him through this shit.'

'I meant, why not ask Mickey directly?'

'Can't get in touch with him. He and I, we're not exactly on the best terms.'

The door for the holding pen opened. She turned and saw Kennedy, who motioned for her to join him.

'Excuse me,' Darby said to Sean.

'You're coming back, right?'

Darby didn't answer. She walked away.

'*Hey*,' Sean called after her. '*Come back here*.'

Darby stepped into the hall. Mickey was standing with Kennedy. Mickey had showered and shaved and combed his hair and put on some clean clothes. He also reeked of booze.

'He tell you why he asked for you?'

'He wanted the name of a criminal lawyer. I didn't tell him anything, just as you asked.'

'Good,' Mickey said, rubbing the back of his wrist vigorously across his bottom lip. 'That's good. You say anything about my mother yet?'

'Not yet. You bring the stuff you mentioned on the phone?'

'I've got it right here with me. Look, I just got through talking with Detective Kennedy, and he said I can go in there and see Sean, talk to him about my mother instead of having you do it. That okay with you?'

Darby nodded.

'Make it quick,' Kennedy said. 'And remember, cops are watching you on the feed.'

'Good luck,' Darby said to Mickey.

'I want you to come with me, to tell him about the lawyer stuff,' Mickey said. 'It will have more, you know, weight coming from you.'

She followed Mickey back into the holding pen. Mickey took a folding chair and set it up in front of the bars. Sean, his arms wrapped around his stomach, leaned forward but wouldn't look up from the floor. He could see them from the corners of his eyes, though.

'Lenny Glazer,' Mickey said after he sat down. 'You remember him?'

'The fuck you doing here?'

'Do you remember him?'

'Why you asking me this shit?'

'The lawyer I have in mind; she not only kept Glazer out of jail, but represented two of Glazer's button men – Jimmy Flannery and some Italian guy named Ricci. They never did a day of time.'

'She?'

Mickey nodded. 'Her name is Rosemary Shapiro.'

'This broad any good?' Sean asked.

Darby answered the question. 'This *woman* is the best criminal attorney in the city. I use her myself.'

'Okay,' Sean said. 'Make the call.'

'She's next to impossible to hire,' Mickey said. 'But Darby agreed to call in a favour.'

'Make the call.'

'She's also very expensive.'

'How much?'

'Probably around a hundred grand for a retainer.'

No hesitation from Sean: 'Make the call.'

'You got that kind of scratch?'

Sean nodded. 'Get in touch with her.'

'That depends on you.'

Sean's eyes clouded.

'You help me,' Mickey said, 'and Darby will contact the lawyer.'

'Help you with what?'

'What you did to my mother.'

'My ass is on the line here and you want to rehash shit that happened –' Sean cut himself off when Mickey got to his feet. 'She left us. End of story.'

'A month after she left, she mailed a package to Jim Kelly's house, along with a note. That note said she would be coming back to Belham.'

'Your point?'

'How'd you find out where she was hiding?'

'If I knew that, don't you think I would have brought her back home?'

'Not without giving her a good beating first.'

'I got no idea what happened to your mother.'

'You went away for a few days, remember? On business? Of course you do. You came home and called me into the backyard and delivered a speech about how she wasn't coming home, that it was time for me to accept it and move on. And maybe I would've bought your story but I happened to see your suitcase on your bed and decided to do a little investigating.'

Mickey reached inside his back pocket, came back with a pair of plane tickets so old the paper had yellowed with age.

'Tickets to Paris in the name of Thom Peterson,' Mickey said. 'The guy in the passport photo bears a strange resemblance to you. Want to take a look? I've got that too . . . Nothing to say?'

'Thought I'd lost that passport.'

'Thing is, you hate to fly. You're claustrophobic. That's why you're sweating like a pig right now.'

Darby, who was standing to the side and watching Sean carefully, saw the words hit home.

'And yet,' Mickey said, 'you hopped on a plane and flew all the way to France – under a false identity. Why is that?'

'We can talk about this with my lawyer – this Rosemary Shapiro. Make the call.'

'I'll call her. But first you're going to tell me what you did to her. You don't, Shapiro isn't going to take your case. That's a fact.'

Sean gritted his teeth, balls of cartilage popping out along his jawline. 'You don't want to go down this road with me.'

'I hear the cells at Walpole are like POW cages,' Mickey said, getting to his feet.

41

'You never told me about finding the tickets and the passport,' Big Jim said.

Mickey shrugged. 'Didn't see the point.'

Big Jim didn't answer. He used a pair of tongs to flip over the steaks and chicken breasts cooking on the charcoal grill he'd set up outside on the porch.

It was good to be outside in the fresh, cold air, even after only a few minutes inside the holding cell. Mickey knew he looked a little rough around the edges. And, much as he wouldn't have minded pounding back a few beers with Jim, he decided to stick with water, rehydrate. Besides, there was a bottle of Maker's 46 waiting for him at home if he decided to indulge again – and he might.

Or he might not, which proved that he was *not* an alcoholic. An alcoholic would be drinking right now. He wasn't.

'I'm surprised Sean never confronted you about the passport,' Big Jim said.

'He told me he thought he'd lost it.'

'And you just held on to it. That, and the tickets.'

'You think I should have given them to the police?'

'They thought Sean was responsible for your mom's disappearance. If you'd told them, shown them the tickets and the passport –'

'It wouldn't have done any good. Back then Sean had cops on his payroll.'

Big Jim sighed. 'True.'

'Plus,' Mickey said, 'I was, what, eight at the time? I remember thinking that if Sean found out I had the tickets or the passport, I'd probably be lying somewhere next to my mother.' Mickey checked his watch. 'I should probably get going.'

'Stay for dinner.'

'Can't. I'm going to see Heather.'

'About your old man,' Jim said. 'A week ago I was watching this TV programme on how you can donate your body for cadaver research at medical colleges. You'd be surprised at how easy it is. All it takes was some minor paperwork. You should consider it.' Jim grinned at him through the smoke. 'Sean's brain would make an interesting specimen.'

Mickey started his truck. He was about to pull out of the driveway when his phone chimed. He glanced down at the console and saw that he had received a text from Darby. It read: Check your email. Call & I'll explain what happened.

Mickey grabbed his phone. He didn't find an email from Darby, but he did see one from someone named 'MHager@shaprioandhager.com'. Shapiro, Mickey knew, was Rosemary Shapiro, the name of the lawyer Darby had recommended.

He didn't know 'MHager', didn't need to; his eyes were glued to the subject line: 'IMPORTANT: From Sean Flynn'. With a sense of dread, Mickey pressed a finger against the screen and opened the email. The message read:

Mickey,

I was denied bail. Not that you give two shits. You made it crystal clear where you stand. Now let me tell you where I stand.

My lawyer wants $50,000 as a retainer. Money's in a floor safe. Peel back the carpet in your old bedroom closet and you'll find it. Combo is 36-24-36. You'll find some stuff that belonged to your mother.

They got me locked up in Cambridge until my trial. I'm meeting with my lawyer tomorrow at 10. Get your ass there at 9, give my guy the fifty, and I'll answer all those questions you got about your mother. After that, you and me are through.

Believe what you want about me, but know this: I got nothing to do with burning that man.

Darby called Mickey almost an hour later, just as he was taking the Rowley exit off 128 North.

Mickey had been nursing his anger during the entire drive. He didn't give her a chance to explain. 'You told me Shapiro wouldn't take the case unless she got the go-ahead from you!'

'Yes,' Darby replied, sounding contrite but also a little angry. 'That's exactly what I said.'

'So what happened?'

'Your father bypassed Shapiro, is what happened. Sean went straight to her partner, Martin Hager, who also practises criminal law. Told him if he took the case, Hager would be looking at a bonus of twenty-five thousand, cash. And if Hager got him off, then he was looking at a bonus of a hundred grand – in cash. *Cash* is the operative word here. You understand what I'm driving at?'

He did. In addition to whatever percentage the firm would give this Hager prick for taking Sean's case, he was looking at a potential bonus of $125K – all tax free, since Sean had agreed to pay him in cash. No records, no way for the IRS to come knocking, looking for their cut.

'Hager care Sean's money is dirty?' Mickey asked. He knew he sounded desperate and weak even as he said it.

'No, he doesn't,' Darby replied. 'I hear he's got his eye on a new Bentley.'

'Sounds like a helluva guy.'

'Why didn't you tell me your father had that kind of scratch on hand?'

'I have no idea if he does or doesn't,' Mickey replied. Sean had never been a flashy guy. He owned a couple of nice suits, but he didn't dump money into clothes or houses or fancy cars or big vacations. His house in Belham was a one-floor ranch with a basement, and there was a time, during those first few years when he got back from Vietnam, when money was real tight. At least that was what his mother had told him.

'Look,' Darby said. 'I get you're pissed. I would be too, if I were in your shoes. And, for what it's worth, Rosemary tried to talk Hager out of it, but he wouldn't budge. Sean's case will give him something no one else can give him.'

'What's that?'

'Publicity. Hager's a walking hard-on when it comes to TV cameras.'

Mickey wasn't pissed at Darby; he was pissed at himself. He had been so consumed by the idea of having Sean cornered that he hadn't stopped to consider Sean might have cash stored somewhere.

And let's not forget about all the time Sean has spent in Florida. Who knows what kind of jobs he did while he was down there?

He pulled into Heather's driveway. 'I've gotta go.'

'I'm sorry,' Darby said.

'Thanks.'

He hung up and got out of the truck. A FOR SALE sign was posted on the front lawn, another brutal reminder of how his old life was gone, and how everyone, it seemed, was moving on except himself.

Heather looked amazingly well rested and put-together, with her dark jeans and ivory shirt with a long, sloping V-neck. Her hair was different too, cut shorter and with highlights. He hadn't seen her in person for months, and, as he took her in, he was slightly amazed at how this woman he'd known since high school, this girl who had once lived in sweatshirts and sweatpants and thought a fun day was tailgating at a Patriots' game with friends and drinking beer, had morphed into this other woman, one who took great care in picking out her clothes and spent weeks travelling through Europe.

And now she was moving to New York. Not a dream or an idea but a stone-cold reality.

Mickey stepped into the foyer, a hollow pit in his stomach. She surprised him when she hugged him.

Holding her like this brought back the larger memories, the markers that had defined their lives together: comforting her at her father's funeral; dancing together at their wedding; holding each other after the neonatal specialist came in and told them that Claire had successfully fought the lung infection she'd contracted shortly after being born. He felt all the smaller moments too, the seemingly inconsequential ones he had taken for granted every day: laughing during a movie or at a party; kissing her goodbye as he left for work. There was this entire history, this entire world, that still existed only between them but also didn't, and knowing this made him feel frantic and lost and powerless.

'I'm so sorry,' she said against his chest. 'I'm so, so sorry.'

He wasn't sure if she was sorry for him, or sorry about Byrne's dying without having confessed, or sorry about all of it.

'I'm sorry too,' he said, his throat feeling thick. 'For everything.'

Heather eased herself away from him. She didn't know what to say – or maybe she didn't want to say anything, at least not yet. She walked away from him, into the dining room, Mickey noticing the majority of the furniture was already gone.

'When are you leaving?' he asked.

'Tomorrow, maybe. Or the day after.'

Mickey said nothing, his chest tight, as though someone were standing on it.

'This is the best I could do,' Heather said, making a sweeping gesture with her hand at the various plastic plates holding sandwiches and coleslaw and potato chips and a fruit platter.

Mickey sat down and listened to Heather explain how the pots and pans – pretty much everything from the kitchen – was on its way, along with a few select pieces of furniture, to New York. He vaguely heard her mention something about a moving company coming in and doing all the packing, how expensive it was.

'What's wrong?' she asked.

He was thinking about his conversation with Sean. Talking about him was a safe subject, and one of the few areas in their marriage they had both agreed on: Sean was trouble and inviting him into their lives in any way, shape or form would be the equivalent of contracting an incurable cancer. But he opened his mouth and said, 'I packed up Claire's room.'

Heather's eyes widened – not in anger but in surprise.

'Not all of it, just some of it,' Mickey said. He didn't know why he had clarified it.

Heather folded her hands on the table, waited patiently. She was looking at him the expectant way his therapist did, like he was going to have an emotional breakthrough or some such shit. Or maybe Heather was looking at him this way because he very rarely talked about his feelings.

Mickey couldn't meet her eyes. He kept his attention focused on his plate of fruit, the melons and strawberries, as he spoke.

'It felt wrong. Like I was telling her I didn't have room in my life for her any more.' He took a deep breath, not wanting to tell her the rest. And then he did: 'I wanted to put everything back just the way it was.'

'Did you?'

'No. But I still want to.'

'Maybe you're not ready to say goodbye,' she offered.

That's the thing, he wanted to say. *I don't know if I'll ever be ready.*

'The jacket on the Hill,' Heather said.

'What about it?'

'It's really Claire's?'

'No question.'

It took something from her, knowing that. He thought about reaching out and taking her hand in his, but she had leaned back in her chair and crossed her arms over her chest, as if bracing herself for another blow.

'Is that why you're angry?' she asked gently.

'I'm not angry.'

'Your neck is beet red.'

'I think I'm coming down with the flu that's going around.'

'You're avoiding looking at me. You only do that when you're trying to avoid a difficult topic – or avoid a fight.'

She was right, of course. Heather was a pro when it came to recognizing the signposts for all of his moods, knew all the emergency detours and exit ramps he used to back his way out of painful conversations.

'It's okay to be angry, Mickey. It's a part of grieving.'

But I don't want to grieve, Mickey thought. *I want to be angry. It's the only thing that's keeping me alive.*

42

Shapiro and Hager operated out of an old brick building that had once been a candy factory. It was in Post Office Square, in Boston's financial district, the building directly across the street from a two-acre park, the popular lunch-time area during the summer for local workers, with its ample seating, abundant plants and flowers, and a pergola around a central lawn.

Darby reached the building after a brisk walk from the parking garage. She had just got off the phone with Mickey and was thinking about the one thing she hadn't shared with him: that Martin Hager had called and left her an odd voicemail that said Sean Flynn had a package for her.

Darby had called Hager back to get more specifics and instead got Hager's secretary. Hager wasn't available, the woman explained, and she had no idea what was in the package, or what it was about. Darby could come into town to pick it up or the package could be messengered to her. Darby decided to drive to Boston.

She didn't entirely blame Hager for taking the case. Purely from a business point of view, she got it: Sean Flynn, one of the last old-school Irish mobsters, was getting a lot of press, which meant a lot of free publicity for Hager, and probably a lot of other cases would be thrown the firm's way. She didn't agree with it, but she understood it.

The marble lobby was warm and dimly lit. Darby stood at the security desk, watching the guard, an old timer with hair as white as snow, hunt-and-peck the information from her driver's licence into the computer system in order to print out her visitor's pass. While she waited, she decided to try Glassman's office again. She called the pathologist's direct number and got his voicemail. She left another message, and, after leaving multiple unanswered messages for Glassman, Judith Levenson and Nancy Hamilton, without even a simple text-message reply – the frustration she felt had gone from annoyance to frustration and then to anger. It must have shown on her face, because when she went upstairs, people quickly got out of her way.

Hager's insufferable secretary, a prim older woman named Sandy who loved telling people she lived in Beacon Hill, was standing outside Martin's office door, which was open. The office, Darby saw, was empty.

'He's not here,' Sandy said. 'He asked me to give you this.'

She picked up a sealed white envelope, with Darby's name written on the front, from her desk.

Darby ripped open the envelope. Inside, next to a folded letter, she saw a thick stack of 5 × 7 photographs bound together with an elastic band. The top one showed Heather – a much younger Heather, her hair longer – climbing into the passenger's seat of a red car. A man was behind the wheel. It wasn't Mickey. Darby couldn't see the man's face, just part of his profile – a Caucasian with a squared-off jaw and neatly trimmed black hair. He wore a dark, navy-blue suit jacket with a red tie.

Darby unfolded the piece of paper. The letter had been written on a computer and printed out.

Doc,

Mickey and I got ourselves what you shrinks call a 'toxic relationship'. But I don't got to tell you that since you got to see it for yourself. That boy blames me for every single thing that's gone wrong in his life, and quite frankly, I'm sick and tired of it, of being his whipping post. All the things I've done for him, and the first time I ask him for help, what does he do? Turns his back on me so I can rot in prison for something I didn't do.

Well, fuck that, I say – and FUCK HIM.

Since Mickey is so goddamn interested in digging up skeletons, tell him to start with his ex-wife. Ask Heather all about the guy she was screwing at the bed and breakfast in Maine the month before she and Mickey got married. I'd love to be the one to tell Mickey all about it, see the expression on his face when I shove it up his ass, but I've got to talk to him about his mommy issues, and after that he's not gonna want to have anything to do with me (which is fine 'cause I don't want nothing more to do with him, after the shit he pulled). Besides, anything I tell him about his ex, his mother, he's gonna accuse me of lying.

Since you got a degree in shitbags, I've decided to let you be the one to tell him about Heather. Or not. I don't give a flying fuck. That boy is dead to me – as dead as the granddaughter he never allowed me to see and get to know.

Mickey's finally gonna get what's coming to him.

Peace and Love,
Sean

The pictures, thirty-six in all, told a story: she saw Heather getting into a Volvo with a man who wasn't Mickey and the two of them driving north to New Hampshire (she saw several pictures of the Volvo on the highway, the photographer, who, she assumed, was Sean, capturing the signs for Route 128 North and Route 3 North and a sign that said WELCOME TO NEW HAMPSHIRE), parking in a bookstore parking lot (the bookstore was Waldenbooks, which had gone out of business decades ago) and then walking across a busy street and climbing a set of steep, concrete steps leading to a white house that gave off a bed-and-breakfast vibe. The last three pictures culminated in Heather and the man from the Volvo walking down the stairs together, both of them looking dour, Darby thought, and getting back into his car. In the last picture, they were kissing, or hugging, she wasn't sure which, given the angle. But it was definitely intimate. There was no question about that.

Darby flipped the pictures over and went through them, looking for writing, a date the pictures had been processed, and came up empty.

Darby looked up at Sandy. 'What are the visiting hours at Cambridge?'

'Mr Flynn won't talk to you.'

'Is that right?'

'Yes. Martin said you would ask.'

'Well, what does Martin expect me to do with this shit?'

The woman flinched. 'There's no need to take that tone with me. I'm just the messenger.'

Darby needed some relief. She got some when she was outside, heading to her car: Judith Levenson, the mother of Byrne's second victim, Elizabeth, was finally returning her call. She hadn't spoken to the woman since taking on the Flynn case, knew next to nothing about her. Well, that wasn't quite true. Byrne had shared about Judith

Levenson that day at his home, calling her a serial philanderer who engaged in violent and degrading sexual acts.

'Thank you for calling me back, Mrs Levenson.'

'Yes. Well. I'm sorry it took so long. I was away for several days, at a . . . retreat, I guess you could call it. For couples. With . . . marital problems. They didn't allow phones.'

Judith Levenson was in her early sixties, Darby remembered reading in the file, but she sounded two decades older. She also sounded as though she'd been crying – and drinking. Her words were slightly slurred.

Judith laughed bitterly. 'But you don't want to hear about that, I'm sure.'

'If you'd like to talk about it, I'm more than happy to listen.'

'You're far too kind. Mickey said you might be calling me. Said you were helping him with his daughter's investigation. You're calling about Father Byrne, I'm guessing.'

'I was, yes,' Darby said. 'I was hoping to find out more about him.'

'Well, ask away. Not that it's going to do much good, is it, now that the bastard is dead?'

The sigh that exploded across the receiver made Darby flinch. It was full of so much pain and anger and regret, but what caused the knot in Darby's stomach was the woman's loss of hope. With Byrne alive, there was always a sliver of hope that he might confess. Now that hope was gone, and Judith Levenson, like Mickey, was struggling to come to terms with it.

Darby was about to speak when the woman said, 'He's leaving me.'

'Your husband?'

'Yes. Ted. We went to this marital retreat – my idea, yes, sort of a last-ditch effort to save our marriage. He played along the entire time and now he's told me he accepted a research position at the University of California in San Diego. I told him I wasn't going – that I would *not* leave this house.'

Darby sensed the woman wanted to keep talking. She had to bear down hard, to follow the tendrils of thought hidden inside the woman's grief.

'You know what he told me? He said, "Do whatever you want, Judith, but I'm going." It's his way of punishing me. Like keeping the dining table. Father Byrne sat at that table and had dinner with me and my family. Can you believe that? I invited the monster to my table and fed him – I mean *it*. I fed *it*.'

Judith blew her nose. 'You know what I finally came to realize? Just how alone I am. What happened to Elizabeth . . . people don't understand. They can't. They try to, because they're good people and want to help, but my friends . . . they've drifted away. Not because they don't care but because they don't know *how* to care. It's been draining, I'm sure, having to listen to me all these years.'

Darby conjured up an image of the woman in her mind's eye: Judith Levenson wrapped in her bathrobe even though it was late in the day, her eyes puffy and bloodshot from crying, a Kleenex balled into her plump fist.

'I don't know why I'm telling you all of this,' Judith said. 'You want to know about him, don't you?'

'Only if you want to speak about it.'

Judith sighed.

'It was a different time back then,' she said. 'It's still a nice little community where I live, but back then? Back then we knew all our neighbours. Our kids grew up together. They hopped on their bikes and rode wherever they wanted and you thought they were safe. When you enrolled them in a church's after-school programme, you didn't *think*, let alone worry, about priests molesting children or the Church covering it up. You didn't question priests, and you didn't question the Church.' Judith blew her nose again. 'I had that man in my *home*. I confessed my sins to him. I *trusted* him.'

Darby recalled another fragment from her conversation with Byrne: *I cast no judgement or aspersions on her sexual proclivities, or on the fact that she'd had an abortion, which, as you know, is a big no-no in the Church. What I took exception to was Judith's weak moral fibre . . .*

'Can you believe I still own that dining-room table?' Judith said, sounding clearly disgusted with herself. 'My husband refused to get rid of it. Elizabeth had been missing less than a year and Ted went into her room and packed up all of her clothes and gave them away without telling me because *he* said I needed to move on. But the dining-room table? Oh, no. We can't get rid of *that*. It didn't matter how much I hated looking at it, day after day, I had to keep it because it belonged to his precious mother. I stopped eating there, but do you think Ted cared? Of course not. Do you know why?'

The woman genuinely seemed to want Darby to ask the question, so she did. 'Why?'

'To punish me. For what happened to Elizabeth. For refusing to go with him to Cambridge when Harvard offered him a research position. There was no way in hell I was

313

going to move. Never. I had to think of my other children. I didn't want to disrupt their lives any more than they had been. But Ted kept pushing for a fresh start. I finally told him if he took that position at Harvard, I'd leave him.'

Judith Levenson sniffed away her tears and then she said, 'I don't deserve this.'

'No one deserves this.'

'The doctor said these things happen.'

'There is no way you could have known about Byrne's past.'

Judith's breath hitched. 'I meant the baby,' she said.

'I don't understand.'

'There was a baby before Elizabeth. Ted and I thought the pregnancy was going along fine.' The words, while slurred, came out sounding as if they were being torn from her chest. 'The middle of the fourth month came along and we found out that the baby didn't have a brain. The doctor gave us two choices, and Ted . . . Ted convinced me that the right thing – the humane thing – was to terminate the pregnancy. That was the word the doctor used: "terminate". Made it all sound so practical. It didn't matter. In the eyes of God, I had committed murder. I knew that and yet I went along with it anyway.'

Judith Levenson was most likely cut from the same die-hard Catholic mould as Darby's mother – Sheila had been the product of Catholic schools at a time when nuns cracked your knuckles with a ruler. You went to mass every Sunday; you took an active interest in the religious education and formation of your children; you followed the rules and did what you were told; and you most certainly did not, under any circumstances, participate or approve of the great evil known as abortion. Such matters were left to God.

'I couldn't live with the . . . burden of it,' Judith said. 'I wanted the Act of Contrition, but I couldn't confess this to Father Byrne. I was terrified he'd judge me. So I went three towns over and talked to a priest named Father Morgan.'

Judith burst into tears. 'I'm sorry. I don't know why I'm telling you all of this – why I'm *burdening* you with all of this.'

'Don't apologize.'

'I don't even know you – I've never even *met* you. And here I am, spilling things I've only told my husband.' Judith laughed abruptly. 'Maybe it's because you're a woman and also a stranger and I'm not afraid of being judged. I lived that way for far, far too long.'

'Keep talking. Please. I'm here to listen.'

'You're being far too kind.'

Darby heard an approaching car. 'No, I'm not,' she said, turning to look down the street at the approaching car. 'I want to know. What happened with Father Morgan?'

Wrong question. Judith cried even harder.

'He screamed at me, in the confessional,' she whimpered. 'Said that I had no right to make that decision. That I should have delivered the baby, so the baby could have been baptized and buried properly and his soul sent to heaven. But I didn't do that. I took the easy way out and damned his soul to hell.'

Darby didn't know what to say. She was good at dealing with the emotional landmines of psychology, not religion. So she said words she believed were true. 'If there is a

God, I think he has a secret window into all of our hearts. I think he's the only one who can see us for who we really are – the only one who truly knows.'

'Father Byrne ... he knew something was wrong. I couldn't hold it in any longer. I told him. And he was so gentle with me. So incredibly kind. To be that way and then to turn around and do whatever he did to Elizabeth and the others – I just don't understand. I just don't understand.' The sobs being ripped from her were ones Darby recognized all too well from other victims: the wails of those unfortunate few who had been damned, through no fault of their own, to a special level of hell that most people would never comprehend.

'I'll let you go,' Judith said.

'I'd like to talk to you – not about Byrne, but about your daughter.'

It took Judith a moment to clear her throat so she could speak. 'What do you want to know?'

'Everything,' Darby said, removing her car keys from her jacket pocket. 'I want to know everything.'

43

The following morning, just shy of nine, Mickey drove to Sean's house – and, make no mistake, it was *Sean*'s house, he and his mother nothing more than guests, really. The last time Mickey had set foot inside he had been a couple of months shy of eighteen. After Sean had left for work, Mickey had packed up everything he owned into two boxes and had driven over to the Kelly house to live in the bedroom once occupied by Big Jim's two older brothers, both of whom had long since moved out.

That was several decades ago, and the neighbourhood had undergone a conversion. Most of the ranch homes that had once occupied the area had been levelled and replaced with nicely sized Colonials, a few of them with two-car garages. A part of him felt he had taken a wrong turn into the wrong neighbourhood.

And then he saw the house where he'd grown up, a small Cape, untouched by time.

Mickey parked against the kerb and stared at his childhood home, thinking about Sean's note. Sean was giving him a one-shot deal. If he didn't show up with the cash tomorrow morning, it was over. Like Byrne, Sean would gladly take all his secrets with him to the grave.

Mickey killed the engine.

No good can come of this. You know that.

The voice speaking to him was the rational, sensible

one that had kept him out of a good deal of trouble most of his early life. Sensible and rational. Just like his mother.

Mickey got out of the car and shut the door. He fished the key out of his pocket as he walked up the sloping lawn of dead grass.

When it came to his actual living quarters, Sean applied the same lessons on orderliness that he had learned in the military. The low-pile tan carpeting in the living room still looked new, not a stain anywhere. The white walls didn't have a mark on them — and they were empty, not a single framed picture or print.

The small kitchen, though, was another story. He saw scuff marks left from shoes on the white linoleum floor. He saw cabinet doors hanging open and dishes placed on the counter and the contents of drawers dumped on the table, traces of black fingerprint powder everywhere. Right. The cops had searched the house.

Mickey moved down the narrow hallway, stopped when he saw Sean's bedroom. Everything had been torn apart, but what caught his attention was a framed photograph of Claire.

No, not one; there were *four*. Four pictures of his daughter on Sean's bureau and each one had been taken outdoors. Each photograph had captured Claire at various ages: Claire, around two, walking barefoot on a beach Mickey was pretty sure was in Old Orchard, Maine; Claire smelling a dandelion; Claire playing with Ericka Kelly at the jungle gym at the Hill; Claire dressed in her pink snowsuit, holding Mickey's hand as they waited for their turn to go down the Hill.

The photos looked familiar and unfamiliar at the same time. Seeing them — it was like he'd been kicked in the stomach. Mickey had never given Sean *any* pictures of Claire. Heather wouldn't have done it either, which left only one answer: Sean had taken them. Sean, who had never met Claire and never would. Mickey and Heather had both agreed to keep that murdering scumbag son of a bitch away from their daughter, their family. But Sean had sneaked around and taken these pictures, had captured and stolen these moments – probably using a long-focus lens so he could stand in the shadows. A camera phone would have required that he get closer, and Sean wouldn't have wanted to get caught by Mickey, no question.

Mickey wanted to search the rest of the house – wanted to rip it apart, from rooftop to basement, to see if there were any more pictures of Claire. He could do that later, when he had more time, when he wasn't thinking about what was stored in the safe relating to his mother. He removed the Swiss Army knife from his jacket pocket as he walked into his old bedroom.

It was completely empty. He opened the closet, found it empty too, then got down on his knees and used the small knife to cut away a corner section of the carpet. Once he got a strip, he grabbed it and gave it a hard yank, pulling up the construction staples.

Sean's safe was square and made of solid steel, with a flush cover plate that was perfect for concealment under a carpet. Mickey knew a thing or two about safes, and he was willing to bet Sean had gone all out and sprung for a drill-proof model built to provide protection against forced entry with something like a sledgehammer. The safe had been set in concrete, making it impossible to pull out unless you happened to have some serious construction machinery.

The safe hadn't been there when he was a kid. It also had to be less than ten years old. When Claire had been abducted and before Byrne became a suspect, Belham PD had their sights locked on Sean and had ripped apart every square inch of this house, the thinking being that Claire had been kidnapped by one of Sean's past associates. Mickey had never heard anything about a safe in the floor – or about pictures of Claire, for that matter.

Mickey worked the dial. The combination entered, he turned the hinge and heard the safe click open.

Two rows, stacks of crumpled $100 bills bound together with elastic bands. Mickey grabbed one, counted it.

Ten grand. And that was just one stack. There'd be a hell of a lot more, depending on just how deep the safe was.

Five minutes later, he knew.

'Holy shit.'

Half a million dollars – in *cash*. In a safe hidden in his old house.

Of course he'd hide it here, Mickey thought. If Sean had placed this amount of money in a bank, the government could have swooped in at any moment and frozen his accounts.

An envelope was at the bottom of the safe. Inside was a stack of pictures, but not of Claire. Well, at least the top one wasn't. The top picture, the colours slightly off and yellowed by age, was of people walking through a crowded, brightly lit alley of brick buildings.

At first Mickey thought the place might've been Faneuil Hall in Boston. But this area was more enclosed and had a foreign feel to it.

Like Paris.

Mickey studied the faces in the photo. He didn't recognize them. By the way people were dressed, it was either spring or summer. He turned the picture over and saw the developer's date stamped on the back: 16 July 1976.

July.

July was the month Sean went to Paris.

The next picture was of a woman with frosted blonde hair sitting at an outdoor table under a white awning covered with ivy, a pair of round black sunglasses covering her eyes as she read a newspaper. People sat around her, reading newspapers and books, talking, drinking coffee. Mickey flipped to the next picture, a close-up of the same woman, only she had taken off her sunglasses and was smiling at the man now seated across from her. The man's back was towards the camera, but the woman's face was as plain as day.

It was his mother.

Mickey flipped through the rest of the photos. His mother was in every one of them, as was her companion, this unknown man who was a good deal taller than her and had a very sharp, hawk-like nose, long sideburns and thick, wavy, black hair. He wore a suit that had long since gone out of style, and Mickey pegged the guy for an investor or a banker – something in finance. The guy had that feel to him.

What was clear was how much his mother cared for this man. In every picture she was holding either his hand or his arm. In the last photo, the man had his arm wrapped around her shoulder as they walked together down a crowded street, his mother's wide smile turned away from him, his mother safe and happy, relieved to be back in Paris, lost in the streets of her birthplace and hometown, her other life forgotten.

44

The prison guard took out his keys to unlock the door. Through the glass panel, Mickey could see Sean, dressed in his orange prison jumpsuit, sitting in a chair with his head bowed, studying the handcuffs secured to a chain wrapped around his waist. Under the fluorescent lighting, he looked withered, the skin under his eyes bruised from lack of sleep, his thin lips bloodless.

'You've got thirty minutes,' Martin Hager said to Mickey. The lawyer, his black hair slicked back à la Gordon Gekko from *Wall Street*, wore too much cologne and sucked on a peppermint Lifesaver. 'And try to show some compassion to your old man, okay? Your father was throwing up all night, the shakes, everything. They had to take him to the doctor, give him some meds to treat his PTSD. That stands for post-traumatic stress –'

'I know what it stands for.'

'Good, then you know why your old man's acting like he's crawling out of his skin. Look, I don't know what the deal is between you two, and I don't care. I'm not a therapist. What I do know is that the man in there is a war hero, and, while you may not like him, now's not the time to be busting his cherries, know what I mean?'

The door opened. The small room held a desk and two folding chairs. Sean sat in a swivel chair bolted to the floor. He looked at his lawyer and said, 'He give you the money?'

'We're good,' Hager said. 'Sean, you need anything, I'll be standing outside the door with the guard.'

Then the lawyer left, and Mickey was alone with the creature that shared his DNA.

'You find the pictures inside the safe?' Sean asked.

Mickey slid out the chair. He sat and folded his hands on the table.

'Where'd you get those pictures of my daughter?'

'What pictures?'

'The ones on your bureau,' Mickey said. 'You take them yourself?'

'What, you think I hired a photographer?' The words came out slurred and cotton-mouthed, and his eyes were dull. What had they given him for his anxiety? Xanax?

'That wasn't right, keeping my only grandchild from me,' Sean said. Drops of perspiration ran down his forehead. He smelled of soap and shaving cream. 'You are one cold son of a bitch.'

'I had a great teacher. How did you find out where Mom was hiding?'

'*Hiding?*' Sean laughed.

Mickey pointed a finger at him. 'Back out of your promise, and I swear to Christ I'll take the rest of the money I found and donate it –'

'Arthur Lewis.'

'Who's that?'

'The Kellys' mailman,' Sean said. 'Artie was a regular at McCarthy's – came to the bar every Friday night. One night he asks me why *your* mail is getting delivered to the Kelly house. I said to him, I don't know what you're talking about, and he tells me about this package you got all the way from

Gay Paree. We get to talking, I buy him a few beers, and I asks him to keep an eye out for any more mail with your name on it, tell him if he hand-delivers it to me personally I'll give him two hundred each and every time.'

'So she sent a second package.'

'More like a note. It was written on one of those heavy, expensive note cards. Then again, your mother always valued expensive things. Did I ever tell you how she almost bankrupted me? No, of course I didn't. Why would I? You always took the bitch's side.'

Mickey felt warm underneath his clothes. Sean might be drugged up, but Mickey could tell his old man was working up to something, sharpening his knives.

'Money was tight in the beginning,' Sean said, 'but that didn't stop your mother from treating herself to nice things. She always hid them around the house, thinking I'd never find them.' His eyes were no longer dull. 'You ever see her do anything like that? Your mother?'

'What did this letter say?'

'She tell you the story behind that blue scarf of hers? You know the one I'm talking about, right? The one she hid downstairs in those boxes of hers?'

'Doesn't ring a bell.'

Sean tilted his head to the side, confused. 'I thought you came here for the truth? Or are you looking for me to back up the bullshit she sold you?'

'She said her father gave it to her.'

Sean chuckled. Shook his head.

'What's so funny?'

'Her old man was a waiter who could barely afford the groceries,' Sean said. 'Her mother died when René was four.'

Mickey searched his memory for stories his mother had told him about her parents – something to set against what Sean was saying, prove he was lying. He couldn't come up with anything.

'The note,' Mickey said. 'What did it say?'

'I don't remember the exact words, but it was something along the lines of how much she missed you, that she carried you in her heart and in her thoughts. That sort of shit.'

'That's it? That's all she said?'

'You mean did she say when she was flying back to the good ole US of A to come rescue you? She did not.' Sean licked his lips. Grinned. 'You don't believe me.'

'You're right. I don't.'

'I still have it.'

'Have what?'

'The note. Would you like to read it?'

Mickey felt his pulse quicken in his throat.

Sean didn't speak. He made Mickey ask the question.

'Where is it?'

'You sure you want to read it?' Sean asked. ''Cause once you read something, you can't, you know, erase it or –'

'Where?'

'Basement,' Sean said. 'Top drawer of the Gerstner.'

The Gerstner was a solid oak tool-chest made by H. Gerstner & Sons. Sean stored his wood-working tools in it. Mickey said, 'So in this second letter, she had to have included a return address. That's how you found her.'

'Look at you, playing detective. I'm proud of you, son.' Sean winked.

'And once you had her address, you just hopped on a plane to Paris.'

'I did. Didn't *want* to, mind you, given how much I hate flying, but I did it because –'

'Why use a fake passport?'

'There was a misunderstanding between myself and the authorities at the time. They believed I might have had something to do with the theft of certain electronic items from a warehouse in South Boston, which was ridiculous. Stealing was never my thing.'

'Just murder.'

Sean smiled. Said nothing.

'Only you hate to fly because you're claustrophobic.'

'I don't fly because I don't trust planes.'

Mickey waved it away. 'So why not call her? You had her address; you could have found her phone number. Why bother hopping on a plane?'

'Boy needs his mother,' Sean said, Mickey feeling the heat in his old man's voice, words coming together to form a fist.

Why is he acting so confident?

Mickey knew why. Sean was setting him up. But for what?

'Your problem is you always considered your mother this great saint,' Sean said. 'The day she left? She took all the money I had in our bank accounts, left us with nothing. She's the reason I don't trust banks.'

'She –'

'You forget about all the things I did for you – the ball games, all the equipment you needed for football and baseball. Your tuition for St Stephen's. Who the hell do you think paid for that after she drained my bank account? Your mother?'

Mickey had no idea whether or not that was true – and didn't care.

'And when you and Jim started your business, I offered you money. You turned me down, being the spiteful son of a bitch that you are, but did that stop me from steering clients your way? Making sure you two had money coming in? Anything you ever needed, I gave you.'

'Including beating the shit out of me.'

'You needed toughening up. Your generation? You're a bunch of pussies. You whine to your therapists and to each other about how unfair life is, have meltdowns when you get the wrong coffee order at Dunkin's. Your generation gets off on being treated unfairly. What's that shit they taught you in AA? Accepting life on life's terms? You ever catch me bitching and moaning about my life? About losing my brother in a shit war or spending almost a year in a POW camp?'

'Tell me what you did to her.'

'What do you think I did? I tried talking her into coming home.'

'I don't believe you.'

'Did me and your mother get into it over there in frog land? Absolutely. Sometimes our tempers get the best of us. You, of all people, know what I'm talking about.'

'I'm nothing like you, Sean.'

'Oh, yeah? Then let's talk about that night you went over to Byrne's. I mean, let's *really* talk about it. I'm sure you convinced yourself you didn't go over there with the intention of beating the living shit out of him, but *you* told *me* something else that night at McCarthy's. You told me you were going to kill the son of a bitch, and I said –'

'We didn't talk that night.'

'I'm not judging you, or what you did. But don't try selling me your bullshit, 'cause I'm not buying it. And if you want to believe I hurt your mother, killed her, whatever, then you go right on believing it along with Santa Claus, the Easter Bunny and Jesus Christ. You don't want to accept the truth the way it is, warts and all, feel free to get the fuck on out of here.'

'The guy in the pictures,' Mickey said. 'Who is he?'

'Timothée Peltier.' Sean searched Mickey's eyes. 'Name doesn't ring a bell?'

'No. Who is he?'

'You sure? He and your mother were real close – thick as thieves, you could say.'

'I already answered your question; now answer mine.'

'They grew up together – were *quite* an item when they were young. Inseparable, from what I was told. Then your mother moved to the States. She was fifteen and hopelessly in love. She and Timothée kept in touch by mail, by phone – only Timothée had to do the majority of the calling since your mother's father wouldn't have allowed phone calls to France. As Timothée got older – would you like for me to continue, or have you had enough?'

'Keep going.'

'You sure? You look drained. I'm a bit tired myself.'

'I said keep going.'

Sean yawned. 'So, Timothée. When he was nineteen, he flew here to meet your mother. He could afford it. He was working in his father's papermill business when your mother moved here and was being groomed to take over the company. Peltier Paper. Big company over there – check it out online if you don't believe everything I'm saying. Anyway, Timothée, he just loved showering your mother with expensive gifts. Like that blue scarf.' Sean's smile felt like a knife. 'Expensive gifts popped up from time to time around the house.'

Unconsciously, Mickey rubbed his forehead, found it slick and greasy.

'Having a hard time believing your perfect saint of a mother could possibly be involved in something so seedy?' Sean searched Mickey's face and smiled. 'Admit it. Your life was so much simpler when you were busy hating me.'

'If she was having an affair, I don't blame her.' Mickey's voice sounded oddly calm. 'I don't blame her for it at all.'

'An affair? She was in love with him the day we met.'

'Then why'd she settle for you?'

'Timothée's family was very successful and very rich. Prestigious background, lots of inventors in the family, politicians – all that fancy pedigree shit that makes a woman's panties get soaking wet. And nothing, and I mean *nothing*, got your mother more excited than the topic of money, as in having lots of it. And Timothée had shit-loads of it. Timothée's old man, though, wasn't about to let his boy get involved with common trash, even if that trash was as beautiful as your mother. Got to think of the bloodlines, you know?' A sharp smile. 'I had no idea about Timothée when me and her got together – had no idea she was still holding out hope for him even after we married. I always knew those pictures were bullshit.'

'What pictures?'

'The ones in the photo albums,' Sean said. 'I know she showed them to you.'

The photo albums she hid in boxes in the basement – the ones she packed up and took with her back to France – Mickey remembered how she would sometimes sit alone down in the basement and go through them. The handful of times he had caught her there crying she would bring him over and go through the pictures with him and narrate the story of her family.

'Those pictures?' Sean said. 'They were of Timothée's family, not hers.'

'Never saw 'em.'

'He was around Belham a lot when I was away during the war. I found that out later, after I caught them together in Boston when you were four? Five? Even after that he kept coming around. That son of a bitch was, well, one stubborn son of a bitch. One time, I broke his hand in a car door and he –'

'You knew about the affair?'

'I had my suspicions. Fresh flowers every now and then, and she'd tell me some bullshit story about how she bought them at the florist. Or how, when I spotted a silver picture frame or a nice pair of shoes in her closet, she'd make up a story about finding them at Goodwill or some place like that.' Sean leaned forward a little. 'Your mother could be very persuasive with that soft, gentle voice of hers. Smoothest liar I've ever met.'

But Mickey was only half listening now, trying to recall times when he'd seen his mother all dressed up and heading into someplace like Boston to meet this Timothée guy. He couldn't picture her as anything but the person he knew and loved: a kind and loving woman in frumpy, used clothing. A penny-pincher who cut out coupons, her only extravagance, as far as he could remember, the makeup she used to cover her bruises. That image was fixed in his mind because it was true – and here was Sean trying to poison it with his lies. To believe Sean would ever come clean about anything had been both stupid and foolish. The man lied for a living, and he was lying right now.

'Those pictures you found in the safe?' Sean said. 'Your mother knew I took them. I showed them to her. I –'

'We're done.' Mickey felt anger flush his face and explode through his limbs, but it didn't find his voice. 'The next time you see me will be when I'm on the witness stand, telling everyone about that morning you came by my house and told me about how you'd been inside Byrne's house.'

'That's what legal douchebags call hearsay.'

'I bet the police haven't found the listening devices you left there.'

'And they never will.'

Mickey put his hands on the table as he got up and leaned forward. 'You will never see daylight again. I'm gonna make it my life's mission to ensure you fucking *die* in here. That's a promise.'

'Timothée loved your mother, but he hated kids,' Sean said. 'So he gave her a choice: life with him in the city of love or life with us. Which life do you think she chose, Mickey? Any ideas?'

45

The hotel didn't have a gym, but there was a fitness centre in the strip mall across the street. She exercised with weights, did four miles on the rower, showered and headed back to her hotel. She was walking through the small lobby when the young black guy working the front desk waved to get her attention.

'Got something for you,' he said.

He handed her an 8 × 8 white envelope. Her name was written on the front, in black marker: DR DARBY MCCORMICK. No stamps or post-office marks or a return address, just her name.

'Who gave this to you?' she asked.

'Just some guy. A messenger, I think. He came by here an hour or so ago.' He looked at her, puzzled. 'Something wrong?'

'No. Not at all,' she said. 'Thank you.'

The envelope was extremely light. She opened it upstairs, in her room.

Someone had unspooled rolls of audiotape and cut them up into thousands of small fragments that nearly filled the envelope. A notecard was also inside, the writing, done in blue ink, performed by an unsteady hand.

The card read:

I could have answered so many questions about your parents and your brother and shared other insightful details if you had played nicely during our afternoon together. But I can't say your actions surprised me. What else should I have expected from such a blunt killing machine?

In the spirit of confession, I will admit I so envy your experiences in that arena. Killing is one of the few delights I never indulged in – not that you believe me.

Now you'll die without ever knowing who your parents really were. I take great comfort in knowing that you are suffering. But don't despair. It will bring you closer to Him.

46

The Gerstner was exactly where Sean had said it was: in the basement, stored at the bottom of one of those self-assembly plastic shelving units. The oak tool-chest was locked, which surprised him. Mickey thought the police would have found a way to open it during their search of the house. Maybe they found whatever they needed and skipped it, or maybe they had been lazy since they already had the evidence recovered from the crime scene in Byrne's backyard.

Rather than wasting time searching for a key, Mickey used Sean's drill and bored a hole through the lock. When Sean wasn't out and about, or when he got into a particularly nasty fight with his wife, he would come down here to the basement and putter around on some project. Sean had a talent for wood-working, but he didn't have the patience. It was here, using Sean's tools, that Mickey had made the birdhouse he had given his mother.

The chest opened without a problem. Sitting inside the walls of green felt were six neat stacks of envelopes bound together by elastic bands. They were all addressed to René Flynn in Sean's trademark chicken scrawl. Most of the paper had yellowed over time, the stamps either missing or curling at the corners, about to fall off.

Must be Sean's war letters, Mickey thought. Odd that Sean would have kept them. It was such a sentimental act, and

Sean was hardly sentimental. Even odder that he'd written them in the first place, since he rarely talked about what had happened over there.

Mickey removed one stack and set it down on top of the long counter that stretched its way down one length of the wall. He unfastened the elastic, which snapped because it was so old, and picked up a random letter written in faded pencil.

13 May 1965

Dear René,

The sun here doesn't let up, and everywhere I go there's this thick, wet heat. Mail over a fan when you get a chance.

Things have been heating up here in Gookville. The other day we were choppered into Dodge City and immediately got stuck in the middle of a firefight. I had my helmet and flack gear on, otherwise I wouldn't've made it. Damn gooks had us pinned down for two hours. Never been so damn scared in my entire life. Keep trying to talk some sense into my brother. I don't want him over here.

Please write. Your letters will get me through this. How's Mickey? What's he doing? Send a picture of him. The two of you are always in my thoughts.

Love,
Sean

'Scared' and 'love'. Words Mickey had never heard Sean say but had used here.

Mickey opened another envelope. This letter was dated a week later.

They have us guarding a road next to a graveyard. Every night
I'm sleeping next to a damn tombstone made out of wood.
We're losing about a man a day here, most of it 'cause of
the heat.

You and I had some words before I left. I know money's tight
and things are tough on you and Mickey. I'll come home and
make it up to you and him and give you the life you've dreamed of.
That's a promise.

There were a dozen more letters like this one, Sean describing the hell around him and practically begging his wife to write to him. The last letter in the stack read:

I'm sure you already know about Dave Simmons. He was
standing right next to me and sneezed and it made me think of
you so I said God Bless You and the back of his head blew apart.
It keeps replaying over and over and over in my mind.

Please stop punishing me with your silence. If you don't want to
write a letter, okay, fine, I get it. But send a picture of Mickey. Just
one picture. That's not a lot to ask.

A card-sized envelope was on the bottom of the chest drawer, resting on top of an envelope for Brick's Photos, the words THANK YOU FOR TRUSTING US WITH YOUR MEMORIES printed across the top in letters so bold it read more like a scream than a simple thank you. The card inside was addressed to Mickey Flynn at Jim's old address – just as Sean had said.

The card had a return address in the corner. It was from Paris, France.

Mickey removed the envelope from the pile of pictures.

The back flap's seal had been torn open. He lifted the flap and prised out the heavy note card.

Dear Mickey,

I'm sorry it has taken me so long to write back to you. I've been actively searching for a place big enough for us. Paris is incredibly expensive, especially here on the Île Saint-Louis. There's first and last month's rent to consider, and things like security deposits. I'm working as a waitress at a café, but money is slow coming in. Looking back, I should have taken the money I put aside for your tuition and used it to set us up here, but, after all the setbacks you've suffered, I didn't want you to endure the pain of having to move to another school and be away from James and all your other friends while I got settled in Paris.

I'm coming for you. I know it's taking longer than I said, and I know you've been patient. I need you to keep being patient. You can write to me at the address on the front of the envelope. Don't let your father get this address. Hide this letter where he won't find it. If your father knows where I'm hiding – well, I don't have to remind you of what he is capable.

No matter how bad it gets, always remember to have faith. And always remember how much I love you, how special you are and will always be.

She signed the letter in the way she always did, using the French word for 'Mom': *Maman.*

Mickey slid the note card back into the envelope. His eyes were hot and his throat felt raw when he swallowed.

Pieces of this morning's conversation with Sean came back to him. *The day she left? She took all the money I had in our bank accounts, left us with nothing. She's the reason I don't trust banks ... Your tuition for St Stephen's. Who the hell do you think paid for that after she drained my bank account? Your mother?*

Mickey opened the Brick's Photos envelope.

No pictures. Nothing. It was empty.

Were they somewhere down here, or in some other part of the house? Or were they gone forever? He didn't care, and he didn't feel like moving either. His feet felt like they had been welded to the floor. He felt lost.

Who could he go to in order to find the truth?

Mickey searched his memory – his mother had been close to Father Keith Cullen, the priest all too well aware of Mickey's home life with Sean. He remembered asking Father Keith if he knew anything about where his mother had gone (this was before the letters came), Father Keith looking shocked before saying no, he had no idea – no knowledge of where his mother could have run off to. If it was an act, it was a damn good one. He took out his phone and dialled Father Cullen's cell phone number and got a 'No longer in service' message. He called the rectory and, after telling the secretary who he was and why he was calling, she told him to hold on while she transferred the call. Mickey felt some relief, and a sense of building anxiety, when the phone on the other end of the line picked up.

'Father Cullen.'

'It's Mickey Flynn. Sorry to bother you, but I was hoping you could help me with something ... I had a quick question about my mother.'

'Your mother?' he said.

'Yes. I was wondering . . . I know this is going to sound odd, but I had a conversation with Sean today, and he told me he paid for my tuition at St Stephen's. Is there any way to find out if this is true?'

'It's true.'

'You're sure.'

'Positive. He came to me personally and paid me in cash not long after your mother . . . went away. Every year he paid in cash.'

'Cash,' Mickey said. 'Sean.'

'Yeah. He's the only parent I know who ever did that. You remember a thing like that.'

'I see.' Mickey felt cold all over.

'Mickey, I hate to cut you off, but I've got to –'

'Go. Thank you for your time, Father.'

Mickey hung up, blood thrumming in his ears, his vision swimming.

Sean said he had paid the tuition, and Father Cullen had just validated Sean's story. Which meant his mother had lied to him. His mother had written: *Looking back, I should have taken the money I put aside for your tuition and used it to set us up here, but, after all the setbacks you've suffered, I didn't want you to endure the pain of having to move to another school and be away from James and all your other friends while I got settled in Paris.*

His mother had deliberately lied to him. Why?

Timothée loved your mother, but he hated kids, Sean had told him. *So he gave her a choice: life with him in the city of love or life with us. Which life do you think she chose, Mickey?*

Mickey imagined Sean wandering the streets of Paris, following his wife and her long-time lover, snapping pictures and thinking about how he was going to get René alone, confront her, get her to come back home.

He leaned forward and splayed his hands across the countertop, his head bowed and his eyes tight shut, wondering how much grief a heart could hold, how many truths it could be forced to accept before it ruptured.

47

The thought of going back to his house and Claire's nearly empty room made Mickey want to drink. Not just a couple of pops or whatever it took to get him buzzed and comfortably numb but the entire bottle. He knew the reason behind the urge: he was terrified of being alone.

Big Jim, Mickey knew, was going out for a well-deserved night on the town with his wife. What would he do tonight? When the idea came into his head, he didn't question it. He dialled the number, feeling a burst of gratitude when Darby picked up.

'You free tonight? I'm asking because I'd like to take you to dinner. To thank you for everything you've done and to apologize for, you know, being somewhat of an asshole.'

'Somewhat?' Darby teased.

It surprised him, the grin that spread across his face, how good it felt. Mickey sat with it for a moment.

'I'm only busting your balls,' Darby said.

'I know you are. And thank you for that.'

'For breaking your balls?'

'For treating me like I'm a normal human being instead of some sort of freak show. Like I've got the plague or something. So, how about it?'

Darby agreed, and had only one condition: she wanted to get out of 'Bedlam', which was fine by him. She suggested one of her favourite restaurants in the city, an Italian place called Antonio's in Beacon Hill. They agreed to meet on the earlier side, at five-ish, to avoid the long wait for a table.

The few memories Mickey had of Boston's Beacon Hill area were from his early twenties: drunken nights spent running from bar to bar with Big Jim, Heather and some of their other friends. His recollection was that of a brick-lined haven for the elite and the superrich, complete with bad parking and antique lantern streetlights that had been converted from gas to electricity. Beacon Hill seemed small until you actually walked through it and then it resembled a hedge maze, its narrow one-way streets lined with brick sidewalks and tall brick-faced condos and townhouses, the price of one more than the cost of three or four upscale homes in the north side of Belham.

The narrow streets and bad parking still held true, as did all the brick, but the streetlights had been converted to solar power. As Mickey walked across Charles Street, taking in the neighbourhood feel of Beacon Hill, he found himself actually enjoying the winter evening, the distraction of watching people going in and out of stores or on their way to dinner, the college students with backpacks drinking coffee and talking and texting on their phones, parents out pushing strollers.

Antonio's was small, located right across the street from the entrance to Mass General, and inside it was roughly the size of a large bedroom. It fitted ten tables, all of which were full. He didn't have to search for Darby: she was sitting in a corner table by the window. She was dressed in the same clothes he'd seen her wearing since she arrived in Belham: nice jeans and a collared white shirt and dark-brown harness boots. A lot of bikers he knew had them, and she wore them well, Mickey thinking how she was the only woman he had known who could dress in something so basic and simple and yet make it look sexy and elegant.

He slid into the chair across from her, Darby smiling – a bit wearily, he thought, like she was in possession of an uncomfortable piece of information.

'Everything okay?' he asked.

'Long day. You?'

He nodded. He had spent the day resurrecting ghosts.

The waiter came by to take their drinks order. Darby ordered a bourbon neat – Knob Creek, the single barrel.

'Great choice,' Mickey said, and then surprised himself – and Darby – when he ordered a soda water, which they didn't have, only sparkling water, which probably came in a fancy bottle and cost more than a pack of cigarettes. He wanted a break from the booze. Not permanently, just for right now – which, in his estimation, proved that he wasn't an alcoholic.

When the waiter left, Mickey sensed Darby was tense. She lapsed into silence, Mickey getting the feeling she was trying to figure out, exactly, what to talk about, what topics were safe. He didn't want to talk about himself or his day with Sean. He wanted to get out of his own head for a bit.

'Why this place?' he asked.

'I came here a lot when I lived here.'

'You lived in the Hill?'

'Had a condo here for a long, long time.'

'That must've been nice.'

'It was. I miss it.'

'Why'd you move?'

'It was time,' she said.

'I haven't been here, Christ, in years. My mother liked to come into the city, especially around Christmas. Back when I was a kid, she'd always take me into the city and we'd go to see the Christmas tree on the Common. After that, she dragged me to this holiday-stroll thing where we'd get a walking history tour of the Hill that always ended up in that square there, you know, the one where the Kennedy family lived once upon a time.'

'Louisburg Square.'

Mickey snapped his fingers. 'That's the one.'

'Louisa May Alcott lived there too.'

'Who's that?'

'Writer from the late 1800s. She wrote *Little Women*.'

Mickey smiled a bit. 'I'm pretty sure she read that. My mother was a big reader. Carried books with her everywhere she went. You probably would have liked her.'

'I'm sure I would have.'

'And she would have loved to live here – especially Louisburg Square. She loved to –' Mickey cut himself off, a memory stabbing him.

It must have shown on his face, because Darby said, 'You don't have to tell me. I'm not trying to pry.'

'I know you're not. Something just occurred to me – something I didn't realize until now, about our last Christmas together. I remember her walking around Louisburg Square, and the homes there, those big Greek Revival homes, some of the windows facing the street

344

didn't have the curtains or the shades drawn, and you could look inside, see the people who lived there, catch a glimpse of these enormous Christmas trees. My mother would point them out to me, and I just realized how sad she sounded when she talked. She sounded real sad towards the end, you know, before she left, and I always thought it was because of Sean, being married to him. But now I think she was also sad because she knew she'd never be like one of those people – wouldn't have nice things.'

'Not too many people get to live like that.'

'True,' Mickey said, but he was thinking about what Sean had told him earlier about how much his mother had loved expensive things. *And nothing, and I mean nothing,* Sean had told him, *got your mother more excited than the topic of money, as in having lots of it.*

There was something else he remembered about their last Christmas together – something he'd forgotten, or blocked out, until now. The last time they had come into the city for the Christmas tour, after it ended his mother had lingered around because she said she was waiting for a friend. Mickey remembered how it had surprised him, his mother saying that, because she didn't have any friends – at least none that she'd spoken about to him. And he remembered how he'd been even more surprised when this friend of his mother turned out to be a man.

Mickey didn't know the man's name, or whether his mother had introduced him. He couldn't recall what the man looked like or how he had been dressed, but Mickey had a vague memory of shaking the man's gloved hand before he and his mother moved away so they could talk privately, the conversation seeming to go on forever.

Mickey felt sure he was recalling an actual memory and not something his mind had constructed to give weight to Sean's story.

Was this man Timothée?

The waiter came back with their drinks and told them the dinner specials. Darby said they needed a few more minutes. Then she moved her glass to the side, put her elbows on the table and leaned forward.

'What's going on?'

'I'm fine,' he said. 'Let's talk about you.'

'I'd rather talk about what's bothering you.'

He wanted to talk about it and didn't want to talk about it. *What the hell?* he thought, and said, 'Can I get your opinion on something?'

'Sure.' Darby gave him her full attention, another trait he admired, the way Darby could not only listen – but really *listen* – and make you feel as though you were the most important person in her world, but also actually empathize.

'Back when we were together,' he said, 'I told you about my mother, how she just packed up one day and disappeared, right?'

Darby nodded. 'You never told me specifics,' she added.

Mickey started with the day his mother had left and the reasons why she did; took Darby through his conversation with Sean at the prison; and ended with the second letter in Sean's tool-box, and the lie about St Stephen's.

'So now you're thinking your mother never had any intention of coming home,' Darby said. Her voice was low, almost fearful, like she was afraid to ask the question.

'Did Sean go over there and take pictures of my mother

with this guy? Yes. Do I now think she was having an affair? Most likely. Do I think my old man tried to talk her into coming home? I highly doubt it. People who cross him disappear. That's a fact.'

'True,' Darby said. 'Still, we're talking about your mother here.'

'The guy lies for a living. It's as natural to him as breathing.'

'He was telling the truth about paying for your tuition. You said the priest confirmed it.'

Mickey held up a hand, willing to concede the point. 'Still, my mother wouldn't just vanish. If she were alive, she would have written or called, you know? She would have done *something*. When she disappeared, the police came around. *A lot*. Sean had those pictures. He knew exactly where she was and who she was with. All he had to do was to hand those pictures and that information over to the police and he'd have been free and clear of any suspicion.'

'If he had done that, the news would've spread through town. What if you'd found out about the affair? Imagine what that would have done to you. How old were you then? Nine? Ten?'

'Eight,' he said. 'I see where you're going, but I just don't buy it. This guy is – okay, this one time when I was a kid, around fifteen, I was sitting in the car with Sean, driving through Charlestown, when he suddenly stopped the car, told me to keep my ass parked in it. He reaches under the seat, comes back with a lead pipe and gets out. I find out later this guy was big into debt with one of Sean's buddies. Guy's on the ground, crying, begging for his life, saying he's sorry, and Sean keeps beating the shit out of him. Then Sean gets in the car, acts like nothing happened, like he had just stopped to grab a newspaper, and when we get home he goes and takes a nap.'

'Mickey, I'm not going to try to suggest your old man isn't a son of a bitch. He is. What I'm saying is, it's *possible* that, instead of showing you the pictures of your mother, he decided to shelter you from the truth.'

'You honestly believe that?'

'"Believe" is the wrong word. I'm only responding to everything you've shared with me about him while taking into account his actions. We know he took the pictures of your mother. Maybe he wanted to use them to confront her. Maybe he had plans on showing them to you. Maybe he's not even sure why he did it, as strange as that may sound. What we *do* know is that he kept those pictures from you all this time – kept the truth from you. The question is why.'

'What do you think?'

'I think it's possible that on some level he believed that having you hate him would be easier than your knowing the truth.'

Mickey felt a sudden exhaustion that seeped all the way into his bones. He rubbed his eyes.

'Look,' Darby said. 'I could have this all wrong. Having a degree in nut-jobs doesn't mean I know everything about them. What I do know is that people are messy. That's all I can say with any authority. Good people, healthy people, the sick and the demented – everyone is messy.'

'What's your advice?'

'About Sean?'

'About my mother. All this time I thought, you know, Sean had done something to her. Buried her somewhere. Because if she were alive, she would have come back for me, like she promised in her letters. At least that's what I've told myself all this time.'

'And now you want to see if you can find her.'

'The second letter my mother sent me had an address on the envelope.'

Her expression changed, Darby putting on what he called 'cop face' – her features turning flat and her eyes looking empty as she retreated deep within herself. 'And now you want to see if you can find her.'

'I take it you don't think that's a good idea,' he said. 'Trying to find her.'

'It doesn't matter what I think.'

'You're – what do you shrinks call it? – deflecting?'

'I'm not. This is a decision you have to make because it affects you. There's no right or wrong answer. What it comes down to is whether or not you're ready to open these doors.'

'Because I might not like what I find.'

'Or may not find.'

'I've been thinking about that all day,' Mickey said, nodding. 'And the thing is, I don't think I can walk away from this. Actually, that's wrong. I *know* I can't. I need to know what really happened to her. Will you help me, Darby? Will you help me find my mother?'

48

Finding people, Darby explained to Mickey, wasn't her area of expertise, so she promised to put him in touch with Sue Michaud, who, coincidentally, worked as an investigator for Shapiro and Hager. Sue, she explained, was not only great at her job but also known for her discretion and professionalism, which wasn't always the case with private investigators.

Alone in the car and driving back to Belham, Darby got in touch with Sue and told her about Mickey's situation. Sue agreed to take on the case, and Darby gave her Mickey's contact info. Sue, thankfully, did not ask if Darby had come to a decision involving her own family drama.

The question of whether or not her parents had given up a child for adoption when they had been in high school had been eating at her for days. Every time she pondered it, like now – when she thought of those torn shreds of audio tape sitting inside the envelope – it felt like a blade dunked in ice water was resting against her heart.

Her phone rang. Chris Kennedy was calling.

'You're calling to tell me you've arranged a personal tour of Byrne's house, aren't you?'

'I am indeed,' Kennedy replied. 'Where are you?'

'Driving back to Belham. In fact, I'm almost there.'

'Good. Head on over to Byrne's house. Blake will meet you there.'

'I hate to ask, but why are you calling me instead of Blake?'

'Let's just say he's not interested in becoming a member of the Darby McCormick fan club.'

'We'd probably have to reject his application anyway. It's a very select group.'

Roger Blake was not waiting for her at Byrne's home. Instead, she found a plain-clothes cop sitting in a cruiser parked along the side road that abutted the former priest's backyard – an older, Irish guy with a bloated face caused by too much drinking. She recognized him.

'You were the first responding officer that night,' she said. 'Officer Rich, right?'

He nodded and, as on the night she'd met him, he made no effort to hide his contempt. Rich knew who she was – had made a point telling her so when she'd met him after finding Byrne's body and calling 911. Just to make sure she knew where he stood, Rich had called her 'a rat'.

'Detective Blake won't be joining us,' Rich said.

'Oh? And why's that?'

'He got tied up with something.'

Rich didn't want to talk, which was fine by her. He stuck close by her side and took out his notepad when she entered the bedroom.

The evidence cones were gone, but the floorboards where Byrne, she assumed, had hidden the pictures, Claire Flynn's snow jacket and the cassettes of the girls crying hadn't been placed back in their slots. The bed, which was on rollers, allowing Byrne to move it to access the floorboards, was pushed aside, to the left – the same position she'd seen it in on the night Mickey had called her.

She looked around the room, at the toys covering the bureau and nightstand. The floor. Everywhere she looked she saw clean surfaces. She turned to the patrolman.

'Why wasn't the crime scene dusted for prints?'

'Because there was no crime,' he replied, clearly uninterested in the topic. 'We were dealing with a suicide, not a homicide.'

'But you didn't know that at the time.'

The patrolman looked at her, his boredom reaching his features.

'Just because something appears as a suicide doesn't mean it is one,' Darby said. 'You can never assume. You have to rule out homicide first. That means processing the scene correctly, treating it –'

'Blake is the investigator, and he ruled it a suicide. You got questions, ask him.'

'I would, only he's not here, is he?'

'Not my problem. Now get on with it. I'd like to get home to my wife. We're binge-watching *Game of Thrones*.'

She ignored him and turned her attention to the ceiling beams. On the one Byrne had used to hang himself, the rope was still there, only it had been cut in half. The section tied around Byrne's neck had gone to the lab for analysis. The other part hung limply from the beam.

She doubted the patrolman had a folding ladder in his cruiser, didn't want to ask or engage in any more fruitless conversation. It was clear he wasn't going to cooperate.

She went downstairs, to the kitchen. Rich followed her, jotting down notes on his pad. When she returned to the bedroom with a kitchen chair, she turned on all the available lights. He wrote that down too.

Darby examined the knot. It was called a trucker's hitch, a popular knot she used herself to secure a mattress or some other large piece of furniture to the roof rack of a car or an SUV. She fished a pair of latex gloves out of her back pocket.

'Detective Blake doesn't want you touching any evidence,' Rich said.

'You just told me no crime was committed here. Therefore, there isn't any evidence, correct?'

'Doesn't mean he might not find something down the road, so –'

'I'm going to take a look at this knot. Write that down in your little book.'

Darby moved the knot to the side and, using her flashlight, examined the wood.

'What are you looking for?' he asked.

'Termites.'

'If you're going to be a smartass, I'll remove you.'

No, you won't, Darby thought. The reason Blake had allowed this quid pro quo was because he was worried she might come across something he'd missed. Blake was hedging his bets. If she found nothing, no harm, no foul. But if she did come across something, he'd want to know about it. Only he was too lazy to go there himself.

Darby traded her flashlight for her phone and took several pictures at different angles, the patrolman keeping a close eye on her and writing on his pad.

For the next half-hour, she used her flashlight to carefully examine each of the beams. When she got down from her chair, she examined the bedroom door.

'What are you looking for?' the patrolman asked again.

'Home-decorating tips.'

The man gritted his teeth.

'I'm looking at a bedroom door,' Darby said. 'Before that, I was looking at the ceiling beams. Now I'm going to look inside the other bedroom.'

Darby brushed past him and moved down the narrow hall. It took her a moment to find the light switch.

This bedroom, which clearly belonged to an adult, had the same fifties vibe to it – same ugly colours and furniture that had gone out of fashion decades ago (and, ironically, was probably worth a lot of money in vintage circles). The bedroom didn't have any exposed beams, and the space looked neat and clean except for the areas where the cops and forensic people had been.

She examined both sides of the door and then turned to the patrolman.

'I'm all set,' she said.

'And?'

'I didn't find anything. It was a bust.'

'I think you're full of shit.'

Darby smiled.

'You keep something from us,' he said, 'we'll kick an obstruction charge so far up your ass you'll choke.'

'Duly noted. Any other words of wisdom?'

'Yeah. You're no longer a part of this case. It ends here. That means no more talking to Grace Humphrey, Father Cullen, Mickey and Sean Flynn.'

'Not even to say hello? Seems rather rude, don't you think?'

'If you're smart, you'll pack up your shit and leave Belham,' the patrolman said. 'If you don't, well, you're not going to like what happens next.'

49

Last night, after leaving Byrne's house, Darby had called Heather and asked to meet in person, unaware that the woman had already moved to New York. What Darby wanted to discuss with her was something that was best handled in person. It was easy to hang up on a phone call, harder to walk away from a face-to-face conversation – although Heather, Darby was sure, would have no trouble in doing such a thing. A shuttle flight was cheap and convenient, Darby told her, and she had no problem going to her. Heather had agreed, albeit reluctantly, to meet.

To Darby, New York City always felt like Boston on steroids: taller and wider, meaner, ready to devour you if you were careless or clumsy or just plain stupid. The first time she had gone there had been on a junior-high-school field trip that took place over two days, the big highlight being a stay in an actual New York hotel that, to her, seemed as tall as a skyscraper. The rule she had learned then still applied now: make every effort not to look like a tourist. That meant keeping up with foot traffic and watching where the hell you were going – not like the country bumpkin across the street, who was trying to divide his attention between reading street signs and finding his location on his phone while his family looked around, slightly nervous about the sheer number of people, how fast they were moving, and the homeless-looking

355

person standing few feet away with a big white sign that read THE TIME FOR REDEMPTION IS NOW, ASSHOLE!

That was the great thing about New York. They were never short of free entertainment.

The day was unnaturally warm for winter, in the low sixties, and sunny, not a cloud in the sky. Everyone on the Upper East Side seemed to be out, enjoying the weather. Darby had Kennedy on the phone.

'Can you hear me okay?'

'I can hear you fine,' he replied. 'What's up?'

'Reason I'm calling is that I got in touch with Glassman this morning. He was on vacation. His daughter's wedding, down in Texas.'

'And what did he have to say?' Kennedy's tone made it crystal clear that he didn't have much interest in the answer.

'Cause of death is acute mechanical asphyxiation. The physical markers that Glassman found were all consistent with a case of strangulation: presence of a discontinuous groove on the neck and petechial haemorrhages in the skin of the face and beneath the conjunctivae; a frothy, blood-stained fluid in the air passages; mucus in the back of the mouth and slight acute emphysema, from years of smoking; and oedema of the lungs, with scattered areas of atelectasis. Glassman listed the death as accidental and not suicidal.'

'And, what, you don't buy it?'

'How much do you know about auto-erotic asphyxiation?' Darby, threading her way through the crowds on the sidewalk, saw more than one person glance in her direction.

'I know I don't want to do it,' Kennedy replied.

'Good to know. But I was referring to actual cases.'

'Byrne would be the first one.'

'Okay. I've had experience.'

'Professional or personal?'

'You're on a roll today.'

'My way of blowing off steam. You were saying?'

'Asphyxia is a form of sexual masochism. It's a paraphilic disorder, which means a recurring disorder that involves intense, sexually arousing urges, behaviours and complex fantasies. The key word here is "recurring". Men – and they're predominantly men, and white – who engage in this activity have a history of it.'

'And, I'm guessing, judging by your tone, you found something you didn't like.'

'Glassman found no evidence of prior trauma during the autopsy. No bruising beneath the skin, nothing. A person with a history of this disorder would have it. Before the autopsy, I specifically asked Glassman to look for it.'

'Why?'

'Because I wanted to be sure,' Darby said. 'Which brings me to what I found in Byrne's bedroom last night.' She turned a corner, stopped and glanced around the streets. She got her bearings and continued walking. 'I examined *all* the ceiling beams. There weren't any grooves in the wood or slight abrasions left from repeated usage of rope.'

'That's not exactly a smoking gun.'

'Men who perform this act do it repeatedly, and often in the same place. There would be evidence – rope abrasions on the wood, grooves, like I said. There was nothing, Chris. Byrne hasn't engaged in this activity before. The crime scene was staged. Everything points to it. The physical evidence I found, the fact that the pictures scattered on the floor weren't sexual, that handwritten note he gave me about having had nothing to do with those girls –'

'Don't tell me you honestly bought that shit.'

'Why would he mention it? What's the reasoning?'

'I'll tell all of this to Blake.'

'He's not going to do anything with it.'

'Well, what do you expect me to do with it?'

'I think we need to look into the possibility that someone framed Byrne.'

'*We* can't look into anything. I'm off the case, which means you are too. Besides –'

'Byrne's toxicology screen said he had a lot of morphine in his system. Person with his levels wouldn't be able to put up a fight. He would be totally out of it. The other important thing is his bedroom door. It didn't have a lock on it.'

'The guy lived alone.'

'I know. But men who engage in this activity do it behind locked –'

'Darby, the man was *dying*. He probably didn't give two shits if someone caught him. And who, exactly, was going to catch him? Oh, that's right, *he lived alone*.'

'He wouldn't want to get caught. He wouldn't want a secret like that to get out. He'd go out of his way to protect it even if he were dying.'

'Has anyone ever told you that you have an uncanny ability to induce a migraine-level headache?'

'Someone staged the crime scene. I'd bet my reputation on it – and that's not something I say often.'

'The Byrne case is closed. Blake's there to dot the *i*'s and cross the *t*'s. And, even if you find a smoking gun – which the autopsy info, while interesting, is *not* – Blake isn't going to listen to you or, by extension, me.'

'The night Byrne called in the jacket. Were his body-guards with him?'

'No. He gave them the night off.'

'And that just happens to be the night the jacket is found.' She spotted the restaurant where she was meeting Heather and crossed the street.

'Darby, do you consider me a friend?'

'The guy who attacked me is still out there. He's involved in this.'

'Let this go. They can't all be winners. Cash your cheque and move on to . . . whatever.'

'I'll relay that to Mickey Flynn and the others.'

'Darby –'

She hung up.

Darby got a table near a large window that overlooked the street. The waiter came by for her drink order.

She was sipping her soda water and watching another out-of-towner trying to find out where he was when she saw Mickey's ex-wife heading her way.

50

Heather wasn't smiling but she was clearly enjoying the relief from the bitter cold and, possibly, the gift of being anonymous in such a big city. Her demeanour changed, became more guarded, after she entered the restaurant. Darby stood and waved to her.

She shook the woman's hand. Heather's grip was stiff, her body tense, on high alert.

'So,' Heather said, taking a seat, her tone all business. 'What is so urgent that you had to fly all the way to New York to talk to me in person instead of on the phone?'

'Would you like a drink?'

'I'd like you to tell me what this is all about, so I can put this ugly business behind me.'

'Does Mickey know I'm here?'

'Last night, when we spoke, you asked me not to tell him.'

'Good. I'd like to keep this strictly between you and me.'

Darby could see the unease growing in Heather's eyes.

Where to start? The pictures seemed to be the best way to ease into the conversation. Still, as Darby slid the envelope across the table, she knew full well she was about to drop a torpedo on the woman's life.

'These belong to you,' Darby said, and handed her the envelope holding the pictures and Sean's note.

Heather tried to read Darby for some hint about what

was going on. Then she turned her attention reluctantly to the envelope. Her hands were steady when she opened it.

The first picture showed her and her boyfriend, lover, whoever he was, holding hands as they walked down the steps of the bed-and-breakfast.

Heather's lips parted and the blood drained from her cheeks. Then she caught herself. She swallowed as she looked up, her eyes narrowing as if to say, *I won't let you break me.* It was the same expression she had used that day when Darby had shown up unexpectedly in Rowley: everyone in the world was an adversary. Get ready to fight.

Seeing the pictures, though, had broken something in her, and the fight . . . it didn't so much leave her as it was placed on pause. Darby saw this when Heather slowly turned her head away, to the street, where her gaze jittered over the cars and taxis, as if someone were about to emerge from one of the vehicles to come and rescue her.

Darby said, 'You should read the note.'

Heather snapped her attention back to Darby, her eyes burning with anger.

'I'm sorry to hit you with all of this,' Darby said, and explained how she had come by the pictures through Sean Flynn's lawyer.

'Does Mickey know about the pictures?' Heather asked.

'I haven't told him. And I won't. It's not my place. I thought you should have them.'

'That's very . . . kind of you. Thank you.'

'I take it Sean took those pictures,' Darby said.

'Oh, yes.'

Heather shook her head at some thought as the waiter came by and placed a soda water in front of Darby and asked if they were ready to order lunch. Darby said no, and the waiter stormed off, miffed at the small tip this bill was going to generate.

'When did Sean show these to you?' Darby asked.

Heather slid the photos back into the envelope and dropped it on the table. 'Why are you asking?' She leaned back against her chair, glaring at Darby from across the small table. 'Are you working for Sean?'

'No. I wanted to give these to you.'

'Then why are you asking?'

Darby leaned forward, crossing her arms on the table. 'I'm not here to hurt you or punish you or whatever it is you're thinking. I wanted to give you these pictures, as I said, but I'd be lying if I didn't say that you, Byrne, Sean, what happened to your daughter – they're all connected somehow. I just don't know how.'

'I made a mistake – a huge mistake – and it has torn me up in ways you'll never understand. But I've forgiven myself. It was a long road, but I've forgiven myself, and I've moved on. As for that part of my life' – she pointed to the pictures on the table – 'it's over. I'm not revisiting it.'

Heather snatched her handbag from the ground and got to her feet. 'Please,' Darby said. 'Sit down.'

'Don't ever contact me again. If you do, I'll –'

'Byrne has you on tape.'

Heather resumed her seat. She pulled the chair as close to the table as she could, to keep their conversation as private as possible.

'What do you mean, he has me on tape?'

'I should have said I *think* he has you on tape,' Darby said. 'Let me explain.'

She told Heather about her mother's recorded confession with Father Cullen. Hearing the priest's name caused the colour to drain from the woman's face.

'Did you ever go to Father Cullen for confession?' Darby asked.

Heather struggled to get the words out. 'Yes,' she said, swallowing, her gaze skittering across the table. 'Yes, several times.'

'What about Father Byrne?'

'Only a few times, then I stopped.'

'Why?'

'Because he asked me very personal questions I didn't want to get into.'

'Heather, I'm not trying to pry, but it's important that –'

'I'm not discussing it.'

'Okay,' Darby said. 'Okay.'

Heather looked pained. Mortified.

'I don't know if he has you on tape,' Darby said. 'I do know that Elizabeth Levenson's mother, Judith, sought out Byrne for confession many times and confessed to a lot of things. I thought you should know in case –'

'Where are these tapes now?'

'I don't know. I could be completely wrong in what I'm about to say, but, if I had to make an educated guess, I'd say that Father Cullen has them. If he does, my guess is that he destroyed them.'

'Provided Byrne, in fact, gave him all the tapes.'

'Yes.'

Heather rubbed her face. 'I can't believe this is happening,' she said under her breath.

'I have to ask you a delicate question involving Byrne,' Darby said. 'Did he ever . . . were you ever alone with him?'

'A few times. Why?'

'Did he ever look at you sexually? Speak to you in a sexual way?'

'What kind of question is that?'

'Did he?'

'No. Absolutely not.'

Heather, Darby could tell, was lying.

'I said no.' Heather glared at her, trying to sell the lie. She saw the waiter approaching and sighed. 'Thank God. I need a drink.'

Heather ordered a white wine, Darby a bourbon neat.

'Actually,' Heather said, 'I'll have a bourbon. Make it a double.'

Heather didn't speak until the waiter came back with their drinks.

'Aaron. That was his name.'

'The man in the pictures?' Darby asked.

Heather nodded. Darby sipped her drink. Waited. She didn't want to rush this; there was no reason to rush.

'It happened the year Mickey and I were engaged,' Heather explained. Her voice faltered and she pressed a hand against her mouth as she looked back out at the busy street, at the sea of people moving back and forth across the sidewalks, going about their lives.

Heather said, 'I met him at a party. He was in his late thirties and worked in the financial district in Boston. He was so different from Mickey and the people you and I grew up with – you know, the blue-collar types.' She spoke haltingly, as if the act of speaking was draining her of blood. 'He was so smart in that . . . that bookish way, I guess you could say. Every morning he read the *New York Times* and the *Wall Street Journal*. My father only read the sports section of the *Herald*, and my mother . . . she couldn't have cared less about what was going on in the world outside of Belham. Aaron was passionate about art and architecture. He rented a villa in Tuscany one summer. He had all these stories about travelling through Europe. He loved sailing.'

Heather paused to drink some of her bourbon. She grimaced. 'I don't know how you and Mickey can drink this stuff.'

'I'm Irish,' Darby said. 'We drink anything that tastes like gasoline. It's part of our heritage.'

Heather flashed her a sad, fleeting smile. 'Aaron was . . . he was so well put together. I didn't know anything about investing, and, at that point in my life, the furthest I had ever travelled was to Newport, Rhode Island. But he was interested in me and I was attracted to that. Into discovering why he could like someone like me, I suppose. I didn't understand why. I certainly didn't plan on falling in love with him.'

'It happens,' Darby said, thinking about Coop.

'He knew about Mickey. Knew I loved him – and I did. I didn't hide anything from him. From Aaron, I mean. He knew I was afraid of losing Mickey. Losing what we had. When you fall in love with someone for the first time, especially when you're young, it's so . . . intense. It feels, you know, so special. So *permanent*.'

Darby nodded in understanding. She had felt that way about Mickey, once upon a time. That cliché – you never forget your first love – rang true. Clichés often did.

'Mickey told me about you,' Heather said. 'He loved you, you know.'

'I know.'

'At that time in my life, I believed – I truly believed my heart was only built to love one person. And I thought that person was Mickey. In the end, I chose him because I thought that was where I belonged.'

'Is that why you broke it off with Aaron?'

Heather licked her lips as she shook her head. 'I met Aaron during the summer – another one of my summers in Newport. When September came around, it was time to go back to work, back to Belham. I was a special-education teacher. And Aaron . . . I had convinced myself that someone like him couldn't be seriously interested in someone like me, so I told myself I had made a mistake and broke it off.'

'Only he didn't want to break it off.'

'No,' Heather said quietly. 'He kept coming around. I tried to do the whole let's-be-friends thing – I know that sounds naive and ridiculous – but a part of me wanted him to remain in my life. And we were attracted to each other. That was never going to go away.'

Heather took another pull from her glass, swallowed it like bad medicine. 'What I did was wrong. I was engaged to Mickey. It should never have escalated the way it did with Aaron, but it did, and I knew I had to put an end to it. No matter what Sean told you about that night, I was in the process of breaking up with Aaron.'

'What night?'

'The night I saw Sean at the restaurant.'

Darby nodded as if Sean had, in fact, shared this with her, which he hadn't.

'I met Aaron for dinner at a restaurant in Charlestown,' Heather said. 'I told him it was over, that I couldn't deal with it any more. I went to the ladies' room, and there was Sean standing in the hallway with a big shit-eating grin on his face. When I came out, he was still there. He escorted me back to the table, told me how nice it was to see me, how good I looked, and then he dropped the pictures on the table, just like you did.'

Heather sighed, wrapping her arms around her chest. 'He told me – told us, Aaron was there – that it was time to end this thing. Said if he saw me with Aaron again, he'd show Mickey the pictures. Then Sean said that it would also be in my best interests to broker, you know, some sort of peace treaty between him and Mickey.'

'Did you?'

'I tried. Mickey had no interest.' Heather glanced up at the sky. 'Mickey and I were living together at the time, and every day when Mickey came home from work, I worried that Sean had said something to him. I should have come clean and told him, but I didn't. Maybe I should have.'

Darby didn't know what to say. Sometimes it was better to say nothing. She kept quiet.

But, for whatever reason, her silence had the reverse effect. Instead of comforting Heather with a sense of understanding and sympathy, it seemed to anger her. Tears spilled down her cheeks, and that stony resolve that carried her through her days came roaring back.

'You have no right to judge me,' Heather said, her voice clear and strong.

'I'm not judging you.'

'Of course you are. Everyone does.'

Darby was about to speak when Heather cut her off. 'Did I blame Mickey for allowing my daughter to go up the Hill all by herself? You're goddamn right I did. But I never told him that. I had to be the good girl and swallow it back because of what I'd done to him. I wanted to scream it at him, but I never did because I knew how those words would cut him to the bone. Accidents happen, and what happened to me was an accident too. When I found out I was pregnant, as much as it killed me, I had to do it. I knew it was wrong and immoral and I knew that I was committing murder, but I had to do it. I couldn't bring this other man's baby into our marriage. It was wrong, but I did it. I did it because I chose Mickey. Because I loved him. And then God punished me.'

Darby stayed very still. Heather had admitted to having an abortion. Judith Levenson had also said she'd had an abortion. Was that the connection? What did it mean?

'It was a mistake,' Heather said, her face crinkling, on the verge of breaking into full-blown sobs. 'Everyone should be allowed one big mistake in life. You shouldn't have to pay for it forever, but I did. The doctor screwed up the procedure – it was a miracle Claire was born – and even though I told Father Byrne how sorry I was, how much what I'd done was killing me, he said that he couldn't forgive me. He told me I was a monster – a sinner, and that God would never forgive me – and he was right. God punished me and took my baby away. *My* baby. *My* Claire.'

Heather couldn't stand up fast enough. The top of her thigh hit the underside of the table; it tipped over and Heather's highball glass fell on to the floor and shattered. Heather grabbed her handbag and stormed away. Darby got up but she didn't go after her. She stuffed two twenties, more than enough to cover the bill, under her highball glass and then she grabbed the envelope with the photographs with one hand, and reached for her phone with the other.

51

Darby thought about the photos. The moments they had frozen in time weren't about cheating; they were about comfort. Aaron wasn't kissing her; he was hugging her, consoling her after the abortion.

Did Mickey know? Darby suspected he didn't. If Heather hadn't told him about her affair, why would she tell him about aborting another man's child?

But Byrne knew about it, because Heather had confessed it to him.

Judith Levenson had also had an abortion and confessed it to Byrne. Darby knew this because Byrne had shared that information with her, that day at his house.

Two women who had had abortions and confessed their sins to Byrne when he was a priest were also the mothers of young girls who had been abducted, allegedly by the same priest. That was one hell of a coincidence.

Darby needed a reasonably quiet spot where she could make a phone call – a near-impossible task in a city as busy and as loud as New York. The restaurant was too noisy, but the alley she found outside, between two buildings, would work.

Judith Levenson answered the phone.

'I'm glad you called,' Judith said. 'I feel horrible about the other day.'

'Don't. I was glad I was there to listen. I need to ask you a question.'

'Okay.'

'When we spoke, you mentioned having your pregnancy . . . terminated. I know this is going to sound like an odd question, but may I ask you where you had it done?'

Darby heard the woman take in a long breath.

'I know this is personal, but it might be important.'

'I don't mind your asking.' Her voice, though, sounded stiff. Cold. There was a long pause, and then she said, 'Concord, New Hampshire.'

'Describe the place to me.'

'It looked like a house. That's the first thing I remember. And there wasn't a sign out front. Back then, if you had that . . . procedure, you did it in secret. It's not like it is nowadays, when you can go on the Internet and find a clinic.'

'Describe the outside of the house to me. What did it look like? Was it blue?'

'White,' Judith said without hesitation.

'You're sure.'

'I remember everything about that day. How I had to climb this really steep set of concrete steps. I'll never forget those steps. It was climbing the mountain to judgement, is how I felt.'

Just like in the picture, Darby thought. Judith was describing the building Darby had thought was a bed-and-breakfast in the photo of Heather and her lover, Aaron.

'When I came out,' Judith said, 'I was in so much

discomfort and still so woozy that Stan had to hold on to me, help me down the steps because they were so steep. I kept feeling like I was going to fall.'

'Thank you.'

'Does that help?'

'It does. I appreciate your candour.'

'Does this have to do with Father Byrne?' Judith's tone jumped, brightening with hope. 'Is there some sort of break in the case? Something new?'

Darby didn't want to get into it, give the woman any sense of false hope. 'No,' she said. 'Not at the moment. But Judith?'

'Yes?'

'If I do find out *anything*, I will let you know. You have my word.'

'Thank you.'

The first girl Byrne abducted was seven-year-old Mary Hamilton, from New Bedford, Massachusetts. Darby didn't have the case file with her, but she had programmed the phone numbers listed on the file into her iPhone. She dialled Nancy Hamilton's home number first and got the woman's voicemail.

She didn't hold out much hope when she dialled the woman's cell, as Nancy Hamilton hadn't picked up a single time or returned any of her calls. Darby was surprised when someone on the end of the line answered.

'Mrs Hamilton?'

'Dr McCormick,' the woman said curtly, 'I want you to hear me and hear me now. You are to stop calling me, you are not to come by my house. Do you understand? I have no interest in discussing –'

'I'm sorry for bothering you, but this is in regard to your daughter's case.'

'I don't want to talk any more to you people.'

'I understand. I –'

'You've called day after day, and I've told you people everything I know about that goddamn monster, and I'm done with it. Do you understand? I'm *done*.'

'Are you Catholic?'

Nancy Hamilton reacted as if Darby had reached through the line and slapped her face. 'What did you say?'

'I need to know if you're Catholic. Wait, *do not hang up*. This is *extremely* important.'

A moment of silence, and then the woman said, 'I was Catholic. Emphasis on *was*.'

'Did you ever go to Richard Byrne, back when he was a priest, for confession?'

The woman didn't answer.

'Mrs Hamilton, please, this could be very important.'

'Several times. Satisfied?'

Not yet, Darby thought. She didn't want to plunge ahead, but she could tell the woman was moments away from hanging up. Time to roll the dice.

'I'm going to ask you one last question. It's very personal but it's critical that you answer it.' Darby closed her eyes and took in a deep breath. 'Did you ever have an abortion?'

A dead, ringing silence came from the other end of the line.

When the woman spoke, her voice teetered between fury and tears. 'My daughter has been dead for twenty-four years. I'm not reliving it any more. You're not going to steal this life away from me too.'

'Mrs Hamilton, I –'

The sting of the dial tone came next.

Darby thought about calling Kennedy. But what could he do? He'd been sidelined.

She had an idea. She dialled another number as she left the alley to wave down a taxi.

52

That morning, Mickey woke up early, showered, dressed and headed into Boston.

Sue Michaud, the investigator for the law firm, had called him yesterday morning, and, after Mickey explained what he needed, she offered to dig in for the low, low price of two hundred an hour. Mickey didn't hesitate. He said yes.

What surprised him, though, was how fast Sue got back to him. She had called him back later that evening, as he and Jim were wrapping up for the day at the job in Newton.

'That was quick,' Mickey said.

'We're one big happy global family, all of our secrets loaded on the Internet.' Sue Michaud had the kind of rough, deep voice, with a thick Boston accent, he associated with women who smoked and drank beers and got into fistfights at Bruins hockey games back in the old days at the Boston Garden. 'The address on the envelope you gave me belongs to a café in Paris. Your mother never worked there – at least not under the name René Flynn.'

Sue told him she spoke French – definitely not the sort of skill a woman who got into fistfights at hockey games would have – and went on to say how she'd spoken to the owner of the café, who told her how the business had been owned and operated by the same family for two generations, the family having also branched out and built two very successful restaurants in the area. He had no record of a woman named René Flynn working at either place, nor any memory of her, but not all his records had made their way into the company's computer system. It was possible, Sue said, his mother had gone by another name when she arrived in Paris, maybe even had legally changed it for fear of Sean finding her.

Mickey had now caught his mother in two lies: paying for the tuition at St Stephen's and working at the café.

'Timothée Peltier,' Sue said, 'is still alive. He's still the owner and operator of his father's paper company, Peltier Paper. He's sixty-eight and still lives on the Île Saint-Louis. He married only once, a woman named Margot Vermette. The marriage happened about two years before your mother married your father. Timothée divorced Vermette in November of 1976.'

'That was the year my mother moved back there.'

'He never remarried. No kids either.'

Mickey recalled Sean's comment about Timothée not wanting children.

'He's constantly on the move, Timothée,' Sue said. 'He has multiple phone numbers. I finally managed to get his contact info by pretending to be the vice-president of some big-name paper company here in the States.'

'What did he say about my mother?'

'You asked me to track him down for you, and I did. You didn't say anything about my talking to him.'

'I don't speak French.'

'But he speaks English. A decent amount, anyway. I can

be on the other line, translate for you, when you talk to him. *If* you want to talk to him.'

'I do,' Mickey said. 'Absolutely.'

Now, though? As he drove, he wasn't so sure. He was afraid of what other lies his mother had told him. He was afraid of discovering Sean had been telling him the truth. He was afraid of a lot of things right now.

He recalled two lines from the first letter: *And remember to keep this quiet. I don't have to remind you what your father would do to me if he found out where I was hiding.*

And now the second letter: *I'm coming for you. I know it's taking longer than I said, and I know you've been patient. I need you to keep being patient . . . Don't let your father get this address . . . If you father knows where I'm hiding – well, I don't have to remind you of what he is capable.* Mickey pictured his mother dropping each of these letters off at a mailbox or whatever they called them over there in Paris, his mother knowing exactly what she was doing, mailing him lies. He knew that now.

And yet . . . and yet, on some level, even before he'd found out about Sean's trip to Paris, hadn't a part of him believed his mother wasn't coming home? Hadn't he known that, over the course of the months she was gone, if she had *really* wanted to come back for him, wouldn't she have made some sort of arrangement? Some sort of effort? Wouldn't she have tried *something*?

Your mother could be very persuasive with that soft, gentle voice of hers. Smoothest liar I've ever met.

Funny thing about the mind – how it could take each trauma and shave off the parts it didn't like. Made things easier to store, he supposed. Or maybe it was a survival mechanism. Maybe the brain simply couldn't handle cata-loguing the polarizing depths of how some people could love and hate and kill in equal measures. Maybe the rea-son why he couldn't see himself as an alcoholic with a violent temper that mirrored his murderous father's was the same reason why he couldn't see Claire willingly walk-ing off with Byrne or his mother never coming home because she didn't have any room for him in her new life. To accept the truth was to accept all of it, and he could feel his mind starting to crumble under the sheer weight of it.

And now here he was, heading into Boston, to con-firm it.

Sean's words from that day in prison came back to him: *Admit it. Your life was so much simpler when you were busy hating me.*

53

Darby woke up that morning, in the uncomfortable hotel bed with its stiff sheets, and stared at the ceiling with her hands clasped behind her head. She couldn't shake the feeling she was grasping at straws.

Still, she couldn't discount a few key facts.

Fact No. 1: Byrne's body did not exhibit the physical signs of someone who had engaged regularly in auto-erotic asphyxiation. She did not believe he had suddenly decided to try it out, at his advanced age, while hovering close to death, and in pain.

Still, it *was* possible.

But *if* he didn't hang himself – and her professional experience kept telling her he had not – then someone had killed him. Maybe the same man who had tried to kill her. Or maybe the two were completely independent of one another. Byrne had a lot of enemies. A lot of them, Darby was sure, wanted him dead.

But wanting someone dead and putting a plan in place and – this was the important piece – actually going through with the plan were two completely different things. The only person she knew who had tried to kill Byrne was Mickey Flynn.

Could Mickey have killed Byrne? If given the opportunity, yes. He had gone to Byrne's home once to kill him, and, on the second time he returned, if Byrne hadn't already been dead, Darby was sure Mickey would have tried to beat the truth out of the former priest, maybe even have gone so far as to torture the man.

What Darby kept coming back to, what kept gnawing at her, was the actual crime scene. The easiest thing would have been to smother Byrne with a pillow. Or shoot him.

Fact No. 2: The pictures of the girls were not sexual, or sexually provocative. They seemed too neat and clean too – not something you'd find stored underneath a dusty floorboard. Same with Claire Flynn's snow jacket. And, regarding the pictures: they showed no sign of wear. They were too crisp, like something hot off a colour photo-printer.

And there was Byrne's note to her, where he stressed that he'd had nothing to do with killing the Snow Girls. That he was, in fact, dying with a clear conscience.

If the crime scene was staged, someone had put a lot of thought into it. Someone had hanged Byrne and put all the props – the pictures of the girls, the clothing – on the floor.

Three people had access to Byrne: Grace Humphrey and the two bodyguards, one of whom was dead. The Humphrey woman didn't look strong enough to physically handle Byrne by herself. Then again, Byrne was most likely physically and mentally incapacitated by the morphine. Maybe she had given him an extra dose. Maybe she'd had help. Maybe, maybe, maybe.

What Darby needed was motive, and she didn't have one.

Money might be a motive; Grace Humphrey had been listed in Byrne's will. Did Byrne tell her? Had she taken the money? Darby remembered the woman had said she was going to donate it to charity. Did Humphrey follow through or was she blowing smoke? There was one way to find out.

Darby whipped back the covers, and, as she headed to the shower, she considered Fact No. 3: Judith Levenson and Heather Flynn were both Catholics and had had abortions. Both had sought forgiveness from Father Richard Byrne. Both of their daughters had been abducted and were never seen again. Father Byrne was the prime suspect in each case. And, while Nancy Hamilton hadn't come out and confirmed she'd had an abortion, she had certainly reacted strongly to the question.

So Darby had two, possibly three, women who'd had abortions and gone to confession to seek absolution from Father Byrne. Two, possibly three, women who'd had young girls who were abducted and disappeared, with Byrne as the main suspect. That was too much of a co-incidence to ignore. Belham PD, though, would ignore it. They weren't going to devote time and manpower – both of which required money – to chasing down a wild theory.

Darby had the luxury of time. She didn't report to anyone. Showered and dressed, she headed out and drove to Grace Humphrey's house. The only available parking spot was at the far end of the street. Darby parked and walked the rest of the way.

Two cars were parked in the woman's driveway. Darby climbed the front steps. The front windows were open but the blinds were drawn, and there was a two-inch gap between the windowsill and the shades. Darby wanted to check to see if Grace was awake – it was 8.30 a.m. – so she bent down and peered through the screen, relieved to see a shadow moving across the far wall. Grace Humphrey was home and, judging by the faint *chick-chink* noise Darby heard, the woman was probably unloading her dishwasher.

Darby walked to the front door and rang the bell, expecting to hear footsteps. She didn't. Darby waited almost a full minute and then went back to the window and bent down. Grace's shadow was no longer moving; she was standing absolutely still.

'Miss Humphrey, it's Darby McCormick. May I talk with you for a moment?'

A pair of legs came out from the kitchen. By the time Darby had stood up, Grace had cracked open the front door. She looked slightly embarrassed.

'Sorry, I thought you might have been a reporter,' she said. 'Please, come in.'

The air inside was cool and heavy with a lemon-scented cleaner. The bookcases were bare, the contents most likely packed away in the neatly stacked and labelled boxes near the window.

'I didn't know you were moving,' Darby said.

'Neither did I until a few days ago.' The woman brightened. 'This amazing opportunity came up and, well, I decided to jump on it.'

'Judging by that smile on your face, I'm guessing it has nothing to do with the hospice business.'

Her smile gained some wattage. 'A good friend of mine works at this very high-end spa in Phoenix, Arizona. She called the other night and we got to talking, and she started telling me how they're looking for a new massage therapist. Sally – she's my friend – knows I used to be a massage therapist years ago. So Sally was telling me about how nice the weather is out there, you know, warm and sunny all the time – great weather if you suffer from fibromyalgia.'

'How long have you suffered from it?'

'For years. Doctors don't know the exact cause, but people who have it suffer from constant pain and fatigue, and cold climates and places like New England, where the weather is constantly changing, only aggravate the condition. I'm really looking forward to it, especially after everything that's happened here.'

'Sounds exciting.'

A short and uncomfortable pause followed. Darby said, 'I'm sure you're sick and tired of answering questions.'

Grace's smile was polite. 'I'd be fibbing if I said no.'

'Reporters are still bothering you?'

'The calls have pretty much tapered off, but every now and then someone will drop by unannounced.'

'I'm sorry. I should have called.'

Grace reddened with embarrassment. 'I wasn't referring to you.'

'It's okay. I understand where you're coming from, I truly do. I've come across some information and wanted to run it by you.'

Grace looked puzzled. 'I thought the case was closed – at least that was what Detective Blake had told me.'

'I'm just trying to tie off a few loose ends.'

'He said I shouldn't talk to you. That you're not working with the Belham police.'

'I'm not. I'm working for Mickey Flynn. I'm sure you'd want to help out in any way you could.'

'Of course. Here, let's sit.'

Darby took the same spot she'd had the last time she'd been invited inside. She caught sight of the gold crucifix the woman was wearing. 'Did Father Byrne ever talk to you about any special work or service he did for the Church?'

'Such as?'

'It seems a lot of women went to him for the sacrament of reconciliation after they elected to have their pregnancies terminated.'

The shock on Grace Humphrey's face barely masked her disgust.

'It's a different time now,' Darby said. 'I know the current Pope has allowed all priests to absolve women who've had such procedures. But, go back a decade, and only a bishop could grant forgiveness for this sin. A bishop or a priest who specialized in this area. Not many priests were permitted to do it.'

'As well they shouldn't. We're talking about murder.'

Darby didn't want to get into a political debate. 'I hear you,' she said.

'I know some priests forgive that sort of thing – just as some priests and cardinals knowingly shuffled sexual predators to other parishes and then covered up their disgusting actions. To use your power to hide such things – to forgive such things – is an absolute disgrace.'

The room had an awful stillness to it.

The indignation set in Grace's face slowly melted away, her features softening, slipping back into the bright and pleasant woman who had greeted her at the door.

'I'm sorry,' Grace said. 'I didn't mean to get on my soapbox.'

Darby's instincts told her to probe further. 'No apology necessary,' she said. 'I completely understand.' Then, to establish a rapport, she lied: 'I feel exactly the same way.'

'It's just . . . what happened here in Boston with Cardinal Law, and now what you've just told me about Richard – it makes it hard to keep believing.'

'In God?'

'The Church,' she replied. 'When I was growing up, I never considered the Catholic Church a political organization. But that's exactly what it is. A business. It's always been that way, I suppose, but it didn't sink in until my sister tried to get her first marriage annulled. She'd been married for two years and had a baby girl, when her husband just packed up and left. Wanted nothing to do with her any more. The Church wouldn't annul her marriage on account of the baby. Now take that example and compare it with the son of late senator you-know-who here in Massachusetts who was married for something like twenty years and had four children. The Church granted that annulment right away. It's disheartening, but that's the way things get done in life – and in the Catholic Church. You wouldn't believe the stories Richard told me.'

'Like what?'

'He just talked about how political the Church was. I'm

sure some of that – well, maybe a lot of it – came from the bitterness at being defrocked. He missed it. Being a priest, I mean.'

'And the cloak of secrecy it provided for him.'

'Yes,' Grace added bitterly. 'The side of Richard that hurt those girls and kept those things hidden under the floorboards of his bedroom – I didn't know anything about that man.'

Darby felt her heart skip when the woman talked about the floorboards – a detail, she was sure, only the police knew. She kept her face neutral, nodded in understanding.

'I just knew the man who had cancer.' Grace shrugged. 'I've told you everything I know now.'

Yes, Darby thought. *You certainly have.*

54

Sue Michaud was a thin, striking older woman with short grey hair and stylish glasses and she had an office the size of his bedroom, the walls full of Boston Red Sox and Patriots memorabilia, including a signed football from Tom Brady. Her handshake packed a lot of punch.

'Sorry I had to push our time back,' Sue said, shutting her door. It was made of glass, as were the walls, Mickey surprised at how busy the law firm was on a late Sunday morning, everyone moving or reading with a wired, under-the-gun energy. 'Had a little family emergency. My dog shat all over my kitchen floor this morning.'

Hearing the relaxed way she spoke eased something in him, Mickey having gone through life with a chip on his shoulder at how a lot of 'educated' people looked down at – and talked down to – blue-collar workers.

'Sorry for my language, and for being blunt,' Sue said. 'I'm not good with small talk and BS. A lot of people have a hard time with that, especially men, which probably explains why I'm still single.' She pointed to a small table in the corner. 'Take that chair over there.'

Mickey sat down at a small conference table. The big bay window overlooked Post Office Square, which was empty, given that it was the weekend.

'So,' she said, sitting. 'Timothée Peltier.'

Mickey waited.

'I'll try his home number first,' she said. 'If he doesn't answer, don't leave a message. We'll work our way through the numbers I've got.'

Underneath the table, Mickey wiped his palms on the thighs of his trousers.

'I'll be sitting at my desk, listening on the phone. You probably won't need me – his English is pretty good, like I said – but, if you do, I'm here. Unless you want to speak to him privately.'

'No. No, that's fine.'

'Would you like some water? Coffee?'

'Water would be good.'

She came back with a bottle of Evian. He nearly drained it, his mouth was so dry, but Sue wasn't watching. She had gone back to her desk, where she now sat, dialling the number. She nodded to Mickey to pick up the phone in front of him.

The receiver felt slick and greasy in his damp hand. Mickey heard the connection go through, heard the ring and felt his stomach clench, a part of him wanting to hang up.

Click, and a man's voice said, *'Allô.'*

Mickey's breath caught in his throat.

'Allô?'

'Timothée Peltier?'

'C'est Timothée.'

'I'm sorry, I don't speak French. I'm calling for –'

'This is Timothée.'

'My name is Mickey Flynn. I'm René Flynn's son.'

A long pause came from the other end of the line. Mickey spoke into it, spoke quickly, suddenly terrified that the man was going to hang up: 'I have pictures of you and my mother together in France. I know she moved out there to be with you. I know all about you, your . . . connection to her.' The words were tripping over each other in their rush to get out.

Trickles of silence as Mickey drew in a sharp breath, picturing Timothée dressed in a sharp suit and wearing one of those scarf things around his neck and sitting in some fancy antique chair in his mansion or whatever they called them over there, Timothée debating whether or not he should speak – or just simply hang up.

Mickey said, 'Five minutes is all I'm asking. Five minutes and I'll let you get back to your life.'

'*Jésus doux et humble.*'

'Look at it from my point of view,' Mickey said. 'If you were in my shoes, wouldn't you want to know what happened to your mother?'

On the other end of the line Timothée sighed heavily against the receiver. Mickey propped an elbow on the table and dropped his forehead against his palm and rubbed the area above his eyebrows.

'This is . . . I would rather not have this conversation.'

Mickey tightened his grip on the receiver. 'I need to know,' he said. 'Please.'

The silence gathered, Mickey wanting to scream into it, when Timothée said, 'Francine Broux. Your mother's name, when she returned to Paris.' His voice was hesitant. Nervous. 'She changed it. She was terrified of your father.'

'My father flew over there and found her.'

A pause. 'Yes.'

'You know all about it?'

A longer pause. 'I do.'

'What happened?'

'He beat her. He broke her nose. Two of her ribs.'

Mickey rubbed his tongue against the roof of his mouth, finding it dry.

'She had a life here – a nice life,' Timothée said. 'I loved her very much.'

There was a hitch in Timothée's breath that told Mickey to hang up and run.

'It happened about a year ago,' Timothée said. 'Chest pains. In the middle of the night. I rushed her to the hospital but it was – it didn't matter. She was gone.'

All this time his mother had been alive.

Mickey felt the sting of tears and tried to blink them away. 'I met you once, didn't I? In Boston? I was with her, doing a Christmas tour in Beacon Hill. She introduced you as a friend of hers.'

Beats of silence. Mickey was about to speak when Timothée said, 'Yes.'

'Only you didn't plan on her showing up with me.'

Timothée didn't answer.

'So that night,' Mickey said. 'That night was about, what, her trying to convince you to take me in?'

'Early on, I knew one thing about myself for sure: I did not want to be a parent. I'm very selfish. Very self-centred and self-absorbed. I have to be, in many ways, in order to conduct my business. But I also –'

'She never had any intention of coming back for me, did she?'

Timothée didn't answer.

Mickey said, 'She dropped those letters in the mail,

and, when she didn't come for me, she knew I'd blame Sean because of the violent history they shared. She knew I'd think Sean had killed her because, well, that's what he did for a living.'

'I did not agree with your mother's choice.'

'But you don't regret it either.'

'We were young,' Timothée offered. 'When you are young, you do foolish things. You do not often stop to think through the consequences. How you'll have to live with them, your choices.'

'Did she ever regret her decision?'

'I cannot speak for your mother.'

'You just did,' Mickey said.

55

Darby had found a kerb spot about two blocks up from Grace Humphrey's duplex, a spot under a tree that offered a good view of the woman's front door, porch and drive-way. She'd been here for a good two hours and nothing had happened. A part of her said she was wasting her time. The other part, the stronger part, told her she was on to something and urged patience.

Her seat tilted back, she was wrapping up a conversation with Sue Michaud when she got an incoming call from Kennedy.

'I've got to take this,' Darby told Sue. 'Thanks for your help.'

Then, to Kennedy: 'You got my message?'

'You said you had some news,' Kennedy replied. He sounded tired. Uninterested.

Darby told him about the abortions, and Grace Humphrey's reaction.

Kennedy sighed like a teacher dealing with a student who wouldn't stop asking questions, who refused to leave him alone and go away. 'And?'

Darby, parked down the street, had a clear view of Humphrey's driveway. 'You don't find it the least bit odd three women —'

'Two,' Kennedy said. 'You told me Nancy Hamilton didn't confirm it.'

'She didn't come right out and say it, but, fine, I'll give that one to you. So we have two women who had abortions and also have young girls who are missing and sought out Byrne for confession. Oh, and Byrne was also considered the prime suspect in those abductions.'

'It's interesting, that's for sure.'

'*Interesting?* What about Humphrey's reaction?'

'The woman's a proud Christian. Wears a cross outside her blouse at all times. I'm not surprised she had a strong reaction.'

'Would you go on a religious rant like that in front of a cop or a stranger?'

'It happens more than you think. She probably –'

'She said the items were stored under the floorboards in his bedroom. That information hasn't been printed anywhere, as far as I can tell.' After leaving Humphrey's house, Darby had used her phone to go online and scour the Internet for any mention of the floorboards or the items recovered from the bedroom.

'Blake probably mentioned it to her,' Kennedy said.

'Come on, Chris. Blake wouldn't go into that level of detail with her. He wouldn't share key aspects of the case.'

'You don't know him. The man's an idiot. This one time, he –'

'What do we really know about her?'

'We did a background check on her. She's clean as a whistle. No trouble with the law – the woman has never had so much as a parking ticket.'

'She said she's been speaking to a friend in Arizona, this woman named Sally.'

'And?'

393

And I had my friend Sue Michaud look into her cell-phone records, Darby wanted to say. *There isn't a single phone call to Arizona.*

Darby was on shaky ground here. Obtaining someone's phone records or recording their conversations without consent was considered illegal in the state of Massachusetts and punishable by law – as was hacking into someone's medical records. Sue had also shared with her some other interesting news about Grace Humphrey: the woman didn't suffer from fibromyalgia, at least according to her medical records, which were scattered all over the country. Grace Humphrey moved around – a lot.

'Let's just say I have reason to believe she's lying about a number of things.'

'I don't want to know,' Kennedy said.

A cream-coloured Lexus came to a stop at the corner of Dibbons Street and then banged a quick right into Humphrey's driveway.

'In fact,' Kennedy said, 'I'm going to pretend this conversation never happened.'

At first, Darby thought the Lexus was going to back up and turn around; then Grace came out of her front door and down the stairs, one hand clutching both a bulky, black leather briefcase and her handbag. She looked around the street, to see if she was being watched.

Darby had already sunk further down in her seat. She peered over the dashboard and saw Grace leaning into the passenger's-side window of the Lexus.

'This suddenly got interesting,' Darby said.

'What?'

Grace was no longer holding the briefcase, just her handbag. Darby said, 'Something's going down.'

'Where are you?'

'Watching Humphrey's house.'

'Jesus Christ.'

'The guy that attacked me,' she said. 'I stabbed him in his right knee. A driver has just stepped out of a Lexus? He's limping, Chris. He's putting all his weight on the left leg.'

'You recognize him?'

'No. I've never seen his face before. He's about six-one, salt-and-pepper hair, medium build. He's wearing a white shirt and chinos.'

'And Humphrey? What's she doing?'

'She's behind the wheel of the Lexus . . . Now she's backing out of the driveway. You got a pen? I have the plate number.'

'Darby –'

'Grow a sack, will you? Look, you brought me into this – and don't hand me that bullshit that the case is over. Send someone here to watch the house until you arrive, okay? Just do that for me. And run that plate.' She gave him a number. 'I'll follow Humphrey. Keep your phone handy.'

Darby hung up and started the car. The Lexus had turned left and was now driving up Grafton. Darby pulled out from her spot and followed.

56

For the next two hours, Darby followed Grace Humphrey as the woman drove on Route 93 and then 89, passing through a good chunk of New Hampshire and then heading into Vermont with no sign of slowing down.

Tailing someone when there are no cars between you and the target is difficult. Right now, Darby and Grace were travelling on a quiet, two-lane stretch of highway lined with trees on both sides, the Lexus a good way ahead but still visible and still moving at a steady six-five. Grace Humphrey hadn't sped up once. Either the woman wasn't in a rush to get to her destination, or she was being a stickler for the speed limits, possibly – maybe – because she didn't want to take the chance of getting pulled over.

What was she up to?

Her phone rang. Kennedy was calling.

'About time,' Darby said, half kidding. 'I left you two messages.'

'I know. And I texted you back and told you I would call when I had something to tell you. I now have something to tell you. You still have eyes on Humphrey?'

'Yep.'

'The Lexus she's driving belongs to a gentleman named Gregory Young. He's from the great city of Medford. Married, two kids, used to be a cop and took early retirement about six years ago – I don't know the reasons why yet.'

'But you're working on it.'

'Of course. My job in life is to serve you, be at your beck and call.' Kennedy had gone back to sounding like his old sarcastic, ball-busting self. *He must have found something*, Darby thought. 'I can tell you two things about Young, the first of which is that he was arrested for disorderly conduct – this was after he retired – for . . . wait for it . . . protesting at an abortion clinic.'

'Look at you, being a cop and putting the pieces together. What's your second piece of info?'

'The man is a regular Mr Clean. For the past hour, I've been watching him through my binoculars, scrubbing down the walls in Humphrey's apartment. I'm thinking of hiring him to clean my place.'

'Say it.'

'Say what?'

'Say that I was right.'

'I will say this is starting to stink. I will say that he looks like he's in a lot of pain and most of it seems to be centred on his right leg. I will also tell you I had an interesting conversation with Halloran's father.'

'About what?'

'You told me Halloran said his old man spoke to him about you. Turns out that's a crock of shit. The father said he never spoke to his son about you. Said he was hardly on speaking terms with Danny.'

'I'm still waiting, Chris.'

'Stay on Humphrey. Don't lose her.'

The sun that had greeted her this morning was now gone, replaced by dark-grey clouds. Darby watched the Lexus dip over the horizon. She stepped on the gas a little to catch up, wondering if Humphrey was heading to Canada.

Then Darby encountered a long stretch of empty road, the Lexus nowhere in sight. A flutter of anxiety brushed the walls of her heart, and then she saw, on the far right, a Mobil station and a Burger King. *If she didn't pull in there, she must've taken the exit right beyond the gas station.*

Less than a minute later, Darby had her answer: the Lexus was parked at one of the full-service pumps. She didn't know whether Humphrey was in the car; maybe she had left for a bathroom break or to get out and stretch, grab something to eat. But it was her car, no question.

Darby did a three-point turn and parked at a self-service pump three lanes over, near the back of the station, figuring she might as well get gas since she didn't know how much longer Humphrey was going to be driving. Darby's car wasn't exactly concealed, but Humphrey would have to look behind her in order to see it.

Darby was in the middle of refuelling when she saw Humphrey walk out of Burger King's front doors. She had her handbag slung across a shoulder, a bag of food in one hand, the other gripping a bladder-busting-sized soft-drink cup with a straw. Humphrey couldn't see her: her back was towards Darby, and, as Darby watched her, she noticed the woman took her time walking back to the car – and she wasn't looking around as she had earlier, when she'd left her house. Grace Humphrey seemed relaxed. Good.

Humphrey climbed back in the Lexus and started the car. Darby waited a moment, wanting to give the woman a head start. Then Darby climbed back into her car, her tank full, and she saw Humphrey drive across the lot and park in front of a coin-operated air-hose pump and a relic from her childhood: an honest-to-God payphone. Humphrey got back out of her car and walked towards the payphone.

The call lasted thirty, maybe forty seconds. Humphrey returned to her car but she didn't drive way.

Two minutes passed.

Five.

Humphrey was still here.

Was she eating her lunch? Darby couldn't see Humphrey, only the back of the woman's car.

What if she was waiting here for someone to arrive? She had just used a payphone, not her cell. Why? Was she afraid of having the call logged on her cell? Did she know she was being followed?

Darby was bothered by the idea of someone coming here to meet Humphrey; she couldn't follow two people at once. There was a chance, possibly, they'd hop in one car and drive somewhere.

Right now Grace Humphrey was alone. Darby decided not to take the chance and wait it out. She started her car, pulled away from the pump and parked on the opposite side of the station. After she pocketed her keys, she grabbed her phone, got out and started to run.

Darby opened the passenger's door and threw herself inside. Grace Humphrey jumped in surprise, the burger and fries spread out on the waxy yellow paper on her lap spilling to the floor.

'No one from Belham PD told you where Byrne's items were stored,' Darby said. 'And yet you knew they were stored underneath the floorboards in Byrne's bedroom. How is that?'

'I overheard the police talking about it. Detective Blake and his partner. That's the truth.'

'Good. Then you won't mind talking to the police.'

Grace showed no surprise – at least none that Darby could detect. 'Who did you call from the payphone?' Darby asked.

'A friend. Her name is Tina Simpson. She lives in Woodstock, Vermont.'

'Why didn't you use your cell?'

'I can't get a signal up here.' The woman saw the doubt creep across Darby's face. 'Go ahead and check if you want.'

'Why aren't you on your way to Arizona?'

'I need to visit a friend first.' Then, with a bit of indignation, she added, 'Is visiting a friend in another state a crime?'

Grace Humphrey, it seemed, had an answer for everything. Darby said, 'Let's take a drive.'

'Where?'

'Belham. I'm sure you're anxious to get back there to return this car to your friend Gregory Young.'

Again, Humphrey showed no surprise. 'I'll do whatever you want,' she said. 'Just please don't hurt me. May I put on my seatbelt?'

'Be my guest.'

Darby sat half twisted in her seat, watching the woman carefully as Grace slowly fastened her seatbelt. Grace pulled out of the station, turned left and drove back down the highway. She stuck to the speed limit and kept both hands on the steering wheel, at two and ten o'clock. There was something creepy about the calm way she was conducting herself.

'Your friend Young,' Darby said. 'What's he doing inside your house?'

'Knowing Gregg, he's probably cleaning.'

That took Darby by surprise; she'd been expecting to catch Grace in a lie.

Grace said, 'I'm in a lot of pain right now, so I called Gregg and asked if he would come over and help me clean.'

'And here you are, driving to Vermont.'

'Gregg said I should get away, in case any reporters came by the house. That way I wouldn't have to deal with them.'

'You have an answer for everything, don't you?'

'I'm telling you the truth.' A grin tugged at the corner of her mouth. 'You'll see.'

'You don't have fibromyalgia,' Darby said.

Still no change in Grace's expression.

'And you never received any phone call or made any phone calls to Arizona,' Darby said. 'We've had you checked out.'

Grace said nothing. She looked relaxed.

'Not going to try to deny it?' Darby said.

'You've already made up your mind about me.'

'We also know your friend Young was arrested for protesting at an abortion clinic.'

'That was a long time ago.'

'You seemed to have a rather strong reaction when I told you about Byrne's role in forgiving women who sought him out for confession.'

'God will deal with those people when it's time.' Grace said *those people* with acid, but the rest of her words rolled calmly off her tongue, any trace of the nervousness she had felt earlier now gone, Grace acting as though she were alone in the car, enjoying a leisurely drive through the countryside.

Keeping an eye on Humphrey, Darby reached into the back seat, found the zipper for the black leather briefcase and opened it. Her hands found a MacBook Air.

'Why'd you drive all the way up here with this?' Darby asked.

'My hard drive crashed. I can't retrieve any of my files, so my friend Tina offered to help me. If you want to call her, be my guest. She'll share the same story with you. But I'm not answering any more of your questions until I have my lawyer present.'

'Guilty people ask for lawyers.'

'No,' Grace corrected, 'smart people do. I've seen plenty of TV shows and movies, read countless books at how law enforcement screws up cases – screws over innocent people. Or, in your case, kills innocent people.' Grace turned her head slightly to her, her eyes burning with righteousness. 'I know all your sins.'

'You're an excellent liar, Ms Humphrey. In fact, you're an extraordinary one. You want to know what I think? I think the MacBook I'm holding is going to reveal a lot of interesting things. Maybe I should take a look right –'

Grace Humphrey slammed on the brakes.

57

The moment the woman hit the brakes, Darby realized her mistake: she had forgotten to put on her seatbelt. Her right hand flew up to protect her head as she slammed against the windshield, white balls of pain exploding across her vision. She was thrown back against her seat as the car skidded across the highway, into the shoulder.

Grace floored the gas. Darby, her head spinning and screaming, tried to gain some footing when Humphrey hit the brakes again. Right before Darby's eyes slammed shut, she saw the glowing blue numbers on the radio clock. Her forehead slammed against the radio and more balls of white light exploded inside her head and across her vision, and when she fell back against her seat, dimly aware that the car had pulled off the highway and was now bouncing its way down a slope off the road, she caught sight of Humphrey releasing herself from her seatbelt.

Grace Humphrey threw herself from the car and on to the grass. The door hung open as the car bounced, a steady *ding-ding-ding* chime filling the cabin.

The car was still bouncing as it moved forward, towards a section of woods. Darby got a hand on her door and opened it. The car wasn't going very fast, but when she got out she stumbled and hit the ground hard. She scrabbled to her feet, her skull pounding from having been used as a batting ball, and saw Grace running twenty, maybe thirty feet ahead. The woman was surprisingly fast – she moved as though she were running for her life. She had the MacBook gripped in a hand.

The Lexus hit a tree with a dull thud and branches snapped as Darby removed the SIG from her hip holster in one smooth, practised motion. Her thumb clicked off the safety, the nine came up, and she was already in the shooter's stance when she yelled, 'Stop right now or I'll shoot.'

Grace came to a jarring stop and spun around, Darby thinking for a brief second the woman was about to surrender until she saw the hatred burning in the woman's face; the snarl and gritted teeth. Then Darby saw the handgun clenched in a fist – a snub-nose revolver.

Darby's usual policy was simple: put the target in a body bag. But she wanted Grace alive. A slight adjustment down to her left and she squeezed the trigger, boom, the report echoing through the air.

The round hit Humphrey in the meaty thigh of her right leg. The MacBook fell from her hand as she went down, collapsing against the ground, Darby advancing slowly, looking down the target sight.

'*Drop the weapon.*'

Grace didn't. She held on to the revolver but didn't point it at Darby, deciding instead to scrabble for the MacBook. Darby fired a warning shot; the round hit the ground in front of Humphrey and Darby yelled, '*Drop it. Now.*'

Humphrey had her own agenda. She pressed the revolver against the MacBook and squeezed the trigger, the report no louder than a firecracker. She moved the revolver a few inches and fired again, Darby breaking into a jog and looking down the target sight, ready to fire – wanting to fire.

Do it. Take her down.

Darby squeezed the trigger. The shot hit the woman high in the chest, near the collarbone. Humphrey yelped and tumbled backwards, on to her side.

A dark-red spot was on the leg of Humphrey's jeans, another spreading across her jacket. Grace Humphrey looked up at Darby, hissing and grunting in pain but smiling in triumph. Humphrey was still holding on to the revolver. Darby brought her boot down on the woman's wrist, and, when Humphrey yelped, releasing her grip on the revolver, Darby kicked it away.

'What did you do to the girls?'

Humphrey ignored her. Her eyes closed, and she brought her hands together and began to pray, her lips moving wordlessly.

Darby placed her heel on the wound on the woman's thigh and brought all her weight down on it.

Humphrey's eyes flew open. The plaintive howl that roared past her lips wasn't so much pain but more a scream of defiance.

'Tell me,' Darby said.

Humphrey was gasping and panting like a woman trying to breathe her way through an excruciating labour. Sweat popped out on her dirty and grass-stained face, her eyes glazed over, staring in that vacant way that brought to mind a dark, empty house.

'The police are already investigating,' Darby said. 'This thing you're involved in –'

'Is so much bigger than you.' Another crazy smile of triumph. 'You can't scare me, you can't threaten me. God and God alone will protect me.'

'God's not here. I am.' Darby applied more pressure to the wound.

Humphrey's screams roared through the air, echoed and died, echoed and died again.

'Tell me and I'll let you live.'

'I don't bargain with sinners and whores. Sinners and whores will not be shown God's mercy. You'll all face judgement, just as Father Byrne did. When the rope was slipped around his neck, he didn't fight it because he knew that, by forgiving those murdering whores, he'd become a sinner in God's eyes. He will face the Lord's wrath because God's punishment is swift and just and –'

'It was you who abducted the girls, wasn't it?'

Darby saw the words hit home. It was fleeting – just a flash of the woman's eyes widening as if to say *Who told you? How did you find out?* Then it was gone.

'That's why all the girls were taken during snowstorms,' Darby said, going with the thought, feeling it building into something solid. 'It's cold out, you're all bundled up in men's clothing, no one can see your face. So everyone thinks it's a man out there, when it's you, because a strange man wouldn't be able to calm a frightened girl. A woman could, but not a man. A child would be much more willing to believe the lies of a woman because they think a woman would never hurt them.'

Humphrey spat on her.

'The girls,' Darby said. 'What did you do to them?'

'We killed them.'

'You're lying. Where are they?'

Humphrey smiled her blood smile. 'Only God knows what is true.'

'I understand,' Darby said. She felt calm. In control. 'Truly, I do.' Darby returned the smile as she continued to grind her boot into the woman's wound. Humphrey writhed in agony, screaming until the cords in her neck stood out, straining against the skin, her eyes tracking a flock of birds from a nearby tree that had jumped into the air and were flying swiftly away, as if trying to put as much distance as possible between them and the two-legged animals that had brought horrors to the land.

58

Mickey was on his way back from the call with Timothée when he felt a burning need to go to the cemetery. He didn't question it. He simply drove.

The cemetery was quiet. He stood in an almost trance-like state at Byrne's grave.

The day he had lost it out here, when Heather called from France – he had cried for Claire, absolutely, but he hadn't been able to *release* her. A part of him refused to give up hope. When he'd packed up her room, a cry of hope rose up and told him that what he was doing was wrong. Now, as he stood at the graveside, he found the hope still there, still digging in its heels. *Don't give up on me.*

Byrne lay six feet under, sealed inside wood, preserved in embalming fluid. The grass had been recently cut. Mickey saw wet clippings sticking to the sides of his loafers, and a memory came to him of Claire, the bottom of her feet stained with dirt and covered in fresh grass clippings from their backyard, running through the house and dirtying up the carpet and floor. It amused him, but it had driven Heather, a neat freak, crazy.

He remembered how Claire loved to scoop the cheese off pizza – 'Daddy, it's the best part, and I only want to eat the best part' – and he remembered how she would throw a fit if she wasn't allowed to pick out her own clothes or decide the number of blueberries she wanted on her pancakes. When he thought of Claire, it was always these moments of toughness that came to him, the small ways she had of trying to control her world, to prove that she was independent and had a mind of her own and God help you if you got in her way. Remembering Claire in this way – this spirited toughness that she used to move through life – maybe that was a distraction too. Maybe he didn't want to see her as willingly walking off with Byrne, no matter how upset she was.

Why didn't you kick and scream when Byrne picked you up, Claire? Why didn't you have one of your patented meltdowns? I would have heard you. Why did you just walk away and leave me?

Byrne's coffin held not one body but four – Claire's, and those of the two other missing girls. And it would be that way forever, unless he wanted to hold a separate service for Claire, maybe bury her snow jacket when the police released it, if they ever did.

Only you didn't bury things. You buried people. You prepared them for their journey into the ground and whatever lay beyond it. You didn't say goodbye to a snow jacket.

How do I say goodbye when I don't even know what happened? When was the right time to give up on the people you loved?

The answer came to him later, at home, after half a bottle of bourbon.

High-end bourbons and Irish whiskies always set his head right. They shut off all the noise of the outside world, stripped away the bullshit. They put his mind and soul at ease. They brought him to a calm, inner place where he could hear The Voice.

Mickey believed in God, and, while he would never say

409

out loud that he believed God spoke to him – that was the realm of lunatics and preachers looking to rob people of their hard-earned money – he truly felt that The Voice was a conduit to some higher plane. The Voice was full of wisdom and understanding and acceptance. It spoke the truth. The Voice had helped him to navigate through those awkward and frustrating teenage years when everyone treated him like a zoo animal because he was Sean Flynn's kid; had helped him through the rough patches in his marriage; and then, when the thing with Claire happened, it had helped hope stay alive. Right now The Voice was telling him that, yes, Claire and his mother were gone, but he shouldn't give up hope. He could see them. All he had to do was to go upstairs and get the gun.

The thought didn't sicken or repulse him. After Claire vanished, during those dark moments when he was sure she was dead, he had contemplated suicide. The nine upstairs in the gun safe was equipped with hollow-point rounds. Press the muzzle in the roof of his mouth, squeeze the trigger, and it would be done. A couple of times – well, more than that – he'd put the gun in his mouth or pressed it against his forehead, and The Voice would say, *No, don't do it, Mickey. Not until you have proof that Claire is dead.*

And now he had proof. Okay, not hard evidence, but still. She was gone, she wasn't coming back to him, but he could go to her. *You should go to her,* The Voice said. *It's time, Mickey. You've suffered enough.*

It took a moment for Mickey to get to his feet. The room swayed a bit, but that didn't matter. He didn't have far to walk.

The doorbell rang. The sound startled him. He glanced

at the clock on the microwave: 2.32 a.m. Had to be Jim, he thought.

Don't answer it.

The doorbell rang again, followed by a fist pounding on the door.

'*Mickey.*'

Not Jim; Darby McCormick. What was she doing here? At this hour?

More pounding. '*Mickey.*'

He had to concentrate on walking. His head was swimming and, while he could see his hand reaching out and grabbing the lever for the deadbolt, a part of him felt far away, as though he were watching this from the other end of a long tunnel.

Darby was standing on his front doorstep, all right, and she wasn't alone. Detective Kennedy was with her.

Darby invited herself in.

'Come on,' she said, 'let's sit down.'

'Sit down? For what? What's going on? And what the hell happened to your face? You get in a fistfight?'

She exchanged a glance with Kennedy and then looked back at Mickey. It was a look Mickey recognized, a reserved one with a hint of disgust, a look that said, *Oh, shit, we've got a drunk on our hands.*

'I'm allowed to do whatever I want in my own home,' Mickey said.

'Absolutely.' Her tone changed, became more sympathetic and less urgent. 'Come on, let's go sit and I'll tell you what's going on.'

Mickey made his way to the living-room couch without tripping. Darby hadn't followed. She was in the kitchen, her hand inside his refrigerator. She came back with a bottle of water, twisted off the cap and handed it to him.

Darby sat on the ottoman, facing him. 'It's about Grace Humphrey.'

'Who?'

'Byrne's hospice nurse.'

'Right. What about her?' Mickey's gaze slid away from her to the grave-faced detective, who was leaning against the archway to the living room, his arms crossed over his chest, watching.

'You're going to have questions,' Darby said, and Mickey wondered why she was speaking so slowly. 'I'll tell you everything I know so far.'

'I don't even know what you're talking about, why you're even *here*.'

'Remember the day of Byrne's funeral, those people dressed in white who were picketing, holding up those signs?'

'Yeah. The Truth Soldiers.'

'The Soldiers of Truth and Light,' Darby said. 'The FBI has had them on their watch list for years. What the Bureau didn't know – what they're finding out right now – is that this group has been operating, in one form or another, for the better part of thirty years, they think. What this group does is abduct young children from parents who've had abortions. Then they brainwash these kids –'

'What?' Mickey looked to Kennedy, who was staring down at his phone. 'What's she talking about?'

'Mickey, look at me.' She waited until he did. 'The kids are abducted and brainwashed into thinking their parents are dead,' Darby said, holding her eyes on his. 'Then the kids are placed into Christian homes – members of this group who, for one reason or another, can't have kids of their own. The majority of these families live in Canada. They operate in this Al-Qaeda-like fashion, using encrypted email on private servers. They have members working in abortion clinics all over the country, gathering data on various women who –'

'Who told you this?'

'Grace Humphrey. Well, not so much her but her friend, this guy named Gregg Young. Which is a good thing, since Grace can't talk right now. She's recovering from surgery.'

'Surgery from what?'

'I shot her. We'll get into that later,' Darby said. 'Grace had a laptop with her. She tried to break it but the FBI – they're involved in this now – they were still able to access the hard drive. What the FBI has been able to uncover so far is a contact list with the names of the people in this group – names, addresses, even phone numbers. You with me so far?'

Mickey nodded. The Voice, though, told him he had blacked out and was dreaming. *Claire's dead, Mickey. I'm sorry, but she's gone.*

'There was quite a lot of information on Byrne in these emails,' Darby said. 'Grace's group went after Byrne because he represented – and this is a direct quote – "the continuing moral decay of the Catholic Church". So they took matters into their own hands and pinned the disappearance of your daughter and the other girls on him.'

'Wait, you're saying Byrne was innocent?'

'I'm saying he's not a paedophile. I'm saying he didn't abduct your daughter or Elizabeth Levenson or Mary Hamilton. I'm saying –'

'Those items in Byrne's bedroom – the pictures and clothing, and those tapes of the girls crying.'

'Grace planted all of it. She and her pal Young and her group – they're the ones who had the evidence and took the pictures. This group had . . . scouts, I guess you could call them, who conducted surveillance on the families and took pictures. This group was extremely organized – I've never seen anything like it – and we've only scratched the surface. Their goal was to make their victims suffer psychologically – to torture them. Young, by the way, was the one who planted the jacket on the monument. It was pure coincidence Byrne found it that night. But it didn't matter who found the jacket. When it turned up, you would ID it, and then the police would head straight to Byrne's and put him under the microscope again.'

Byrne's voice from the night he had called: *I'm going to die in peace. You're not going to take that away from me. Not you, not the police, not the press. You stay away from me or this time I'll send you to jail.*

Mickey said, 'Why go through all this when they knew he was dying?'

'To prolong his suffering,' Darby said. 'Byrne admitted to Humphrey he was terrified of dying alone in a prison cell. When it didn't look like the police were going to arrest him, Humphrey and Young decided to punish him another way: burning him alive. Another thing Byrne was terrified of. Young was the one who threw the Molotov. And he already had someone lined up to pin it on.'

'Sean.'

Darby nodded. 'This group bugged Byrne's house – pinhole microphones and cameras. They were watching

414

and listening to him *all the time*. Young told us your old man broke into Byrne's house and set up his own little surveillance system.' She looked at him with a level gaze and said, 'That's how you knew Byrne talked in his sleep.'

'What?'

'You told me Byrne talked in his sleep. You found out because Sean told you he'd been inside Byrne's house – at least that's what Sean told us a couple of hours ago.'

Mickey sighed. 'Yeah. Yeah, it's true, but I didn't ask him to do that. I didn't –'

'Forget it,' Darby said, but there was no anger in her voice. 'Young knew your old man was poking around Byrne's house, so Young set him up. Dropped Sean's lighter and some cigarette butts at the crime scene, and guess who the police are going to nail to the wall.'

Kennedy spoke up. 'Young is also the one who attacked Darby in the South End. He thought – the group thought – she was getting too close to finding something out about them, so he paid a visit to Danny Halloran and his boyfriend. Had them shoot up, had Danny call Darby, set her up, make it look like she'd been a victim of some lunatic who's running around the South End, targeting gay people.'

Mickey looked at Darby. She said, 'I survived so they decided it was time for Byrne to die. Their plans weren't working out. They staged Byrne's death to make it look like a suicide. Grace loaded him up on morphine, and Young did the heavy lifting. Police come in, find the tape with your daughter's voice on it – and they recorded those tapes, not Byrne. Young told us. They'd recorded those audio-tapes years ago – that's how organized this group is. They were going to plant the tapes, the pictures and your daughter's snow jacket inside the house after Byrne had died in his sleep. But, given how everything worked out, they had to change their plans. They had the jacket shipped to them, and the tapes. Young printed out the pictures of your daughter and the other girls from a colour photo-printer at his house. We come in, see all the evidence, find the single ligature mark around Byrne's neck, and it looks like he died during an auto-erotic asphyxiation gone wrong. The extra morphine in his system didn't raise any red flags because Byrne was dying of cancer.'

Mickey felt a cold sweat break across his skin.

'When Young fitted the noose around Byrne's neck,' Darby said, 'he told Byrne what they had done to him and then let him hang. It's all detailed in the emails between him and Humphrey.'

Kennedy cleared his throat. He looked up from his phone and said, 'Darby, a moment?'

Darby got to her feet. Mickey stared down at his hands, feeling numb – feeling like this couldn't be happening, even though he knew he was awake. He had heard every-thing Darby had told him but, at the same time, he hadn't heard it, because he was drunk and because he couldn't believe what was happening.

And he thought of Claire. She had to be alive. God wouldn't bring him this far, this close, only to make her disappear again. God wouldn't be that cruel twice.

'Mickey?'

Darby's voice. He looked up at her. She was smiling. Kennedy was too.

'We've got her,' Darby said. 'We've found your daughter.'

59

'I'm not one of those, you know, nature dudes,' Jim said to Mickey, 'but even I can appreciate a view like this.'

Jim was wrong. The view wasn't impressive; it was spectacular. Everywhere you looked there were valleys of blooming trees. The farmhouse, with its sprawling maze of rooms, was completely isolated. It was a safe house, Special Agent Mark Quinn had explained, a place generally used as a temporary shelter before people were placed in Witness Protection. With the media frenzy surrounding Claire's story, the FBI thought it would be better to have the reunion here, in upstate Vermont, without cameras and microphones, to give Claire some time to adjust.

Behind him, coming from inside the house, Mickey heard a landline phone ring. He whipped his head around and, through the windows, caught sight of Agent Quinn walking across the hardwood, talking on a cell phone. Darby was on the phone too. Mickey could see her profile, sitting at the big farm table inside.

Mickey had spent yesterday afternoon and a good portion of last night talking to Darby, listening as she explained how to approach Claire, what to expect.

The most important person in all of this is Claire, Darby emphasized. *She's going through a whirlwind of emotions right now, which is normal. There's a lot she has to adjust to, Mickey: that her parents are alive; that you and your wife are divorced. She may even be angry. She may not want to talk. All of that is normal. The Smith family has been very good to her.*

The Smith family, Catholics, no children, Dina Smith unable to conceive and unable to afford adoption, Dina and Albert Smith, part of Grace Humphrey's radical pro-life group. It was the lead story everywhere – and, according to both Darby and Agent Quinn, was only going to get bigger. Mickey couldn't absorb what was going on; he couldn't imagine how Claire was dealing with all of this.

Jim said, 'You talk to Heather?'

'Not yet,' Mickey replied. Heather hadn't even been in New York for a week before deciding to take advantage of some last-minute tour deal to Australia. She had been halfway through her twenty-four-hour flight to Australia when the news about Claire broke. When the plane touched down, the Australian police came on board and explained the situation. Right now Heather was on a flight back home. Her plane was due to touch down sometime later tonight.

Agent Quinn came out of the house. He saw Mickey and smiled, his blue eyes looking bright and unclouded. Mickey liked him. No question seemed too stupid or too repetitive. The first two days, Mickey kept asking, between Quinn's questions, 'You're sure the girl you found is my daughter? You're absolutely sure?' and Quinn would flash a smile and then reaffirm what Mickey had already been told: *There's no question. We matched her fingerprints, and fingerprints don't lie.*

Still, Mickey felt a creeping fear, waiting for someone to come to him and say there had been a terrible mistake. And then they would drive him back to Belham, back to his empty house, where the reporters would be waiting, and he would get up in front of all those microphones and look into all those cameras and say, *Sorry, this was all just a big misunderstanding*. And then they would all leave, Darby included, and go back to their lives, and he'd be alone.

'Your daughter's en route,' Quinn said. 'She'll be here in an hour.' Then he turned to Jim, had to look up. 'Mr Kelly, I know you're her godfather –'

'I know, strictly family, we don't want to confuse her because she's already confused enough,' Jim said. 'Darby already filled me in.'

'Car's waiting for you out front,' Quinn said. Then, to Mickey: 'Dr McCormick would like to speak to you, go over a few things before your daughter gets here.'

Your daughter.

Claire was on her way here.

To see *him*.

To come back *home*.

The joy filled Mickey up to the point where he thought he was going to burst.

With the joy came a new set of fears.

'What if she doesn't recognize me?' he asked Darby.

They were sitting in the living room, Darby in a chair facing a window overlooking the long, winding driveway. Mickey sat on a couch, leaning forward and rubbing his hands between his knees as he stared at the old hardwood floor.

'She might not at first,' Darby said. 'She was six when she was taken.'

'And a half.'

'Pardon?'

'She was six and a half when she was taken.'

Darby smiled. Beneath her tough exterior, she had a well of empathy he hadn't thought she possessed. He found himself wanting to open up to her, put his heart on the table and dissect it – anything Darby wanted. She was the one who had found his daughter. She had kept digging, refused to give up.

'How many memories do you have from when you were six?' Darby asked.

Mickey could cough up only fragments: wandering across the street to the neighbour's yard; getting into a rowboat with Sean; arguing with his mother at the store, wanting two colouring books instead of one.

Darby spoke slowly and deliberately, navigating her way through a verbal minefield. 'Claire may have memories of you and your wife, but they're most likely buried. That's temporary. These memories will come back to her, but you have to give it some time. What Claire's going through right now is extremely traumatic. She was brainwashed – all those kids were. That's why this group only took young children. Dina and Albert Smith told Claire you and Heather had died. She's been living with a new family in a new country and then, out of nowhere, the police barge in and take her away. Not only does Claire find out her parents are alive, she also finds out the Smith family essentially kidnapped her. It's also possible Claire has overheard bits and pieces about the Smiths being a part of this radical Christian group. In any case, it's a lot to absorb. And Claire may not want to absorb it right away – and that's okay. Remember how you felt when you found out the truth about your mother.'

Mickey nodded. He had told Darby all of it yesterday.

'What if she wants to go back to them?' he asked.

'That's not going to happen. They're going to prison.'

'Still, she *may* want to go back to them. She was with them longer than she was with me and Heather.' Mickey's eyes slid up to hers. 'It's possible, right?'

'You're her father, Mickey.' Darby's tone was gentle but firm. 'Nothing is going to change that fact. Are there going to be some bumps along the way? Absolutely. Will there be times when you get frustrated and pissed off at the unfairness of everything that has happened? Without a doubt. But you *will* work it out. She's coming up on seventeen. She's still young. You have the gift of time. Some of the other families don't.'

Darby was right. He thought of Elizabeth Levenson, now in her late twenties, engaged and living in Italy; Mary Hamilton was in her early thirties, married with two kids and living a mile down the road from her adoptive – was that even the right word? – family in New Brunswick, Canada. Would he rather be in that position, trying to reconnect with an adult child?

Two black Lincoln Navigators were coming up the road.

'That's them,' Darby said.

Mickey sprang to his feet, his heart pumping so fast he was sure it was going to quit on him. He could see the headline now: FATHER OF MISSING GIRL REUNITED ONLY TO DROP DEAD OF A HEART ATTACK.

Why was he so terrified? He had wished and prayed for this moment how many hundreds of thousands of times over the past eleven years, and now here it was, coming right at him, and his skin felt clammy and electric with fear and joy and anxiety and hope. His stomach was doing double-flips, and he felt light-headed.

It's going to be fine, he told himself.

It's going to work out, he told himself.

The pair of Lincolns came to a stop in the driveway.

'Mickey?'

He wiped the sweat away from his forehead. He tested his legs. A little wobbly, but okay.

'You're her father,' Darby said. 'Don't forget that.'

And with that Mickey opened the door to meet his daughter.

60

Claire was tall – much, much taller than he had imagined, around five-foot-nine.

And thin – not from lack of food but from exercise. She probably had Heather's metabolism.

Her glasses were gone.

So was the pigtail (*obviously*, he corrected himself. She wasn't a little girl any more). Her hair was shoulder length, the way it was when he dreamed. Her hair was so blonde, so fine, it looked white in the sun.

No earrings. No jewellery. She was dressed very plainly, jeans and white Converse sneakers and a puffy North Face goose-down coat.

What he loved most – what made him almost crumble right there in front of everyone – was seeing her face. He could still see the stubborn traces of the six-year-old girl who had refused to grab his hand that night at the Hill.

Claire stood among three FBI agents (or so he assumed), her hands folded in front of her, her head bowed, staring at the tops of her sneakers. She was upset. Like when she knew she had done something wrong, she would bow her head and stare at her feet, the floor, anything to avoid meeting your eyes. Seeing her like this made him want to run to her, grab her and hug her close, take the fear and pain and all the questions she carried in her eyes and transfer it to him, just as he had when she was little. When she was his.

Only it wasn't going to work that way.

Mickey gripped the railing and took the steps one at a time, wanting a chance to absorb her but more afraid that, if he moved any faster, he'd trip and crack his head open, end up having the reunion in a hospital room. When he stepped on to the gravel, he kept his hand on the railing, squeezing it.

Darby addressed the crowd: 'Why don't we give them some room?'

Everyone nodded and moved away, Claire's eyes coming up and tracking a chunky woman in jeans and a powder-blue shirt. Probably the psychologist, Mickey thought. Darby had told him the FBI had provided Claire with a psychologist who specialized in trauma.

The woman had moved only a few feet; she stopped and leaned against the hood of the Lincoln.

Mickey walked over to his daughter but didn't get too close, wanting to put some space between her and all the eyes pinned on her – and him.

'Hi,' he said, pleased that his voice sounded strong. Confident.

'Hey,' she said softly.

Hearing her voice for the first time made him want to reach out and touch her, make sure she was real.

'How was your ride?'

'Long,' she said quietly, her eyes still downcast, locked on her sneakers.

'You want to stretch out, go for a walk?'

Her gaze cut to Mickey. Those eyes had once looked up

424

from her crib into his, had once sought him out in their house, been excited to see him when he came home – those eyes he had helped to create and shape now stared back at him, studying him, wondering who he was.

Claire, remember our last Christmas together? You were so excited that you came and woke me up at four and whispered in my ear, 'He came, Daddy, Santa came again!' Remember how we didn't want to wake Mom up, so you and I went downstairs and made pancakes and burned them and you tried one and said yuck so you gave it to Diesel? Remember how you don't like olives but you always kept trying them and kept making that grossed-out face? Remember that Saturday morning when you brought all your dolls and stuffed animals downstairs into the TV room and seated them on the couch and then stood up on top of the coffee table because you thought it was a stage?

He had hundreds of little memories like that – thousands. But they didn't mean anything to her right now. What she had right now were memories from the Smith family – memories and stories and events he didn't own, let alone know about yet.

Claire remained quiet.

Tell me you remember me, Claire. At least tell me that.

'I could use a walk,' Claire said.

Behind the house were a barn and a stable for horses. No horses, though. There was also what Mickey believed to be a small skating rink. Claire, he saw, was eyeing it too, probably wondering the same thing.

As they walked down the slope, heading towards the trails, he debated whether he should talk first or wait for her to say something. Right now she seemed to be enjoying the peace and quiet and fresh air. She probably hadn't had much of those things during the last few days, so he decided to wait for her to initiate the conversation.

Ten minutes passed, and he couldn't bear the silence any longer.

'I know you're feeling very confused – maybe even scared,' Mickey said. 'If you don't want to talk, that's okay. This is about you. What you're feeling.'

Claire didn't nod, didn't respond; she kept walking, eyes straight ahead. He wanted to take the chasm he'd been carrying inside him for the past decade and shape it with words she would understand, words that would form a bridge she could cross, so she could see the hell he'd gone through.

'They said you'd died,' Claire said.

Mickey nodded, trying to keep the anger from reaching his face.

'I remember them sitting in their kitchen,' Claire said. 'Both of them told me you'd died and that bad men were looking for me, and that's why they changed my name to Susan Smith. It was the only way to protect me from these bad men, they said. They said if I told anyone my real name, the bad men might come looking for me, hurt me and them both.'

Mickey wanted to speak, stopped. This was about Claire. His job right now was to listen.

'Mr and Mrs Smith were always so nice to me,' she said. 'They never yelled at me. We went on vacations – went to Disney World twice. I went to church with them. They punished me when I lied to them. And this whole time they'd been lying to me.'

They're religious fanatics, Claire. They all share the same sick belief that God spoke only to them – that they were special. Chosen.

He didn't see the need to tell any of this to her. Not now, anyway.

'Sometimes,' Mickey said, 'you can believe in something so much, with such intensity, that it blinds you. When that happens, when you believe with all your heart and mind that what you're thinking or doing is right, it's all you can see. In their hearts and minds, the Smiths believed what they were saying and doing was right.'

'But they *lied*.'

'I know. And I wish I could change it, but I can't. The older you get, the more you'll find people will lie to you – sometimes even people who are close to you. It's sad, and it hurts, but it happens. That's why it's important to think about the good things. Like this.'

Mickey reached into his back pocket and took out his phone. He had already had the pictures loaded on to the screen.

He handed Claire the phone. She slowed as she studied a picture of Heather.

'Your mother will be here sometime later today,' he said.

Claire stopped walking. She studied the picture, Mickey waiting to answer questions, if that was what she wanted. And if she wanted to hand the phone back to him, that was fine too.

Claire flipped to the next picture.

'Oh, my gosh,' she said with a smile. 'Is that a baby bear?'

'That was your dog, Diesel. He was a bullmastiff.'

'He's *huge*.'

'And a big-time drooler. Flip to the next picture and you'll see him as a puppy.'

Claire did. She wasn't staring at Diesel, though; her eyes were locked on the little girl with the glasses and crooked teeth sitting next to the sleeping puppy. Mickey had chosen the photo, hoping it would trigger a memory.

He moved closer, debating about whether or not to put his hand on her shoulder, when she flipped to the next picture, a colour photo he had downloaded from the *Globe*'s website: Sean Flynn leaving prison.

'Who's this?' she asked.

'He's . . . he helped me find you. His name is Sean Flynn.'

'That's your last name.'

It's your last name too, he wanted to say.

'Is he related to you?'

'He's my father,' Mickey said. 'Your grandfather.'

Claire handed back his phone. Her face had closed up. He had pushed her too far.

Mickey took the phone and smiled, but it was forced, and holding it was an effort.

'I'm hungry,' she said. 'I think I'm going to go back and get something to eat.'

'You want some company?'

'Maybe later.'

Later.

It's okay, he told himself, watching Claire move back up the path, back towards the house where Darby and the psychologist were waiting.

It's okay, he told himself again. He and Claire had been given the gift of time.

Darby watched the interaction from a vantage point behind the house.

Her intention wasn't to spy. She couldn't hear what they were saying, did not want to eavesdrop on this incredibly private and powerful moment. Her intention was to keep an eye on Mickey, to be there in case he went to pieces. He had stopped drinking, which had caused him to go into a minor withdrawal of headaches and anxious nerves that was complicated by the tremendous fear – and pressure – of not being able to reconnect with his daughter. She promised to be there for Mickey, and she would be.

Claire had walked away. Mickey stared off into the distance, his face twisted in pain.

Should she go to him?

No, she decided. *Give him some time.*

She moved away. When she was sure she was alone, Darby took out her phone.

That day in New York, while she was in the back of the cab, on her way to the airport, Darby had decided she wanted to find out about the boy her parents had given up for adoption. She'd called Sue Michaud and asked her to investigate. And this morning, Sue had sent an email with her results. Everything Darby wanted to know about her biological brother was attached in a Word file.

Her phone rang. Kennedy was calling.

'I thought you'd like to know Father Cullen finally agreed to cooperate,' he said.

For days, she and Kennedy had been wondering what had happened to the tapes of the confessions that had been in Byrne's possession.

'Your theory about Byrne having traded those tapes with Cullen in exchange for last rites and a Catholic funeral,' Kennedy said. 'You were right. When you left that message with Cullen's secretary, Cullen headed straight to Byrne's house, just like Grace Humphrey told you. It was important that Byrne, for reasons Cullen couldn't – or wouldn't – explain to us, that he be given the full Catholic treatment on his way out.'

'Where are the tapes now?'

'Cullen said he destroyed them. Took them to an incinerator. I believe him. He wouldn't want evidence like that lying around. Cullen also maintains that he had no idea Byrne was recording the confessions, but he did say that Byrne did it to amuse himself. In any event, we'll probably never know the entire truth about it, but I thought you should know you don't have to worry about him airing any dirty laundry. Your secrets are safe.'

Darby planned on having a long, frank talk with the priest.

'It's not going to happen,' Kennedy said.

'What's that?'

'Paying him a visit. Cullen's lawyer went back to court, to get an extension on the restraining order.'

'For how long?'

'The maximum number,' Kennedy said. 'Five years.'

'You need to look into Cullen. The man's a liar. He hides behind the collar.'

'That's also not going to happen.'

'He was close friends with Byrne. That wasn't an accident. People like that –'

'We can't get everyone, Darby.'

'If I took that attitude, I wouldn't have found Mickey's daughter and those other kids.'

'Point taken. Take care of yourself, okay? And take a moment – just a moment, that's all I'm asking – to be happy with what you accomplished.'

Darby hung up and thought about what Kennedy had said. He was right, of course. The important thing here was Mickey had been reunited with his daughter. And Richard Byrne, while not a paedophile and murderer, was a truly evil man who had got what he deserved. Win-win.

Darby stared at her phone. The attached file in Sue's email was on her screen.

All she had to do was to open it and she would know his full name, age, address, everything.

She pressed her finger against the screen.

Deleted the email and file.

Then she went into her deleted folder and permanently deleted it so she wouldn't be tempted to look at it later.

She didn't regret her decision. She had been giving a lot of thought to what she should do, when it occurred to her that she shouldn't do anything. If her brother had wanted to find his biological family, he'd had plenty of time to look. If he'd wanted to find out about his birth parents – or her – he would have done so by now – and he hadn't. There were things in this world that shouldn't be disturbed, even for the right reasons and with the best of intentions.

61

A few minutes shy of midnight, Mickey stepped out on to the front porch for a smoke. The sky was black, bursting with stars, the air cold but not freezing. He lit a cigarette and sat in the rocking chair, feeling the weight of the day in his bones.

Darby and the shrink had spent a good part of the afternoon with Claire, who suddenly didn't want to talk any more, just wanted to hang out in her room with the door shut.

'She's overwhelmed,' Darby explained to him. 'It's a lot to process. Just give it time.'

He had given it eleven years. Claire didn't need all this talking. What she needed was to be home, not here, out in the middle of nowhere, inside this sprawling farmhouse full of strange rooms and strange faces. She needed to be back in her house, in *her* room and sitting on *her* bed, and he would sit next to her and the two of them would go through all the pictures he'd taken from the day she was born until the day she was taken from him – go through each picture and the videos he'd taken over and over again until Claire finally turned to him and said –

'Smoking's bad for you.'

Mickey turned, saw Claire in the doorway. He hadn't even heard the door open.

'You're right,' he said, and mashed the cigarette out on the floor. Then he flicked the butt into the darkness.

Claire came out, dressed in grey sweats and a denim jacket over a thermal shirt. Mickey wondered who had bought her the jacket, if it was a birthday gift or something she had picked out for herself, a reminder of her home for the past decade now comforting her as she waited in this strange house, about to go to another strange house and another strange bedroom.

'Can't sleep?' he asked.

'No.'

'Long day. Stressful too.'

Claire nodded. There was a problem; it was written all over her face.

She's here to tell me she wants to go home to her other family.

Only that wasn't going to happen. Claire wasn't going back to Canada. But the warm, good feelings and memories she attached to the Smiths were very real and weren't going away.

'This scar,' Claire said, pointing to the skin near her right temple.

Mickey couldn't see it. He got to his feet and took a closer look.

The scar was faint, about an inch long and jagged. He hadn't noticed it earlier.

'I can't remember where it came from,' Claire said. 'Do you know?'

Mickey thought about the dried blood he's seen in her hood.

'No,' he said. 'I don't.'

He wanted to ask her about what had happened that night on top of the Hill. He had so many questions.

Claire crossed her arms over her chest. She seemed on

433

the verge of tears. He resisted the urge to reach out and hold her.

Don't force it, Darby had told him. *Let her come to you. And, most importantly, listen. Listen without judgement, without anger. Make this about her, not you.*

Mickey said, 'I'm sorry you have to go through all this.'

Claire said nothing. She turned her head and stared out at the trees, the leaves rustling in the wind.

'Today, when we were walking, we saw a skating rink,' she said. 'At least it looked like a skating rink.'

'That's what I thought.'

'I was in bed thinking about it – about the skating rink, I mean. At your house, was there a pond out back?'

'Not out back,' Mickey said. 'It was about a mile away. Salmon Brook Pond, it's called.'

'It's out in the woods, right?'

Mickey nodded. 'You learned to skate there.'

'You put these, like, crates or something on the ice.'

'Yeah. Plastic milk crates. I'd stack two of them together and you'd hold on to the top. You didn't like them after a while; you wanted to skate on your own.'

She saw him smile from the corner of her eye and turned to him, serious. 'What?'

'Sorry, I was thinking about when you fell on the ice. Each time you did, I'd reach down to pick you up and you'd get so mad. Each and every time.'

'Why?'

'Because you were stubborn,' Mickey said. 'You wanted to learn how to skate on your own, liked doing things on your own, ever since you were a baby. Skating, swimming and sledding. Especially sledding.'

The last words came out before Mickey realized what he'd said.

It was okay. The words washed right over Claire. She went back to staring out at the trees, only now she had this faraway, dreamy look, as if the memories he'd been describing were being played out for her.

'But,' she said, 'I got better.'

'Oh, yeah. You really took to skating.'

'And we played a game. You held me up in front of you while we skated.'

A chill washed through him. He wanted to speak, wanted to urge her on, but was too terrified to say or do anything that might break this fragile connection to her hazy, fragmented memories.

'You held me up,' Claire said, 'and I'd call out names. These really silly names.'

Mickey swallowed. 'Your favourite was "Fighting fish".'

Claire nodded slowly, lost in a time they had built together and shared.

'Yeah,' she said with a shy smile. 'I remember.'

UNCOVER THE DARBY

'A scary, breakneck ride with thrills that never let up'
Tess Gerritsen

1

'Chris Mooney is a wonderful writer. Compelling, thrilling and touching'
Michael Connelly

2

'This will keep you up past your bedtime'
Karin Slaughter

3

'An exceptional thriller writer. I envy those who have yet to read him'
John Connolly

4

McCORMICK THRILLERS

'If you want a thriller that will chill your blood, break your heart and make your pulse race, Chris Mooney is your man'
Mark Billingham

'One of the best thriller writers working today'
Lee Child

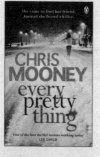

'Harrowing, gripping, haunting, gut-wrenching and beautifully written'
Harlan Coben

'The smart money has long been on Chris Mooney, one of crime fiction's rising stars'
Laura Lippman

He just wanted a decent book to read ...

Not too much to ask, is it? It was in 1935 when Allen Lane, Managing Director of Bodley Head Publishers, stood on a platform at Exeter railway station looking for something good to read on his journey back to London. His choice was limited to popular magazines and poor-quality paperbacks – the same choice faced every day by the vast majority of readers, few of whom could afford hardbacks. Lane's disappointment and subsequent anger at the range of books generally available led him to found a company – and change the world.

'We believed in the existence in this country of a vast reading public for intelligent books at a low price, and staked everything on it'
Sir Allen Lane, 1902–1970, founder of Penguin Books

The quality paperback had arrived – and not just in bookshops. Lane was adamant that his Penguins should appear in chain stores and tobacconists, and should cost no more than a packet of cigarettes.

Reading habits (and cigarette prices) have changed since 1935, but Penguin still believes in publishing the best books for everybody to enjoy. We still believe that good design costs no more than bad design, and we still believe that quality books published passionately and responsibly make the world a better place.

So wherever you see the little bird – whether it's on a piece of prize-winning literary fiction or a celebrity autobiography, political tour de force or historical masterpiece, a serial-killer thriller, reference book, world classic or a piece of pure escapism – you can bet that it represents the very best that the genre has to offer.

Whatever you like to read – trust Penguin.